M

SALTATION

BAEN BOOKS by SHARON LEE & STEVE MILLER

THE LIADEN UNIVERSE®

Fledgling

Saltation

Mouse and Dragon (forthcoming)

The Dragon Variation (forthcoming omnibus)

Duainfey

Longeye

SALTATION

A New
Liaden Universe®
Novel

SHARON LEE &
STEVE MILLER

A Baen Books Original

Baen Publishing Enterprises
P.O. Box 1403
Riverdale, NY 10471
www.baen.com

ISBN-13: 978-4391-3345-3

Cover art by David Mattingly

First printing, April 2010

Distributed by Simon & Schuster
1230 Avenue of the Americas
New York, NY 10020

Library of Congress Cataloging-in-Publication Data

Lee, Sharon, 1952–
    Saltation : a novel of the Liaden universe / Sharon Lee and Steve Miller.
        p. cm.
    Includes bibliographical references and index.
    ISBN 978-1-4391-3345-3 (hc : alk. paper)
    1. Life on other planets—Fiction. I. Miller, Steve, 1950 July 31– II. Title.
    PS3562.E3629S25 2010
    813'.54—dc22

                                        2009053082

10 9 8 7 6 5 4 3 2

Pages by Joy Freeman (www.pagesbyjoy.com)
Printed in the United States of America

· ·

*The authors would like to extend special thanks to the
following people, all of whom made Saltation a more fulfilling
experience for us and helped bring these words to you:*

*Mike Barker, for his continued unflappable good
nature, and deft touch with a wiki*

Judith Tarr, who pointed out the Perfect Word

*Charlie Schlenker who voiced, and Sam Chupp, who
hosted and promoted the Saltation podcast*

*Shawna Camara and Angela Gradillas, for their
ongoing promotion work in Second Life*

Toni Weisskopf of Baen Books, our esteemed editor

Jennifer Jackson of the Maass Agency, our marvelous agent

*The many active supporters of the Saltation online project,
and especially the denizens of the Theo_Waitley Live Journal
Community, who made it all happen, and happen well.*

· ·

. . . .

Saltation : That which proceeds by leaps
rather than by smooth and orderly progression.

. . . .

FIRST LEAP

ONE

· · · · · · · ·

Shuttle Approach
Anlingdin Piloting Academy
Eylot

"CONSELEM!"

Theo didn't think that the gentle off-center nudge of reaction jets had deserved a sneeze, much less a cuss word. And the shouts and cackles of self-important glee when the second nudge was followed by a firmer push were just mean.

"We're all gonna die!"

Theo resisted the urge to look toward the front of the shuttle, having recognized *that* voice. Should've known. Sighing, she rested her head resolutely against well-worn padding. She'd drawn a seat without nearby viewports and was just as happy not to be sitting with the three student pilots, their flight wings shiny on their collars, who'd started chancing her back on the *Vestrin*. They were coming back to Anlingdin from the Short Break, so they said, and were determined to party as long as possible.

Snickiots.

At least she wasn't alone. Apparently they didn't much care for . . . Theo squinted at the legend scrolling across the main screen: "Student Pilot Kern Vallee at controls, please strap in." Right. They didn't much care for Kern Vallee, either.

"Conselem!" the ringleader yelled again, to the loud delight of his friends.

"You know," the second-rank snickiot said, sounding way too

3

serious. "Kern flunked his first three landings. Good thing for us he's got Ablestum and the Short Wing sitting with him. We've got a good chance of getting down in one piece!"

There was another cycle of jets then, as if the pilot was testing controls, and then a tremble followed by a push Theo judged to be fairly firm, which brought more cuss words and shrieks from the front.

Eyes closed, Theo tried to ignore the noise and mentally recited her schedule. Landing, free time, then Admin Roundup. She sighed, longingly. In a half day or less she'd be in a quiet bunk. Alone. She hadn't been properly alone since she boarded *Vestrin* at Delgado Station, weeks ago. At least, she'd only had to put up with the three party-boys since Rooba, two ship-days.

And the descent to Eylot, of course.

She felt the jiggle of acceleration, the twisting on her gut as front and down changed place, guessed the maneuver upcoming, and grimaced.

"Oh, no! We're in for it now!"

The punch came in four distinct bursts of power, each one bringing shouts of fake terror from the three rowdies.

Theo felt her hands curl into fists. She took a deep breath, and deliberately relaxed them, trying to distract herself by imagining Father—or, better, Captain Cho!—shutting them up. Instead, she saw Win Ton inside her closed eyelids, fingers flicking in his own *binjali* hand-talk rendition of *regard them as mere passengers*.

That thought led to others closer to her heart, and she regarded those things rather than the noise until the shuttle's very gentle touchdown on the Anlingdin Piloting Academy's own landing strip.

The newbies had been directed to the so-called passengers bay to collect their baggage, while the returning students—among them, the trio of snickiots from *Vestrin*—rushed off elsewhere. Theo breathed a sigh of relief. Good. That was probably the last she'd see of them—at least until year-end.

Someone jostled her, and she sighed again, this time in irritation. There was a lot of random motion going on, like everybody had a lot of energy to work off after the shuttle trip. She was feeling kind of jittery herself, like she wanted to dance and sleep at the same time. Still, milling around wasn't going to get their baggage out any sooner, so she tried to find a place to stand that was out of the way, but still gave her a good view of the gate.

The room was tall, and voices echoed noisily off of the ceiling, adding a headache-making depth to the nonstop chatter around her. She was apparently the only one among the newbies who didn't have a best friend with them. Well—her and a tall, awkward-looking girl in a bright green jacket, who was standing sort of in the middle of it all, adjusting her jacket with one hand, the other hand under her chin, like she was the only one in the bay, and wasn't too sure what to do next.

A baggage sled came through the gate, piled high with bags and crates. The crowd surged forward. Theo stood where she was, not wanting to get crushed. She could wait.

Another sled came through the gate; the crowds made way and re-formed with a minimum of fuss and a maximum of quick activity.

Theo looked about in sudden realization. This was so unlike either Delgado or Melchiza. On Delgado it felt like everyone older than her was in charge, and on Melchiza there was never any doubt who was in charge. Here, no one seemed in charge but everything was in motion. No one on guard, no one watching for miscreants, or antisocial conditions. It was . . . strange, she thought. And then she thought that she liked it, this tacit admission that they could sort themselves out. She relaxed, and watched, practicing advertency, like any good scholar, or traveler.

Around her were scores of young trainees standing by piles of baggage or looking hopelessly at the incoming field carts, watching for some last item among the confusion of the large hall. There were two large bags where the girl in the green jacket had been standing—and here she came back, dragging two more!

More carts arrived. Theo made herself stand patiently: her bag was well marked and would be easy enough to see once everything was brought in by the quick-moving workers. They all moved so easily, so much like pilots—

She lifted her eyes to the ceiling, feeling more than a little bit dumb. Of course they all moved like pilots: she'd been told that most of the work at Anlingdin Piloting Academy was performed by pilots-in-training; eventually she'd be doing the same thing herself.

Looking around, Theo wondered how some of her fellow students could possibly have moved all their stuff between ship and shuttle. Could they really need piles and piles of whatever it was they'd brought?

True, she had shed some solemn tears in making the first hard decisions for herself, but as time went on she'd thought about the Melchiza trip and the extra carrying she'd done for that, and about how little of what was in her room would be going with her after she was a pilot, so it might as well stay home now. Like Coyster, and Father, and Kamele. They, like her things, would be there when she came home to visit; that would never change.

Kamele's reaction to Theo's first attempt at packing had been an astonished, "*Two* bags? But you have an allowance for three times that much!"

Father had laughed. "Be gentle—it is her first attempt! She'll soon learn better," he told Kamele, at the same time flashing a bright bit of hand-talk to Theo—*pilot to pilot*—and she'd laughed, then, though a heartbeat before she'd been ready to cry.

He'd managed to get much of the contents of her second bag into the first with astute repacking, and had eliminated other things with quick questions and comments like, "No library on Eylot?" and, "Outworld is not the same as frontier, youngster: I am almost certain that they will have tea" and even "This mumu will be inappropriate on Eylot. Perhaps you should take your files with you and turn this back into the Wall for reuse."

She'd checked his face and seen only serious interest there: not a joke. And in the end, she'd copied her files and turned the mumu back to the Tech Department. In the end, she'd whittled things she brought to only the necessary.

Father said that pilots used the Three Pile Rule for deciding what to take with them. The first pile consisted of the things she really needed: ID, money, "your license, eventually, and a keep-safe, if you wish." Those things ought to fit into her jacket, vest or travel kit and always be to hand.

Things that she'd need later went into the second pile, and were packed in luggage.

Those things that she *might* need, except for extra air or water, went into the third pile—which was left behind.

Theo shifted from one foot to the other. She was getting tired of waiting in all the din and confusion, and was beginning to think longingly of her nice, quiet bunk, soon to be achieved— There!

Yet another sled came into the hall, her bag with its tag clearly visible perched on top of the pile. The gate snapped closed smartly behind it; a student work gang including—to her surprise and regret—the three troublemakers from *Vestrin,* ran for the cart to toss the last items off.

Ah, she thought, that explains it! The three knew exactly where their luggage was, and hauled it free with a fine disregard for physics. The surrounding bags shifted and tumbled. Her bag slid from its high perch, caught, and fell. Theo jumped forward—

Just before her bag hit the floor, one of the crew caught it, neatly and without flourish, looked down, blinked, and turned to display it to his friends. Maybe he was checking the tags, though she didn't know why they should care.

Theo continued toward them, and was almost knocked down by the tall girl in the bright green jacket, who had been looking lost earlier. She didn't look lost now. She looked mad.

"That box need not be thrown!" She sounded mad, too.

Indeed, the tallest of the three from the ship was hoisting a small box as if he meant to toss it to the floor.

He glared, put the box down hard on the cart, off-handedly caught another bag tossed to him by the stubbier guy, dropped it to the floor, and picked up Theo's bag. He made a show out of reading the tag, and laughed too loud.

"I'll take that, thank you."

Startlement.

Theo flushed; her words had come out louder than she'd expected, and into a lull in the racket of the hall, turning heads and dropping conversation levels all around.

"Yours? It's got a pilot tag on it!" This from the ringleader who'd offered, several times and pointedly, to permit Theo to accompany him—or all of them—to his cabin on the *Vestrin.* The oversize pilot's wings glittered on his shirt collar, just as it had when he'd leaned toward her conspiratorially on the ship, as if his offer had been some kind of favor.

"My bag." Theo nodded, trying for Kamele's crispest, most efficient voice. "Thank you."

A flick of fingers from the stubby one; quick and with an accent she wasn't sure of, though she caught the sense: *Throw me now run catch back toy's bag.*

"Don't!" Theo snapped, accompanying that with a slashing

STOP ALL! that brought a laugh from an onlooker and a too-loudly muttered, "Miss Purity strikes again!" from the ringleader.

"And *I* want my box," the girl in the green jacket said imperiously. "You make me late for lunch."

The guy holding Theo's bag sat on the box and looked down at her, ignoring the girl in the jacket.

"This tag—" He held the bag up and shook it at her, like she needed help understanding which tag he was talking about. "This tag is from Melchiza, in case you don't know that. I can read the sight-code, and that's a pilot-rated clearance. I bet you don't have a pilot ID, do you? If you do, now's the time to show it. If you don't, I'm filing this as stolen."

Theo glared, and touched the patch on her jacket, that still carried her *Vestrin* photo pass-card and—

As if from all the walls at once came a lilting, if loud, announcement.

"Attention. Registration jitney leaves in two minutes from door four. Load now."

"This tag," Theo said, showing the strip she'd gotten at Melchiza Station, "matches *that* tag. I got them on Melchiza, and they're current for the Standard. My name is on both. My bag. Sir."

She spoke calmly, and the *sir* was almost gentle, but she couldn't stop herself from dropping into a posture of alert waiting—nor, judging by the murmurs behind her, was that lost on others. She sighed to herself. Father had warned her—

"Oho, Wilsmyth, I think you ought to give the pretty her bag," said someone Theo couldn't see. "Before she breaks you."

"I want my box!" snapped the girl in the green jacket. "Rise, oaf! I must have lunch! I must register!" She moved forward purposefully, jacket billowing.

Wilsmyth hesitated for another fraction of a second. He rose then, fast and sudden, and threw Theo's bag at her, hard. The other girl ducked beneath it to grab the box.

Theo fielded the bag one-handed, feeling a pull in her shoulder, and used the other hand to sign a curt *receipt acknowledged*, before she turned to seek door four.

TWO

. . . .

New Student Orientation
Ozler Auditorium
Anlingdin Piloting Academy

THE WOMAN IN THE PLAIN GREY UNIFORM HAD THE ROOM'S FULL attention as she strode about the low stage, left to right, right to left, talking at times as much to herself as to the group. The simple acts of walking on stage wearing a Jump pilot's jacket, slipping it off and casually throwing it over a nearby chair, had caught them as much as the quick hand-and-voice: *Welcome and listen up.* "I'm Commander Ronagy."

The basic intro was about what Theo had expected, a highly condensed repeat of the information in the school's orientation packet, but the follow-on was not.

Commander Ronagy came to the front of the stage and stood, legs braced, hands at ready, looking sternly out over the first four center rows, which were all the newbie class filled in this big auditorium.

"If you have any doubts about being here," she said soberly, "please, there's a shuttle scheduled to lift in the morning. If you're here under duress, come talk to me tonight, and we'll get you out of here as soon as we can, as neatly as we can. If you don't want to be here, we don't want you here."

Her right hand rose, fingers dancing briefly, several subdued metallic rings marking time in the spotlight, before she turned to pace again. Theo turned her head slightly and saw that tables

9

and tray carts were being moved in the side door and rolling silently toward the back.

"I can tell you that not every pilot trainee has survived the course at Anlingdin Piloting Academy," the Commander continued. "The records speak for themselves and I suggest you avail yourselves of them if you haven't already. But you're here now, and this is what I can tell you without doubt: This will be one of the most physically and mentally challenging periods of your life. You may succumb to any of the hazards that claimed those of your less successful predecessors here at the academy: carelessness, bravado, inattention, suicide—these are the more common.

"You'll study some of the more dramatic errors in your training sims and if they don't leave you shaken, then perhaps you're in the wrong field. Our testing is designed to ensure that you're always at your peak, and always up to the next level of instruction. If you find you're falling behind, speak up."

Here she stopped in midstride, appeared to look at all the students at once and emphatically finger-yelled *GET HELP*. Her hands fluttered into a more subtle motion . . . she might, Theo thought, have been reminding herself of where she was in her presentation—*point six*.

"I can tell you that, statistically, your chance of survival and graduation is higher than the average. That's because you—this group—are something special. On the whole you're older than the school cohort groups we get for first and second semester. There's a compelling reason to start you now, rather than with the freshman class starting in a few months. Someone we trust told us you don't need to be babied or coddled, that you'll be able to do the job of becoming a pilot on your own terms. On the whole your recommendations have come directly from pilots who know you, and who are teachers in their own right.

"I can also tell you that if one of you errs to the point of death, it will greatly sadden us all, and we will mourn, but we will continue, as we have for three hundred years."

Theo caught the quick hand motion: *point seven*.

"Remember, yours is the interim group, and you're replacing those who washed themselves out, who flunked, who were asked not to return, who were claimed by their families for other duties, or who got drafted by their governments. Those ahead of you are technically your seniors. As we're at midyear, you will be moved into classes already in progress—and if necessary into remedial classes. Our charter with the planetary government requires the academy not only to enroll so many pilots per year, but to graduate so many a year. We are depending on you to be able to graduate, and while you'll get as much help as we can give to make you ready, your group is not supported by the general rebates and fees Anlingdin pays for local students and you'll generally not have the option to retake entire semesters."

Boy, was that ever true, Theo thought. She'd seen what the annual fee was, and it would have taken three years of Kamele's base salary to pay for her first year here...without Captain Cho's sponsorship she'd have never been able to enroll. And if she didn't keep her grades up, she wouldn't be able to afford to stay.

Point eight.

"If we were at the beginning of either half-term, I would be able to tell you how many of you will be sharing dormitory rooms, and give other housekeeping details. As it is, you will be scattered among existing housing arrangements, and might have anywhere from one to three other students with you. Generally, one student in each suite will clearly be the senior. Though we're not strictly military about these things—pilots are flexible, after all!—allow me to strongly suggest that the senior student be regarded as a mentor and guide, at least during your first semester. Your housing and meal information will be delivered at the tables which will be set up here while we all take advantage of the meal being laid at the back now. After the break, please have your Anlingdin cards at the ready and we'll get your piloting career under way. For the safety of all, please, no bowli balls in this room!"

There was an undercurrent of laughter as the Commander pointed out the tables piled with plates and food being being uncovered and set to serve.

The next signed but unspoken command was clearly *all eat.*

The buffet was surprisingly lavish, especially after the stifling sameness of *Vestrin's* menus. There was a mix of what Theo considered to be morning food and day food, to accommodate different personal times and preferences. Theo grabbed what looked like a cheese sandwich on dark bread, and a salad plate.

Real, green vegetables! Carrots! And whole slices of tomato! She hadn't seen anything so good in weeks.

She located a vacant seat at a table for four, sent a nod and quick *seat taken?* to the sole occupant, a kid who was already deeply involved with a slice of pie. His unoccupied hand sent back a laconic *help yourself.*

"Thanks," Theo said, and parked her eatables before going off in search of a beverage.

The real tea was filed on a small table away from the coffee urns, fruit juice dispensers and carafes of water. Theo flipped open the keeper and flicked through the packets on offer. Again unlike *Vestrin*, which had offered Terran grades of so-called "tea," here were more familiar—and vastly more welcome!—packets interleaved with the Terran leaf.

Her hopes rose. Maybe they'd have— Yes! She grinned and plucked the packet of day tea from its cubby, turned—and all but fell into a man hardly any taller than she was. She danced sideways and made a recovery, the precious packet between her fingers.

The man smiled, and gave her a brief, pretty bow, murmuring something quick and lilting. The sound was so liquid that it took her a moment to realize that it was neither Terran—the official language of the academy—nor Trade, but Liaden.

She gave back a nod, found her hands had already asked *Say again?* while she blurted out in what she was sure was the wrong mode and probably the wrong tense, too, "Pardon, I have very small Liaden."

The man—the tag on his jacket read "Flight Instructor Orn Ald yos'Senchul," and the right sleeve of his crisp, tailored school jacket was empty—inclined his head.

"I'm sorry," she gasped, feeling her face heat. Using hand-talk to somebody with only one hand. *Way to be advertent, Theo!*

Flight Instructor yos'Senchul's fingers formed an elegant sign she read as *expectations betray*, while he smiled and murmured in accented Terran, "My pardon, as well. I was speaking a small Liaden jest, of two with exquisite taste who search for the same treasure." The fingers moved again, shaping the air effortlessly, *Apology unnecessary.*

"Oh, the tea!" Theo showed her packet. "This is the kind we drink at home."

"Is it, indeed? And you have so little Liaden?"

"Sleep learned, mostly," she confessed. "I know my accent's terrible. We speak Terran at home on Delgado, but the tea, I learned from my father."

His focus went distant a moment and the single hand signed a word she read as *wifechoice*. "Yes, of course. Delgado is quite cosmopolitan in its beverage choices, is it not, quite unlike... Melchiza."

She snorted, hands signing *squashed fruitwater* very nearly on their own, and he laughed.

"An excellent description, and their wines are not much better. Still, they do appreciate pilots... and I deduce, from rumor, that you must be Theo Waitley. I am pleased to make your acquaintance. You will be in my classes starting in two days. Enjoy your meal, and your tea!"

"Thank you, sir," she said, but he had already turned to the tea chest to make his own choice. She caught up a brew-cup and moved off to her table, now full except for her place, and felt her face heat again as she went over the encounter.

Squashed fruitwater, she thought, and sighed. There must be a better sign that that!

"Erkes!" the van driver called out. "All excellent exopilots exit energetically..."

Theo went down the ramp on the heels of the tall girl in the green jacket from the baggage claim. The two of them pulled their bags from the rack, Theo wordlessly helping the other girl move her ridiculous pile out of the path of vehicular traffic.

"Thank you," the girl said as the van pulled away. She looked down at Theo and nodded. "I am Asu diamon Dayez," she said, pronouncing it like she expected Theo to recognize it, which she didn't. "And you are?"

"Theo Waitley." She hefted her bag, glad all over again to have only the one to deal with. "I'm in suite three-oh-two," she said, watching Asu diamon Dayez tether her bags together.

The taller girl looked up, shaking tumbled black curls out of her eyes. "So am I." She straightened, handle in one hand, and the all-important box tucked into the crook of her left arm. "Well! Let us be off, then, to discover this suite. If you will be so good as to open the door?"

✳   ✳   ✳

Suite 302 was no bigger, Theo thought, than the apartment she and Kamele had in the Wall back on Delgado, but it was a lot better arranged. The door opened into a common room, with chairs, table, vid-screen, and a built-in counter already sporting a coffeepot and a minioven.

At the far end of the room, to the right, was another room, door open to reveal two bunks, two desks and lots of built-in storage space. To the left was a room slightly larger than the bunk room with a single bed and its own vid-screen.

She turned as the door to the hall opened to admit Asu, who was already sliding her key away into a pocket. "It works, and a good idea to test both at once," she said, giving an approving nod, which she probably meant to be friendly, but which for some reason irritated Theo.

I must be really tired, she thought, and swallowed her irritation, as she turned away to point at the bunk room.

"Which do you want, top or bottom?"

"Surely neither," Asu said crisply, steering her baggage train toward the single room. "I shall take this one."

Theo frowned. "That's probably the senior's room, do you think?"

The other girl turned her head, eyebrows up in surprise. "And I am senior, am I not? Eighteen Standards, plus a half."

She waited, her attitude one of challenge, and it wouldn't do to have an argument with her roommate on their first day, Theo reminded herself. She shrugged, hiding the sigh. "Plus a half? You're older than me," she conceded, and Asu nodded, apparently mollified.

"Please," she said, like she was giving Theo a present, "take whichever bunk pleases you." She glanced around again, frowning slightly. "Surely this can't be all the space. I will look more closely, but first, let us be secure."

She turned to the box she had placed on the table in the joint room. Theo carried her bag into the bunk room and set it down on one of the desks.

To her eye the top bunk was the best. The storage was good—more than she needed—the lighting abundant and directional, and twin fans—

"There!" Asu exclaimed.

Theo drifted out to the joint room, more curious about what

was in the mysterious box than she was willing to admit even to herself.

"What is it?" she asked, blinking at the squat console with its array of varicolored lights.

Asu stared at her. "A Checksec, of course. Didn't you bring one? I mean, we've *got* to be careful. People are always snooping to see when you're traveling next, and if anyone's home, and intercepting the banking and everything. You never know if someone's listening with a vibcounter, or using a chipleak detector, or tapping net-calls. I mean, you can with a Checksec...but without one, all your business is public."

"But we're—" Theo swallowed the rest of her protest, suddenly remembering the "bug" Win Ton had found on board the *Vashtara*. Maybe Asu had a point, after all, she thought, warming to her roomie slightly.

That glow had faded by the time Asu had gone on to explain—at length—how in her house each room had a Checksec and they got calibrated every five days, and moved about randomly as well, so that anyone trying to spoof one would have a very hard time. And...it all sounded like too much trouble to Theo. She excused herself as soon as the Checksec had shown all its eyes green, which Asu said meant they were clean, "For now," she'd added darkly; and went to get settled in to quarters.

Some time later, Theo sat very much at home on the top bunk, marveling at the amount of unused storage still available to her, wondering what else she might want to own here that would fill up the space. Chaos, the counter in the joint room had a coffee-pot already, and if she could get a tea maker she'd have storage for all that tea Father had suggested she not bring. Well fuff on him, she thought—and smiled.

Father had been right about her packing, she allowed, and she was glad not to have done all the huffing and puffing that others of her classmates had—

From next door came yet another scrunching noise, and perhaps a swear word she didn't know. Asu was still at work trying to fit a house's worth of goods into a closet's worth of space, now that she was finished setting up her Checksec. Honestly, you'd think there wasn't a Safety Office on Asu's world, whatever it was.

"Oh, Theo, come see!" Asu called.

Theo sighed, but in the interest of keeping peace, slid off her bunk and went to see.

The alcove room had a single bed, with a large expanse of wall behind it. That wall was now adorned with a life-sized—or maybe, Theo thought on quick second appraisal—a larger than life-sized image of a lusty nude young man with amazing ear jewelry, among other fine and entirely visible qualities, standing in front of what must be an ocean.

"Ah..." Theo managed, trying to recall the information about decorating campus suites that had been in the school's orientation materials.

"Yes," Asu said, smugly. "Jondeer had much the same effect on me when I first met him dressed like this on the Ridyea beach. How was I to know he was a full member of the Bovar System Scavage A-Team?"

Theo laughed despite herself—"Well, you could say he was out of uniform, couldn't you?" She sighed, and managed a calm question. "Don't you think he'll be...distracting?"

"No, I think Jondeer will be inspiring! After all, once I have my *own* pilot's license I'll be able to travel to his games whenever I like! You know, he has a pic of me that he puts up in his locker everywhere he goes! I've seen it in the background of his game interviews!"

Theo remembered now. The instructions about images had been particularly clear: Display only group-appropriate images within view of an open door, always use academy-issued hanger tabs...

But, she reminded herself...maybe first day wasn't the time to start an argument. And clearly, someone who was swapping perspix with a top-line scavage player had a lot more experience than she did. Though maybe not, she thought, the kind of experience that was going to make her much by way of that "mentor and guide" Commander Ronagy had mentioned.

Theo sighed as she clambered back to her bunk. Well, the Commander had also said that they were expected to be self-sufficient.

It wasn't like there wasn't stuff to do, so she'd be ready for tomorrow and her first classes. She turned on her commlink and keypad, set up her accounts, checked again to make sure she'd stowed everything, and memorized where she'd put what. Her single piece of luggage had a cubby to itself, and she still had three left over. She felt a small glow of satisfaction. Other than being light-years from home, missing Coyster and Father and Kamele and Win Ton and Cho and Bek, she was in good shape.

She closed her eyes. More noise and mutters came from the other room, in spite of which she felt like she could almost go to sleep. But it was too early, local time, to go to sleep, and besides, she was too twitchy. There was a school store. Maybe she'd go down and see if they had a tea maker and tea. That would use up some of the undirected energy *and* make the place feel a little more like home.

A chime sounded, under the racket that Asu was making. Theo looked around, frowning, but there was no repeat. Shrugging, she swung down from the bunk. Maybe she could go for a walk around Erkes Quad; familiarize herself, and get a little peace.

The door to the hall snapped open, and one of the rude crew from the *Vestrin*—the third-string guy, stocky and quieter than the other two—stepped inside, and stopped, staring around at the disarray of Asu's unpacking, shock apparent on his face.

"What are you doing here?" Theo demanded. "We set the locks!"

He didn't even spare her a glance, his attention focused on the open door to Asu's room, and the abundant display of male flesh plainly visible, his hands moving insistently *remove please remove please remove please.*

"Who are you?" Asu demanded, standing in the doorway with her hands on her hips and a mighty frown on her face. "You disturb our privacy!"

"I'm Chelly Frosher," he said, sounding rushed, but surprisingly firm. "I got nine semesters in grade, so I'm senior here. I rang, but you didn't answer, so I used my key. The locks override to my card," he said pointing at the door and waving his card around. "This here will be my quarters, um, Miss. And that," he continued, pointing more or less toward Jondeer's insouciant grin, "won't meet community standards here at Erkes. This is your basic local frosh house, except for us and the house father. Some of these kids are underage. So, take it down, and move into your bunk. Thanks."

THREE

· · · · · · · · · · ·

Erkes Dormitory
Suite 302
Anlingdin Piloting Academy

"BUNK?" ASU RAISED ONE HAND FROM HER HIP AND USED IT TO sweep the room, like she was proud of the mess she'd made and was putting it on display. "Does this look to you like it will fit into a *bunk*?"

Chelly shrugged. "Not my problem," he said. "Getting into my quarters so I can grab a little downtime before class, that's *my* problem."

"There is a bunk available," Asu told him, with a false sweetness that set Theo's teeth on edge. "I'm sure Theo will be glad to show you."

"Look," Chelly began, his shoulders tensing up toward his ears, and it really *wasn't*, Theo thought, a good idea to fight on their first night together.

She went two steps closer to where the pair of them were staring at each other like two cats trying to see which one could blow themselves up bigger.

"He's senior," she said.

Two pairs of eyes—one blue, one brown—focused on her, which was what she'd wanted, she reminded herself, swallowing.

"Excuse me?" Asu asked, still in that too-sweet voice that was all out of sync with posture that said she was one grab short of throwing something.

19

"He's senior," Theo repeated. "Nine semesters in grade, didn't you hear him say?" She pointed at the joint room screen. "You can probably look him up in records if you think he's smoking us."

"Smoking—" Chelly blinked at her. "Why would I *bother*?"

"Why'd you *bother* on *Vestrin*, you and the rest of your crew?" Theo snapped back. "It's not like *you've* never gotten a note in your file."

"Do I look that stupid?" Chelly demanded, but his fingers were already signing, *Message received*. He stalked over to the screen, slammed his card into the reader and spun the unit round to face them.

Student ID 439285
Frosher Chelly
Meal Plan
Study Score: 23
S1 Erkes 302
Student Pilot Rating: 3.5

"Satisfied?" he asked, mostly at Asu.

There was silence, not nearly, Theo assured herself, as long or as heavy as she thought it was before Asu sighed sharply, nodded once and turned to peel Jondeer off the wall.

"Are there no beaches on this backward, benighted planet?" Asu demanded sometime later. Her stuff was mostly unboxed now; the joint room was awash in *things*, as was every available flat surface in the bunk room and most of the floor. She looked tired and sounded tireder, with a side helping of torqued off.

Theo, who was tired herself and not feeling exactly calm, couldn't work up much sympathy for her, especially since she'd seen the taller girl eying Theo's extra space.

"That," she'd said, pointing at her shelves and built-ins, "is my storage. Yours is down below."

"There is less down below!"

"There's exactly the same amount of storage space for high bunk and low," Chelly said grumpily from the doorway. He shook his head in, as Theo read it, equal parts amazement and disgust. "What's with the beach? You thinking you earned a vacation?"

Asu turned her back on him. "I am thinking that Jondeer's picture was taken at the beach, and that he is garbed appropriately," she said icily. "Surely even the youngest student here has been to the beach."

"If it was a picture of the beach with a guy in it, that maybe would've passed," Chelly said, and it sounded as if he really was trying to explain the problem. "This is a picture of a guy that happens to have some beach in it. *Whole* different perspective."

Theo snorted, and Chelly turned his head to glare up at her.

"You wanna finish out the course, you better lose some of that attitude, Waitley."

This from a guy who'd been making her life miserable for the last—Theo sat up, face hot. "What's the matter with my attitude?"

"*That's* what!" he yelled. "You think nobody noticed you daring Wil to come dancing, there at baggage? You think maybe you don't already have a note by your name that you got aggression problems?"

"*I've* got aggression problems?" Theo shook her head and just stared down at him, absolutely unable to believe what she'd just heard.

"I—all right." She took a breath, and another one, centering herself there on the bunk and letting the tension—well, as much of the tension as she could, flow out of her toes and fingertips.

"Look, Chelly," she said, over Asu's slamming open storage bays. "I don't know what people saw. What I know is that Wilsmyth was trying to make trouble for me. I don't know *why*, but I don't need to know *why* to know that he was, from the very first time I saw him, on *Vestrin*. From *my* perspective, he was trying to get me to lose my temper, or maybe get me in trouble with Admin for having a *stolen bag*, like he said. If I was edgy, I think that's reasonable. And I think anybody who saw me drop to neutral would also have seen why I did it." She took a breath. "So, there might be a note in my file. It wouldn't be the first time. And I'm probably not alone."

Chelly chewed his lip, and looked over his shoulder into the joint room. "Wil gets chaizy when he's not working," he muttered. "He'll buckle, now there's work." He sighed, and shook his head, looking back to Asu.

"You'd think somebody whose family owns tradeships would know how to pack," he said.

Head and shoulders inside the bottommost storage compartment, Asu sniffed. "We *own* them," she said, her voice echoing hollowly, "we do not *live* on them."

"Yeah, well, you think you'll have all this stuff stowed soon? It's gotta be put away—those're regs, and if the house father does an inspect while you're at class, he can clean up anything that's not in its place." He grimaced. "He gets a real buzz outta cleaning up after newbies."

"Thank you," Asu said, emerging carefully from the compartment, and sitting back on her heels. She ran a hand through her damp curls. Unfairly, they sprang neatly back into place, unlike Theo's hair, which had frizzed out into its most uncombable.

"Were you in this room...last semester?" Theo asked Chelly, and then wondered why she cared.

He nodded. "Yeah. I was top bunk. Panvay was senior—she challenged out. Tildenburg was low bunk—he flunked out. *Finally*."

"Finally?" That final word even caught Asu, who gave Chelly an over-the-shoulder look.

"Yeah, he should've been outta here before the end of his second semester, but his family paid the fee and convinced Ronagy he'd stick with the program. Only he just did the same thing over again, like he couldn't help himself, and flunked again, just like the first time and—that was it." He shook his head. "It wasn't like Pan didn't *tell* him, or like he didn't know, it—" Another head shake. "Didn't want to be a pilot, is what it came down to. His parents, they wanted it. Tildenburg, he wanted to be a poet."

"A person may be both a poet and a pilot," Asu said soberly.

"Not," Chelly answered, "if you only work on the poet side." He looked around again and shook his head.

"Look," he said. "I *am* the senior and I'm telling you this straight—" His hands moved lightly: *affirm, affirm.* "You gotta get this stuff stowed and get some downtime. When you start on-mester you get a couple days' slack while you catch on to things, 'cause everybody's slow and sleepy, see? But the off-shift—you guys are gonna go into classes that are already moving and they're gonna expect you to *run* to keep up—and no whining. I'm telling you."

"Thanks," Theo said. "But *why* are you telling us?"

He looked up at her, strong eyebrows pulled over blue eyes. "I'm senior," he repeated. "And I'm on command track. If you two screw up, it's gonna go against me, too."

Asu laughed.

Chelly glared at the back of her head, then transferred his glare to Theo, who did her best to keep her face neutral.

"I'm going to bed," he said, turning away. "Try to get sensible, right?"

"Sleep well, Chelly Frosher," Asu caroled brightly. He didn't answer, and Theo really couldn't blame him.

"Why'd you laugh when he said he'd get marked down if we flunked out on his watch?" Theo asked as Asu climbed to her feet.

The taller girl put her elbows on Theo's bunk and smiled.

"He admits to an interest," she said, around a yawn. "Therefore, we have leverage."

"Oh," Theo said, and looked over the edge of the bunk at the wreckage below. It seemed to her that Asu had managed to get an astonishing amount of stuff stowed while seeming to be ineffective. Unfortunately, that still left a lot to put...somewhere.

"Theo, I cannot help but notice that you have unused space," Asu said, and Theo sighed.

"We've been—" she began, and blinked, remembering the dusty smell of rugs and an old woman's voice: *No dickering here, I see!*

She considered the side of Asu's face, and decided the other girl looked at least as tired as she felt. The sooner the stuff got put away, the sooner they both could get some rest after what had become a really, *really* long day.

"You want some of my extra storage?" she asked Asu. The other girl smiled.

"It would be a boon."

"No, it wouldn't," Theo corrected her, and reached out to tap two of the three empty cubbies. "Trade for them."

Asu raised her head and stared at the mess all around, before looking seriously into Theo's face.

"I cannot promise or incur a debt in the name of Diamon Lines," she said finally, hands giving emphasis to the point.

"Diamon Lines isn't sleeping in the bunk below mine," Theo said. "I want an IOU, redeemable at a future time for one favor. Deal?"

Once again, Asu glanced about her. She sighed, and held a hand out to Theo.

"Done," she said, barely touching Theo's fingers before reaching past her to open the first empty cubby.

FOUR

· · · · · · · · · ·

Academy Flight GT S14
Anlingdin Piloting Academy

SLIPPER FOURTEEN FELT LIKE HOME TODAY; NO LONGER AN ALIEN environment to be overcome but a friendly, trusted place, a place without the constant sniping between Asu and Chelly, a place where her motions were simple and sufficient, a place where the instructor looked over her shoulder only by instrument, his voice brought to her by the ear bud, and that not often; she'd wondered these last five flights if he'd monitored her at all.

The craft's cockpit was tiny, hardly more than a stiffly padded lay-back seat and some hand controls and pedals yoked electrically to the airfoils, with a tight-sealed canopy a hand's-width in front of her face that let the wind slip past. Boarding it was like slipping into her proper skin, especially with the belt-web forming itself to her so carefully after she touched the locking stud.

The tow drone's pace was sufficient for her to test her skill at boxing the wake without being bored: she moved to the right with the tow rope taut, then down below the wake, then left to the other side of the box, up, and centered again, the whole while using *her* slip-string to help guide her by sight as the other instruments.

Otto El, the glider instructor, insisted that each trainee bring and mount their own slip-string; just as he insisted that each trainee personally inspect the craft before each takeoff and after every landing.

"It is good to see what you have done," he'd told the small assembled class of five on their first meeting, "and it is good to *see* that your vessel is able before you trust your life and the lives of others to it!"

The slender wings were well behind Theo's position as the Slipper rose; today's preflight inspection had shown the outer left wing stained and scraped—grass stains. She'd immediately entered that into her logbook, lifted the wing to inspect it, attempted to flex it and probed at it with her hand and stylus. Pilot El had nodded as she made her verbal report and inquired about it.

"Yes, good. There was an awkward moment for someone in a crosswind landing yesterday; we've imaged it and everything is fine. You'll find it noted in the ship's log."

By the third class they'd lost two of their class members, one apparently to basic homesickness and the other to something Asu darkly called a "hyper-dense Code Ten Fifty-Six"—but there, Asu had been in three much larger classes with the boy. The Ten Fifties were the mental fitness codes if Theo recalled correctly, and the result was that Pilot El was pleased to go on an accelerated one-on-one with the remaining three students.

"We can all move to the power segments much faster now," he said, "and you three, very soon, will be able to walk with wings on your shoulders."

The wings he promised were more than metaphysical: while some of the astronautics group went without the atmospheric license, deeming it a useless artifact, there was, after all, still a living to be made in flying atmospheric and near-world craft.

The drone's beeped report echoed what Theo'd already felt: they were comfortably topped out and had a good steady flight, and maybe a chance to ride the front wave down Kirky's Range.

"Academy Flight GT S14," came a trainee's bored voice, "you're set for release in fifteen ticks at my mark. We've got your transponders in good order, you've got great Qs, and the designated landing zone is South, runway seven. Mark!"

Great Qs meant the clouds favored a long flight; she was all for it since the longer she stayed up the longer she could avoid going back to Erkes. Asu busy was better than Asu with nothing to do, but still she found time to complain about how little room she had, about being stuck in with the Erkes kids whenever she used the jitney, and with a litany of Anlingdin security weaknesses...

"Mark, thank you, GT S14 acknowledges."

Theo watched the slip-string as she raised the nose a bit, allowing the tow rope just a bit of slack and then just a bit more. She touched the rudder to dip wing, pushed the stick slightly forward, and the rope went from lifeline to fluttering ribbon, bearing to the right, and away. The slip-string snapped, like it was waving good-bye, and Theo sighed with the joy of finally being free to fly.

Slipper Fourteen gained speed for a moment until Theo leveled it out and then saw the variometer happily indicating she'd hit the thermal. Her key in the flight system jauntily blinked blue once a second, indicating her flight time was logged and mounting properly, and everything else looked good.

Everything. From here, Anlingdin was beautiful, and even the grounds of the academy, spreading out toward the horizon, were worth seeing. Out the other side of the ship the mountain range stood stark and compelling, the blue-grey peaks casting sharp-edged shadows.

She laughed out loud, and suppressed the urge to shout, suddenly mindful of Asu's warnings.

"Remember, Theo, every mic is live at all times. We're all right here, in our suite, because the Checksec will warn us if we're monitored. But out there? Galosh, they can hear everything you say about everyone, and then hold everything against your record."

Theo'd wondered who'd twisted Asu's hair that time... but after all, Melchiza did it, and Delgado did it; everybody was always watched by somebody, for the good of everybody else.

She laughed again, as she looked about her, seeing nothing but blue sky and wonderfully large and billowing clouds. They hadn't outlawed happy at the academy, and flying was a happy thing.

"Flight GT S14, Academy GT S14, acknowledge."

Not flight control, but her instructor. He *was* paying attention!

"Flight GT S14 here."

"Waitley, this is El, on special from control; how quickly can you get down?"

Theo's glance swept the board, gathered in the variometer and altitude; she consulted the map display and clicked the direct route... she'd hardly been worried about getting down fastest; in fact soaring had been working well and she'd been thinking about filing an amendment to extend her time.

"Ship says at standard descent...sixteen minutes, unless I get an updraft."

"Won't do. Want you out of the sky—everyone out of the sky quickly...emergency."

Theo looked away from the instruments, across the sky, to the eminence of Kirky's Range. Local history had it that the first traveler from space had used its spine and plateau as a pointer for his rescuers...

Out of the sky...

"I can stuff it on the plateau in five minutes."

Her hands and feet followed her eyes, as if she leaned toward the promontory.

There was no reply, and she repeated, watching the slip-string on the canopy as it flowed in reply to the ship's bank and turn. Who would've thought that simple piece of yarn could be so useful?

"GT S14 here, please ack—"

"Can you?" The query overrode her. "El here. That's tricky, Waitley, lots of updrafts. Acknowledge."

The ship was already gaining speed as she pushed the stick forward. The plan was...

"I can," she said, absolutely sure of it. "If you want me down quickest. Acknowledge."

Again a pause, but now she realized Instructor El was thinking hard. She was thinking hard, too—while the way was clear to the mountain, even the Doppler radar setting might not be enough for the tricky currents she'd be facing.

"Bad spot, Waitley. Report before you set down; be prepared to abort on my command. I won't jostle your elbow otherwise. Acknowledge."

Theo smiled. "Acknowledged."

She'd cruised distantly along the standing wave the mountains created just once before, in the trainer, when she'd had Pilot El in the second seat. That had brought flutters to her stomach and twinges to her hands as she'd felt the strength of the up-draft.

This time she was going to *use* that updraft; sideslipping the ship several times to lose altitude, and then: yes!

There was the wave! The slip-string fluttered momentarily and the variometer showed a sudden change in the ship's motion. Even though the nose was pointed slightly downward, the whole column of air she was in was rising rapidly. Noise multiplied in the cockpit as the variometer began to sound a rising pitch, while the automaton intermittently spoke rate-change numbers. The most important thing was the rising pitch...

Ahead, the mountain's dark color began to differentiate into rugged columns of weathered rock and deep shadowed crevices.

She'd never had to read the radar so hard before; the twisting currents swept the sleek glider higher, closer to the mountain with each second. Designed for simple soaring, the great wings seemed to chuckle at this unexpected task, the sound unnerving, as they trembled in the troubled air column.

More than three minutes had passed according to the ship's chronometer; she was sweating, listening for the call to abort, fighting to keep the nose pointed in the right direction against wind that made the plane crab and shudder. Her goal was only a minute or so higher; she knew that once she reached the top her work would really begin.

There came a lull in the buffeting, but she wasn't comforted because the rock face loomed. She was close enough now that the fuselage might easily fit into a crevice if air willed it; the beautiful wings she loved so much now as much of a problem as an asset.

Warnings went off: too much lift, too close to the mountain, stall warning...

Theo worked to shut out the sounds of the winds and the warnings: she could only ride this out. She *would* ride this out. She only—there!

The top of the plateau appeared to her left. She sideslipped the craft in that direction, fighting a wicked crosswind that wanted to twist her wings.

Unexpectedly, she continued to rise. She forced the nose down, arms shaking with the effort. The top of the plateau was pocked with wind-worn gullies and rippled dust, but her biggest problem wasn't finding a place to land but in forcing the Slipper into actually setting down.

She had underestimated the winds, she thought. Or overestimated her own ability.

"Not great, Theo," she muttered, "not great."

Then she saw a spot and caught a lull in the wind.

"Waitley, GT S14," she snapped at the comm. "Setting down immediately."

She almost managed it, but her wings built their own ground effect in the jostling wind and the plane hovered as she hit spoilers and then did one more very slight sideslip to meet the ground. The Slipper stayed down, then, roiling grass and gravel, coming to rest on an incline that became a slope that ran out into the abyss below. Distantly, and far below, was a blur of green that was flat land.

"GT S14 here. Down."

She had an immediate acknowledgment. "Waitley, El acknowledging GT S14 down on Kirky's Range. Now, if you can pop that canopy, get out of the plane and find yourself a safe spot to sit. Give me ten minutes, then call back."

What she said was, "Acknowledge."

What she thought was harder: if this whole thing was some weird part of training she had an idea why pilots washed out. A more stupid way to...

The canopy stopped resisting as she hurled some off-mic invective at the world, and then she was too busy keeping dust out of her face to think—

A new sound assaulted her as she tumbled out of the plane: a chunking noise like one of Father's old auto engines gone wrong, then a *whoosh* and another round of chunking noises.

A bright sidewise flash caught her eye: aircraft in the sun. Not just one, but a group of three or four. Now five. They were nearly as high as she was! She wondered if they were there looking for her, but then—

The chunking noise came again and she saw bright streams of fiery dots blast from one of the jets, and then from a second; there was another bright flash then and the lead plane roared low overhead, trailing smoke and debris, while the others...

Understanding rushed through her: *this* was the emergency!

She flung herself between two boulders as the other planes flashed by, and from the corner of her eye she caught a multiple flash, turning her head in time to see the lead plane, already well on the other side of the mountain ridge, explode in a brilliant flare of metal and flame, and fall out of her line of sight.

*   *   *

"Do you know what they've done? They've stolen my safety! They ransacked my security! They've..."

Theo stood stock-still, and closed her eyes against the noise. She'd been interviewed three times by officials. Her bona fides had been checked at least three times. She'd had very little to eat for the last half-day, she was tired, and she needed to put her day bag down before she used it as a weapon.

Chelly's door was closed. Theo strode past it, wondering what was going on now. She'd anticipated being asked questions, not being beset—

"I told you! I *told you* these people weren't good at security! Did *you* think we needed a Checksec? No. Does our *senior leader* think we need a Checksec? No. So what are we going to do about—"

Theo barged by Asu, swept into the bedroom and swung her bag to the top bunk.

"I mean, here they call a campus security alert and ask every-one to stay in room and then they won't even answer a simple theft call..."

Goaded, Theo turned, and Asu stepped hurriedly back.

"He's right, you know?" Asu gasped "Chelly's right! When you do that, you do look like you're looking for a fight..."

Asu started, backed against the door.

He stood there in person suddenly, gingerly stepping in from his room, his face an uncertain mask of tight muscles under blotched skin, framing tired eyes. Uncharacteristically he wore a sleeveless workout shirt—he'd been doing his best to keep the formal edge on his attire ever since he'd been invited to join the—

Theo couldn't remember what it was called right now; it was a bunch of gonna-be commanders, all at work being official.

His hands were carefully neutral, as were his shoulders.

"I just got word that you'd been released, Waitley," he said quietly. "The rumor was that you'd been shot down, or crashed on the mountain. Is there anything we can do for you?"

"The rumor was *what*?" Asu demanded. "Why didn't you tell me? What is going on?"

Theo moved, slowly, hands also carefully neutral, only half suppressing the sigh she felt weighing on her.

"Yes, Chelly, you can do something for me. Break out some

cheese and biscuits, make some tea. I'm not gonna take this stuff they gave me, if I can help it; I got math first thing in the morning and I need to stay sharp."

"Tea. Tea." He said it like it was an alien concept.

Asu shut up and looked between the pair of them as if she just now recognized that Chelly and Theo were both distressed, and not about the Checksec.

"Yes," she said then, "I see!" She hurried out of the room, calling out, "I know your tea setting, Theo. Chelly, you get the biscuits down; if you need to, you may open my cheese."

Theo sat on Asu's bunk and slowly pulled off her shoes and her socks. Who knew that the ancient wooden floor in Erkes would feel so good to bare feet?

FIVE

· · · · · · · ·

Combined Math Lab
Anlingdin Piloting Academy

MATH 376 WAS A RELIEF SO FAR, EVEN WITH A DRILL. EIGHT students and an instructor stand-in were in the Math Lab already; soon they'd be joined by an assistant and the lab section from Math 366, all students who weren't taking an atmospheric component in their training, and maybe even by the instructor herself.

Surprisingly, the drill had helped settle Theo; this time it didn't involve any of the head-spinning dual-reality arithmetic in which numbers had to be solved for both real and imaginary components at the same time they were solved for string expansion and entropy resistance.

She still wasn't sure she wanted to risk her life on her computations, but just to be busy without having Chelly's quiet grief hanging over her head was good, not to mention being free of Asu's sulky nattering about her confiscated Checksec. Asu's paranoia hadn't been helped by Chelly keeping his secret until the second cup of tea—

"What kind of a senior are you if you don't keep us informed? Especially when one of our own...well, no, just because he'd slept in our pod doesn't make him ours—this Hap Harney—but *Theo's* ours and you didn't even *tell* me and she sleeps right over my head?"

"Chain of command," he'd said quietly. "You always have to remember chain of command, Asu. Suppose I'd told you everything and then they'd come for your Checksec instead of the other way around? You might have been in big trouble. And yeah, I think it's good that you didn't know Hap Harney's name until just now: again, think what it would look like if I'd have said something earlier and then you'd gone talking to those youngsters you've been coaching in bowli ball? The whole of Erkes could be under a cloud then. Now the news is out."

Asu'd fumed and fretted; it had taken Theo explaining her view of the whole thing. "I think he was trying to lose them," she'd said, from her new, in-depth understanding of the wind shear problems right there. "I think he knew the mountain from when he was at the academy and was figuring he could break away, gain time—for whatever he was trying to do."

She hadn't explained that one of the planes had strafed the falling pieces, nor that she'd noticed that none of the military guys who'd landed with the copter had their sidearms on peace-bond. She'd come out from between her boulders when they landed, identified herself, and then had to listen . . .

"She's got guts and the goods, bringing that thing down in here with no auxiliary," one had said, and then another, "Right convenient it could have been, too, for Harney, heh? Drop himself off here, then glide off with a cutie while we're looking for his body?"

"*You* run the gonsarned thermal, then. There's nothing here but her and a cold ship. All pure."

Volunteer nothing to an official, she'd remembered Father saying then, as he had several times when listening to her retelling of her time on Melchiza. *When you're in their power, bureaucrats can be more dangerous than a loaded gun. A gun hits the target you aim at. Bureaucrats are another story.*

She'd kept quiet, then, and was startled when the copter pilot asked if she'd like a turn at the controls once they'd left *Slipper Fourteen* and the mountains well behind. She'd been watching—what else was there for her to do?—and taking in the whole process, but . . .

"No, sir. I mean, yes sir—I would. But I don't have any power hours at all and probably I shouldn't."

"Hah, that's great! No hours at all and they made you land that feather up there? Somebody's in need of pilot refresh if you ask me!"

There were chuckles from a couple of the others *in* the machine, and the pilot himself flashed a quick *top landing*, making sure she'd caught it before going into a monologue on the good and bad points of hovering vehicles...

But that would have been too much to tell Asu, and they'd told Theo not to talk about the questions they asked: had she known Hap Harney, had she been told to fly to the mountain, why had she selected that spot, why had she hidden in the rocks—which of course she hadn't, really. They'd gone on and on and on about how long had she been on-world and did she have any opinions on the coming elections and would she call someone who died stupidly a hero just because he'd died and...they were amused, somewhat, that the only drink she accepted was from the water fountain.

So she'd hoped Asu would give over on that topic and Chelly—well, he'd helped, actually. He'd had some idea of what she'd been through—apparently he'd had his time with the authorities when the security team came through.

"Asu, I didn't *give them* your Checksec, they turned it off the moment they saw it and said it was a potential violation of the privacy regs."

"Violation? What's wrong with active protection? Everyone knows you have to take care of yourself! What about my privacy?"

That, it turned out, had been the rub.

Chelly's voice was low and firm while he was talking about it, and he lost some of the blotchiness that looked like it might have come from tears.

"Your Checksec's a pro model, Asu. It not only blocks within a perimeter, but it probes any signals it finds and records them. The thing is, it kept trying to connect to the network so it could report somewhere."

Asu's face and neck darkened; her mouth opened as if she were going to say something, but it took several jaw movements and some hand motions as well before she could articulate anything more understandable than, "Oh no...."

Finally: "I didn't even think! That's the Checksec Jivan gave me—she's head of Security for Diamon. You don't think it was trying to report, do you?"

Chelly's glance may have struck the ceiling before Theo's, but as they looked down at Asu they both shrugged.

Chelly's shrug had turned into a slow hand to the side of his face.

"Could have been calling in, what do I know? I do know that they came in here and swept the place three times, then ran off and did the rest of Erkes. Harney's time here—I guess they had to check everything, since he'd been senior when I got here."

"Same room as us? Right here? In our beds?" Asu's eyes widened.

Chelly hand-talked, *Yes, right, right, yes.*

"I'll need to get some smutch in then. Bad luck to sleep in a dead man's bed, you know . . ."

It was then that the exhaustion really hit Theo, and she'd wished, very much that she'd had a certain Scout pilot to . . . talk to. Or something. Even Bek. He wouldn't have understood the piloting problems, but he would have made sure she relaxed.

Lying in the top bunk, she smiled. Bek had been a good *onagrata*, even though they'd both gone into the First Pair knowing they'd each be going off in different directions.

Despite the tea or because of it, she'd slept deeply, if alone, and managed to get up and dress without waking Asu, whose schedule put her on late-day, and took herself to math class, adding a note to *shop for tea* on the joint to-do list.

Math drill done, and filed, Theo looked around. Others were still at work, which was something she was used to from the Wall, so she did some calculations in her head, trying to keep herself from remembering that there'd been a live pilot in that craft—somebody Chelly had known—trying to concentrate on the drill's final question, which to her mind had two mutually antagonistic answers. She'd chosen the simple one, of course.

Visualizing the other one—no, well, she probably shouldn't use the desk for that, not with others around her still working. She resorted then, like she had at the Wall, to her needle. She slipped it and a length of thread out of a cargo pocket, and bent to work, stretching out a point on the fabric here, and one there . . . and after all, since the fabric was malleable and penetrable she could consider that the needle might be the spaceship and the . . .

The sounds around her changed, which probably meant the rest of the class was finished with the drill. Theo glanced up. Peering at her from the next row was the instructor herself, Pilot Truffant.

"No, Trainee, please don't let me interrupt your work. I'm sure it must be fascinating."

Theo felt her face warm, but she had, she thought, earned some sarcasm. After all, it wasn't very advertent to be discovered doing needlework in math class. The low laughter of her classmates didn't help.

She took a breath and answer the instructor calmly.

"Yes, Pilot."

The instructor moved closer.

"Good, good. We'd hate for you to be bored, here at Anlingdin. Perhaps you'll be kind enough to explain why, in the face of your incoming scores, you find this a compelling way to follow up on a drill."

"Yes, Pilot," Theo said. "I was thinking about the last question on the drill. The work here," she raised the unfinished lacework, "was helping me think."

"Very good. The needle-and-haystack approach to space navigation, I take it?"

Theo looked at the instructor. She seemed more amused than taunting.

"I'm not familiar with the term," Theo admitted, while some few in the class sputtered. "But, on the drill, there was the answer I thought you wanted, and then there was the second answer. I needed—"

"Enough!"

But Theo had already stopped, obedient to Pilot Truffant's hand-talked *stop*.

"You intrigue, Waitley. Please hold your work a moment."

The instructor turned to the larger class.

"The rest of you are done with the drill. How many were concerned about the 'second answer'?"

No one moved or spoke; the instructor glanced down at her handheld readout and said finally, "This is excellent. All of you have the final answer right. I salute!"

She fit action to words, saluting in all directions, and then leaned toward Theo, face intent.

"The answer I expected is the one you gave," she said quietly. "Now, what does your needle say about the second answer?"

Theo looked down at her work, and then up at the instructor again, grimacing as she tried to put words to thoughts. There were more sounds around as several of the lab students from the other class drifted in, pushing a small materials cart.

"The easy answer," she said after a moment—"that answer is missing a dimension somehow. That is, it is right as far as it goes, so I'm glad I have that. But we're—see, the string-contraction effect *needs* to be in here; it may be negligible on a clean-paper arithmetic run but we can't assume that's what we have and—"

The hand-talked *sharp thought hold mouth hold* came quickly, and then:

"Enough, Waitley, enough. You anticipate a lesson some days in the future. I hope you'll have time after the lab to discuss your cloth computer with me."

"Now, Waitley," said Pilot Truffant, "the drill's fine and so is your lab. You just finish that up on your time this evening. I wanted to tell you that I looked at your flight profile from yesterday. You made some wide-awake choices there, some challenging choices. I think that flight'll be flown a few times in the next semester or two, in sim and for real. While I could have done it in your five minutes I'm not sure there's more than a dozen on campus who could have matched it, all things considered."

Truffant cleared the lab stuff away cheerfully, and then insisted:

"Really, I'd like you to show me that other solution you were working on. I've banned an abacus, an antique slide-stick, three kinds of subvocal calculators, and a pet norbear from class in the past. Now I wonder if I have to ban needles and string."

SIX

· · · · · ·

Lunch Break
Anlingdin Piloting Academy

"YOU WALK EVERYWHERE, DON'T YOU?"

"Did the soldiers threaten you?"

"Were you scared?"

"How did you get the Slipper to *do* that?"

"Are you sleeping with anyone?"

The girl who asked that got poked in the ribs by the young man next to her. That sparked some laughter and ribaldry which gave Theo a chance to catch her breath and take a sip without looking like she wasn't paying attention.

If any of the questions surprised her more than any others she couldn't say; the good news was that a couple of the crowd were kind enough to use recognizable hand-talk, and that gave her something to concentrate on, besides trying to eat.

They'd walked her in to the lunch room like she was leader of the pack, but partly it might have been to make sure no one else joined them.

All of them were from the math lab; all had been at the school longer than she had and they all wanted to be close to her, where before they barely acknowledged her.

She managed to answer some questions.

"I wasn't scared," she said after another sip of whatever soft drink someone brought her, "because I was just too busy." Here she interjected with her hands, pointing toward the could-be

39

instrument panel and signing *updown, north, wind speed, drift, drift, updown, clock.*

"The order came and I had to find a way to get the ship out of the air, and the mountain was nearest...

"Afterwards, *then* I was shaky and wanted to dance!"

For some reason that prompted laughter, and she grabbed a bite as people quieted and then looked as the youngster—she recognized him as one of the Erkes local students—blurted into the silence, "You always walk so fast and..."

She agreed, nodding in his direction. "I do. I like to walk, but there's not really enough time to just take a hike, and I'm usually a little late..."

Again, some laughter and smiles, and the pair staring back and forth at each other with furtive hand-talk that looked like *Later alone ask* and an assent and...

"But the Slipper was great," she said, getting back to another question, "except I'd never landed in that kind of a head wind before. I really had to trick her down with a sideslip..."

Here Theo demonstrated with a hand motion and a swing of the shoulders and then a dual slide of hands toward the tabletop. Then she laughed, doubling the attention on her.

"The only time I worried about the soldiers is when I made them hold the Slipper and one didn't understand so good about paying attention. He let the starboard wing loose before I got the tiedowns set and it almost clipped his nose."

"You made the soldiers help?"

Theo snickered.

"Did I have a choice? You think I'm going to let a school Slipper fall off a mountain if I can help it? They insisted I was going with them, and right away, but the rotor pilot, he told them I was right, the ship needed to be tied down else it might run into his machine at liftoff. So yes, the soldiers helped."

The other hand-talkers, not the hormone addicts, were more readable: *saw flight well done* came her way and *bowli ball after?*

That sounded good, but she really wasn't going to have time. *Not today,* she managed and, *thank you.*

Normally lunch was a chance for Theo to think over math or math lab, and even to eat. Today she was having a hard time fitting the food in around fielding questions and watching the hands for words.

The quarter chime sounded, barely discernible above the conversation buzz at table; in moments the group—all carefully nodding, saying, or signing their good-bye to Theo—was off in disparate directions.

Theo heard or felt the presence of someone behind her, and turned to see—

Asu.

Her roomie sighed gently, and without asking pulled out a chair and sat heavily.

"It won't last, you know." she said, waving at the empty chairs. "Once people figure out that you don't want to be friends, don't need to be friends, and can't do anything for them, they'll look for some other fast line."

Theo raised empty hands and shrugged. "I don't know why..."

Asu made a sound remarkably similar to one of Lesset's triumphant I-knew-it noises.

"Have you seen the news, Theo? Do you know how many comm calls I've denied this morning? I mean—you survived!"

Theo looked to the ceiling before hoisting the last of her drink and guzzling it. She was going to need to start walking soon...

"I don't much follow the news, Asu. Not politics, not finance, not even sports."

That last was a bit of a cut, and she was exaggerating, anyway.

Asu wrinkled her nose.

"Look, what's going on is the local newsies—and I mean planetary, not continental!—they've got these great long distance vids, even a satellite shot or two, of you throwing the Slipper around like it's an aerobat while the military chases public menace number one in your direction. Two expert commentators following the chase say there's no possible place for you to land and right there you calmly slot the thing in with a half wing-span to spare, just in time for the public menace to get obliterated, kabloom!"

Asu's sound effects and hand motions brought stares; Theo blushed and looked away. When she looked back, Asu's full attention was on her face.

"Look," Theo insisted, "all I did was land the Slipper. That's *all*. They told me they wanted the sky empty. That's what I did. This other stuff—" Theo found herself looking at the ceiling and its suspended model aircraft, moons, and spacecraft. "This other stuff isn't really about me."

Asu sighed slightly.

"I know—and I'm glad you know. It isn't your fault that Chelly's old bestguy and mentor was idiot enough to get shot down."

Theo looked up, eyes wide, and shook her head.

But Asu was nodding, with a certain amount of grimness.

"Chelly told me this morning. They were bestboys till Hap left and then didn't ever even answer a bit of comm...left him flat."

Theo grimaced. Just what they needed in close quarters, a senior with a problem love life come back to haunt him.

Asu sighed. She looked tired for a moment, then shook herself into businesslike.

"So," she said briskly. "I caught news reports for you; they're filed in your shared inbox, if you want them."

"Thanks," Theo said, not certain if she did want them. Still, it had been nice of Asu.

"You're welcome," Asu said, rising, with a shapeless flap of her hand. "I'll see you later, Theo. I've got to get to class."

Theo had class, too, and ran most of the way.

Commerce and Transport 111 was usually a dry, quiz-heavy class. Long-retired full-Terran cargo master Therny Chibs was the professor. Theo saw his lanky form just ahead and sped up to get to the door of the classroom before he did, squeezing by as he turned to address a question from a student who stood outside waiting.

Theo found classmates making room for her as she hurried to the back of the lecture room, still a bit unsettled by how many of the people acted like they knew who she was. Not likely, given the size of the class.

She'd already memorized and been tested on thirteen common forms for the class, and expected a quiz today on two more. Professor Chibs had never met a form he didn't like, nor a reporting protocol he didn't admire. If she was lucky it would be two more and not three, because she hadn't quite caught up with—

"We'll start," said Chibs in his twangy accent, "by requesting those of you who live by the syllabus or who are taking the class feed for catch-up to disconnect recording devices and save those pre-made form files for next class, when we'll return to boring you all with material that you'll only need to know if you graduate."

He chuckled at the startled looks, the same way he chuckled

when gleefully pointing out some overlooked tick-box on a paper-filed support form.

"We have an object lesson to hand, and we shall use it. It comes to us in the shape of perhaps the most widely known pilot on the planet for the next two days, our own Theo Waitley."

It felt like the whole room turned to stare at her, tucked away as she was in the back corner. She sat up, and watched the professor warily.

"Oh no, you've all seen the news, I'm sure. Good landing, good landing, yes. Everyone knows what she did right, I'm sure. Now, with the pilot's leave, if you will listen to *me* closely rather than staring at Pilot Waitley, I'm going to tell you what was done wrong."

Pilot Waitley. There it was again.

The professor's hands flashed *permission request pilot acknowledge* so fast she almost had to assume it rather than read it.

Well, there. If she'd done something wrong she'd better know about it so she didn't have to depend on luck next time. She answered *here for learning.*

"Good, good," Professor Chibs said out loud, turning his back momentarily on the class before unleashing a large image of a Slipper to every desk top.

"Consider this," he said at volume as he turned back to peer at them, "your ship. You are a pilot, the ship is in your care. At what point does local traffic control, or local military for that matter, get to dictate what you do with it?"

Theo felt wrung out, if only from waiting for her errors to be told. Mostly, though, if she'd understood Professor Chibs correctly, the mistakes that had been made weren't exactly *her* mistakes. It was true that she'd failed to ask landing permission from the Mountain Commissioners, but that was arguably covered under the so-called Port In A Storm protocols.

Still, it was unnerving hearing her name used in terms of "Waitley's liability to pay for the ship if it were damaged" and, "In space, on a job run, Waitley must, and all of you must, take tactical news reports for your flight zones. That she wasn't informed of this is unfortunate, and that mistake is partially the school's curriculum and partially the fault of the equipment or lack of it on the Slipper. Your ship is your life."

He paused then, and an image of her Slipper, sitting on the mountain ridge, appeared. She wanted a copy of that—the Slipper looked beautiful!

"That's it then. No one signed for the ship, no one accepted legal or fiscal responsibility. No one offered, promised, or required a written return-to-ship. No one offered or promised hazard pay or indemnity. No one apologized—well, her instructor did, but none of the authorities on the scene. The debriefing was not done in a neutral location. On-site, the pilot demanded and received, through the intercession of another, more senior, pilot, a very basic securing of the ship, which was well done." Here he fell into hand talk for emphasis: *listen listen listen.*

"Do not undervalue detail, people. Do not undervalue info trails. Do not let the bureaucrats overwhelm you to the point that you, as a pilot, cannot fend for your ship. Do not forget that, on the whole, in a trouble spot, you first depend on your ship and yourself. You may listen to traffic control, but you must depend on pilot sense to survive."

Chib paused again, looked in her direction, and did a sort of half bow.

"Pilot Waitley, thank you."

Then he straightened, disappearing the Slipper from the desk tops, and raised his voice.

"Essay assignment due in ten days is entered into the log. I look forward to your analysis. Next class, back to the forms! Dismissed!"

SEVEN

. . . .

Mail Room
Anlingdin Piloting Academy

"DO YOU SEE THAT?" ASU WHISPERED FIERCELY TO THEO AS THEY took their place in line. "They're still throwing packages around like they don't care down here! Why doesn't the school just pay for a package system instead of using children like that to do the work?"

The *children* Theo was seeing were all bigger than her, and a couple of them were worth watching as they quietly hauled packages from the semi-pods that brought them directly out of the small transport sitting tubed to the building.

Not only that, for all that they were moving the packages rapidly out of the semi-pods, they didn't seem to be harming anything. As Father had pointed out to her on more than one occasion, the more noise you made, the more likely it was that you were using too much force.

The mail handlers were making a minimum of noise, their motions precise and controlled. There was no spinning, no random flinging, no purposeful shoves. Rather each package was selected, tossed gently by the tall young woman in the blue work top or the muscular guy with the strange mostly-bald-but-ponytail hairdo, and caught quietly, with an odd twisting motion...

Asu's complaints were subdued at the moment, and Theo gathered that the young man on the left side of the receiving line, the one with the shorts and—one willingly imagined—overall tan, was the object of her distraction.

45

That interesting twisting motion wasn't entirely a show-off, either, Theo saw. Instead, it looked like the handlers were making sure a read strip on each package was illuminated by a quick rainbow of light...

"'Ware!" cried Blue Top over the bustle of the room, as the package she was in the process of moving took on an uncharacteristic wobble.

"Hah!"

The shorts and their inhabitant moved smoothly, the wobble was corralled, the read strip rainbowed, and the package passed on, no fuss, really, and nothing dropped or broken.

Asu's exclamation followed another pair of transfers.

"Security! The strips are passive, so they don't give off an ID to anyone with a listener. You can't just flash a frequency and hope to get a reading, and you can't get a type count that way, and you—"

"Next, please!"

Next was not them, but they had to move up in the slowly shortening line so the view of the workers was not as interesting. The overhead apparatus was more visible now, though, with multiple light sources and small buttons that were probably actually cameras.

"Guess it makes sense to keep it simple—" Theo said.

Asu harrumphed.

"I guess it works, but it seems slow. The refids are fast and self-reporting, though, and these are slow and require people. People are nosy. People are expensive! And they create lines!"

There was a gentle laugh from behind, which turned into the words. "Economy is such a variable concept, do you know. In some places, people work and expensive machines replaced thereby. Having people, conditions may be noticed without an official record being made. With people, you may reward and advance individuals, and train leaders for practical direction, without using sims and psych tests, both of which have surprising margins of error."

Even on a campus full of pilots and would-be pilots, Theo was becoming unused to being surprised by the silent approach of anyone. Flight Instructor yos'Senchul's voice was as smooth as his bow.

"Pilots," he said bowing to Theo, and then to Asu.

Asu's bow was instant, and probably overdone: obviously she'd been studying *something*, but yos'Senchul hadn't bowed any fancy bows, just a bow of acknowledgment and even a taste of "in this line together" with that motion of his hand...

Theo bowed as if acknowledging a remark from Captain Cho or Win Ton.

The pilot's hand flurry said *is good*, combined with a nod that was almost a wink.

Asu was by now waving a polite hand forward, as if to offer her place to yos'Senchul. He flipped his hand with a practiced equanimity.

"Thank you, but no. This is my off-hour just as it is yours, and as pilots, we ought practice standing in line together as well as orbiting harmoniously, since we need do the first more often than the last—or so it seems."

"Erkes," Asu said with some asperity when they at last arrived at the head of the line, "Suite three-oh-two. Package pickup note."

"Well, we're so glad you could make it! Any longer on all these and we'd have been charging you rent!"

The rather pale young man on the counter tossed a crumpled ball of paper or plastic over a short wall lined with tables, calling out at the same time, "Hey, wake up back there! Bring out that Erkes mountain, will you?"

"Any longer?" Asu demanded. "We'd have been here sooner except we had a line in front of us, you know!"

Theo admired Asu's restraint.

"They've been here for hours!" The counter guy answered. "If you didn't sleep late you could have had this out of here at breakfast!"

Asu started to say something, but then choked the words into a really ugly face and a good seething hiss, apparently in deference to yos'Senchul, standing quietly behind them.

Her accent with her hands wasn't all that good yet, Theo saw, but still, the words thrown toward the floor were quite indignant, and included *rude, useless, slow,* and maybe *sunless.*

"Which Erkes package is that?" came a firm voice from the back, followed by, "Will you recycle your own snack pack, Turley? Not *my* fault you drew the line again. I think they're trying to tell you something!"

Clanks and plastic squeals ensued, followed by a thud.

"That big one fell again!"

"If they've dropped something of mine, I'm going to . . . I'm going to . . ."

Theo grinned and filled in, "Going to go to the Delm of Korval?" she asked, remembering how Father had challenged her as a child, leaning on her favorite book to help bring a sense of proportion to her young complaints.

"Do what?" Asu turned, squinted down at Theo with a wry expression, waving her hands at the same time.

Theo's fingers told Asu *will repeat suggestion* and she said out loud as seriously as she could muster, "Are you going to take this problem to the Delm of Korval?"

"How could he help?" the other girl asked, apparently genuinely puzzled. "I mean, that's silly. He's dead, anyway, even if he could."

"He's *dead*?" Theo stared at her, feeling her grin slide toward a gap. "You mean there *is* a Delm of Korval? Or—was?"

Asu shook her head sadly.

"Yes, there was one, of course there was. But he died. Very sad."

"No, wait," Theo said. "I thought he was a story—a myth for littlies!"

A voice from behind the short wall interrupted their discussion and promised more delay.

"This thing is tagged by you, Turley. I need your signature before I can move it!"

"You got a go from me," the counter guy called.

"I need your signature or a thumbprint, not a verbal!"

Turley sighed dramatically, looked at the line, which had grown considerably at yos'Senchul's back, and called out, "A moment more only, duty calls!" before hurrying toward the back.

Asu shook her head, continued: "Why would you think Korval was a myth? They've got ships *everywhere*. They make Diamon Lines looks small!"

Asu sounded exasperated, so Theo continued in the same tone. "I thought the Delm of Korval was a myth because I saw him in a storybook for kids!"

"Ah . . ."

That was yos'Senchul, who had obviously been listening in with some interest.

Theo rounded on him.

"Well, that's where I knew about him. The book was called *Sam Tim's Ugly Day*, and it was by Meicha Maarilex. I found it at a Try and Trade when I was a littlie, and made Father read it to me over and over—it had the story in Terran at the top of the page and in Trade at the bottom . . . and 'way in the back, it was written out in Liaden. That's how I started reading Trade and Terran together—even though the words weren't always exactly the same as Father read to me from the back."

She sighed, knowing exactly where that book was, and knowing that with any luck at all Coyster would be sitting on the desk under the bookshelf, staring up at the mobile, or curled asleep on the bed or . . .

"And this book was all about Delm Korval? I think I have heard of the author but did not know she had written about Korval."

The instructor's voice was low, but she'd managed to catch his words despite her own distraction.

"No, but that's why it was interesting. There was Sam Tim, you see, and his day was ugly to him. He complained some. Nothing was going right, over and over, and he kept wanting it all fixed. Everyone in his family, and all his neighbors, and the storekeepers, they kept saying to him, 'And if we can't solve this for you, what will you do? Take your problem to Delm Korval?'"

"Ah, an excellent question to ask someone suffering from the day without delight, *Al'kin Chernard'i*, as we have it in Liaden."

Theo nodded, and looked back to Asu.

"See, it was obvious that Sam Tim was always looking too high for his answer, that he ought to be able to solve some things for himself. That, really, you only go to Delm Korval with really important problems. So then we started using that for us. If I was having problems with something, or complaining, Father would ask me, 'So, is this problem worth taking to Delm Korval?' It was a joke."

"Truth, also," yos'Senchul said. "One would wish not to be seen by Delm Korval over matters of little consequence."

"But you say he's real! I thought he was like, you know, Mr. Winter who lives over the mountain and brings the snow."

"No, not so powerful and more powerful too, that is Korval." yos'Senchul raised one hand, fingers curled slightly, as if weighing Korval's power. "A mighty clan, Korval, and very old. They are considered, perhaps, a bit odd, even dangerous, though none doubts their *melant'i*."

Asu nodded as if he'd given a lecture, and blurted out breathlessly, "If you think Korval's a myth you might as well think that Diamon Lines—and me too—are myths!" She waved her hand, not hand-talk, just finger-junk, and went on quickly. "But, anyway, Clan Korval doesn't have a delm right now. He committed suicide!"

"This news..." said the instructor, leaning forward earnestly. "Of a suicide I have heard. Might you share? Is it recent?"

"You didn't know? Delm Korval's life-wife was shot on Liad, right in front of him. I mean, she died, stepping in front of a pellet meant for him. And there, it was like he kept going a few days, and then turned everything over to staff, and left. They say he took his wife's spaceship and just flew it right on into the sun!"

"Ah," said the Liaden carefully. "Do you know, I think that I may have heard this—it happened some Standards ago, if I recall correctly."

Over a sudden clatter and squeaking, yos'Senchul hand-spoke a determined *attend me*, leaning forward so they might both hear.

"Even at the time, there was some measure of disbelief in this death. It seemed...unlikely, at best, given what they say of Korval—and what Korval says of Korval. *Korval is ships*, Liadens say. A delm so distraught as to consider self-death...even such a delm, being Korval, I think would not, and could not, kill a ship. Korval is ships, Korval is pilots."

Asu looked aggrieved.

"Well, have *you* seen Delm Korval? There is none!"

She straightened abruptly, fingers pressed to lips, as if just recalling that she spoke with one of her instructors.

yos'Senchul smiled lightly, his hand signaling a soothing *this will clear.*

"Indeed, this is not the first time that Korval has waited upon a delm—and it is true that yos'Galan never spoke against the reports. Be assured that there will again be a Delm Korval, and Sam Tim's lesson is a good one to recall. Go to Korval Himself only in extremity!"

"Do you guys want this stuff or should we just send it back now?" Turley leaned on the counter in front of them, hands spreading apart in question.

The stuff was overwhelming, and the first five pieces of it, including two large packages requiring signatures and thumbprints both, were for Asu, who cooed over the return addresses, each from one of the stops on the pro scavage tour. Covered in customs stickers, postage marks and symbols, freight notes, and handling instructions, the collection massed more than Asu.

Theo nodded to herself with casual understanding: *this* was why Asu wanted her to come along—not out of a concern that Theo wasn't getting enough "fresh air," but to have help carrying it all! It was a shame, she thought, that most of her hangers-on had found other things more interesting than her over the last few days.

No, on second thought—it wasn't. All that company had made her twitchy and bad-tempered. She'd rather not have to deal with a crowd, even if it would have been useful to have more hands to push Asu's mail across campus.

"Two more," Turley called out.

Asu looked around, spied a community-use handcart across the room and darted off, leaving Theo to cope with whatever came across the counter next.

...which turned out to not be so bad.

Package number six was a white box bearing local postage only—for Chelly. It had the look of a box of candy or pastries. There was no return address and no sign-for; Theo took that in hand with a shrug, as Asu came back, pushing the cart ahead of her.

The clerk from the back tossed the last package over the wall.

"Heads up! That one needs special handling!"

It wasn't a big packet; slightly smaller than Chelly's box. Turley caught it casually, and glanced at the tear slip.

Asu reached for it, but Turley lifted it out of her range.

"Ahem, *student*. This object has traveled light-years to reach us, so I think it ought to go to the person it's for. Erkes, Suite 302, *Theo Waitley*."

He looked at Theo suspiciously, hamming it up for the line.

"Are you a pilot, Trainee? Or do I have to sign this *for you* from my lofty height?" He tapped the stylized delta wing on his collar for emphasis. "This, my friend, is *pilot post*."

He held the package out tantalizingly, as if daring Theo to take it.

From behind her came yos'Senchul's voice.

"If you please, Second Class Provisional Pilot Turley, it would honor me to sign for this package if you feel that Pilot Waitley's bona fides are lacking. In fact, I insist. I'm sure we all know the Terran refrain, 'Pilot post travels faster on the wings of a master.'"

EIGHT

· · · · · · · · · ·

Erkes Dormitory, Suite 302
Anlingdin Piloting Academy

IT WAS ASU'S TURN TO PUSH.

Theo walked beside the cart, keeping a concerned eye on the wobbling stack of packages, especially the thin one in the pale-brown cargo wrap. The wrap was worn in spots—which was, Theo told herself, reasonable for something so well traveled. There was a stub of green stuck askew at the bottom left, which was her part of the school's tear slip; otherwise the package was innocent of the postage and customs forms that decorated every square centimeter of Asu's packages.

Her name and address were written on it in clear Trade block letters on the right, and again, in flowing Liaden cursive, on the left. The return address was in Trade, the sender's name also rendered in Liaden.

She might, she thought, as she grabbed onto the cart to help ease it over a particularly rough bit of sidewalk, have been guilty of over-bowing to Pilot yos'Senchul for his signature. Theo thought the instructor had been amused, though, and he had made her sign her name, too, beside his on the slip, then tore it off and handed it to Turley with a flourish.

Surprisingly, the mail clerk had bowed, and solemnly placed the slip into a small bin at the side of the counter. "Next outgoing pilot," he had said, then looked over Theo's head and called out, "All right! Who's next?"

"Scout Pilot Win Ton yo'Vala?" Asu said, as they and the cart hit smooth surface again.

She'd already said the same thing twice before, and it was getting hard to ignore her. You'd think, Theo said to herself, that a girl who'd just collected five packages with her name on them would be too busy wondering what was in *them* to pay attention to somebody else's mail.

Still, she'd better answer *some*thing; it was important to keep peace—more or less—with her roommates.

"Win Ton's a friend," she said, like she was telling a story about somebody else. "We played bowli ball on the liner when I went to Melchiza with my mother and her team." She felt her lips curve slightly upward. "We beat the dance machine, too. The arcade manager said we had the two highest scores she'd ever seen."

"And he remembers these adventures so kindly that he sends you a packet at school," Asu said, with a smug look that Theo didn't quite understand. "A good friend, indeed!"

"Well," Theo said cautiously, "he *is* a good friend. But it isn't like it cost him a lot to get this to me."

Asu's laugh was quick and sharp.

"Did it not? Are you sure?"

Theo frowned and looked again at the thin box with its notable lack of stickers and forms.

"The favors, you mean."

"Sometimes," Asu said, in that annoying too-old-for-school voice she used to explain obvious details to the kid, "favors are more expensive than cash. And he owes everyone who carried that package a favor." She sighed, stopped pushing, and spent a few seconds fussing with the brake before she looked up again.

"That's a *good* friend," she said and the smirk this time was unmistakable. "Here, it's your turn to push."

"I owe a favor, too, though, don't I?" Theo said when they'd changed places and gotten under way. Asu was eying her box again.

"What gives you—oh." The other girl frowned slightly. "yos'Senchul had you sign too, didn't he? Yes, I guess you do owe a favor, or will, as soon as that receipt gets back to your . . . *friend.*"

Theo gritted her teeth and kept on pushing. "Why?"

"Well, it's clear yos'Senchul expects great things from you," Asu said, matter-of-factly. "There's a hole, Theo, bear left—good. All of the pilot teachers have, ever since you brought the Slipper down like that." She cast Theo a bland, over-the-shoulder look. "You really do need to get your math scores up, though."

"I know," Theo told her fervently.

"So," Asu said, with another glance at the top of the cart, "what do you think it is?"

You had to give her credit, Theo thought; Asu never gave up.

"It's probably just a note," she said, shaking damp strands of hair out of her face. But there wasn't any reason, was there, she asked herself, for Win Ton to send a note this way, incurring all those favors, when they'd been writing via the letter service just fine, her more than him—and her less than before she'd come to Anlingdin.

Asu's sigh could've blown a feather ten feet.

"No, it's probably *not* just a note," she said. "Pilot post is *expensive*, weren't you listening? Why would your...*friend*...pile up all those favors to send you *a note* when he could use a letter service far more cheaply?" She gave Theo a smile. "It's bothering you, isn't it? You can stop and open it now, if you'd like. I don't mind waiting."

Theo put her head down and kept pushing. The steepest part of the path was still ahead; it would take both of them pushing to get the cart up to Erkes. The good part was that the approach hill was short.

"Bowli ball," Asu said, contemplatively, as if speaking to herself. "Our little Theo has a Scout pilot sweet on her and she thinks we'll believe they just played bowli ball. Oh, I'll take a wager that he taught her *all kinds* of hand-talk!"

That was it. Theo stopped, set the brake, snatched Chelly's package and her own from the top of the cart and was half-a-dozen steps up the hill before Asu found her voice.

"Wait! Theo, where are you going?"

"Home," she said, pointing up the hill to where Erkes was silhouetted against darkening clouds. "With *my* package and with Chelly's. You can bring your stuff from here."

"It will take both of us to get the cart up that hill!" Asu cried. "Theo—be reasonable."

"I *am* being reasonable," Theo said sincerely, but she was already slowing. Asu in a snit was irritating. Asu in a snit at *her* was bound to be unpleasant in ways she didn't have time for. Besides, she told herself, as her feet turned her around, Asu did try to be helpful, and to pull her weight as a member of the team. Sometimes. In her own way.

"Win Ton didn't send this to you, he sent it to me," Theo said.

"Agreed," Asu said solemnly.

"I want you to *promise* to quit asking what's in this package—*and* I want you to quit making fun of Win Ton! You don't even know him!"

"That is true," Asu said, still solemn. "I don't know him." She sighed. "I apologize, Theo. To tease about a bestboy or bestgirl is considered . . . friendly . . . in my experience."

"I know some other people who think so," Theo admitted, remembering her team on Delgado. "But *I* don't think so."

"I'll remember that," Asu promised, and moved to the back of the cart. "Now, will you help me push? I think it's going to rain."

They got the cart through the door with a clatter that would have earned a sharp word from Kamele and a sharper look from Father, but didn't even rate an open door and a curious look from their across-the-hall neighbors.

"Chelly," Asu called as soon as they were inside, "you have mail!"

"He's not here," Theo said, jerking her head at the senior's door, with its yellow status light.

"Another round of workouts, I suppose," Asu said in a long-suffering voice, like she was Chelly's mother or older sister. Not, Theo thought, slipping the slender white box into the in-basket next to Chelly's door, that it wasn't worrisome, the number of hours he'd been spending at the gym. Theo wondered if the work helped him feel . . . less sad about his bestboy's—about what had happened to Hap Harney. If it did, she guessed it was a good thing, and, really, Chelly didn't have that tight, bruised look in his face anymore. On the few occasions she'd seen him lately, he'd only looked . . . tired.

Behind her came a prolonged crackling. Theo turned in time to see Asu throw the wrapper from the smallest of her boxes to the floor. The others wobbled, and Theo jumped forward to grab Win Ton's package and slide it quickly into the thigh pocket of her pants.

"Look!" Asu cried, shaking out a long strip of hot pink gauze. Theo squinted. "What is it?"

"A banthawing," Chelly said sourly from the front door. "They're not going to let you use that until you can *at least* get through a board drill without a fumble."

"Why not?" Asu demanded, whirling around so fast the gauze snapped audibly. "It's a—a recreational device!"

"It teaches bad habits, is what it does," Chelly said. He kicked the discarded wrapping as he came into the room and shook his head. "You're gonna clean this up, right?"

"In a moment," Asu said loftily. "I have other packages."

"Hope they're more use to you than that thing. Who sent—oh! The scavage-head. Give him a hint, why not?"

"I would *never* hint to Jondeer that I wanted a present!" Asu said hotly. "He sends what is in his heart!"

Chelly turned and blinked at the banthawing and then at Asu.

"Funny kind of thing to find in somebody's heart," he commented, then threw his hands up in front of his face, half-heartedly, Theo thought, as if to fend Asu off.

"Hey, it's your relationship. I'd just think you'd clue him in on your space situation, so he wouldn't waste shipping on big stuff like this that you don't have anyplace to keep."

"This is not *all* from Jondeer!" Asu snapped. She threw the gauze over the cart's handle and snatched the second-biggest box from its place on the cart. "*This*, for instance, is from my father's head of security!"

"Great," Chelly said without enthusiasm. "I hope she didn't send you another one of those whaddycallits—checksums."

"Checksec," Theo said hurriedly, seeing Asu's face tighten. "Chelly, there was a package for you, too." She jerked her chin at the inbox. "I put it in your basket."

"For me?" He frowned, then shook himself, his mouth straightening into a thin line. Theo thought maybe he was trying for a smile. "Thanks."

He moved toward his door, and Theo turned to go into the room she shared with Asu, meaning to retire to her bunk and open Win Ton's package while both of her roomies were involved in their own business.

"Oh, of all the thought-deprived, careless—"

Theo turned; Asu was holding up a hinged, transparent screen.

"What's that?"

"*This*"—Asu shook the item in question so hard its hinges squealed—"is the *security shield* for the Checksec that was confiscated. Had I had this at the beginning, it would not have drawn the attention—"

"Shit."

It was amazing how cleanly that quiet cuss word cut through Asu's racket. They both turned toward the third member of their party.

"What's wrong?" Theo asked. Chelly was standing like he'd been dipped in plastic and left to dry, staring down into the open white box, the lid held loose in his off-hand.

"Chelly?" She moved forward, carefully. His face was almost as green as his gym shirt and she could see sweat on his upper lip. "Hey, Chelly," she said.

He looked up, eyes wide, face looking—soft. Unformed. He focused, first on Theo, then on Asu; his face firmed and he put the lid back on the box.

"I'm calling Security," he said, his voice absolutely steady. He dug into his pocket and pulled out his key, tossing it underhand to Theo. "You're in charge, Waitley. First Bunk in the absence of the senior, right?"

She swallowed, the card warm in her hand, and nodded, once. "Right," she said, acknowledging the chain of command.

"Good kid." He went over to the comm, not even bothering to kick Asu's discarded wrappings on the way.

Security had come, and Security had taken Chelly into custody, as he must've known they would, Theo thought, as she lay on her bunk, staring up at the dark ceiling. She'd overhead a little of his low-voiced conversation with the two officers who had answered his call—enough to know that the box, whatever was in it, was from Hap. Since Hap was dead, it was probably somebody's idea of a joke, Theo thought—a really cruel joke, too; baiting somebody with his dead bestboy's name. She could see why Chelly would be upset, but calling Security seemed an overreaction.

The Security team hadn't thought so, though. And now she was in charge. Until Chelly got back. Which ought to be, she told herself, as she had every fifteen minutes since he'd gone, Real Soon Now.

She and Asu had cleaned up; Asu had stowed her presents, except for the stuffed octopod Jondeer had sent her. That, she had improbably taken to bed with her, sleeping curled around it, like it was a cat—or a friend.

Theo, alone in the top bunk, envied her, but she couldn't sleep—it didn't seem right to sleep—until Chelly got home. She'd have to let him in; she had his key.

On the other hand, she ought to try to get some sleep. She had an early class. History of Piloting. *Boring.*

Finally, she got bored with the ceiling and her thoughts, sat up, turned on the minispot and pulled Win Ton's package out from under her pillow. Carefully, so she didn't wake Asu up, she slit the wrapping and opened the small box.

It *was* a note; written in careful but perhaps hasty Terran on a skinny sheet with a trick underlay that changed color as the paper moved. *Blevins Transit Services, Gas, Groceries and Gladthings*, it said—and then it didn't, and she could read the words he'd sent.

Sweet Mystery, dear friend Theo, the Terran words ran, *I trust and hope this finds you well, in the aftermath of your recent successful soaring flight made under such trying circumstances.*

She blushed at the memory of telling Win Ton it was stupid of him to call her "Sweet Mystery"...but there, their friendship had survived that setdown, and she was glad they had.

The news of your flight reaches here in the latest of piloting updates, where it is shared among pilots full of admiration, and some with jealousy that one so new to the art should perform so well. For me, I am not surprised that you go on so well, but expect it.

In her head she heard his voice, trying to be both formal and light, and saw him suppress a smile as he did so often.

It is the nature of the universe to provide us with both challenges and frustrations, and this challenge you have borne so well, while I, alas, have labored under the frustration of being a mere two jumps away from you, and thus, close enough to consider coming to you in celebration and far enough away that given time and my duty schedule it is impossible to route myself to you. But there, know that I celebrate and that in honor of your flight, I bestow upon you the enclosed, which of course you must wear only if your grade permits, and only if you desire it, and feel it appropriate.

If it matters, the note went on, *the enclosed was on my duty uniform until I wrapped it here; I have a new one that I was too indolent to attach without good cause, which cause I now have. Please wear it in good health, always. If this scrawl is unreadable it is because a Scout pilot stands waiting to receive it, her ship fueled and at the ready, that it might travel the first of those Jumps that separate us, that your wings should reach you swiftly.*

She smiled at the hyperbole of a Scout waiting a ship for a note to her—and then wondered if it *was* hyperbole.

Below the note, wrapped in a second sheet of the same informal stationery, was a pair of slender silver and onyx wings, engraved feathers glistening.

Theo held them, remembering. She'd seen them on his collar. Yes, she had. And they'd go on hers as soon as she could put them there.

NINE

· · · · · · · · ·

History of Piloting
Anlingdin Piloting Academy

"PERHAPS TRAINEE WAITLEY WOULD LIKE TO RELATE THE HISTORY of the ven'Tura Tables to the class."

Theo started. She hadn't been *dozing*, exactly, though Instructor Johansen's voice did tend to put her to sleep, even when she wasn't working with a short night behind her. But—the ven'Tura Tables? She *had* done her reading, she thought, her stomach tightening in panic. She sent a quick glance at her screen, but if she'd read anything about these tables—whatever they were—she hadn't thought them worthy of even a note, much less a history.

"Well, Waitley?" Johansen purred in that nasty-sweet voice that meant she was about to shave an inch off of somebody—and Theo was apparently today's chosen victim. "I'd think that someone who was sponsored into this academy by the *Liaden Scouts* would be fully conversant with the ven'Tura Tables."

Theo took a deep breath to settle her stomach, and stood—in Johansen's class, you stood to give your answer, so everybody could get a good look at the kid who was too dumb to be up on her work.

"I'm sorry, ma'am," she said, keeping her head up and meeting the teacher's eyes. After all, Kamele and Father had taught her that it was no shame to admit ignorance, though it wasn't going to be pleasant to be chewed out in front of the whole class for not having done her reading thoroughly.

"I'm afraid I don't know the history of the ven'Tura Tables," she said, and added, before she could stop herself, "and I wasn't sponsored by *the Scouts*, ma'am. I was sponsored by *a* Scout."

"By *a* Scout," Johansen repeated, sounding thoroughly disgusted. "Thank you for that correction, Trainee. Sit down." She spun around, glaring at the rest of the class.

"Well? Who can tell the tale of the ven'Tura Tables? *No one?* Not *one* of you has read ahead?"

She shook her head.

"And you aspire to be pilots," she said witheringly. She clicked the autoboard control in her hand and the screen came alive behind her, thick with citations.

Theo touched her keyboard and snatched the info down, scanning the windows as they opened.

"The class will—at your leisure, of course!" Johansen was saying, "—review this material. Each of you will bring to our next meeting an analysis of the Tables, comparing Master Pilot ven'Tura's original effort with the Caylon Revisions. I will expect some insight into those factors which made revision necessary and the role of the Tables—in the original and the revised forms—in shaping piloting as it is now practiced. Go."

The end-of-class chimes were simultaneous with that last contemptuous word, and there was a subdued clatter as the trainees gathered their things up and ran for their next classes.

"*At your leisure*," Theo muttered, as she walked across the quad. She actually didn't have a class right now, though that didn't mean she was at *leisure*. Far from it. For her *leisure* time between classes, she had her choice of activities. She could practice board drills, work through her math tutorials, review the latest sample batch of cargo forms, or she could get started on Johansen's read-and-analyze.

And, really, what she wanted to do more than anything else on this bright, blowy day was to sign out a Slipper and escape into the green and gold sky.

Theo sighed. She didn't *think* she was a slacker, but she couldn't understand how school kept getting harder. By now, she ought to have the rhythm down, and done all the readings listed on the syllabi—she'd *always* had time to read ahead at school. Here at Anlingdin, she felt like she was running all the time, without *any* leisure, and instead of catching up, she was falling further behind!

"Ball!" called an unfamiliar voice.

There was a blur of not-quite random motion in the corner of her eye. Theo spun, feeling her pack shift on her back, snatched the bowli ball out of the air and pitched it at a girl in a pair of faded mechanic's coveralls.

The girl jumped, grabbed the ball and let it spin her in midair, releasing it before she was back on the ground. It danced crazily to the right, then to the left—and then shot straight up, almost clipping the nose of a stocky boy with his hair in a dozen short pigtails.

He made a one-handed recover and rolled the ball off his palm, on a trajectory for Theo.

"Hey!" she protested, but the ball was on its way and there was nothing she could do except field the thing and get it moving to somebody else. Turning your back on a bowli ball was a good way to get beaned—or worse. It wasn't unusual for bones to be broken in an intense bowli ball engagement. Chaos! She'd come away with bruises from playing with Phobai and Win Ton and Cordrey—and she'd been paying attention!

"Ball!" yelled the third player—a lanky, loose-jointed kid Theo recognized from her General Aviation class. She twisted, getting around the ball just in time, and sweating a little, too. She'd let her attention wander, and that was fatal.

"Out!" The lanky player stepped back, hands down at his side. "Duty."

"Find me later," the stocky boy called, while the girl in the coveralls dove for the ball.

"I can't play!" Theo protested. "I've got too much work to do!"

"A pox on work!" the girl answered, sliding into the grass to grab the ball before it touched the ground. It came out of her hands with a tipsy spin on it, and the boy hooted as he ran forward, one up and to the right.

"Forfeit, Kara!" he yelled.

"Frell if I will!" the girl yelled back. "That ball is in play, sir!"

"Didn't touch!" Theo called, feeling like the boy was trying to get off easy—and suddenly there was the ball again, high over her head. She jumped, and almost lost her balance when the pack shifted on her back. Twisting, she released the ball, skinned the straps down, dropped the pack in the grass—and danced sideways, catching the ball on a dip and sending it whirling back.

"That was fun!" Kara panted cheerfully to Theo. Their third had called duty, grounded the ball and taken it with him as he ran toward the landing field. "A shame we were playing with Vin's ball, eh? If I had one of my own we could have continued."

"Not too much longer," Theo said, scraping wet hair back off of her face. "I've got class." She gave the other girl a grin. "It was fun, though. Thanks for calling me in."

"No, *that* was Ristof," Kara said, naming the lanky boy. "He had been telling us that you were much better than you walked, and then here you came, stomping across the grass like a dirt-hugger, and the idea just bloomed." Kara pulled the clip out of her hair and shook her head, loosing a perfectly straight cascade of reddish-gold hair down past her shoulders.

"Be careful of Ristof in the clutch of an idea," she said, stuffing the clip into one of the coverall's numerous pockets. "A warning, because you do not play like a dirt-hugger."

Theo frowned, and looked around for her bag.

"What *do* I play like?" she asked, spotting the abandoned item a surprising distance away. "If you don't mind saying."

"Ah, have I insulted you?" Kara sounded more curious than contrite, walking with Theo toward the bag. "You play, Theo Waitley, like a pilot. More, you play like a pilot who has already flown the stars—I say this as one who has lived her whole life in a House full of such. Indeed..." She paused, blue eyes narrowed in her round, gold-toned face.

Theo bent and picked up her pack, shrugging into it.

"Indeed?" she asked.

"It is a thought, only, but it may serve you. I have heard that you have what my so-excellent Terran friends term 'attitude.' That you 'spoil' for want of a fight."

"I've heard that, too," Theo said, remembering Chelly's advice that she lose her "attitude." She turned uphill, surprised but not displeased to find Kara walking with her.

"Such judgments upon your good nature must be lowering. But what can you expect when you broadcast across two bands?"

Theo turned her head to get a good look at the other girl's face, but she seemed serious. "I don't understand," she said.

Kara nodded. "Yes, yes! It is apparent! When you are at rest, you walk—not like a dirt-hugger, but *like a Terran*. Your eye is bold, your stance is square, and you look—Theo Waitley, you *look* at everything!"

"If I didn't look, I'd wind up walking into a tree," Theo pointed out.

"Accompany me but a step further," Kara said excitedly. "When it comes to action—to bring a Slipper down on emergency landing, or to join into a sudden game of bowli ball—*then*, Theo Waitley, you *act* as a Liaden! You are quick, you are subtle, you grasp nuance—the difference is quite remarkable."

Theo chewed her lip. The sound of an air breather taking off came to them on the wind. *Some*body was having fun in the sky today.

"My mother's Terran," Theo said eventually. "My father's Liaden."

"That would explain much," Kara said, solemnly. "You speak to one who stands in a comparable situation. My family is Liaden, but most of our associates are Terran. I would advise you in your present state to give Liad itself wide berth."

"Stuck-up?" asked Theo, amused by her new acquaintance's busyness.

"One might say. Not long since, I visited my uncle at Chonselta City—allow me to say that I was compelled! Still, kin counts, and it was thought that my uncle might see me established in a piloting school upon Liad, where the politics are—somewhat less effervescent than we have here at home. It was no use, however; I am tainted from my contact with Terrans, and the distressful fact that my House is situated upon an outworld. It was worth my life to bow—and I have, I assure you, been taught the forms!"

"So you came back and took your scholarship here."

"My uncle could not buy me a passage quickly enough!" Kara laughed, shook her head—and laughed again. "There! You see? A properly brought up Liaden woman does *not* shake her head. Alas, the habit is altogether too easy to pick up and far too difficult to put down!"

"Your family are all pilots?" Theo asked, wondering what it would have been like to grow up in a house full of Win Tons and Captain Chos.

"Pilots for hire, the lot of us! Which is what I shall be in my turn, though perhaps," she said, suddenly sounding wistful, "I can convince my mother to allow me to 'prentice at Hugglelans repair yard when I am done here."

"I used to like helping my father work on his cars," Theo said, slowly. "It was fun, but I think I'd rather be a pilot than a techneer."

"Oh, I'll be a pilot, never fear it! But a mechanic who can also jockey ships—that is worth a premium fee! But stay—your father is a mechanic?"

Theo laughed. "My father's a scholar. He teaches cultural genetics. His—I guess you'd say his *hobby* is cars. He races. There aren't that many techs who know the engines on Delgado, so he fixes his own." She hesitated, then added. "My father's considered a little odd."

"What, because he does his own repairs?"

"No-o. Because he lives outside the Wall in his own house, with a garden, surrounded by things that are—*distractions to true scholarship!*" She grinned, remembering what Father's answer had been to *that* bit of high-nosed criticism.

"Pah! *That* has the feel of a quote! Of course, your father heeded this well-meaning advice to conform himself?"

"Not exactly," Theo told her.

Kara grinned. "Your father's classes are well attended, perhaps?"

"Oh, there's a waiting list!" Theo said, remembering. "Students travel to Delgado just to take his courses."

"I see. Thus, he has *melant'i* out his ears, and may safely do as he pleases."

"It does seem to work out that way," Theo agreed.

Kara sent her a sidelong glance. "Your father did not teach you to be a Liaden, did he?"

"Why would he?" Theo asked reasonably. "Delgado's Terran."

"True if you say so, Theo Waitley." Kara raised her hand. "I fear that our ways part here. Come find me the next time you want a game of bowli ball—Kara ven'Arith. I'm in Belgraid."

"I'll do that," Theo said, and meant it.

TEN

· · · · · · ·

Erkes Dormitory, Suite 302
Anlingdin Piloting Academy

THEO'S WORK SCREEN WAS THREE DEEP IN REFERENCE CHAPTERS, each detailing some aspect of the ven'Tura Tables. Her hands were busy with needle and thread.

The Tables—the original ven'Tura Tables—were just lists: numbered lists of numbers, lettered lists of numbers, cross-listed lists of numbers and dates, and more lists of numbers. They weren't nearly as interesting as their history, and for once Theo was glad she'd been more than a little attentive during some of her mother's informal get-togethers where the always-fluid topic of "the history of history" was under discussion. You could always count on someone saying that "you can't judge past actions by the standards of today; you have to look at things from the perspective of the times." "And," Father would add if he was there, "the culture."

Still smarting under Johansen's scorn, she was determined to produce an analysis that did justice to the topic, and placed the Tables into their proper historical context. Culture didn't seem to matter, unless you thought of piloting as a culture, but the times... The original Tables had been developed during a time of trade expansion, coupled with a radical improvement in Jump drives. Those two conditions had created an urgent need for clarifying gravity effects and string constants as tradeships began to travel more than a few hundred light-years from home.

Ships had begun to go missing—lost, or found far too late for the crew to be rescued, because no one had formalized the new conditions. One ship in a thousand was lost, routinely. And all people said—even pilots!—was that piloting was dangerous. Which it was. But what nobody looked at was *why* it was dangerous, and if the odds couldn't be leveled a little, in favor of pilots surviving and ships winning through.

Nobody, that was, until Master Pilot ven'Tura had dared not only to log, but to share with all pilots—even Terrans, which was considered antisocial in his culture—the information that he and his clan had gathered over dozens of years.

Eventually, Master ven'Tura had become the clearing house and editor for the monumental and necessary task, and his Tables became rote companion to thousands of pilots over generations.

Then, over time, the loss of pilots and ships trended upward again. Most assumed it was because there were more ships and more pilots, less training, and...all kinds of things. It had taken someone with keen insight to see that there were tiny and fundamental flaws in the way the ven'Tura Tables were being applied, in the way they were being read by modern equipment...

And so, the Tables had been revised. Recently, within the lifetime of pilots still flying. Again, they were making a difference. Had already made a difference. The number of ships lost was down again, in a statistically meaningful way. The person who had done the revision had been a Scholar Caylon, also a Liaden, though not, it seemed, a pilot.

Theo flicked a footnote to access the next level of information.

Well. It seemed that Scholar Caylon was *Pilot-Scholar* Caylon, though she had come to piloting late, and after her revised Tables had been adopted by pilotkind. She'd been a statistician of a sort, an expert in Sub-rational Mathematics. The text noted that her later work was...esoteric—notably a lengthy proof for pseudorandom tridimensional subspaces that, while illuminating her genius, was of little practical use to working pilots.

The text also noted that her scholarly output had lessened after her affiliation with Clan Korval—

Theo blinked; shook her head.

"Spend your whole life thinking something's made-up and then it starts showing up everywhere," she muttered, and tapped the screen again, calling back the problem she'd set up to help her think.

Trouble was, it wasn't particularly helping her think. She glared at the screen, looked down at the work in hand, and shook her head again.

She pressed the process button, importing the familiar "standard cluster" that the class, indeed, the whole school seemed to depend on for training, into the second set of assumptions. How concrete were the numbers when applied to a tiny, sanitary, best-case situation?

But there, the work in her hands was concrete, while space, which the numbers were trying to describe...

A noise sounded in the hall, a thump—she shook her head. The kids—she felt like she could call them that even though some were several years older than her—the local kids had been all revved up over a sporting event; charging around the building cheering since early morning, though the game didn't start 'til afternoon. Even Asu had gone out to view the victory, leis woven in layers around her neck.

The noise repeated, and resolved: someone was at her door. Theo sighed, locked the screen, and gathered her lace into one hand.

The click came before she was on her feet, and a tired-looking Chelly smiled up at her as he lifted several large bags into the entry, where they thunked solidly on the floor.

"Chelly, they let you come back!"

She felt her face warm slightly—it sounded like she was pleased to see him, after all...

"Treat to see you, too, First Bunk!"

"Well, I am," she insisted, because it was true, after all, "glad to see you."

He laughed and shook his head. "Don't worry, I'm sort of glad to see you too." He shouldered the door shut, making sure it clicked tight, and stepped into the room, leaving his bags by the door, where Asu could complain that she'd almost fallen over them when she came back.

"Not out at the game?" he asked, and peered over the top of her screen. "Oh. Orbital dynamics, huh?"

"I wish," Theo said, settling back into her seat. "History of Piloting."

He blinked. "Yeah? With that screen?"

"We're doing the ven'Tura Tables," Theo said, unfolding the lace bit and spreading it out. It was... *almost* right. She leaned forward and unlocked the screen, frowning between the configuration of stars and what she had in hand.

"Still playing with the needles?"

"No," Theo said absently. "Not playing. *Seeing*." She squinted up at Chelly.

"Why does everybody act like space is flat?"

"Huh? Who said space was—oh, I get it." Chelly held up his hands. "You gotta learn your basics first—the tables and the board drills. The *math*, if you don't mind my saying. After you got all that—"

"The *math* isn't flat!" Theo broke in, feeling a surge of heat, like temper. She bit her lip; it wasn't Chelly's fault and yet—

"What d'ya mean, the math isn't flat?" Chelly was looking at her sideways, which he did when he thought you might be pushing a line.

"The whole *point* of the ven'Tura Tables—the reason they needed revision—is that space isn't flat—and it isn't static! And to describe what a non-static, dimensioned space is doing, you need a math that isn't flat! That's what Scholar Caylon did! She didn't so much revise the Tables, as she revised the math that described the relationships, and the changes—here!"

She held out her incomplete lace, shaking it in Chelly's bemused face. "Look at this! See how the lines hook here—and here—and over here? And then look, if—oh, Chaos, it isn't done! But, anyway, if you—"

"Wait." Chelly held up his hands again, his eyes moving from the lace to the screen. "Wait. That's a *star chart* you're making."

"Well . . ." Theo blinked at him, caught breathless by the tone of his voice. "Sort of, I guess. I think of it as the shape of the relationships, but—that's what a star chart is, isn't it?"

"And this is the kid who needs to pull up her math scores?" Chelly might've been talking to himself. He reached beyond Theo and touched the control on the screen, locking the image again, then put a hand lightly on her wrist and exerted light pressure until she lowered the lace to her lap.

"Okay. Theo, listen up—I got a bunch of info to dump and I'm on a short watch. First thing is, I'm still going to be on the roster here, but mostly I'm going to be working real-time shifts at daily ops so I can get in enough time to be the official exchange student with Galtech over break. That means you're still gonna be in charge here. You been getting the Senior notices?"

She nodded.

"Good. Now, my bunk still being officially here in Erkes, that means you won't get another kid in to deal with right away—not 'til end of next term, when I fly out. I've got it set up that you're reporting to me—you tell Asu that, too. She gives you trouble, bump it to me."

"I don't think she'll give me trouble," Theo said. "She's not dumb."

"No, but she don't *think*," Chelly answered, which she couldn't say wasn't so. "Next thing I gotta tell you—that lace-making thing you're doing. The star map?"

Theo felt her face heat. "It helps me think to—"

"No, no. Hear me say it first, Theo, then argue—right?" He didn't wait for her to nod, just kept on going. "You need to talk to somebody—one of the advisors up—"

"I have an advisor," Theo interrupted.

"Sure you do. And if you'll stop *arguing* for a second and let me tell it, you'll find out where I'm going with this."

She bit her lip. "Right," she muttered.

"Yeah, that won't last," Chelly said cryptically, pulling a pen and a card out of his pocket. He frowned at the card, flipped it over and wrote something on it. "I'm giving you her name and office number. You go tomorrow, and you ask to get an intro hearing—seven minutes. What you want to tell her is just what you told me, about space not being stable, and what the revisions to the ven'Turas did, got that? Take your lace thing there with you and show it. Promise me. You're not going to say or explain anything else. Just that. Then you wait and you listen to what she's got to tell you, Theo, right? I'll send her an intro tonight when I get back, so she's expecting you—and you're not gonna make me sorry I did this."

"No," Theo said softly, feeling a lump in her chest. "No, I won't, Chelly. Thanks."

"Sheesh," he said, shaking his head ruefully. "I think I like it better when you're showing attitude." He held out the card. "Tomorrow, Theo. Skip lunch if you gotta."

"Right," she said, and slipped the card out of his fingers. "But—"

The door clicked and there was Asu, nimbly avoiding Chelly's bags, her dark face glowing and a violet-and-green lei around her neck.

"We won!" she caroled. "And Chelly is returned to us! The day is perfectly attuned!"

Chelly snorted.

"Close the door," he said, though Asu had already turned to do so. "I was just telling Theo that I'm temp-posted to daily ops. My official berth is here, but most times it'll just be the two of you. Theo's in charge, and she reports to me. We got it all set up, and I cleared it with my mentor and the dean of students."

"Of course Theo is in charge," Asu said, with the false sincerity that made Theo's teeth ache. "Theo is very responsible."

"Theo's First Bunk," Chelly said dampeningly. "Duty of privilege."

"While Second Bunk is a social butterfly," Asu answered, looking down at Theo's lap as she walked by. She shook her head. "Still you sit with the needles? Theo, you must study if you—"

"We been over that," Chelly interrupted forcefully. "Now—" He looked up at the clock, which displayed official school time, and said something under his breath.

"Look, you two, I gotta jet. Theo, you move those bags into my room, then lock it down."

"Why must you leave so soon?" Asu asked. "Duty?"

"As a matter of fact. I'm on the Student Review Board. Vanz Mancha is challenging tonight and it's my watch."

"Challenging?" Asu frowned. "Why?"

"What's 'challenging'?" Theo said at the same time.

Chelly shook his head at both of them. "There's trouble at home, and she's wild to get back there and help out. That's what she told me. And she's gotta go as a pilot, 'cause her folks haven't sent any money for fare. So, she's going to challenge—that's when you call the school's bluff, Theo. You bet you're good enough to walk out of the challenge set a pilot, even if you haven't finished your classwork. It's in the school charter, which I guess you didn't bother to read. Vanz—she's good. She'll be fine." Despite saying so, he didn't look all that certain, thought Theo.

"She'll be fine," he repeated, and shook himself, moving with quick grace toward the door. "Theo, you remember what I told you. Asu, stay outta trouble for a change. I'm gone."

The door opened, and snapped firmly shut.

"I'll make some tea," Theo offered to the closed door, and when it didn't answer she offered the same to Asu, who stood leaning against the wall, her face showing some of the exasperation that Theo felt.

ELEVEN

. . . .

Counseling Center
Anlingtin Piloting Academy

"I SEE YOUR WORK, THEO WAITLEY, AND I SEE THOUGHT. THAT is good in a student and in a pilot. The opportunity in this proposition that flight space is unstatic, that I am not clear on."

Theo sat even straighter, looking up at the apparition, as who could not when faced with someone so straight-backed and firm, so immaculately balanced despite the near-aching spareness of her frame, and skin so pale it bordered on a translucent blue. Theo doubted she had ever met a woman so old.

This was Veradantha, who had found seven minutes in her schedule. The counselor had pointedly started the timer on her desk when Theo arrived, and now, it counted down relentlessly.

"These are not so novel, these ideas you have here; the Tables tell the tale, pilots of experience are familiar with these facts. Even these demonstrations you have—true, I have not seen it illustrated thus for the school standard cluster!—even these are used by some teachers and programs elsewhere."

Theo fought a grimace, and then a sigh. It hadn't been her idea that this was all original, just that it was important to her—but Chelly'd put his name on the line with sending her here, so she hoped it wasn't all going to go to dust.

The counselor stepped deliberately from one end of her office to the other—thinking, it seemed to Theo. She paused as she sipped from the coffee cup she held in one hand; bit into the

73

pastry she held in the other. The pastry moved rhythmically up and down for a moment, then caught the cadence of the words, as if it were the pastry making the point and not the woman.

"Understand me, you have insight, and this is good, and it is good that your Senior brought this... energy you have... to my attention."

The pastry indicated Theo's handiwork, still clutched in her lap.

"I took time, Theo Waitley, to review your visit to the mountaintop."

Veradantha spoke very low, and Theo thought she made "Theo Waitley" into one word, to mirror her own single name.

Theo sighed—would she never stop hearing about that?

But if Veradantha had already reviewed that flight, she must be out of time or nearly so already! It was difficult to drag her attention from the woman, to glance at the chronometer, counting down. Except it was *not* counting down from seven to zero any longer, but blinking its way up from 4:45, in half-second increments.

"Nothing to say, Theo Waitley? You frowned when I mentioned your feat."

The timer flipped over from four minutes to five. Theo looked up into the lined, quizzical face and nodded once, for emphasis.

"Everyone mentions it, ma'am," she said, as calmly as she could. "All I did was what Ground told me was needed. But I survived and it makes some people think I was showing off. I didn't do it to show off. I don't like people to say so. I guess I'm still surprised that so many people think about it at all."

The pastry, much diminished, moved back and forth for several precious seconds. Veradantha's thin lips compressed into what might have been a hard smile.

"Yes, I can see that. I also can see why the Senior thought the landing worth my attention. So, Theo Waitley, do you enjoy your flying in the Slippers? I will admit that I do, though I cannot find time and energy together to take as many flights as I might."

"Yes." Theo nodded, feeling wistful. "I do like the Slippers. But now they've moved me into power group training so I can't get time."

"The universe is like that, Theo Waitley. When you are good at something, often you must give it up for something you are not so good at yet. This is inconvenient, but true."

The hand was now free of the disappeared pastry, but fascinating still, adorned as it was with several glittering rings and wrinkles so fine they looked like down.

"So you like the Slipper, and you like powered flight as well. Would you be satisfied to be an air pilot, do you think?"

The question took a moment to penetrate, and when it did, it took her breath.

On the desk, the chronometer hit seven, blinked once, and began counting down again.

"Air pilot?"

Theo heard the quaver in her voice, and winced. True, she was proud to wear the wings that Win Ton had sent her, once she'd confirmed as a rated soaring pilot. Her marks with powered craft were top-notch, too, but to *stop* there...

"Do not be kittenish on my time, Theo Waitley!"

The woman plunked the cup down on her desk, and swept fully in front of Theo, using her height and posture to loom better than anyone had ever loomed over her, including Father.

"You must understand that worlds need air pilots; in fact, in many places air pilots who fly to orbit and back are what citizens think pilots are. It is worthy work!"

Theo felt heat on her face and tried to keep it out of her voice; her stomach felt as if she'd been in a mountainside downdraft. It didn't help that she was looking up—how could someone so skinny be so formidable?

Taking a deep breath, she replied, slowly: "Yes, air pilots do worthy work. I want to know how to fly—that's useful. It's fun. It's more than fun. But, I'm here to learn to be a spaceship pilot. I don't want the sky to be my roof!"

She took another breath, suddenly struck by a terrible thought. She looked carefully at the counselor's face and asked, quietly, "Is my math *that* bad?"

"Piffpuff, Theo Waitley, I have not accused you of being incompetent. I asked if you would be satisfied with the title of air pilot."

The flip of hand and the huff were unnerving, but Theo resisted the urge to stand.

Veradantha tugged a bright blue notetaker or comm from her belt, her frail-looking hands flowing over the keys. She glanced at the chronometer, murmuring something that sounded like "*what* time?"

Theo itched to see what was on that screen but the woman cradled it and walked away from her, peering out the window overlooking the campus airfield and back at the screen, inputting something, glancing outside again. The timer was flashing now and—

"Well, Theo Waitley," Veradanth said. "I am clear that you are not dumb. I am also clear that you are inconvenient. Worse, you are inconvenient in a way that is inconvenient not only to me—I have the habit of being inconvenienced!—but to you, and to the school itself."

Veradantha stood before her, looking down with solemn eyes.

"What we shall do, you and I in our turns, is we shall be convincing when necessary and if that is not sufficient, we shall contrive. I have sent to your regular advisor to ask permission for this, of course, and then we shall see if the threads you string are useful."

The counselor paused, looking away for a moment before peering down at Theo again.

"With luck you have not seen the last of me, as I have some tests you will need to take. I have some forms for you to fill out, a questionnaire or two, they will arrive soon, as soon as permission is given, in your campus mail. These tests will perhaps not be so comfortable for you, but they will clarify things."

Clarity was something she could use, Theo knew.

"Thank you," she began, but her words were waved off.

"I see you are nearly late to your next class, unless you run, which you will do. Thank you for your time."

Theo arrived at the door barely ahead of the crowd off the hourly shuttle, her key sticking first in her pocket and then to her sweaty fingers. She wondered who'd taught them to be so noisy—yah, and they wanted to be pilots!

Asu, at least, wasn't that noisy and she spoke up—

"Hey, Theo, my key's ready! Let the pro through!"

Theo snickered and stepped aside, the rucksack brushing against the side wall with an annoying hiss.

"I bow to progress," Theo agreed, and the door opened for her.

She might have taken the earlier shuttle herself, but she'd taken the longer walk, down by Belgraid, which was a pleasantly situated second and third year dorm she'd not visited before. Not that she'd exactly *planned* on meeting Kara there, but she'd hoped, and since she was still feeling wrung out from her meeting she'd happily accepted Ristof's polite invitation to a small session, joining Kara and three others for what she thought would be a few minutes.

"Bowli ball, huh?" Asu looked her up and down, scowling. "I'm glad to see you getting more social, but you're going to have to run those leggings through the cleaner a dozen times to get 'em clean, and the shirt twice as many, and that will cost the room a yellow dot, I bet!"

"No! I . . ." but a quick inspection showed her roommate's fears to be not entirely unjustified.

"You can do that indoors, you know? Sign up for one of the leagues or at least stop by the pad rooms and play rated. You won't get more than scuffed. But look at you! You look like someone who walked out of a forest. You even have twigs in your hair!"

The game had been going on, Ristof said, since before breakfast, and with trade-ins and trade-outs they were shooting for third-shift lights-out. Of course there wasn't really a lights-out, that was a holdover time for the locals who'd come through residence schools all their lives, but . . .

"The real goal," Kara explained, "is to get us ready for the senior round-the-clock challenge at term end. Belgraid's gonna knock 'em this time!"

"Come, Asu, you know this was just a fun thing . . ."

"Hey, First Bunk, Chelly'd have a fit if he came in here and found that grass all over the place!"

Theo laughed and shook herself the way Coyster did when he came in from the garden. Just like her cat, she shed leaves and grass.

"How'd that meeting go?"

Asu was into the coldbox, pulling a pair of squeezewaters, calling out over her shoulder. Theo, gratefully unshod, pushed the grass and the twig she'd dutifully finger combed onto the floor toward the recycle bin with her sockfeet.

"I'm not sure," she admitted. "I've been waiting for some tests and forms and stuff."

Over the whuff of the floor suction came Asu's "Hunh, guess that's something." She handed over a water tube and scrunched her nose. "Theo, will you get some antisep on that hand? That's blood!"

It *was* blood, but not much of it, and the game had still been going strong when Theo left. She'd been vaguely trying to get out for some time, but they'd been keeping it five strong all day and it seemed rude to break it just to go back to the room. If she'd had a class to go to, it would have been different. But coming off the interview and a session reciting from memory what anyone could read in the history files, each new charge at the ball had felt as necessary as the last.

"Not dripping. I'll clean it."

"So is something going to happen now? About the math?"

Chaos!

"Asu, will you let up? Didn't I say there were forms and tests and stuff? I don't *know* about the math yet."

Asu laughed. "Most days I can't stand between you and that screen in there when you get in, first thing you do is check for mail. Today..." The laugh came back. "You must think they're here already!"

Theo let her glance drift toward the ceiling, and sighed quietly. Sometimes Asu was just too good.

"I got the shower," she said.

Theo usually didn't take long showers, so today she did. After, she made a cup of tea and unsealed the last of the *chernubia* she'd discovered in the school store, for a quiet one-girl snack in the common area, lights low while Asu fussed about some sports thing in the other room.

Not nearly as good as the fresh ones served by a luxury cruise liner, the snack still bore a passing resemblance to something Win Ton had smiled over, and that in turn made her smile and absently adjust the wings on her collar.

And there, a second cup of tea, and she was standing with cup in hand wondering if requesting an image from Win Ton would be bad form. Not like Asu's pet athlete's image, but... well, maybe, actually...

Asu peered into the common area, began mimicking a terminal announcer.

"Attention. Control to Pilot! Blink-blink-blink, attention, Theo!"

Asu's voice was not quite as emotionless as a good warning mode was. She waved her hands impatiently toward the desk.

"Message waiting light here, First Bunk."

Theo sighed. Sometimes it felt like things were changing too fast, and that all the messages were about her doing something *more*.

She took her cup with her and slid into the seat, "I hear you, I hear you."

The incoming message was from Scout Captain Cho sig'Radia. So was the third. Theo slapped the privacy button, effectively limiting the view of the screen to someone sitting in the spot *she* sat in.

Behind her, Asu made a sound like a *harrumph*.

"Must be expecting something else from the bestboy," she hazarded as she headed for the joint room. She paused. "Aren't you?" she insisted, but Theo was already twisting her thoughts to hear Cho's voice behind the words on the screen.

You have not been at all "silly" to pass the news of your recent flight to me; indeed, it is exactly the type of news one could hope for: success in flight! Being some Standards away from a sailplane run I discover the sim a joy; I hope you will not feel overburdened with the information that I, like your academy, have been pleased to share copies with several pilots. Win Ton professes a lack of surprise in your abilities, but promises his own commentary.

Theo relaxed into the seat, nearly losing the sight circle of the screen when she did. Then she sat straight up.

He hadn't been joking, she thought. If Win Ton's packet had gotten to her before Cho's message, he *must* have sent it immediately, by courier! Someone, some pilot, *had* been standing by, on her account!

Too, Cho went on, *you have followed the forms precisely. I need to know these things not only for the reinforcement of my judgment on your ability, but that we make no errors in dealing with your future.*

My role as sponsor requires that I take an active interest in the affairs financial attending your schooling, and in this case, with only a small and not unseemly amount of prompting, your academy and I have reached an accord on the value of your lessons for the school, and for yourself.

Following in a short while will be the contracts I have entered into on your behalf, as well as a document transferring practical control of the finances accruing to you from income derived from various uses, transformations, and recordings of your flight. Pardon that these are dry and filled with complexities well beyond the complexities of piloting equations, but such are Liaden contracts, as you will no doubt be told many times in your career. For your enjoyment, the contract in Liaden is appended to the Trade version. In short form, we have arranged for your earnings to be set against your expenses, with a 25 percent share coming direct to your spending account until all expenses are met. Please follow the instructions about passwords, account controls, and the like exactly. Once accessed the account becomes yours.

Theo leaned toward the screen. *Contracts?*

I have passed a copy of the sim to your mother in the hopes the pilot who trained you may see it, and rejoice in your flight.

Oh no! Kamele would not be happy. Surely, Father would—

The letters on the screen blurred slightly.

Father would do as he always did, and use his own judgment. Given that Kamele'd spent a lifetime in ignorance of his piloting, as had Theo, she hoped he'd explain the sim appropriately.

Good lift and safe landing, Pilot.

I remain

Cho sig'Radia, sponsor

TWELVE

· · · · · · · · · · · · ·

Number Twelve Leafydale Place
Greensward-by-Efraim
Delgado

THE BLUEBELLS ARE DOING WELL THIS SEASON, AELLIANA SAID, her voice seeming to come from just behind his left shoulder. *Theo will be pleased.*

A connoisseur of formal gardens might have commented that the bluebells danced the dagger's edge between "doing well" and "overexuberant." Aelliana, however, did not admire strict order in a garden. Nor did he.

And the bluebells were Theo's favorites, after all.

"We must remember to send her a picture," he murmured. From his right came the creak and smack of the garden door opening. Kamele was home from her meeting early.

"Jen Sar!" she called, her footsteps quick on the path.

He turned, smiling as she came into sight, her hair rumpled and her cheeks pink with hurry. She had a small blue envelope from Data Receiving and a folded printout in one hand; the paper fluttered as she walked.

"Don't you look the picture of indolence," she murmured, bending to kiss him on the cheek. "Grading examinations, indeed!"

"Indolence is pictured thus: The honored professor lying on the grass, his venerable head supported by a kindly and compliant friend, and the second bottle uncorked," he returned, smiling up at her. "Here you see the professor taking a rejuvenating turn in the garden before returning to his labors."

"Of course I do," she said, and shook her head in mock irritation. "*Compliant.*"

"Also *kindly*," he pointed out.

"That's very true." She nodded gravely, though her eyes were sparkling. "Silver-tongue."

"It has," he acknowledged mournfully, "been a lifelong affliction."

Kamele laughed, her glance going over his shoulder. "The bluebells are taking over the garden! I've never seen them so boisterous."

"I was just thinking that we must remember to send a picture to Theo."

"Yes, we should; she must miss them." She looked back to him, her face still glowing, but tending toward seriousness. "Speaking of Theo, I have a letter from Cho sig'Radia, who sends a present—to you!"

He raised an eyebrow. "A present? To me?"

"We did agree that you are *the pilot who raised Theo*, did we not?"

"I seem to recall being cast in that role, yes."

"If you accept the role, you accept the rewards of the role," Kamele told him. She nodded toward the house. "If your rejuvenation is complete, we might go back inside."

"So we might."

"Would you like some coffee?" he asked, as they strolled up the pathway together. "There was a packet of Lake Country beans in today's delivery."

Kamele sighed. "That sounds lovely. There must be a way to get funding for decent coffee in Admin, but I haven't found it yet."

"Raise tuition?" he suggested, as the door opened.

"Don't think I haven't considered it," she said darkly, stepping into the kitchen ahead of him. She put the letter and the packet on the kitchen table and glanced at the coffeemaker.

"I'll do that," he said, "if you would like to change into house clothes."

Kamele grinned at him. "Thank you, Jen Sar. And by all means, *do* read Captain sig'Radia's letter while I'm gone. Just promise that you won't open the package until I'm back."

"That seems a fair compromise," he said placidly, moving toward the pantry. Kamele laughed; a moment later, he heard her running upstairs.

He measured the beans into the hopper, set the texture, poured water into the reservoir and touched the control. The grinder whirred quietly. He went to the table, plucked up the sheet of printout and carried it to the window, hitching a hip onto the ledge as he unfolded the paper.

I, Cho sig'Radia greet Kamele Waitley, mother of Theo, to whom one has the honor to stand as patron.

Though term evaluations are ahead of us, yet I have received news of young Theo's progress which may put to rest such doubts as may have lingered in a mother's heart. I learn that our fledgling has performed very well in actual flight conditions. Indeed, she appears to have an exact and intuitive understanding of piloting at the hands-on level, which must—and does—gratify a hopeful patron. Theo has gained the attention of her elders in this and has been, so I am informed by Senior Instructor Pilot yos'Senchul, placed upon an accelerated flight path. Instead of remaining the full term with Slippers, over which she has demonstrated superiority, she has been moved up to powered flight and will soon know the pleasure of being wholly the master of her craft. The particular flight which drew special attention has been deemed to have some positive value as an auxiliary teaching aid by the school and by the aircraft manufacturers and permission to reproduce it for these purposes has been requested.

As the hopeful pilot's patron, I have negotiated a royalty contract with Anlingdin Academy in her name. Earnings under the term of this contract will be set against Theo's expenses at academy, with twenty-five percent deposited directly into an account under her sole ownership. As I understand custom, Theo has achieved the status of adult, and thus may take ownership of these financial properties, as well as administering her own contracts. If my understanding is insufficient, please teach me better and I shall make what amends I might.

Appended to this letter is a small gift. I ask, if it does not offend custom, that it be shared with the pilot who, with yourself, raised Theo. It will perhaps be of some interest.

It is my hope that this letter has found you in good health, with your goals well in hand, and I remain

Cho sig'Radia
Captain of Scouts

Jen Sar Kiladi refolded the printout along its creases, and sighed lightly.

From its place on the counter, the coffeemaker chimed; and he heard Kamele's footsteps on the stairs.

The coffee was poured, sampled and pronounced delicious. It being one of Kamele's small rituals to savor and prolong such moments, when the beverage was worthy, Jen Sar recruited himself to patience, and sipped again from his own cup.

He had taught himself to drink coffee; a graduate student could not afford to be too nice about the form in which one found one's caffeine, and Professor Kiladi had been a grad student, so it said in his dossier, on the very Terran world of Barvenna. He had, therefore, and by necessity, developed a tolerance. Later, under Kamele's tutelage, he had learned an appreciation.

The Lake Country was pleasant, medium bodied, aromatic, and with an aftertaste of raspberry. He concentrated on the flavor, and did not glance at the little package, still unopened on the kitchen table.

Kamele lowered her cup and smiled at him. "Aren't you going to open it?"

"I had not wished to intrude upon your moment," he said, truthfully.

"Of course, *I'm* not curious!" Kamele made one of her swooping, ironic gestures, her fingers approaching perilously close to his cup.

He avoided tragedy by lifting the endangered item and looked at her over the rim. "I wonder," he murmured. "Perhaps we had best just put it away."

Kamele laughed, and Jen Sar sighed dolefully.

"As transparent as that, am I? Very well, then, yes. With your permission, I will open it."

"I can't imagine what it could be."

He turned away, placing his cup carefully on the table before taking up the small blue-blazoned packet. It was not heavy, but of course, it would not be; data chips weighed very little.

A sim, Aelliana murmured inside his head, and sighed lightly. *Perhaps it won't be . . . very . . . showy.* She paused. *Of course, it is Theo.*

Of course, he thought, *it is Theo.* He opened the envelope and turned, holding the chip high on display.

"There!" he exclaimed. "Now curiosity is satisfied!"

Kamele laughed again and shook her head. "No, my friend, curiosity doesn't begin to be satisfied." She nodded toward the common room. "Why don't you get the screen ready? I'll refresh our cups."

"Well," he said conversationally, as on screen the little glide-plane played with its tow string. "A flight sim, and very agreeable it is, too."

"Theo is flying this—this craft?" Kamele asked from beside him.

He nodded. "We are seeing from the pilot's perspective—her instruments, her environment. If we wished—and had the equipment to hand—we might fly it with her and thus learn something of her technique; a useful tool for teaching other pilots."

Kamele nodded, her face rapt as she watched *Slipper Fourteen* raise its nose, dip its wing and slip free of its tow.

"That was neatly done," he said for Kamele's benefit. "Ah, and see? She has caught the thermal. With luck, this will be a long glide."

"How beautiful," Kamele breathed. "*Look* at those mountains! I had no idea that flying could be so peaceful."

"It can be," he said cautiously, watching the mountains with mistrust. Treacherous things, mountains, and a glide-plane no equal partner for the winds that often danced around such places.

"Flight GT S14, Academy GT S14," a man's voice, terse and businesslike, broke into the peaceful sail through sunny skies. "Academy GT S14, acknowledge."

"Flight GT S14 here." Theo's voice was—not calm. Bright. Sharp, even. Jen Sar scanned the instruments, took note of variometer and altitude.

"...everyone out of the sky..." the flight-master was saying, urgently. "Emergency."

Beside him, Kamele had gone very still.

"I can stuff it on the plateau in five minutes," Theo said, and it was the utter surety in her voice that made Jen Sar's stomach tighten.

"A drill," he managed, for Kamele's stillness. He touched her hand, and smiled when she glanced at him. "She will need to learn to react correctly in an emergency. Of course, there are drills, so that she may prepare while others more experienced watch over her."

Instructor El is worried, Aelliana commented, which he had thought, too, and which he was not about to say to Kamele's strained smile.

The little ship went sideways, and he felt Kamele tense beside him.

"She needs to adjust altitude, and quickly—Ground had said it was an emergency," he said, keeping his voice soothing. "She is being perfectly safe." Safe, but aggressive. His fingers twitched when she hit the standing wave, the slip-string snapping and the variometer beginning to squeal.

"The nose..." he murmured, but there, she had it; the nose was down, and she was on course. The wings thrummed, protesting the service she required of them, and the radar telling stories to frighten children—

But Theo was no longer a child; she was a pilot in command of her craft. Amid the din of scolding instruments her soarplane dutifully sideslipped, crabbing against the sheer wall. She was in charge, keeping her craft level—and the nose was up; she was rising, far too close to the wall, and—

"Not great, Theo," she said, her voice torn by the wind and the noise of the instruments. "Not great."

He scanned the plateau, saw the spot, and his fingers twitched again, reaching for levers that weren't available to him, and they were down—no! A bounce, sternly brought under control, and then they *were* down, in a chancy location, but safe enough for now, and the pilot had reported her situation and received the order to clear the craft.

Inside his head, Aelliana cheered.

He relaxed into his seat, suddenly aware that he had tensed forward, and sighed.

"That was...dangerous," Kamele said in a small, shaken voice. "Wasn't it?"

"Oh." He turned. Her face was paler even than usual, her eyes wide. "Kamele..."

"Tell me," she interrupted. "If what we just saw—was Theo *in danger*? Yes or no? That was not a drill!"

"There is always a risk, in piloting," he said slowly. "Was Theo in danger—I cannot say—" He raised his hand as she began to speak.

"No. Kamele. I am not softening this for you. The truth is

that *I cannot say*. In my experience, a pilot is in danger when a pilot feels that she is in danger. It seems to me that Theo did not consider herself to be *in danger*. She had a knotty problem to solve, and a good deal of maneuvering to do. But I had no sense—from the action of the craft, or from her voice—that she felt endangered." He sighed, and put his hand over hers where it was fisted on her knee.

"Likely it was not a drill."

"And Cho sig'Radia is *selling* this—this frightening—"

"To pilots," he broke in, remembering to keep his voice soft. "To pilots, such a tape is not so much frightening as—exhilarating." He moved his shoulders at her look of disbelief. "Pilots are a disreputable lot, I fear."

"*You* were worried," she accused him. "You stopped talking, and leaned forward, reaching for—as if you would fly it down yourself!"

He looked toward his hand, still forward on his knee, ready to take the stick, and back to Kamele.

"I was worried," he admitted. "One worries about one's daughter in treacherous moments." He smiled suddenly, pride washing him. "But I worry about her far less now." The smile widened, and became a grin.

"Kamele, on my honor—that was a *beautiful* landing!"

THIRTEEN

. . . .

Ozar Rokan Memorial Flight Center
Anlingdin Piloting Academy

GEAR DOWN AND LOCKED.

Theo felt the gear down part in the touch of the controls, and the locked part firmly through her seat as the well-used and surely misnamed Star King Mark II settled into landing mode. The instruments confirmed what she already knew, and she sang out to traffic, who acknowledged visual politely, and gave her permission to do what she was going to anyway, which was touch-and-go number nine.

For luck, she touched her key, plugged into the board and counting her PIC—Pilot in Command time that was—in one-second increments. The hand-talk shorthand *go good* was sufficient, really, even if not as satisfying as saying the words, but she was learning not to talk to herself so much, and this time she managed not to say anything at all, except what was business. The PIC timer showed 35.5. Not so long to go, after all.

She sighed noisily, communicator button off. No need to share that, either. For a while, after she'd gotten pushed into the Advanced Power, she'd hear mock-cloned, "Not good, Theo," half-whispered or louder when she walked anywhere around the airfield.

More than once she'd also heard "Prissy little attitude case" or worse from students she'd passed in the flight lists.

Still, there were good days when she could smile and wave,

or even chat and play bowli ball with Kara, Vin, and the rest of the crew from Belgraid.

The cross-breeze was minimal and she let the little jet drift a hair left of the centerline before applying a modest correction. The altimeter on the Star King was off by at least a short hop, she was sure, and the stick had a click in it—but what could you expect from one of the planes anyone air-rated had to fly for fifty hours in person and another fifty on sim before they could move on? It rarely got a good cleaning or airing out, or even a proper interior wipe-down.

The problem with touch-and-go for her was that after a while the sheer sameness was boring—no new scenery, and not much of a new challenge. It probably didn't help that the catch-up schedule Veradantha had pushed through meant she was in the plane or in sim every day, no break. And this plane, nearly surplus, was the one she'd been saddled with most times because *she* was the push-through. Serviceable yes; comfortable, not exactly.

On the other hand, next week she was scheduled for a run over the mountain and up the coast for a landing at an airstrip she'd never seen, and a run-back the same day. That would be good . . . whatever plane she was in.

Now, the field zoomed up at her; on the instrument panel the altitude ticked down and she backed the throttle just a hair more. The altitude annoyingly read zero while she flew on another moment, and before the touch of the rear gear, and the front. The craft decelerated and she saw disinterested crew working strip-side and heard the confirming "Touch *AP44*," from a bored voice just as she began to really kick the power up.

That quickly she pulled back, felt the rotation and rise, chinged the gear up, reveling in the pressure on her back, and saw blue—

If there'd been a camera on her face instead of a recorder logging the instruments it would have caught a wide wicked grin. This was her last go-round today and she meant to break her personal best time to altitude yet again. The ship might be an old one, but it was willing to press her hard into the seat and climb out into the clouds.

It was good to get a thrill just before another run at math for dummies.

*   *   *

Theo was peeved. As good as things were going in the air, that was how bad they were on the ground today.

This was the second time in six days *AP44* was stuck in a holding while some student controller bobbled the patterns, and then when things were fixed she'd been last in line for landing, with her math class a forced-march across campus if she missed the jitney.

The final landing, like the touch-and-go series, was quiet and fine, and then they'd backed a shuttle food cart out into the taxi strip where it stalled, and then—

There was only so much hurry-up she could do. Her taxi run finally came to a halt at slot 5 . . .

"*AP44*, can you pull that on down to maintenance bay while you're at it and save the crew a hike?"

AP44 was not a road racer on the ground and she hardly saved anyone a hike since they had to bring by a student ground-guide with his paddles to direct her. She tried not to frown at him— she'd done ground-guide for the first time not long before and knew it to be one of the more anxiety-producing chores at the school. Having all those wings at the ends of things made even small turns potentially dangerous.

Regs being regs, she didn't pop the canopy until the engine was winding down. The key read 36.1 as she palmed it, and she was in such a hurry she kept the helmet on until feet touched ground.

The ground-guide nodded, smiled and said, "Good landings, Pilot, good go!"

She smiled back and waved, hurling, "Thanks," into the air behind her and ran up the ramp toward the Ops office to sign out.

Wilsmyth, her chief tormentor from the *Vestrin*, stood at ramp-top, wearing the blue cap and armband of the shift boss, waiting for her, the official shift book in hand.

"Well there, Waitley, looks like you're doing real good in the air. Real good. Better than a lot of us that's been through on regular time, looks like, even in the old ship. Shame they still got you stuck in backwards math, don't you think?"

When he said "old ship" he waved the book in her direction.

Way being blocked, Theo stopped, hand-sign saying, *next class, can't talk.*

"Yeah, well, we all got classes sometimes, don't we? Look, I was thinking it's a shame you keep getting stuck with the old lady out there, you know? I mean, you got the luck of the draw, I guess. But look, you're doing better than some of us figured you would, and I wonder if you'd like to stop up to Castlin Quad later. Seniors are looking for a couple quick hands to back us up for the bowli-ball challenge at—"

"I have class, Wil. Really. And I've been working out with Belgraid, anyway."

He waved the shift book at her again, not gently, but said her name.

"Theo. Really. Listen, see, come on up to the quad, get some high class bowli ball in, maybe stop in after, for some refreshments—and we can get you set. Chelly said you had a rough upbringing, and don't know how to act any better. He thinks you'll finish the course here, if you get a break. Let Belgraid see who the good hands belong to, see? Get that break, you know? Might even be able to get you into the new Star King. It's type-certified a Mark II, but brand new—practially a Mark III in disguise."

Theo heard what Wil was saying almost as through a filter: no matter what nonsense he was offering, she needed to get moving. But she had to get by him.

"Thanks, no. I'll stick with Belgraid,"

"Just *no*?" He frowned, and his voice was louder than it needed to be. "You think *no* is the right answer?"

This, Theo thought, was not good. She'd managed to make him mad, somehow, even though she'd been polite. He was waving the shift book with energy: she could feel the breeze against her neck.

Theo tensed, fighting the instinct to drop into the ready stance, trying to look peaceful—or at least reasonable.

"I've got to go to class," she said, as calmly as she could. "Let me by."

"Right," Wil said, a note of finality in his voice. "I hear what you're saying. But this isn't all social, you know. I'm shift boss. Click your key in here, so we can sync the records—you know the drill!"

From the Ops room beyond him, someone yelled, "New shift coming in!"

"Right with you, Bell, right with you," Wil yelled back without even a glance over his shoulder. He yanked the plug out of the book and thrust it at her face. "You're on my shift," he snapped. "Key!"

At last! Maybe she'd only miss half of math.

Theo snatched the key from her public pocket, but Wil was holding the plug at an awkward angle. She jimmied her key, pushed—the accept light lit orange, then he almost dropped the instrument, forcing her to let go of the key or risk twisting the connection. He grabbed the book more firmly, peering down at it, and muttering loudly as he manipulated some keys.

"You really think you're something, don't you? Can't figure why it is you got no official math but fly like a vet. Your father was a pilot, hey? Can't nobody find any current pilot time for Jen Sar Kiladi."

"Key," she said around the growing coldness in her stomach, and added: "You can't find current flight time because my father is a *retired* pilot."

Wil snarfed a laugh and waved the shift book, with her key still attached.

"Retired? Or is that 'decertified'?"

He's trying to make you lose your temper, Theo told herself. Problem being, that he was succeeding.

"Key," she said again, between gritted teeth.

"Not going to talk about Daddy?"

"I want my key. Now."

"There you go again, always pushing for a fight. You act more like a smuggler's get than anybody civilized."

"Key," she said, closing in slowly.

"Well, your choice. Play with Belgraid and live down a decert dad if you can. We coulda made it easy for you."

Her key clicked out and he tossed it, nearly beyond her, chuckling as she scrambled.

Key in hand, she was on her way around him, thinking about math and how fast she was going to have to run—

"Close to thirty-three hours on there," Wil said, like he was talking to himself. "Who'd've thought somebody who can't add could've got that far?"

Theo froze, then turned, *carefully*, key gripped in her right hand, helmet in her left.

"Say again," she said softly. "*How* much time?"

Wil grinned and glanced down, too casually, to consult the face of the instrument again.

"You really *can't* count, can you? Three two point nine hours. Says so right here."

He turned the display for her, his grin even less certain.

"Fix it," she said. "I have more time than that."

"No," he answered, "you don't. This is the official shift-read."

"I had more time than that when I started today."

"The key count's official," he insisted. "This is your official time, which will be entered into your log."

"*Fix it.*"

"You're really pushing it, Waitley. You can't expect everything to go your way if you don't work with seniors . . ."

The shift bell sounded, yanking Theo's attention back to the rest of the world.

Math!

"You'll fix this when I come back," she said, turning back toward Ops, but he used the shift book like a shepherd's crook, blocking her way.

"Thumbprint, Waitley. Validate it."

"It's in dispute," she snapped.

She started for Ops again, ducking under the shift book.

"Waitley, validate this record or lose it all!" he yelled, following her into the room, where Bell was lounging against the desk, an interested expression on his face.

"Thumbprint!" Wil shouted. He shoved the book at her face, almost striking her, but she fended the thing off with an elbow. He waved it again, catching her a stinging blow flat on the cheek and ear, and before she realized it, Theo was moving.

She swung her helmet into his gut, but he danced partly out of the way, now using the book to prod at her face. She knew the counter for that, though. She ducked, twisted—and she was half behind him, fending off his elbow with her forearm as he tried to strike, rather than dance.

He swung hard, cussing and yelling; there was blood dripping from somewhere, but this move she'd seen on the ship when the other pilots were playing and all you needed to do really was that duck, right into the pelvis and—

Wil was flat out on the floor, dazed, his breath coming in large gasps. The shift book lay against the desk at Bell's feet. Bell, eyes wide, was standing with hands low, nonthreatening, looking between Wil and Theo in wonderment, and then directly at Theo.

"One-handed! I can't believe it, you took him one-handed!"

His face changed, ruddy cheeks going white. He reached to the desk, slapping a button.

The security gong rang about the time Theo realized that the blood was coming from the stinging area on the side of her face. She held her hand there, to stop the blood, but the gong kept ringing.

FOURTEEN

· · · · · · · · · · · · · · · · · ·

Sturtevan Hall Dispensary
Anlingdin Piloting Academy

FLOOR TILE CAN BE VERY INTERESTING, ESPECIALLY WHEN IT'S A floor carefully, nay, *perfectly* set with borders of local stones from local artisans, and then sealed and bonded with a transparent, diamond-hard finish. The subtle blues and greys, combined with a flash of silver and the rare but welcome reds and oranges created a free-form flowing image of waterfall and fish, or stream and birds, depending on the focus of the eye, and the angle of the light.

Theo sat, staring at the beautiful work, thinking. When you have a school or college and someone gives you money to name a hall after their particular heroic family member, you can do that kind of stuff, like make a med clinic into a work of art.

Here, the floor did not merely meet the walls, it curved up and seamlessly became the wall. No errant dirt allowed, no buildup of dust, no collection point for contagion, no dimming of the beautiful floor of Sturtevan Hall's dispensary.

Theo sat in a chair, sorb-pad held to the side of her face, tension singing from her shoulders, studying the pattern of the tile, doing her best not to think too much about how she'd managed to get into a fight. She *never* got into fights. Well, not *that* often . . . and that made the tile much more interesting until the attendant came back with the med techs.

They'd shaved her hair on the left and a patch a little higher

97

to get at the cut, the slender med tech with his grad-student tags soothing her with his quiet voice and gentle fingers as the other wielded the shave wand with dexterity.

"We have permission then, to heal these problems?"

When he said that he pulled back so she could see his startling grey eyes and serious gold-toned face. He drew his hand down the side of her face in front of her ear, perhaps illustrating *these problems*.

She nodded, her fingers repeating *yes*.

He sighed, the corners of his mouth quirking.

"Were you speechless, I would accept, but you are not speechless and we must both hear you say so; it is in the nature of being witness to each other, you understand." Again he gently touched her face. "So, I may heal these problems?"

"Yes," she managed, "you may heal this problem."

"That is well said, Theo Waitley. No concussion for you, and none I hear for the gentleman in the next room. You may relax, please."

She tried, thinking of a dance Bek had taught her, all languid circles and limpid ovals, but the sleepy patterns kept morphing into the sharper moves of defense dance.

"It is adrenaline," the tech murmured lightly. "You are well served. Here, let me look again."

He bent close; she could hear his breathing. He spoke several syllables she didn't understand, to which the other tech made a quick reply. She heard the rustle of a lab coat, and from the corner of her eye saw a small object trade hands.

"Please, then, sit back, and be comfortable. Two steps here, if you will pull your patience together."

She smiled and managed a weak laugh, nodding. He bent forward again, his voice so low it almost put her to sleep.

"This is fine, this is fine, ah, in a twelve-day your boyfriend will kiss it and all will be well. A clean cut after all, which the blood has cleansed, as it should. This, this stings, in a moment, but it will be well."

Theo shivered then, the sudden thought of having Win Ton being close enough to touch her face reminding her somehow that now she had a lot of explaining to do, to Father, Win Ton, to Cho. To Kamele!

She heard the other med tech giggle something about Theo

"needing a boyfriend with quick moves" and then there came the *zzzizzizit* of a cool spray, which, after a moment, *did* sting. When her concentration came back the med tech with the spray said said, "A moment, Theo Waitley, let me check the scalp here; your muscles are quite tense."

His fingers touched her scalp above and then behind her ear, traced a curve down toward her shoulder.

"Dancer," he said, so soft he was probably talking to himself. Theo relaxed under his touch.

"You will wish to dance gently tomorrow and the next day— call it a prescription: you must dance gently. You should dance every day. This will be good practice, for as a courier pilot you will need to stand as ready as you did today. A moment more, if you please, Theo Waitley; you will relax, we will together permit these muscles to relax even more..."

He did something with his hands, touching one close to the affected area and one to the other side of her head, spreading warmth—

"One additional therapy," he said gently, "and your skin will find itself and we shall soothe it together and cover with just a slight tape...she who flies gliders, these muscles we need to relax, we need them to relax so that the parts of you go together properly. You need not always be on the verge of fight, which is wearing and tenses muscles. So, accepting the capability to act, that is good. What is needed, now, is for you to let these muscles relax, to let the skin be natural. This is how we refuse scars the opportunity to form. Let you dance a moment in your head, with your eyes closed, the move that most powers you, then the move that most relaxes you."

With eyes closed she saw Win Ton, dancing beside her, his eyes glinting mischief; felt her own move in response to his joy and the pattern—and sighed.

"Yes, that is fine, that is fine. Ah, excellent, let those emotions work for you. And now the coolmister..."

There came another *zzzizzizit* of spray, like fog on her face, and the touch of fingers and a flower smell that reminded her of bluebells and Coyster and home.

When she opened her eyes, the grey eyes of the med tech were surprisingly close, as if he were watching her whole face and person.

He gave a half bow, and reached about to pull a touch pad to her.

"If I may have your thumbprint, Theo Waitley, there will be two pills for pain, which you will not need tonight, but which I am required to issue. The skin cover will come off in the shower in three days; it is best if you not touch it before."

"Thank you," she managed, and stood. She felt…light, and… calm. Comfortable in her own skin.

"Thank you," she said again, and bowed.

FIFTEEN

· · · · · · · · · · · · ·

Adminstrative Hearing Room Three
Anlingdin Piloting Academy

THERE WAS A HEARING, SCHEDULED IMMEDIATELY, ACCORDING TO regs. Immediately in this case being the first hour of evening watch.

Theo was glad of the delay. Math for dummies was long dismissed. She wrote a note to the instructor, explaining her absence, which was required, then took a shower, being careful not to get the covering over her cut wet, and dressed. She pinned Win Ton's wings to her collar, and made herself a cup of tea.

Good tea, Father used to say, was worth more than its weight in rare wine. She didn't have rare wine, but she did have some tolerably good tea. She sat in the comfiest chair in the joint room, making sure to lean back into the cushion, closed her eyes and sipped.

Carefully, she did a self-assessment. She was still feeling kind of floaty, which she thought might be let-down from the adrenaline, like the medic had said. The calm . . . *inner calm*, she thought, savoring her tea.

Pilot, that's what *that* was. Pilots had *inner calm*. The sample reports they'd been reading made that clear enough. Pilots acted for the best good of ship, passengers and cargo. That meant more than having good reaction times; it meant being calm enough to *think well* in emergencies.

Since she *was* going to be a pilot, no matter what Wilsmyth and the people like him tried to do to stop her, it seemed like calmness was going to be a good habit to cultivate.

She sighed, and finished her tea, wondering how the scene with Wil would have played out, if she'd managed to stay calm. Whether she'd reacted well to the emergency—well, she guessed she'd find out. Opening her eyes, she looked to the clock.

Real soon now.

Veradantha and Pilot yos'Senchul were waiting for her at the door to Hearing Room Three.

"Waitley," yos'Senchul said, his hand giving her a simultaneous, *Welcome*. He bowed slightly, which was perhaps a sign of the seriousness of the moment.

Veradantha merely nodded. "You are prompt, Theo Waitley. This is good. You display a becoming lack of anger. This is also good. The matter before us should not take much of our time. Be sober, be thoughtful, be alert, and all is well."

"Yes, ma'am," Theo said, looking between the two of them.

"We are here as your advisors," yos'Senchul said, moving his hand toward the door. "Please, after you."

At the table between her two advisors, Theo made sure she had her back against the chair, folded her hands on the table, and advertently noted the location of the second door.

As she settled and looked around, she was aware of the solemn patience of both of her tablemates.

Between them they'd had a lot of practice being patient, she supposed, with Flight Instructor yos'Senchul having to deal with wannabe pilots all the time, and Veradantha—and Veradantha having had more years than Theo could imagine to . . . and there, so much for patience. Veradantha placed a small flat object on the table, flashed her hand over it, and settled back, at ease now that the clock was running.

People were settling into place at the other tables. Wilsmyth sat with an administrator or teacher she didn't recognize, pointedly looking away from her, mostly at the pile of hard copy in front of him.

Chelly was at the head table, such as it was—it was hard to have a head table with three rectangular tables arranged in a triangle shape and each with three chairs sitting behind it—but there he was, very busily not looking at her and not looking at Wil, either. Since Wil sat in the middle of his table as she did at hers, that left Chelly a tunnel straight ahead to look at, along with his notebook, and the people who flanked him. Wil's table still lacked his second advisor, but it wasn't quite the hour yet, according to Veradantha's clock, which was official enough for Theo.

The door opened, admitting Commander Ronagy, who looked around, frowned and pulled the door sharply closed behind her.

"Mister Frosher," she said, "please designate one of your associates to take the empty seat; I'll sit to your right at head table."

Chelly looked to his right and left.

"Dorts is a pilot," he said quietly, "so someone in Admin, it looks like. Goueva, that fits you several times."

The plump woman lifted a hand in acknowledgment, gathered up her notebook, and moved over to Wilsmyth's table with a minimum of fuss. The Commander slid into the newly vacated chair.

Right, Theo thought. *Veradantha is here as Admin, too. Keeping track of jobs is hard.*

Chelly nodded all around as if counting, rapped quietly on the desk in front of him, and began the session.

"Thank you all for coming on short notice; as desk man on Ops the decision to convene is my responsibility. This is an informal fact-finding session convened by the officers of the watch as per standing orders in instances where accidents or conflicts involve the need for medical intervention or staff attention; no notes are to be taken and no notes are to be taken away. Should no consensus be reached over the items under discussion this evening, a formal process will begin, possibly as soon as the close of this session."

Chelly's voice was good and strong for all that he was reading from a cheat sheet, with the head of the academy by his side. "Does any member of this fact-finding wish to go directly to formal process? If so, please state your case now."

Peripheral vision is a wonderful thing, except that it almost cost Theo an inadvertent laugh as hands on both sides of her flashed quick instructions, Veradantha's *No* perhaps a tenth-beat behind yos'Senchul's *silence.*

Chelly looked around, checking with the others at the front table before looking toward Wil, and then, almost pointedly, at Theo. She refolded her hands—left over right—and looked right back at him. *Inner calm.*

Chelly let the quiet stretch a moment longer, then nodded, naming all present so that he was sure who was who, and so they could be too, then returned to the cheat sheet.

"With the consensus of all present parties I will state the situation as it came to the attention of Ops."

Inner calm.

Chelly's recitation was bare-boned: a call for medical assistance with security backup came during the early evening free-flight period, with a witness reporting "a discussion or something" between a pilot and the acting field coordinator during which one person "was just about knocked out one-handed" and the other was "bleeding to beat Betelgeuse."

"A moment, Mr. Frosher."

Chelly stopped, head turning rapidly. The Commander's hand motion was a soothing *For clarity* toward Chelly—and a scathing *discussion talk talk discussion* as she glanced between Wil and Theo. Her look was less than warm and Theo wished she had some tea to sip on.

"I've been called from my dinner to *discuss* a *discussion* between two of our students? I see. Please continue."

Theo felt as if she'd shrunk, but the flight instructor's briefly fluttering hand was calm: *fly the ship.*

"Accounts vary somewhat," Chelly continued. "The witness suggests he became aware of an animated discussion in progress as the principals arrived, one which, I guess the word is 'escalated' because both parties were focused on different goals. The witness indicated that perhaps Pilot Waitley was refusing to thumbprint something and during the insistence, accidental contact occurred between the individuals and—"

Theo's twitch was calmed by Veradantha's *smooth, not a problem* hand-sign. Wil, meanwhile, jerked 'round to glare at Theo.

Chelly went on.

"The result was that both parties went to the infirmary. Pilot Waitley suffered a flesh wound to the scalp; Wilsmyth suffered contusions and a few moments of disorientation."

"First strike, Mr. Frosher?"

This from the Commander.

"The cameras might tell for sure, ma'am, but the sequence seems to have been an accidental...ummm...an accidental swipe of the notebook Wilsmyth carried, which caught Pilot Waitley by surprise. Pilot Waitley's response was, I gather, a move of the dance, a trained response."

"Thank you. Please continue."

"I ask the involved parties if the summary of events to this point is accurate."

Theo sat back, thinking hard, willing away her blush, willing away her anger. *Inner calm.*

"Yes, but—" Wilsmyth began, and stopped as a hand came to rest on his arm.

"I think yes," Theo managed. "That's what Bell would have seen. I mean, that's what happened, I guess. I got swiped upside the head and yeah, that dance move was right there. Automatic."

Chelly glanced around, then down at his cheat sheet, nodding as if he were mentally clicking off options as he read them.

"We have a situation that was not the result of an inherent fault in the physical plant of the academy, nor was it the direct result of catastrophic equipment failure, nor of procedure."

He paused, nodded once more with authority, and went on.

"Does any member of this fact-finding wish to go to formal process now? If so, please state your case."

Theo could see Wilsmyth staring at his pilot advisor, and saw a flurry of low to the table hand-talk she couldn't get much out of. For her part, her hands were still after acknowledging Veradantha's low-voiced, "Please wait."

Chelly looked about carefully and nodded. "Who will assert being a victim?"

The relocated administrator was whispering urgently into Wilsmyth's ear, while at Theo's table, yos'Senchul signed an unruffled: *best stay course.*

After a few moments Chelly tapped his cheat sheet, looking relieved.

"We now go to a short discussion of events prior to the witness account. As no charges have been brought to this point and neither party has indicated a claim of victim, precedence goes to the senior."

Theo vibrated with anger and tension, the phrase *inner calm, inner calm* bouncing around noisily in her head. Her advisors walked on either side of her, Veradantha professing a preference for something out of the ordinary, it being so late in the evening, while the flight instructor was saying something Theo wasn't quite catching about a simple snack from Toovil that could be had for a half-hour's flying.

They left the building, cool air and silence flowing over them. Lost behind were Wilsmyth and his companions, who'd gone right when they'd taken the left at the end of the hall. Wil had been laughing, though she didn't think he had anything more to laugh about than she did.

At that, she wiped her hand on her jacket sleeve again, She certainly hoped never to touch him again. Without a doubt laying him out on the floor was something he'd deserved, no matter how accidental, and shaking his hand may have satisfied custom in a way Father would have approved of, but it *certainly* hadn't satisfied her.

"Orn Ald, that's fine for you to say, but some of us have meetings and classes in the morning."

Hand-talk, compressed and sudden. Theo caught *fix now quick* and then realized they were heading at quite a pace toward the faculty airstrip.

"Why did we have to act like losing my hours was an accident?"

Theo tried not to whine but wasn't sure she'd succeeded.

Veradantha spoke, gently, but not in answer to either the question or the tone.

"Theo Waitley, my good friend Orn Ald and I wish, evidently, to speak with you outside the range of official ears."

yos'Senchul's flashed a general *query yes?*

"You are hungry, Theo?" he asked aloud.

"Still mad," she confessed. "I ought to be hungry, I guess." She walked on, glad of the brisk pace, tension in her shoulders and *inner calm* starting to sound like a bad joke.

"I understand your dismay, Pilot," yos'Senchul murmured. "Would you be kind enough to fly us to dinner? The flight will do us all good, I'm sure, and your choice at this point falls to deciding if you'd like to partake of local fried-and-spiced night snacks or a quiet dinner at an A-class restaurant?"

She laughed.

"You're serious? Fly us to dinner? I'm always hungry after."

"Indeed. We all have had our routines disturbed by Wilsmyth's antics. Dinner will help. But what kind of meal?"

"I'm not good for real fancy, I think."

"Excellent. If you will step this way, there's a Star King VI to which I hold the keys." He pointed. A shiny, very new craft occupied the tie-down he indicated, "Also, if we choose carefully, we shall more than make up the 'split difference' between the account hours you've earned and those as recorded by Wilsmyth. In the bargain, we shall certify night hours."

Theo almost stumbled, suddenly seeing what had happened—not only *seeing it*, but *recognizing it*. How many times had she seen Father bow his head, and seem to cede an argument—to her or to Kamele or to a visiting colleague—only to later deftly turn his defeat into victory?

"Thank you," Theo said, fervently. "I should have known! Liadens know how to manage around red tape! Thank you for being on my side! I—"

"Silence!"

They all three stopped, the glare of the runway lights making them a tableau of dark cutouts across the access paths.

Instructor yos'Senchul's jauntiness was gone, and before Theo stood a dangerous man. She felt some of the dance roused in her, and went back a step, wariness answering the set of his shoulders, the warning in his pose.

Carefully, she raised her hands, fingers spread in the sign for *no danger here*.

"Ah." Threat melted away; he inclined his head, hand-sketching an emphatic *attend*!

"Student Waitley, this confrontation with Wilsmyth should teach us all much, but what it should not teach *you*, what you should *never* learn, is to trust and rely on someone simply because they are Liaden."

Theo lowered her hands, slowly. "Yes, sir."

"In this situation," yos'Senchul continued, "our goals align. As an instructor, I wish that a promising student is given the opportunity to prove herself without falling victim to petty politics and power struggles. You have acquitted yourself well this day, and I approve.

"Always know where you stand with a Liaden, student. Do they deal with you as friend, then that is a rare gift—and one to be examined, closely. If they deal with you in business, deal carefully and accurately, and promise nothing you cannot perform. When dealing with pilots, treat as a pilot and you will be treated so. Assume *nothing*, however, about someone simply because they are Liaden. If you are not affiliated with a clan, a Liaden will treat you as disposable, if that is convenient. If you display *melant'i*, as you do, expect to be treated with respect. Do not expect *benefits* from Liadens. As with anyone, expect what you are given, assuming neither hostility nor grace—and be on guard for either."

It left her breathless, his quiet vehemence. Theo did the only thing she felt able to do; she inclined her head.

"Well put, my friend," Veradantha said, moving slowly but smoothly down the field. They followed, her voice trailing behind her like a silken scarf.

"There is something in pilot lore which speaks to this, in fact. As a pilot, the usual rules of behavior on duty are assumed to include a number of things. Let us see—you may number them later if you like, and I will miss some." She raised a long forefinger in emphasis.

"Always know where your ship is and in what state. Always carry an extra weapon—this assuming one always carries two weapons to begin with—your extra is preferably one you are willing to use for a last stand. Be prepared to fight—we know you know this one!—but be prepared also to run and to be small, for a dead, jailed or administratively restricted pilot flies no ship. When you walk in strange places be aware of those who may follow you, and though sitting with your back to the wall is useful, it is not always sufficient. Always know more than you tell, and share all of your secrets, even on your deathbed, only with those who will properly treasure them."

They were close to the plane now, which shone with a flawless beauty.

"And," said yos'Senchul, "except under extreme duress, always perform a pre-flight. Here is the key, Pilot; you will wish to do the walk, and then you will let us in to observe while you are PIC for this flight. I suggest either DurzAnn's, with the guaranteed grittiest Gar-grilled, or Hugglelans, where you may have anything, as long as you eat it under red sauce."

SIXTEEN

· · · · · · · · · · · · · · ·

Conglomeration of Portcalay
Eylot

"I DOUBT I'VE MANAGED TO CROSS ALL FOUR OF THOSE LAKES on one flight before, Pilot. Well plotted!"

Theo had filed a flight plan with those crossing points in it, recalling the Ts, as they were called: *Turn Time Twist Throttle Talk* of her early training; it gave her an excuse to see, if there *was* anything to see, and to practice timing the turns, adjusting the throttle, talking to air control...

"Thank you, sir," she managed, wondering if she'd overstepped somewhere, but by then she was on the landing leg and had less time to be concerned than during the middle of the flight, when she was essentially flying on instruments above the dense blackness of a lake.

The "King Six," as yos'Senchul had it, could have flown itself from campus to Portcalay if necessary. Theo daren't waste flight time, though, and she hugged every second to herself like a precious thing. The night challenge was not as daunting as she'd expected, though no doubt the fine weather helped that. If either of her mentors noticed that she took the sightseers' route, crossing the mountain as well as three rivers and four lakes, they chose not to mention it, beyond yos'Senchul's remark.

The instruments were familiar enough, as were the flight controls, and from her vantage in the pilot's seat she couldn't see the handspan difference in rated wing length, though she certainly felt the more powerful engines from the instant she touched the throttle.

The details though: remembering the right way to sync with the local and regional traffic control, remembering to use the correct aircraft designation, remembering to use a social rate of climb in general airspace, making sure she covered everything in the pre-flight check. Theo sighed. The King Six sure was pretty!

The flight instructor took the radio briefly, calling ahead to reserve a table, using her flight plan numbers without hesitation and without consultation, declaring himself, "yos'Senchul, sitting second."

That was both a thrill *and* a chill—surely she had a lot to learn before she rated a copilot!

The plane was so well-behaved that Theo did get to sightsee, both over the mountains and the lakes, and now across plain and lake, looking north to the nearly edge-on lights of the planet's largest spaceport and manufacturing center, and south across the sudden divide into the crisscross of the commercial farm belt. The radar kept her company, and ground control; several times she sighted the beacon lights of aircraft in the distance, and identified them by the scan.

Ahead was the Conglomeration of Portcalay; within it were several millions of people, and the air strip center she was on course for.

The maps and positioning were fine so far; what she hadn't expected was that the place would be so bright. The runways themselves were lit, of course; Theo read the various beacons as they came to view—*this* was the emergency strip, *that* was backup for regional commutes, the pair of general strips were at right angles, one north-south to the east of the vague square that was Portcalay and the other well to the south of center, running to the west for her.

Conversation in the cockpit had been quiet, then nonexistent after Veradantha fell asleep; yos'Senchul sat the copilot's seat as observer only and several times appeared to be drowsing himself.

The excitement of the flight itself kept Theo awake, though she managed not to comment on it to herself, out of respect for Veradantha's rest. She did, though, need to give air control a verbal ack for touchdown on Portcalay G East.

Quiet as it was, her confirmation woke both her passenger and her copilot. Both were chattering away about sauces of choice, and the taste benefits between whole grain and spelt, when Theo guided the King Six into the final turn for landing.

Well before her, the white line became thicker; Theo unlocked and touched the landing gear switch, felt the drop and lock, and now the thick line was a runway, gleaming in the night, marks of myriad previous landings approximating her landing zone, the lights guiding her true. She backed the throttles slightly, looked at a sudden wind speed change, confirmed that with the ground, and sighed. Almost over. The headwind bobbled the nose, and she trimmed out the elevators with a touch.

The King Six smoothed into the final seconds, the wind allowing her just a hint of flare at the very last moment and...

They were down.

Chaos, did this plane have great suspension! She couldn't feel the gear bottom out, instead there was simple, smooth settle. Soft as a pillow.

She glanced to the screen then, and wrinkled her nose.

"And there is a problem worth a grimace?" Pilot yos'Senchul sounded interested, but unconcerned.

She felt her face warm, but the instrument lighting wouldn't betray her blush.

Theo reduced throttle, letting the craft slow, watched for the runway ahead to take on a green stripe, to the left, and she followed the green stripe, toward those bright lights.

"According to the chronometer, I was seventeen seconds late on touchdown," she admitted.

From the back came a sneeze that might have really been a strangled laugh, while the flight instructor peered into the night, his reply bouncing off the windscreen.

"By so much, Pilot Waitley? Where do you think your error lies?"

She pondered that while steering the plane through a sudden maze of lights and lines, the beacons and strobes of a dozen or more craft in her sight.

The arrows guided her left once more, around the large hangar and maintenance areas she'd spotted from on high, into a kind of courtyard. The lead lights flashed, steadied—

"The Howsenda Hugglelans," yos'Senchul intoned, entirely unnecessarily, since the name was emblazoned in intricately flashing purple signs taller than the control tower.

The parking slot for the King Six was there: Number Eleven. There were picnic tables just ten or twelve plane lengths ahead, and beyond that a bulky building that was all balconies and torches, with smoky fire pits and...motion.

People. Dozens. Hundreds! Some were waving at her plane, some were seated at benches, some were moving in a strange line, right hands on the hips of the people in front of them, some...

Theo checked clearance carefully, and used the correct brake to slide the plane into position, trying not to gawk at the same time.

"Part of it was the head wind," she said, in answer to yos'Senchul's question. "Maybe a second or two, there."

"*Part* of it, no doubt," he said dryly, reminding her of Father's tone when something obvious escaped her, "is that the flight plan did not extend to switching runways. The default is north, but that would have been a nasty little crosswind, indeed, and traffic didn't warrant making you fight it on manual. In any case, late or not, we are here and I, at least, am hungry. Let us eat!"

Theo looked at the menu painted above the reservation desk, knowing none of the names of things, and shrugged at her mentors, who asked, almost in unison, "Today's special?" One nodded, and the other bowed—to each other and to the desk manager, who whistled sharply into the din, producing someone to guide them.

Theo didn't mind following the guide—he was dressed in a tight sleeveless vest over a smooth, muscled chest, and moved quite well for a non-pilot, his bell-bottomed slacks encasing what was probably a dancer's body. His stride was forthright, his eyes, when he looked behind to see that they were still with him, compelling. He carried a bundle in each hand, and Theo was finding it hard to remember that the evening had started out with a fight and an administrative hearing.

Everyone they passed seemed to be having a good time; everyone was eating—well, not everyone. At the smaller and less well-lit tables sat shadowy couples, sipping together with straws from tall, glowing cylinders. Some of the couples were awfully close together, and perhaps getting closer.

Their own table was at terrace edge, with a view of the airport, and a fire pit right there, with a small tabletop leaning against it. Veradantha chose her seat, and perforce, Theo found herself between her hosts while their guide bent in front of them and busied himself with the fire pit.

Surprisingly close came Veradantha's whisper.

"Admirable, is he not? It is a shame we can do no more than admire, Theo Waitley. I, for not having the energy beyond my eyes and nose, and you, you for being Pilot tonight, and thus too tightly scheduled to wrestle three falls with someone who wears *vya* so extravagantly."

She opened her mouth—and closed it. Yes, she knew what *vya* was, and obviously so did Veradantha.

As if oblivious, yos'Senchul turned to them, hand waving wide toward their guide. "And now, the show!"

As if he had been waiting for the announcement, their guide deftly picked the tabletop up from its lean against the pit. A small spindle depending from it was placed precisely into a matching notch, leaving about three quarters of the thing over the fire zone.

Wait, now she saw it! Their guide was their cook, too!

The cook spun the "table" hard with his hand and it continued to rotate. With a practiced air he wiped it with a small paper cloth, gave the table an extra spin, and waved at the pit, which dutifully roared into flame, as he proceeded to carefully portion stuff onto the cook surface.

Theo did as she was told: she watched. His implements were wood and ceramic, his hands quick and sure.

"Thus we clearly see," Veradantha said, bringing their attention to herself, "that the universe encompasses more than the classrooms and grounds of Anlingdin Academy. The choices are varied, and the methods, as well. Some assume that a proper education instills particular beliefs and necessities as much as it instills knowledge; indeed, some would have it that the failure to assume these beliefs indicates a lack of knowledge."

Theo took the cue, offering, "The Simples are like that on Delgado—in fact Delgado is like that on Delgado!"

Her companions looked on, alert, interested, so she continued with, "I mean, the whole thing about the university is that they want to raise people to do what they do, the way they do it."

The flight instructor coughed lightly. "Yes, and after all, pilots wish there to be more proper pilots. This is the way of the universe, is it not?"

Theo paused as the cook flashed his knife rhythmically across something on the inner section of the whirling disk, heard it sizzle as a flash of vinegar was added...

She put her hand to the side of her head, where it itched, then drew it away suddenly, glancing at her hand to make sure she hadn't compromised the dressing on her wound.

"No," she said after a moment, "there's a difference. If an instructor tells me that I ought to use landing gear, and I don't, then I have probably made a mistake, a bad one. A demonstrably bad mistake! If someone tells me that I need to read a particular chapter of a book three times each year and repeat a sentence from that book every day else the universe will collapse on itself... that is not demonstrable."

Neither of the pilots spoke: still they watched with intent interest. Maybe she hadn't explained fully—

"We need pilots. We need people who know about rugs, and people to sell things, to cook, and...but they're all *doing something*. I want to do something. I don't want to go to a meeting and...I mean look, my mother and father have to go to meetings and spend time—waste time is more like it!—because they have all these silly levels of things to keep track of, all these holes to put people into.

"Adjunct," she said firmly, holding up her left hand, one finger up. Using her right to tap that hand she said, "Assistant adjunct. Associate adjunct. Associate assistant adjunct. Assistant associate adjunct."

She stopped, gathered herself. "I don't want to spend my life worrying about how many credit-months I've sat listening to someone tell me about something I know about already!"

She made a face, scrinching up her eyes, and when she opened them found a beverage cart.

So many choices...but, "Nothing with alcohol," she said austerely. "Not for me, I'm flying."

"Of course, Pilot. Something to increase attention? Soft drink, tea, water, coffee?"

"Do you have real tea? Liaden tea?"

The cart driver laughed.

"Yes, *real* tea, Pilot. It could be worth my life to offer anything else."

✳   ✳   ✳

The meal was served with flourish, each plate filled first with a third of the food on the outer circle of the wheel, then with a third of the next orbit, and finally from the center, each expertly scooped, each precise.

The sauces were extravagant, and Theo too busy eating to speak. The cook stayed, using the now still disk over the warm pit to encourage a slowly rising bready dessert, which was covered in fruit and folded on itself before serving.

"And so," yos'Senchul offered as the cook was arranging their final dish, "what would you, Theo Waitley, if you had no need to sit in classrooms for a certain number of hours? If your flight time was counted and found adequate, what would you do? Would you hire yourself off to Tree-and-Dragon?"

Theo waited a moment, raised her hands from the table, palms up, in question, then flashed *repeat query please.*

The instructor sighed, very gently.

"Do you not sit with your classmates of an off-hour, pining for a ship—perhaps a cruise liner or a yacht? Don't you wish for a berth with a particular company, or have plans to own a freight line of your own?"

Theo shook her head, nibbling delicately at her dessert.

"This pilot, your father." Veradantha took up the questioning. "He did nothing to aim you to a company, a preferred ship? The Moon-and-Rabbit, perhaps, if not the Dragon?"

Theo put her fork down, suddenly finished with dessert. There were questions in back of the questions Veradantha was asking. She could feel them, but she didn't understand them. Sighing, she answered the surface, hoping the back questions would come clear. Sometimes, that happened.

"My father didn't even tell me *he* was a pilot until Captain Cho offered to sponsor me to Anlingdin. Then he warned me how dangerous it is!"

The instructor touched the empty left sleeve where his arm should be.

"Danger, yes. There can be danger, after all."

Theo nodded. "I'm learning that. On Delgado—on Delgado, danger isn't acceptable." She looked down at her plate. "My father did help me bring my math up, and he taught me how pilots pack. When I was ready to ship out, the last thing he told me was to remember that really big problems went to Delm Korval. I thought he was making a joke, to take my mind off—" She looked up at yos'Senchul's eyes. "But that might have been advice, too."

"So it might. As you say, Liadens place a certain value on subtlety—and a father would wish to care for his child."

She nodded again, fiddled with her fork, but didn't pick it up.

"I played bowli ball with some cruise liner pilots—there are like six on at a time, working as a team." She paused, then looked to Veradantha.

"I'm not sure I'm good with people, really. I'm not sure about being part of a six-team. I just want to...pilot, to fly. If I had everything Pilot yos'Senchul said, and all the choices were mine—that's what I'd want."

"To pilot, eh?" yos'Senchul waved across the terrace. "You'll have your chance to pilot on the way home, I assure you. Look!"

She'd been so busy eating and talking that she hadn't noticed what she should have: the breeze off the lake had filled the sky with fog.

"You have a morning class and I have an early meeting," Veradantha said conversationally, "and I intend to sleep through the return trip. Please, Pilot, do your duty."

SEVENTEEN

. . . .

Ops
Anlingdin Piloting Academy

THE KING SIX SIGHED, OR MAYBE IT WAS THEO. SYSTEMS COUNTED their fingers and toes one more time, reporting in to the pilot so she could shut them down or bank them as needed; the only oddity was waiting for her passengers to finish gathering themselves together. She'd never had *passengers* before this trip.

Her copilot had been awfully active. He'd watched without comment as Theo used the plane's credit to top off the tanks, heard her call in an amended flight plan to avoid a towering storm predicted for Lake Sawya, and carried on a running hand-talk conversation with Veradantha the entire time they were on the runway and lifting to cruise. For that matter, he'd periodically turn during the flight, chattering by hand for extended periods that seemed to have nothing to do with the progress of the flight. For all she'd vowed to sleep through the return trip, Veradantha's fingers were often active on her small keyboard, the tiny rhythmic clicks distinct in the plane's otherwise steady aural background. When the clicks stopped, that was when yos'Senchul would hold forth.

At one point, Theo had turned her head to pointedly *look* at him, since his level of discussion had gone from active to agitated, and the motion was distracting. She'd caught what might have been *inadequate preparatory curriculum* but, given the syntax and motion of the single hand doing the work of two, could just as well have been *weakly unbaked circles*.

To his credit he signed *apologies to the ship, I rest now*, which she'd also acknowledged with a quick one-handed *yes thanks*, but in only a few moments, after a spate of clicking from the back seat, he was again signing, albeit in a more subdued manner.

The amended flight plan the King Six followed put it over the continent's largest lake, where the venerated and light-spangled Thirty Islands could be paralleled but not directly flown over. The sky was clear enough that she could see lights below and stars above, and if she'd wished she could easily have flown entirely by eye, ignoring the track line on GPS as each island's distinctive shape showed clearly. This part was fun as she threaded the needle in several places, making sure the while she was both above minimum attitude and between the noisier flight modes, enjoying the comfortable g-forces of the banking turns.

Approaching the last of the islands, though, the plane gained altitude suddenly, and a column of cloud leapt out of the darkness, enveloping them, as the sigh of air passing around them changed timbre.

The King Six bounced. She brought it level and began descending very gradually, the while keeping the variometer a focus. The plane behaved itself really well when they hit a quick burst of rain and hail that clattered on the skin, startling her, then they were through, the ship on course but tending downward...

Veradantha spoke, gently, from her place: "We often forget, when we fly, that valleys and channels well below us are mirrored in the sky. You have flown through what some call 'the smoker.' You will look it up and send me your reaction in the morning, if you please."

The variometer telling tales, Theo nodded, and increased throttle, watching the crosswind which threatened to bring the ship uncomfortably close to the no-fly zone.

Advertency won out—just. Then it was time to run a check of the backup instruments, and the flight resumed the comfortable silence, enlivened until the end with near random bursts of hand-talk and the low clicks of Veradantha's fingers on her notepad.

They filed through the small terminal, yos'Senchul's, "Follow me if you will, Waitley," recognized as more of an order than a request.

Passing by the Ops desk, they went down a short hall. yos'Senchul used a swipe key and bowed Veradantha and Theo into a brightly lit conference room.

Theo shivered, belatedly recognizing that it was cool and damp outside, something she'd not noticed when leaving the plane. Maybe it was the hour, too, or concern about this sudden change of course.

Veradantha sat at the table, pulling out her ubiquitous timer. Without looking up, she patted the place next to her, so Theo sat, too.

yos'Senchul paced, his hand describing gestures that were not quite signs, his shoulders moving with a rhythm and beat—with a shock of recognition she realized that this was a calming routine, a tension reliever. Father sometimes—

"The thing is, Waitley, that you are dangerous." The words were spoken gently, which concerned her greatly.

Theo sat forward and steeled herself, admitting, "I don't understand."

He used his hand for emphasis and said again, "You are dangerous. We, between us, have seen you tonight to be an adequate and more than adequate pilot for one of your flight time, background, and training. At flying, you are precocious, as your flight in the sailplane showed. That isn't dangerous, that's good."

Theo sat back a little, unmollified.

"Precocity has pitfalls, Theo Waitley," said Veradantha from beside her, "which I know myself from myself, and which I have agreed with Orn Ald we know for you."

The old woman tapped the table twice and went on, speaking as much to the wall as to Theo or the flight instructor. Theo watched her face, drawn to the precise way Veradantha was moving, as if she were recalling and acting out something rather than merely talking.

"You see, when unfettered, you walk as a pilot of experience does. With confidence. With power. With, let us say, the air of one infinitely able to cope."

Theo sat straighter, trying to marshal her thoughts and words. *Crack!*

She snapped to her feet, twisting up and out of the chair, turning toward the danger, hand up, muscles ready—

yos'Senchul slapped his hand flat against the table again, all the while watching her.

Veradantha continued as if nothing at all had happened.

"And you react so quickly, as if you are threatened. Part of this is because you are fast, and you are strong, and you are young. Part, I do not know. It may be that your genes are at work, or your hormones are balanced in such a way. Perhaps you are, pardon me, frightened. As calm as you are dealing with your flying, as alert and accurate, you are not quite calm among quite ordinary circumstances."

Her hand motion was barely perceptible, but yos'Senchul began speaking immediately.

"This is why you are dangerous, Theo Waitley, because your presentation is often one of being prepared at all times to escalate discussion to disagreement, disagreement to confrontation."

Theo stiffened. "But I don't mean to..."

He held up his hand, *wait* signed as well as intimated.

"Yes, that is a problem. You don't mean to be fast, but you *do* mean to walk as if you are infinite. This problem will need to be addressed quickly, because the course of your learning will put you on flight decks where people will misjudge you to be arrogant, to be pushing, to be trying to provoke. Why seem you to have this attitude... is something you will need to work on... have you an idea?"

Theo sat back, eyes glancing here and there around the room as she searched her mind for an answer, overturning mental bookcases and tables, allowing the instructor to perhaps be right before...

She sighed, eventually, and settled back into the chair, letting it support her back.

"Delgado," she said with an air of finality. "Delgado is a bully. And on Melchiza, at the Transit School, they wanted pilots to be—strong."

She sighed, and added, feeling the truth, "And that's how I think I should be."

There was silence and then the small sound of Veradantha, chuckling.

"Theo Waitley, I think perhaps you are correct. And so I agree, and say 'Delgado is a bully,' as is Melchiza. I ask you to know that so is Terra a bully to its children, and Liad, and Jankalim and Theopholis. And I will posit something more: the planets in their orbits are not the source of your discontent, but nonetheless you are correct. It is culture that is the bully, which is something many of the better pilots learn. As for Melchiza wanting you to be strong, that is, perhaps, an overstatement. But again you are precocious."

yos'Senchul hooked an ankle around a chair leg and pulled it to him. He sat down, fingers moving—*something to start now, something for next time*—and went to voice.

"What we can do, now, is to be sure you do not isolate yourself so much. People—are necessary; even enjoyable. Take the opportunity to be with others outside of class. Go to dance class, perhaps join the cultural diversity club."

Theo sighed. "I haven't done real well with clubs, historically. That Delgado bully thing again. I mean, people thought it was *strange* that we lived in Father's house, instead of in the Wall. They thought it was strange that Kamele didn't... switch her *onagrata* at all. And, and I knew all along he was my father, but it was like it was supposed to be some special adult secret. Then, I got put in the class for misfits... and so I didn't fit. I'm not..."

"Misfit?" said yos'Senchul experimentally. "Misfit. What a useful word."

Theo looked hard into his face, but he was apparently serious, as he tried to form the word with his fingers at the same time.

Veradantha tapped the table briefly for attention.

"What we would like you to consider, Theo Waitley, is this idea. This semester is well in progress, and your schedules should not be altered yet again. Go to classes, take time for these clubs and activities."

She paused, tapping on the desk quietly, nodding to herself before going on.

"It is not that you need to be popular, but that you need to watch others, to learn to be less, let us say, *strident*. To be easy with other people. Speak with me again soon—I will send an appointment to you—and then we will craft for you a schedule allowing a less general curriculum. You will be wishing to take these courses: advanced trade language, the cultural diversity cluster, and..."

Chaos, she was tired! Theo shook her head, and spoke before she meant to.

"I am not ignorant. My father teaches cultural genetics, and he hosts students; I've been—"

HOLD!

yos'Senchul rose, and bowed very slightly, signing *day of many parts, this over soon.*

He continued aloud, with a casual *if I may* signed toward Veradantha.

"What we seek is to be certain you will be adequately prepared for the sophonts who are not prepared for you. Dance will help, as will more language training, and something—we shall discuss and refine these points, all of us when we have a day less busy around us—something so that you do not present as quite so busy, quite so much on the verge of taking action, at all times."

Veradantha broke in then, with some energy.

"We wish to also remove you from petty local politics as much as we may. Now some, like the excellent Mr. Frosher, they have the way of it. He will be an adequate pilot, I am sure, but he has a path in mind, one that involves administration, one that is also likely to be local. It is not surprising he came so close to the edge of things, and it is not entirely surprising that he has survived this error, and grown from it. Eventually he may grow to be a functionary of some merit.

"But you—*you*—do not wish to study the tables of dead grand-fathers, nor to be liable for not knowing them. This altercation with Wilsmyth is built partly of history you do not know, and assumptions he does not realize he carries. This is what we wish to minimize for you. And for the academy, too.

"With your consent we shall construct for you an independent study option. I suggest a goal as an outworlds pilot. We may fine-tune as we proceed and details become clarified. You will need to study ships, but start tomorrow and not tonight. You will need some more languages—start tomorrow and not this night. We shall also see what we might find on-world for your off-time between semesters, unless you will wish to return to Delgado..."

Theo saw the quirking of the mouth for what it was and man-aged a laugh and a quick sign *abort that launch.*

Despite herself, she yawned.

Preliminary accept, she signed. She stood and bowed to them both, the very best bow she could muster.

"We have started tonight," she suggested. "We will start more tomorrow."

SECOND LEAP

EIGHTEEN

. . . .

Diverse Cultures Celebration Team
Anlingdin Piloting Academy

DCCT WAS HOUSED ABOUT AS FAR AWAY AS IT WAS POSSIBLE TO get from the rest of the campus and still be in the residential zone; that was her destination after her last scheduled class for the school week.

Theo walked instead of taking the shuttle, sure that some of her classmates were letting the ease of a quick ride stifle their need to move. How they could expect to keep reaction time up while being sluggards was beyond her.

She'd had defensive dance early, which was a good thing. She'd waked a moment before the timer went off, dreaming the ship-route math she'd studied the night before in prep for lab. That had been happening of late, the dreaming about classes, especially math, like she'd finally cleared some cobwebs and gotten to work. The independent study was a good motivator, and she felt almost like she owed Wilsmyth thanks for the now-healed gash on the side of her head.

Another reason she liked this particular walk, besides the fact that it was often deserted, was that it gave a good view of the planes on final approach to the airfield. A few days before she'd seen a really awkward turn-in and approach, while high and away between the field and the mountain a pair of soarplanes rode brilliant in the aqua sky. She had seen a couple of her landings on video and was really glad that none looked as nervous as that one, which had ended more in a series of bounces than a proper landing.

That was the problem, of course—lots of people around the field also saw that landing—and later in the day there was talk of yet another of the local students being sent home before school end. It was eerie the way the school population seemed to be thinning out as the final grading period approached.

Unexpectedly, she heard voices ahead of her where the path rounded a copse of lush red brambleberry. She stepped to the side of the path as a group of fast-moving DCCT members appeared, Kara in the lead.

"Theo, just in time! But you're going the wrong way!"

Kara stopped, bringing the whole team to a crowded halt, familiar faces and unfamiliar together.

Theo signed blankly *none there*, pointing toward the dorm parapet rising above the trees in the distance.

"Might be, but there's a ship coming in, and we're going to go down to see it."

"There's always a ship coming in . . ." Theo pointed out as a Star King IV obligingly dropped down through the clouds toward the main landing strip.

Theo's hand-sign was flip—*overlooked obvious*.

"I mean a *spaceship*." Kara's hand adding *new info just in*.

"The shuttle is still parked . . ."

A shake of heads, and from the back, a voice she didn't recognize—

"*Spaceship*. You know, *interstellar*. We got a call from the field, they thought we might want to see this."

"Here? Where will it fit? What is it?"

"Right. That's what we want to see . . . Come on down with us! DCCT is on the move!"

The Seriously Official Recognized Name of the organization was the Diverse Cultures Celebration Team. Like almost all the other clubs on campus they managed to do something sometime that earned points or competed with other groups or that got them all out at one time cooking and eating foods that they'd never faced at their milk tables, so they got to call themselves a team.

Some of the upperclassmen in the club were part of the DCCT dorm, which had odd floor names and was repainted every few weeks to celebrate this or that significant event in some culture somewhere. The club met there in a permanently assigned room which was certainly furnished in an amalgam one could call diverse, if not outright strange.

Most of the campus just called them the Culture Club, and Theo was feeling oddly comfortable as its newest member. Maybe it had to do with the feeling that no one was actually in charge, except, maybe, sometimes, Kara. It might have had something to do with the tea selection, which was downright amazing. Or it might simply be that compared to the local students, she was as diverse as anybody else.

Delgado, of course, was a world that celebrated education, cultural enlightenment, and diversity. From experience, Theo knew that diversity stopped just outside Delgado's Wall, and if Anlingdin Academy was different she had little way of knowing.

Theo's first visit to DCCT had been the day after her flight with her mentors, and she'd been pleased then to discover the tea, and almost as pleased to be involved in a discussion, by agreement limited to hand-talk, of the best morning foods. Anlingdin's musch meal was widely regarded as the boringest breakfast food in the galaxy, and she had been surprised to find herself both missing some foods from home, and interested enough in those described by others to get hungry.

Theo'd seen a tall, underspoken fellow who was in her math class hand-wishing the school could make a decent maize button, and she burst out laughing.

Button quick easy she signed confidently, *if time breaks clear could make some for both of us, good choice.*

For some reason that launched the group into chuckles and ignited a flare of signs she wasn't clear on, and a few she was, but couldn't see how they'd got *there*...

In the midst, Bova Yenkoa, a very pretty young man with a small beard, signaled *time out*, and addressed Theo in Trade, laughing and shaking his head.

"Now see, that's a problem. On Finifter if an unmarried woman invites a man to breakfast at her house and doesn't mention that a mother or sister or someone else female is going to be there, that's an invitation for a bed-party."

Theo waved her hand—*incomplete information here query.*

"And similar on Grundig," Bova went on. "And on Grundig,

once you make an offer, it stands until the next house-blessing. Got to be careful what you offer to whom *there*, I tell you!"

More laughter ensued and some maybe not-quite-true stories about friends who had problems with such things, and by the time the stories had worn out, it was late and Theo was surprised at how relaxed she felt.

The second time she'd visited, the ongoing argument in hand-talk was about ships, and about companies you didn't work for, and worlds that were too much trouble to visit so the pilots going there just stayed on ship for the duration. She'd been pleased and surprised to find Kara there—and then just pleased.

She'd gone again, gotten more of the names down. She missed Kara by a few moments that time, but found others to talk to.

It was at DCCT that she found the Book of Clans, supposedly a list of all the Liaden clans and their member Lines. A search on "Korval" had brought her the information that it was composed of two ascendant Lines—yos'Phelium and yos'Galan—and a subordinate Line—bel'Tarda. Clan business interests were given as shipbuilding, trade, piloting, and general commerce. The clan sigil, there at the top of the screen, was a dragon poised on half-furled wings above a tree in full leaf.

"Tree-and-Dragon," she muttered, and brought up the search box. She typed in *Moon-and-Rabbit* without much hope, but the database obligingly loaded a page for Clan Ixin, ascendent Line ven'Deelin. Clan business interests were trade, manufacturing, and general commerce.

Theo sat back. yos'Senchul had been testing her, then. She supposed it shouldn't surprise her—he was a teacher, after all. Theo, the child of two teachers, knew what *that* meant.

"There you are!" Kara called, her footsteps brisk across the floor. "We're trying to get up a round of bowli ball. Are you in?"

"Sure," Theo said, slowly.

"What's that you have—the Book of Clans? Research?"

"In a way." Theo turned in her chair and looked up into Kara's face. "I'm trying to figure out why my father would have wanted me to go to—the delm of a trade clan, if I was ever in really big trouble, and why there was a book about—"

"Trade clan?" Kara peered past her to the screen. "Ixin *is* High House, you know. They'd—"

"Not Ixin," Theo interrupted. "Korval."

Kara blinked.

"Korval?" she repeated. "Are you—*of* Korval?"

Theo shook her head. "I'm a Waitley of Delgado, from a long line of scholars," she said. "My father, though, said that I should go to the Delm of Korval for really big problems—but only for really big problems. I thought it was a joke for—for a lot of reasons, but apparently, he meant it."

"Well." Kara frowned slightly and hitched a hip up on the table holding the screen. "Korval is—beyond High House. It concerns itself with pilots and with ships, so its interests are . . . broader than the interests of, say, *my* clan. Most delms solve for the members of their clan. Korval is said to solve for pilotkind. Delm Korval—of course, you *wouldn't* want to take anything other than life or death to Delm Korval." She paused. "Your father was a scholar, you had said."

"He is. But before that, he was a pilot."

Kara's face cleared. "That explains it, then. He was passing pilotlore. Perfectly reasonable—and good advice, too, though of the kind you hope never to use."

"Oh." Theo thought about it, then shook her head. "There was a book—a book for littlies, *Sam Tim's Ugly Day*—and it was all about how you didn't take problems you could solve yourself to Delm Korval."

"And very good advice that is, as well!" Kara had said warmly. "There are all *sorts* of books written about Korval, Theo. Are you in on the bowli ball game, or not?"

The academy shuttle usually landed in a long, relatively flat trajectory from the north-northeast, with a one-hundred-sixty to one-hundred-eighty degree turn to do a final lineup for touchdown. Theo stared off in that direction while Kara, shoulder comfortably against hers, was on comm with someone who was observing from the control room.

Rather than being right down strip-side for the landing they stood on the slight bluff overlooking the field, not wanting to crowd the operations crew and knowing that the ship coming in would take a few minutes to cool down once landed, anyway. Of ordinary traffic—a couple of Sky Kings circled to the west among scattered clouds, and a soarplane was well to the east, bright amidst a clearing sky.

There was movement close by, and Kara leaned into her shoulder.

"Ops says we're all looking the wrong way. The ship is coming straight on in—it isn't orbiting first."

Theo turned, hands slinging *straight run, power pilot double double*. Kara grinned, sharing the news with the rest of the crew.

"Freck says we gotta watch toward south. Expect a—"

Karroom BOOM! The field shook, and Bova brought his long-glasses up to search the sky.

Kara laughed, and finished, "...sonic boom."

"Got 'em!" Bova yelled, pointing.

Theo shaded her eyes, staring upward—and there it was, a hard, glittering point with a pulsating beacon that looked larger than the craft itself. It palpably dropped, occasional contrails wisping behind it.

"This is a courier class ship, Team," said Bova. "Ought to be flashy, ought to be about the size of the shuttle or a smidge smaller, they say, closer to a packet boat for those of you from outworlds."

Theo heard chatter from the other team members—"Dropping quick; pilot's got an iron stomach" and "Not a sign of drift and we've got a hefty breeze here!"

Kara read more info from the comm. "Often run solo, the *Torvin* can carry a crew of three plus three passengers on need, built thirty-seven Standards ago at the Korval-Mugston Yards on the Yolanna platform..."

Now the ship was taking shape as a gleaming golden stripe angling rapidly above them, a stripe with shiny wing-tip stabilizers on each end and now the stripe showed a bulge above and behind the central nose, all gleaming gold, the beacon under its nose still bright but now echoed by underwing green and red.

"Still zooming!" Vin said, and Theo felt the landing tension in her arms and shoulder, the thing was too low, too fast, too short of the runway and—

"Ah!"

The relief was vocal across a dozen mouths as the glitter caught the light, the ship flaring out and riding the airwave in front of itself, touching down discreetly after passing over the blast pad and the threshold and somewhat ahead of the persistent dark marks occasioned by generations of student pilots.

Theo still had her mouth open as the sound of touchdown reached her, a barely distinguishable *barrup* as the ship actually

settled, as the golden thing gleamed by at twice the rate a Star
King landed at . . .

A sudden hissing reached them as a brief cloud obscured the
bright beacons well down the airstrip . . .

"Retros," came knowledgeably from behind her. "Look at that
thing slow down!"

The sound of the rocket hiss almost obscured another comment.

"Scouts!" said Bova, lowering his glasses and shaking his head.
"You like 'em or you hate 'em, whichever, they sure can pilot!"

Theo stared at the ship, still slowing on the runway.

"Scouts?" she said to Kara quietly.

"Come on, Theo, let's go down!"

The Commander strode by the group, headed toward the Ops
room, and so did yos'Senchul, who flashed *excellent progress plans
move forward* to the lot of them before heading in.

"Ops must be crushed," Theo said to Kara. They and the rest of
the team were waiting while the distant *Torvin* was attached to a
small fleet of tractors and towed toward the shuttle's usual spot.

Now that the spaceship was down, craft were again circling and
descending, while several on the flight line were moving slowly
toward the live deck for takeoff.

Kara was muttering about dinnertime coming right up and
she'd been hoping to get a chance to—

But Theo caught sight of yos'Senchul and the Commander, walking out toward the strip from Ops, carrying on a quick hand-talk.

*Certified routing/newest off-limits/warning zones for graduates/
direct and secure* was the gist of yos'Senchul's communications
while the Commander's were more like *Noisy obvious unscheduled
bad-form non-orbit show-off.*

Theo looked away, feeling a bit as if she'd eavesdropped on
one of Kamele and Father's private conversations. Likely if she
hadn't spent so much time with yos'Senchul she wouldn't have
been able to read . . .

"Theo, look, come on, they've got it settled. Let's go see!"

Kara grabbed her by the hand enthusiastically, tugging and not
letting go until Theo picked up speed and together they outran
most of the team to the orange-chained stanchions.

The ship gleamed in front and overhead, warmth still radiating into the cooling evening, several tiny beacon lights having taken over the duty of the flight lights. Theo could see herself in the fuselage where it bulged to become wings, she could see Kara too, and the Commander and yos'Senchul standing with a small group of seniors dressed with their formals and wings close behind.

"Look at the size of this thing," a pilot used to Star Kings said, and Theo blurted out, "This is so tiny! It could fit in a cruise ship ballroom!"

That started a heated discussion, and quotes of cubes and relative engine power and, "I've sat jump seat on something bigger than this..."

Theo basked in the glow of the ship. *Yes, this is it. Something like this.* She felt as if her pores absorbed the moment and her hands already knew the need to fly such a thing.

The Ops guy came out to the stanchions, comm in his hand, and then opened the gate for the Commander.

"Sorry," he said, "the tug crew forgot this is Liaden, so the ground hatch is on the other—"

yos'Senchul waved him away with a salute and hand-sign, leading the small contingent to the proper side of the ship, just as there came a hiss, then a whir that must have been the hatch opening.

The strip-side crowd quieted as the gangway slid almost all the way to the ground, and then there was hand-shaking and bows, all seen on the other side of the ship. Two of the seniors became honor guard to the ship, flanking the gangway. The others fell in behind the Commander and yos'Senchul and the pilot with his rakish hat, as they walked back toward the stanchions.

"Theo—what?" Kara whispered at her, then jammed an elbow into her side.

The man moved like a pilot, after all, that must be it—her stomach though, apparently had another theory.

"Theo?"

She stood very still, watching as the group came through the gate.

"He looks familiar. He kinda walks like a friend of mine," she managed.

Kara snickered. "Oh, he does?"

The pilot had been scanning as well as walking and talking with his hosts, she could see that. Suddenly his eyes met hers; he did a dance-step pause, a half-smile twitching at the corners of his lips as he looked at her fully face on.

"Pilot Waitley, my compliments." This was spoken in a formal measure as he bowed quickly. "I am extremely pleased to find you here, Theo," followed in a lower tone, for her ears only, then, loud enough to strike the ears of those crowding behind her, "I hope to be in touch."

"Hi, Win Ton!" she got out, waving as the procession swept on, the grin on her face not at all subdued.

The Commander also nodded at her, perhaps sternly, and yos'Senchul bowed an acknowledgment, his hand fluttering with a *this pilot clarifies this pilot clarifies*, and the honor guard looked at her perhaps in consternation as they got back into step.

Then they were gone and Kara was yelling in her ear, "Who *was* that? You *know* him? Who? Why didn't you *say something*?"

"I've never seen Win Ton in a hat before," Theo managed, realizing she was giggling.

"You do know him! How?" Kara was delighted and demanding at once. "That was a bow between equals!"

Theo laughed. "He's a friend, Kara. He gave me my bowli ball. We beat the dance machine together."

Some of the other DCCT people crowded in close to find out what was happening, but the gate was being drawn back and more waiting students surged past, and she didn't have to answer, "What dance machine?" right then.

"Rule is you can look but not touch!" yelled the Ops guy on guard as the official contingent moved into the building.

"The pilot will give tours as time permits," he went on. "Tomorrow."

NINETEEN

· · · · · · · · · · · · · · · · · ·

Erkes Dormitory, Suite 302
Anlingdin Piloting Academy

SHE'D PUT ON HER BEST PAIR OF BLACK SLACKS, AND WAS DITHERING between the black shirt and the cream-colored sweater when Asu came in and leaned a hip against the door.

"It *is* true!" she said, with such a note of finality in her voice that Theo blinked, trying to recall if she'd called the other girl on something at breakfast.

Well, only one way to find out, she thought, refolding the black shirt.

"What's true?" she asked over her shoulder.

"The Scout courier *is* your friend! The one who sends you jewelry!"

"The one who sent me a *pair of wings*, you mean?" Theo shook out the sweater.

Asu frowned. "What are you doing?"

"Getting dressed."

"You're going to wear *that*?" Asu asked, like the cream sweater was—gym clothes or something.

"What's wrong with it?"

"Nothing's *wrong* with it," Asu said in her too-patient voice. "It's a nice, warm, serviceable sweater with a high neck and long sleeves."

"I'm not taking your point," Theo said, yanking the sweater over her head, as the hall door giggled. She emerged, and looked over her shoulder.

135

"Hey, Chelly!" she called, pulling the sweater straight.

"Chelly," Asu commanded, without turning her head, "come here and be of use!"

"What now?" he wondered, pausing beside her and giving Theo a nod.

Asu flung out a dramatic hand, encompassing Theo, their shared room, and quite possibly the entire Anlingdin campus. "*Look* at that sweater!"

Chelly blinked. "Looks okay to me."

"For a date with a star pilot?"

"Well, why not?" Chelly said reasonably, and shook his head. "Should've known you'd get *that* rumor," he added.

Asu looked at him over her shoulder. "It is not a rumor! He spoke to her in front of the Commander, yos'Senchul and all gathered! He called her by name and said he'd be in touch!"

"Said he *hoped to be* in touch," Theo corrected hastily. "Which doesn't mean he's going to *be able* to get in touch. He's here on business, after all. Nothing to say that the Commander won't be sending him off tonight. She might have—" She gulped, suddenly panicked.

"Easy, it's still on the field," Chelly told her lightly.

Theo sighed, and went over to the mirror to fix the wings to the sweater's collar.

"The way *he* flies we would have heard the boom when he lifted," Asu said, acidic. "Honestly, Theo, you might have told *me* he was coming!"

Theo stared at her. "I *didn't know* he was coming!" she protested. "Why would I?"

"You correspond," Asu said loftily. "He sends you gifts."

"One gift," Theo corrected. "And, in case you hadn't noticed, that *is* a courier ship. He might not've known himself that he was coming to Anlingdin until he got his flight orders."

"True enough," Chelly said, firmly. "Give it up, Asu." He gave Theo another look over the other girl's shoulder. "Sweater looks nice, Theo. Don't let her bully you."

"Bully!" Asu swung around, but Chelly was already back in the joint room, pulling open the shared coldbox.

"I will have you know," Asu said, following him, "that I do not *bully* Theo."

"Yeah?" Theo could imagine the look of skeptical interest on Chelly's face as she turned back to the mirror.

The sweater *did* look nice, she thought, and the wings, too. Her hair, of course, was a disaster area... She ran her fingers through it, trying to force it into seemliness. From the other room, Chelly and Asu's voices continued. In the mirror, her hair sprang back into wild disorder the second she took her hands away.

Sighing, she walked out to join her roommates.

"So, Chelly, what're you doing here?" she asked.

"Going to get the rest of my things out," he said, giving her a straight look. "I talked to the house father, Theo. You'll take my slot, Asu'll move up to First Bunk, and you'll be getting a new Second Bunk start of next term."

"Theo's not a senior," Asu objected.

Chelly gave her a bland look. "Don't gotta be a senior to be unit senior," he said.

Asu drew a breath.

And the doorbell rang.

"A pleasant evening to the house." He bowed slightly to Asu, who'd beat them both to the door. "I am Win Ton yo'Vala, come to call upon Theo Waitley, if she will see me."

"I see you," Theo said softly, feeling kind of fluttery and light in the chest. Win Ton, she noticed, had changed out of what must've been his dress uniform, into a dark sweater and pants—and his jacket. He looked at her over Asu's shoulder with a smile.

"I see you, also, Sweet Mystery. Is this everything that will be allowed us?"

She laughed. "Asu, you're not my aunt! Let him in."

"Certainly," the taller girl said. She took a fluid step back, and swept her arm out, head inclined very slightly. "I am Asu diamon Dayez. Be welcome, Pilot yo'Vala."

"My thanks." Win Ton stepped inside, brown eyes flicking to Chelly, who gave him a matter-of-fact nod.

"Chelly Frosher, Pilot Admin trainee." He paused, and added, thoughtfully. "Friend of Theo's."

"I am pleased to meet you, Admin Frosher," Win Ton assured him gravely.

He turned slightly, and Theo felt her stomach tighten, which was silly. This was *Win Ton*, not some stranger, or—

"Pilot yo'Vala!" Asu said, sharply.

Win Ton's eyebrows rose, and he turned, perhaps faster than he had intended. Asu went back a step, and he became very still, hands belt high, palms out, fingers spread in the sign for *no threat*.

"I was wondering," Asu said, sounding breathless, "if it is in fact yourself who taught Theo to play bowli ball." She tossed her head and smiled, nervously to Theo's eye. "She's coy with names, our Theo."

"Ah, is she?" He sent a quick look to Theo, the corner of his mouth tight with the effort of holding the laugh in. "Shall I reveal all?"

Theo felt her cheeks heat, but she met his eyes firmly. *"All?"*

He flung a hand up, as if in surrender. "No, you are correct! Word might yet reach my captain! But, to answer Pilot Trainee diamon Dayez—in fact, I was one of three pilots who introduced Theo to the joys of bowli ball. As you know, the best game can be had with a foursome, and the other pilots must need work around their shifts, so we did not play as often as any of us would have preferred."

There was a small silence, broken at last by Chelly. "Theo learned to play bowli ball from a Scout and two working pilots."

"Indeed." Win Ton turned, gently, to face him. "It would hardly have done to allow her to play with the passengers."

"Make that, a Scout and two *cruise line* pilots," Chelly added, and laughed softly. He shook his head at Theo. "No wonder you got an attitude problem, Waitley."

"I don't *have* an attitude problem," Theo told him, but Chelly only laughed again.

"Who here has not had their temper fail them?" Win Ton asked, possibly rhetorically. "Theo, are you hungry?"

"Yes," she said, though she wasn't, exactly.

"Then we are well-met, and well-matched! I am famished. As I am in receipt of the coords to a *binjali* restaurant, perhaps you will join me for dinner?"

Light spilled from the ship's at-rest lights, casting a circle that faded from ruby to pink along the tarmac. Walking at Win Ton's side, Theo crossed that magic circle and tried not to stare around while he spoke with the security team.

"This pilot and I will be lifting to coords provided by Master Pilot yos'Senchul very shortly. Thank you for your care of my ship."

"That's all right, Pilot," one of the two answered, both saluting with a snap. "Will you be returning?"

"This evening, yes. We will, of course, file with the Tower."

It was said gently enough, but the guards seemed to take it as a rebuke or setdown. Another pair of salutes and they were gone, marching briskly down toward Ops while Theo followed Win Ton up the ramp and into the ship.

The lights came up as they entered the piloting chamber, Theo walking as lightly as she could, as if she would bruise the ship if she set her feet too firmly. It seemed as if Win Ton had forgotten her; he walked to the board, leaned over and touched a rapid sequence of keys and toggles. The ship woke with a soft, welcoming chime. He turned and gave her a smile as bright as the one she remembered.

"Hovering at the door? But that will never do! Come, you must sit second for me!"

Theo stared at him, suspecting a joke at her expense. "I can't sit second on a spaceship," she stammered. "I don't have the hours, or—"

"Tut and tut, Sweet Mystery!" He came back and took her hand. His fingers were warm, patterned with callus.

"The pilot has asked you to sit second," he said, looking into her face with all of Win Ton's mischief. "It is, of course, a signal honor."

"Well, it is," she answered, defensively, but she let him lead her over to the second chair and show her how to adjust it, and where the webbing was. She tried to relax while he settled into the pilot's chair, her eyes drawn to the board, and something like...hunger in her middle...

"Now," Win Ton said calmly, his fingers dancing on a touchpad. "The pilot would take it kindly if Pilot Waitley would ride comm, and clear us with the tower. Coords—"

"Win Ton," Theo's voice cracked. She cleared her throat and tried again, watching the side of his face, seeing concentration and...something else. "Win Ton."

He glanced up, eyes soft with concentration. "Yes?"

"What are you doing?" she asked carefully, twisting her hands together on her lap so she wouldn't reach out and touch that tantalizing board, though she wanted to!

His gaze sharpened somewhat. "I am offering opportunity," he said, his tone precisely as careful as hers. "Will you grasp it? Or will you be shy and orderly?"

She knew better than to take a dare... well, mostly she did. But, that board... She swallowed and nodded, leaning forward.

"Comm is lit yellow," he said quietly. "The rest of the board is slaved to mine, so you may follow, if you like."

"Yeah..." she whispered, and raised a hand to finger the yellow toggles.

"Tower, this is Theo Waitley, sitting second on *Torvin*." She paused, glancing to the amused Scout, who signaled *there now*, and her screen lit with ship numbers and info in proper sequence for her to read out, which she did, adding, "Out of, Solcintra, Liad, local berth Number 9F. *Torvin*'s pilot requests a tow to a launch pad at your earliest convenience."

There was a moment of perhaps shocked silence, then a voice she didn't know answered calmly in the affirmative. "Acknowledge, there, *Torvin*, we see ship systems coming live. We'll call out the horses and camels now, if you can wait that long."

Theo was grinning like a fool, and only part of that was the joke and Win Ton's resultant raised eyebrows.

"Where are we going? By way of where?"

"Very good, Second!" Win Ton said. The info flowed to her screen and she recognized the sequence out of class a few days before, catching her breath, and then laughing.

"Ballistic? That's some g-work, isn't it?" She must have whispered because Win Ton half-bowed, and whispered in reply, "Yes, it is."

He continued in a more normal voice, "Watch the screens: is that a camel or a horse? And what is funny, Sweet Mystery?"

They'd brought round the tractor that towed the shuttle, and as she watched, Win Ton enumerated the camera views, showing her how to change them. She paid scrupulous attention, saying, "That must be the camel, that's the one they only use on spacecraft. And what's funny is the ballistic routing. Asu told me, before you knocked, that everyone knew you were still on port because there hadn't been an outgoing sonic boom!"

She glanced at him, saw him manfully straighten the smile off his face.

"Ah, did she? Then her reputation is mine to save. Please note these amendments, and file the corrected figures when queried."

They felt the tow start as Win Ton went over radio and feed sequence with her, bailout sequence, and how to set vessel on autoland. With each quick lesson he looked at her, and it was hard not to keep looking at him, except she had to show that she'd heard by using the keys on her quiet board.

The tractor pulled free, and tower's voice was live:

"*Torvin*, your flight plan will be accepted by link, since we're getting good feed, please file, and we'll acknowledge."

Theo glanced at Win Ton.

"It is good form to strap in before liftoff," he said conversationally, "and please, file the plan."

Theo touched the send switch and yanked the strap. It was clear they were in the tower's eye, because the response was instant, and she couldn't hit the acknowledge switch right back, because she was tangled in lap strap.

"Be sure to file intentions with your destination, *Torvin*. You may lift at will after your launch signal. Enjoy dinner!"

"Send the duplicate routing on, Second, and we will..."

Theo did that as Win Ton seemed to go half quiet before saying, "...please Asu diamon Dayez, no doubt."

The klaxon sounded tinny through the ship's outside ears.

"Now," Win Ton said, and engaged lift.

By the time they'd set down at the field by Howsenda Hugglelans, with Theo riding comm, her head felt like it was in...some other place; like it wasn't directly attached to the rest of her body. She'd followed the board lights, listening to Win Ton's soft-voiced explanation of what he was doing, interrupting only once, with a question.

"How do I get to do this?"

"This? Become a Scout?"

"No—fly this."

"Ah!" He'd laughed, softly. "Much less difficult! Courier pilots need only be first class, with a demonstrated willingness to fly like a lunatic on any occasion." Her attention on the board, she'd felt, rather than seen him grin at her. "You would do well, I think."

"I think so, too," she'd answered, and lapsed again into rapt silence.

Hull cool, they exited *Torvin*.

Win Ton offered an arm and she leaned on that, grateful for the support as they approached the desk.

A familiar-looking man in a sleeveless vest met them, with a grin and a nod to Theo.

"You return!" said the waiter who wore too much *vya*. "And

this time, you have forgotten your aunt! Very good, Pilot. A terrace table for you and your . . . friend?"

"Yes," Theo said, straightening, but keeping a firm grip on Win Ton's arm. "Please."

They followed him up the ramps and let him seat them together on a cushioned bench by a secluded table overlooking the field. Win Ton laughed softly as they were momentarily left alone.

"You are known everywhere, Theo Waitley! And rightly admired."

She shook her head at him. "I was here a while ago with Pilot yos'Senchul and Veradantha. Happens we had the same server—luck, is all."

"Indeed," Win Ton said with a grin. "Luck." He leaned forward and touched her hand. "Now that the fascination of lift has evaporated, tell me of yourself."

"There's not much to tell," she protested, "outside of what I've been writing to you."

"Ah. Then tell me this: Why does Admin Frosher claim you for an attitude problem?"

"Oh, that," Theo said, as their server came back with the requested tea.

"Service, Pilots?"

"Today's special," Theo and Win Ton said simultaneously—and laughed in the same heartbeat.

Their server smiled. "Today's special, it is. A moment while I gather what is needful."

"Now," Win Ton said, "tell me."

So, over tea and befores, she told him. Win Ton was a good listener, asking questions only when she'd gotten off track; willing to wait while she sorted out her narrative. When she got to the part about Wilsmyth jigging her flight time he said something sharp in what she guessed was Liaden, though it wasn't in the lexicon she was laboriously sleep-learning, with Veradantha's permission.

"Where did he strike you?" he asked.

Theo raised her hand to her head. "It's healed now."

"Let me see, if I may?" He smoothed her hair back from the place; she shivered at the touch of his fingers, even as she leaned into it.

"So soft, like sea mist . . ." His breath was warm against her temple; his lips were gentle against the place where the cut had been.

Theo closed her eyes, feeling a not-entirely-unpleasant roiling in her stomach.

"Yes," Win Ton murmured. "It has healed without a scar." He kissed the place again, and Theo reached—

"Will it please you to have dinner now, Pilots?" their server asked, amusement lacing his voice.

Win Ton eased back and considered him before looking to Theo. "Pilot?"

She sighed, and met the server's interested gaze. "Yes," she said levelly. "Dinner would be most welcome."

"So," she ventured, after they had been served. "Now that you've heard my boring news, don't I get to hear yours?"

"That would appear to be a fair trade," Win Ton agreed slowly, and from the depths of an apparent minute study of the table's centerpiece. His shoulders rose as if he had taken an especially deep breath, and he raised his head, meeting her eyes with a startling degree of seriousness.

"Alas," he said, and she could hear him making the effort to keep his voice light, as if he were telling a joke. "My news is even more tedious than your own." He extended his hand to touch hers where it lay on the table next to her teacup.

She didn't look down, but met his eyes, and tried to keep her voice light, too.

"A star pilot trumped by a student's tales out of school? Hard to believe."

He laughed, low in his throat. "Yes, but what could be more tedious than to learn that one's clan has finally found a use for one?"

She blinked. "They're calling you home?" *But*, she thought, *he's a pilot! What would he do at home, if—*

"For a short time only," Win Ton's voice interrupted these unsettling thoughts. His fingers tightened over hers. "My delm has decreed that I'm to wed, Theo. On Liad."

"Wed?" She blinked at him. "But you joined the Scouts so you didn't have to be on Liad."

He laughed, not happily. "No, I was given to the Scouts because I was more trouble to my honored kin than my then-current worth. But alliance is alliance, and unless I wish to stand *eklykt'i*—which I assure you that I do not!—I shall make my bow to duty." He looked at her earnestly. "You understand that it is merely a contract marriage, and after—" His face lost some of its tension and the grin he gave her was very nearly his usual mischievous expression. "After," he said, "I shall be free to do real work."

"Real work," Theo repeated. "Aren't you doing real work now?"

He lifted his hand from hers and made a short gesture of dismissal. "It is real, but—not preferred. My goal had always been to be part of a survey team. My duty to the clan done, I may embrace it—I hold the word of my delm on the matter! So..." He raised his teacup, as if he offered a toast. "Let us put that topic behind us, if you please, and speak of pleasanter things."

True to his word, he did just that, chattering away through the remainder of the meal until she was laughing, and matching him absurdity for absurdity. They were still laughing when they climbed the ramp hand in hand and *Torvin* let them in.

Theo looked to the second chair, took a step—and Win Ton's fingers tightened on hers. She paused and looked into his face, saw...something...and swayed back, as if it were part of a dance.

"Win Ton," she began, and—

"Theo," he started—

They *both* laughed again, somehow in the middle of it becoming tangled into a hug. His lips burned against her temple, and she hugged him tighter, wanting to, to melt into him, to—

She moved her head, and kissed him on the lips. He started, then pulled her closer, his arms so tight she could scarcely breathe, but that really didn't seem to matter. She slid her hands inside his jacket, feeling his back through the sweater. He dropped his head to her shoulder, nuzzling the side of her neck. His hand moved and she felt him touch the wings on her collar.

"You wear them," he murmured.

She laughed, shakily. "It's your gift to me. Of course, I wear them."

"Good," he breathed. "Excellent." His lips charted a lingering course up toward her ear.

"There's a bunk," he whispered, his voice not at all steady. "Theo—your choice. I—"

"Yes," she said, shaking, needing, *wanting*. "I'm not—Win Ton; I haven't had a lot of practice."

He choked—no, it was laughter, and the look he gave her was brilliant with delight.

"Well, then," he said unsteadily, "I stand ready. You may practice on me, if you wish."

"I do wish," she said, and reached up to kiss him again.

TWENTY

· · · · · · · · · · · · · ·

Piloting Praxis
Anlingdin Piloting Academy

"ONCE YOU'VE SAT FIRST OR SECOND SEAT ON ORBIT AROUND AN inhabited planet you'll see that being Pilot in Command of a space vessel makes being PIC on a two- or four-seat air-sucking cloud hopper an order of magnitude less dangerous to all concerned."

The casual dismissal of their progress to date shocked the room; the palpable intake of breath became a uniform over-the-shoulder glance in her direction from the front—and Theo imagined those behind her staring at the back of her head. As far as she knew there were exactly two people in the room who met that criteria: Instructor yos'Senchul and herself.

That she had exactly two-hundred-and-fifty-one minutes as orbital second board, certified C&C—Comm and Control—by a Scout was known across the campus, and as the instructor went on to explain, far beyond the campus.

"In many ways being on orbit in controlled space is safer than flying through the air. It takes far longer to hard-land a spacecraft than a Star King; and there are many more resources in place to ensure that you do not fall out of the sky.

"Make no miscalculation about it, Pilots, most of these resources are brought to bear not because you are personally more valuable, but because the damage you might do with even a minor lapse in judgment is exponentially greater with each step you take."

The instructor looked pensive for a moment, which Theo thought was a teacher's act since Liadens she knew rarely showed such emotions. Even Father needed to exaggerate his normal expressions to make them obvious to people who didn't know him.

The one-handed motion made next was also artful: a toss emphasizing the empty sleeve.

"Mistakes are expensive. A Slipper striking a home in a small subdivision of a dozen houses might kill the unlucky pilot and damage the home. A Star King doing the same could wipe out the pilot, family, and house, perhaps even two houses. The shuttle..."

He paused for effect then, allowing everyone to digest the thought.

"But no, we need not speculate on this, because we have available, courtesy of the Scout who recently visited, a virtual museum of recent pilot error accidents. Some are complete with tapes permitting you to fly the error right into the ground, or not, on your own time, in sim. All of the master-adjudicated errors we share today have occurred within the last two Standards. These are not pretty. They are, however, instructional."

Of the six errors yos'Senchul deemed most instructive, only one was by a trainee, and that trainee already licensed as a Second Class Provisional. Somehow that heartened Theo, when perhaps it was meant as a warning to all of them.

She took the long-way-around walk to lunch to think through not only what she'd seen, but also what she hadn't. Some of her classmates had simply not reacted at all to the vids, as far as she could see, as if they hadn't recognized the problem instantly. For her part, her hand still ached where she'd clenched the offending palm, trying to take it back from the motion that she hadn't made, that she knew better than to make, already.

She danced out that realization momentarily, feeling this move *here* and that move *there* and seeing that, of course, with the hands and body flowing properly, as compared with dance, even strapped in—especially strapped in—this move, this move that hurt her hand to think about, this move that had killed a pilot and a field boss and injured a dozen farmworkers, *this* motion went entirely against the warm-up exercises and the way you worked with a bowli ball. Well...

The dancing was combat. The dancing was prep for bowli ball

which was prep for moving *now*. The dancing was board drills. The dancing was what had convinced Win Ton that she...

Chaos!

Yes, she missed him. Missed him. Not like she missed Father and Kamele, or the way she still sometimes missed Bek. Still, it was difficult not to look at everything she was doing now knowing that Win Ton also shared this information or moved this way, or would understand—

Well, maybe he'd even understand why it was she'd been spending quite so much time at sim-ship, and why it was she was busy, busy with extra dance, busy with a sudden interest in packet and courier ships, busy avoiding the sometimes just-too-stealthy questions and insinuations from Asu.

Really, what was it to Asu exactly what they'd done or hadn't, or when, or who started what? The first three days after her return from orbit she'd felt like Asu was peering at her neck, looking at her shoulders, for Simple Sake, checking out her feet and legs for marks and bruises!

Win Ton was Liaden, and thoughtful and gentle, and *Liaden!* That meant careful, in many senses.

And *everybody's* questions about, "How was it in orbit?" *Pfui!*

Yes, Win Ton was a Scout pilot... which meant a master class pilot, as it turned out, and so yes, not only *could he* certify her orbital time but he also *should*, because that's part of what master class pilots were supposed to do. He'd also been very clear that once they lifted, it was all about the ship.

She smiled to herself. Yes, when she'd rolled the *Torvin* through the sun-cooling routine, Win Ton's smile had been good. But she'd rolled it properly on axis, and then she'd offered her calculations to him and the board for the deorbit burn that would bring them down on the longest, flattest, slowest, quietest possible landing the ship could make, according to all the information the ship so willingly fed second board. And it *was* all about the ship, and about being a pilot.

Taking the long way to lunch meant a visit to DCCT was out of the question before afternoon class, but it also meant one more chance to avoid Asu, who needed to be in class at about the moment Theo reached for her last cheese muffin, counting teatime in her head. Now that math was falling into place for her she'd been getting in extra dance as well as extra bowli ball and those calories needed to be replaced, and she and Asu were suddenly out of the habit of companionable late night snacks....

Theo continued the count in her back brain even as she thought about Asu. She was senior bunk, after all, and so she needed to be in some touch with Asu, just in case someone asked.

Count reached, she said, "One hundred thirty-two" out loud and gently sipped at her second cup.

Out of the side of her vision appeared a familiar hand with rings on it, fluttering *query query* before the rest of Kara appeared, bonelessly dropping into the chair opposite, tray carefully isolated from the flump of the body.

"What?" Theo felt her eyebrow rise and tried to suppress it, without luck. Genes!

"Counting flower petals odd and even?"

It was Theo's turn to flutter *query* with one hand as she sipped again. It was really hard to get the tea *exact* when the available hot water varied by so much, but...

"I distinctly heard you counting," Kara said, unzipping food from her tray. "Bova informs me that there's a well-known Terran custom of offering a potential night-friend the opportunity of counting flower petals together. I gather one actually pulls the flower apart in the process. Should both parties reach the last petal with a 'Yes, I will'... then the night is decided."

Theo thought a moment, scrunching up her face seriously, cup still in front of her lips.

"How many choices are there, I wonder? Or is it binary?"

Kara bowed, laughing.

"Yes, it is binary. I think you begin to see, O Pilot."

"And so if one knows the number of petals a particular flower generally has..." Theo sipped, put the cup down in favor of finishing the muffin.

The grin got wide.

"Thus speaks a pilot! It is, in fact, pilot's choice. If one is in need, as one may be, one picks the proper flower and starts with the proper count. If there is but one flower to hand, the same result might be obtained."

Theo chuckled around her swallow. "Fast head or fast hand, it's no gamble."

Kara sighed gently. "Temptation is always a gamble, my friend, even a temptation one welcomes!"

Theo theatrically took the last bite, looked toward her empty hand. "None left to tempt me."

Kara sighed again, ending with a laugh.

"If it was all only so easy! But I digress. I saw you here and haven't caught you at DCCT lately." Her hands waggled *busy busy busy*. "Session ends become full with duty to school!"

"Not over," Theo said, "there's ummm..."

"Thirty class days," Kara said, "after today. Many of us will be wandering offworld very soon now. Are you going home to Delgado and kin?"

Theo sipped, shook her head. "The time, the money, the tickets!" Her free hand emphasized *do not mesh*. "I don't want to spend all my money and time in between, as much as I'd like the travel..."

"Hah. Will Win Ton your Scout friend be available to—"

Theo shook her head, hands saying, *would do, more do not mesh.*

"Don't mesh?"

Theo looked at the cup, seeing small particles in it.

"*My Scout,*" she said carefully, "Win Ton. He's on his way to Liad, to be married."

Kara opened her mouth, her shoulders leveling after she managed not to spill her drink. After putting the drink down she gave a short head nod and a hand-fluttering repeat of *don't mesh*.

"Oh, Theo—this is an unexpected lack of luck! In an orderly universe delms would have something more to do than looking for ways to discommode those of the—well, no, the delm's job is the clan after all. Liadens! He could be tied to clan-strings for a year or more!"

Theo sighed, wishing there was more tea at hand.

"He told me. I mean, he was careful to explain all of how it works. And then after that marriage, he's put in for a survey assignment..."

"Survey! Theo, that's wonderful for him." Kara's face was bright. "A good assignment and a way to stay out of the delm's sight." She paused and, Terran-style, pointed a finger at Theo. "And he bowed equal to you. This is not an act, done so publicly. He meant it!"

Theo smiled wanly.

"I believe he does mean it," she said with a sigh, "but that still means no visit during break, right?"

"Indeed," Kara, said, suddenly sounding like yos'Senchul in her seriousness. "That would shatter the Code in so many places..."

Theo shrugged. It wasn't like the Code, whatever it was, had anything to do with her.

"So you are just *staying* at the academy?" Kara shook her hand into *rethink plan.* "The break dorms aren't much fun, you know. They crowd everyone into Plummer Hall, and have hard-set meal schedules, and..." She paused and gave a conspiratorial wink, "and they keep strict compliance hours. Check rooms even. I did it first time around. It is to avoid!"

"You're going home, too? Who will I talk to?"

"I am *not* going home. That is also to avoid! If luck is not mine I'll spend session break with an uncle who has a small repair shop at Portcalay. My best hope is to pick up something at the Hugglelans job fair."

"The what? Are you going to be a cook?"

Kara raised her eyes to the ceiling, and not finding the answer there, she opened her hands wide and gave Theo a stern look.

"Where have you been, Pilot Waitley? Do you think Hugglelans is just the Howsenda?"

Theo shrugged again.

"Well, I mean, they do have the restaurant..."

Kara covered her face in mock despair.

"Theo, Hugglelans is the largest fixed-base operator on the planet! They run the port—the landing zone, all the public spaces, the hotels and dayrooms, the maintenance shops, the cantinas, the whole thing! The Howsenda is...a sideline. No, I misspeak. It is a *melant'i* game, a show of strength, a brag...a *hobby* for the owners. Well." She paused.

"So, be as may," she went on, "they offer all members of DCCT a chance to come to the job fair. They'll send an aircraft, they'll feed us, we take some tests, meet some people—you should come!"

"Do they *all* wear too much *vya* over there? And besides, that's a long commute!"

"Theo, you've got to start getting the DCCT message-mail! They offer room and board plus a small stipend—and you end up with a work record in the industry...Of course, if you think they might not take you, I guess it makes sense not to apply."

Theo nodded, but then held hand to face.

"But suppose they offer me a cook's job?"

"Don't apply to the cook program, my friend. I'm applying to maintenance first, field crew second, flight support third...And honestly, to be out of here for a change, I'd take cook duty if it wasn't one of their reserved for executives specialties. At least try it, Theo, there's free lunch and dinner at the Howsenda."

Theo laughed, hand fluttering *assent, assent, assent.*

"Excellent. Very good. So you have to go right after class to sign up for the job fair. Bova's on desk or maybe Ristof. If Bova is on deck, I ask you to resist the counting of flowers until you have studied your botany and your necessity!"

Theo laughed, rising and pulling on her pack.

"No flowers with Bova, you say. First, I have a class. Then to DCCT, then papers to write. Then letters. Flowers...I have no time for flowers."

Kara smiled, and bowed, seated as she was. "We'll get you work. Your busyness will give you distance, my friend."

TWENTY-ONE

· ·

Howsenda Hugglelans
Conglomeration of Portcalay
Eylot

THE JOB FAIR'S PROMISE HAD BEEN, "REAL WORK FOR REAL PAY!" and while that had sounded good in theory Theo was surprised at how good it felt in practice now that the term was over. Getting up in the morning seemed easier than at school—though how much of that had to do with having Kara as a roommate instead of Asu, she wasn't sure.

Still, getting paid for something besides good grades was a feeling easily as good as a to-the-second touchdown after a three-hour flight. Kara's consternation at discovering Theo's "secret" and her fervid promise to keep it close was still enough to make Theo smile in private.

"First job? You've *never* worked before? How can that be?"

There'd followed a near all-night discussion of how silly Delgado could be, what with the only real work being scholarly work, and how having a job that wasn't with the University was something you hid from your records.

Today, Theo's chores were commonplace. The early morning schedule called for inspecting tie-downs and parking clearances on the civil aviation side, with Derryman opting to drive the cart and update the logs while she spotted the gear and attached tension meters to the ties. The craft in this section were a mixed bag of private and corporate with one thing in common: they all

153

paid extra for the twice daily, premium status checks instead of depending on luck and inertia to keep their wings safe.

Derryman did this every workday, and he was a good teacher, in part because he'd been a teacher before he retired. He had not, as she'd first supposed, taught piloting or anything like it—instead he first sold and then taught insurance sales.

"Outside work is good for the soul," he told her, "and a lot better for health, too. With all the steps I get in a day here . . ."

She looked over her shoulder as he lounged back in the cart and flipped a quick *walk walk walk when query* in his direction before moving to the next tie-down. Derryman laughed.

"You can say that today, but I do this every day, and a lot of the year I don't have no hotshot apprentice pilots to mollycoddle."

She laughed outright this time. For the first five days of the break-shift, Derryman drove the dozen students assigned to him like he was trying to make day laborers out of them. They'd carried cable, rope, tie-twine, twists, pins, and disposable snap readers from one end of the field to the other. They replaced aged and shredded cable tying down display craft, they'd learned the value of gloves—and of choosing the *right* glove—and they learned to respect the gauge color of the temp strips laid in quiet mosaic on the live strips and launch zones.

Her blisters had healed quickly, but by then two of the students had recalled urgent necessity elsewhere, forfeiting the free meals, camaraderie, and income to return to the academy or to make sudden trips home. The afternoon they left, Derryman had turned up with a bowli ball and a round of flavored ice-gel and declared the rest of the day free and clear.

Once the first week's mollycoddling was done the crews had been given split-shift days, with the mornings given over to outside duties and the afternoons to tasks that varied by the day for everyone—except for Kara, who kept getting assigned to the machine shop, doing what she liked to call "belowdecks stuff."

For all that she enjoyed keeping busy and learning new things, Theo was starting to miss the forward motion of school: here every day was clearly the same for most of the staff and workers.

Derryman, who liked being around pilots and flying things, didn't mind the sameness—in fact denying it, claiming each day brought new wonders and different challenges.

Other than having different fingers jabbed by cable fringe, not much seemed to change, but Theo guessed that being out on the tarmac with a breeze in the face and the smell of the water coming off the nearby lake might have something appealing to it year-round, something like watching the sun come up over the bushes and trees at Father's house on Leafydale Place...maybe there *was* something idyllic in it, after all. It was surprising how, among all the noise and motion of the port, one could stand out in a corner of it and feel basically alone and free, even with craft overhead and taxiing nearby.

She bent under the nose of one of the three Indigo Speedsters on the route, admiring it at the same time the voice in the back of her head told her that it was a toy. Derryman had it right: he'd told her the very first time she checked one that, "The thing only has room for a pilot and her lunch, so it's a good thing it can't fly all that long!"

She knew there was a problem with the tie-strap even before the meter's complaining *yeep yeep yeep* broke the relative quiet. The strap looked *soft*, yielded easily to her push...and it shouldn't. The meteorologists were calling for more of the seasonal lake-effect storms late in the day and it wouldn't do for something this light to lift and flip in a downpour, or worse, go sliding out into a taxiway to endanger traffic.

Derryman sighed noisily, calling out, "Do the right wing gear and I'll do the left. That's *Batzer's Bat* and I guarantee they'll all be forty percent light and using last year's recycled cable!"

"Should I call it in?"

"Call it when we have the double check in place."

Right. There'd been some classroom time on these things—always do a double check before disturbing one of the Howsenda's regulars.

Derryman ducked under his wing, a little slowly, heard the expected *yeep* and then a chuckle.

"Guess I was wrong. This one here, it's only thirty-nine-point-nine-seven-seven percent low on the tension! And look out there—we gotta get someone out soon!"

From Theo's vantage the tarmac and flight lines led to the bright line of the horizon, where blue sky glinted behind boiling clouds going from white to grey.

"That'll be a gozwalla of a front when it gets here, Theo. Call this in—then catch me downline."

✳   ✳   ✳

It *was* a gozwalla of a front, and it arrived far earlier than the usual evening rains, from a vector slightly off from them as well. Wind and precocious raindrops buffeted Theo and Derryman as they finished the run—luckily only the one tie-down had needed attention—and Derryman rushed off, one of his rare pilot signs indicating *open windows fragile things home.*

The day locker room was crowded with regular staff and the break crew; ordinary activity of the port slowed as local traffic backed up with the storm's approach, and a call came from the Howsenda offering choice chow seating to crew members since several tour craft were rerouting, despite meal prep in progress.

Kara, Theo, and a crowd of regulars, all wearing staff ID of one sort or another, took the underways beneath tarmac and buildings to arrive at the staff lift to the Howsenda, one wag counting the packed crowd and announcing, "We're one shy of the load limit on this ship—should we wait for someone?"

Theo and Kara managed to duck in, Kara hauling Theo to a supposed spot on the left corner, a spot made by the willing shift of other bodies, and the question was answered by someone close to the door.

She didn't know everyone in the lift, though she recognized most of them by sight and placed a few more from the colors or shapes of their badges. The "outside crew," like her and Kara, wore the blue-rimmed large image badges of maintenance staff; others wore the striped orange of mid-level admin, or the brown of back-house restaurant crew.

"Food before limit tests, Jermy!"

The lift shot to the back corridors of the Howsenda's wait-staff area, laughter still echoing.

Kara grabbed Theo's hand again and they rushed out as the lift door swished open, pointing to a side corridor and—

Directly before them stood the waiter who'd served Theo on her first visits to the Howsenda, both hands held high, instantly quieting the raucousness.

"Folks, I suggest you all stay on board. The Skyliner banquet room is open and there's seating for all of you. We've got a delicious meal just moments from being served, and since it's a non-cancel event, we might as well all enjoy it!"

He smiled generically, then did a double-take as people pushed themselves back into the confines of the lift.

"Ah, Pilot," he said, a sweeping hand gesture picking out Theo and Kara and directing the pair of them back into the car. He nodded to Theo, "I'm so glad you could join us." His badge flashed orange as he waved them into the lift's interior lighting.

The door closed summarily, and Theo grimaced as Kara elbowed her.

"He's something to look at, isn't he? He's..."

Theo lifted a glance to the car top, managing to say, "He might be something to look at, but he always wears too much *vya*!" just before the car reached the banquet room.

Theo could have had cream crackers and soy sprouts and called it a banquet, if only because of the setting. The tables were immaculately laid out, with flowers between guests. The room was composed of three long arms, each with stunning views through transparent walls of the field and city to one side, and the lakes to the other; the ceiling itself was a transparent green. The room lighting was subdued, and the tablecloth itself glowed gently.

The storm walking across the lake threw lightning to the ground carelessly, and the cloud-to-cloud strikes built sudden pink blossoms within the great mass of roiling darkness.

The meal, however, was far beyond cream crackers and soy sprouts; the viands included imported fishes and cheeses, fruit compotes made from berries that blossomed once every five Standards, delicate tendrils of between serving desserts...and no wine or other such beverages. She had tea, as did Kara, though more than one pitcher of near beer made its way to the tables.

When the front hit, the smattering of raindrops on the window-walls were sheeted away instantly, the rain alternately coating and abandoning the wind-driven surface. Lightning strikes nearby brought thunder that shook the port. Most of the diners paused at one point or another in the proceedings to stare into the darkness.

"You're not saying much," Kara chided.

Theo's free hand flickered *watching watching*.

"It is a good storm," Kara agreed.

"We don't much get to see storms like this in the Wall, and even at outside, they aren't often like this."

On the horizon, toward the lake, was a glow hinting at bright sky beyond. The sheeting rains were palpably lessening. Conversation rose; someone from the grounds crew passionately bemoaned the expected fate of a recent planting.

Theo craned her head to look toward the departing storm, only to hear Kara say, "The very definition of wet!"

She turned and saw a bedraggled man, in what might once have been business clothes, moving from table to table hurriedly. His hair was dark and glistening. Droplets rained from his jacket as he stalked across the room. A vague helpful hand at another table pointed toward their part of the room's arm, and the man rushed forward, quelling conversation as he passed.

He was angry, Theo saw, and purposeful. She put her utensils down and placed her hands flat on the table.

"Which one of you is Waitley?" he demanded. "You owe me a dinner and suit!"

Theo was on her feet, standing between Kara and the man. There was commotion around but she was focused on his face and posture, not quite sure how she'd gotten there.

"I'm Batzer," the man snarled, pushing closer. "You called me from my dinner and look at this! Look at this! How did you dare? Why didn't you check them earlier? They were fine!"

The Indigo Speedster! Theo thought, remembering the warning sounds yeeping toward the clouds. No, those ties had hardly been fine.

He shook his arms, splashing Theo and probably soaking half of the room.

He pressed forward. Theo willed herself to relax, fought to change her stance from *prepared* to *aware*, marshaling her thoughts to speak. If he noticed the stance change he didn't react properly, now leaning toward her, crowding her. It should have calmed him, that move, she thought.

She gave ground a half step; aware of the touch on the elbow that was Kara.

"Answer me! I'm Brine Batzer," he yelled, "and *you* owe me a..."

Theo raised both hands slightly, settled her feet flat, prepared to speak or defend.

"Batzer, you are intruding on a private function. Stand down and leave."

The waiter. He came up loudly behind Theo, backing her at first, then standing at her side.

"I'm Batzer. This day laborer of yours called me to tie down my plane and she owes me..."

A rumble of thunder drifted over the proceedings as the waiter took a quarter step forward, insinuating his arm between Theo and the angry man, a surprising twitch of hand fluently suggesting *mine now*.

"I repeat. You are interrupting a private function. This person is an employee and we will not brook this behavior from anyone."

Theo felt Kara's hand tug lightly on her shoulder and took another careful half step back.

"I keep five ships here and you aren't going to threaten me! I'll go right to Hugglelans and have them toss both of you. She's going to apologize, and pay for my dinner!"

The waiter looked across the room, and raised an unhurried hand. The irate figure before them looked, too, and wilted visibly as six uniformed security guards moved in slowly.

"Hugglelans Security will be pleased to escort you to a public area, Brine Batzer. You may leave a note with them and this problem will be looked into."

The man's face whitened and his hands shook.

"I'm Batzer, do you hear? I'll speak to a Hugglelans before I move."

The waiter gave a half nod and shifted the way a fighter or dancer might, tapping his badge, rimmed in solid orange. He looked larger now, and formidable rather than merely respectable.

"Yes, sir," he said, but his voice too, had changed slightly, as if he'd stepped in behind his badge and made it boom. "I am Third Son of the house. You may call me Aito. I will personally look into this matter, Brine Batzer, and take care of it appropriately. You may leave now, and let my people eat."

TWENTY-TWO

. . . .

Erkes Dormitory, Suite 302
Anlingdin Piloting Academy

THE LIGHT FLASHED ON THEO'S MESSAGE QUEUE.

If she ignored it, she could relax until her tutoring assignment.

It might, of course, be a message from Asu asking if they needed anything for the larder, or explaining that she might be *late* again tonight. Maybe it was that, finally, Asu topped the shuttle queue and would be orbiting until tomorrow. *That* would ease the tension in the room.

Stretching into a flat-footed centering pose she closed her eyes, trying to absorb the energy instead of sighing it away. Those inner calm routines worked really well for some people, but the idea that sighing wasted relaxation was one proposed by her latest martial arts partner, and she doubted it.

The light still blinked when she opened her eyes. She sighed anyway.

Asu's schedules and hers diverged more and more now, with Asu concentrating on the basic licensing course—and being a social whirlwind—while Theo's mirrored, according to Chelly, the hard-core tradeship course he'd audited while summering as the school's exchange student.

Maybe she should ignore the message. On the other hand, she hadn't ignored a message since break had morphed into school. While that had happened all too fast according to her work-mates it had hardly been fast enough for Theo, who enjoyed the

161

company and the stipends of break but missed the school constant of hands-on flying.

Break over, she'd looked toward the time she'd be a flight deckhand, and get her own chance to sit first seat on the shuttle. That staffing notice was one she'd waited for, fully aware that each flashing message light might signal her listing on that queue.

Theo did the hand stretch thing that was supposed to be a good antidote to muscle loss if you were in zero g for a long time.

Asu *might* make flight deckhand this year, half a Standard after Theo's first of three deckhand runs and first as PIC. Most recently she'd subbed for Freck the day he broke his thumb at bowli ball. The shuttle was all work and no fun, as far as she was concerned, in part because you had to watch the crew as much as the craft.

She stood down from the stretching, shaking her head. For all that Asu tried to rag her about her math, which was up to snuff, these days, Asu was clearly not looking toward being a professional.

The queue lit up as she touched it—mail call.

She danced another relaxation move—until she saw that it was not yet another one of Jondeer's extravagances for Asu.

Signature pilot post, T. Waitley, Erkes 302.

She felt a thrill of anticipation, and Win Ton's bright face shone in her memory, a quirky smile playing about his lips as—but suppose it was something else?

"Go, Theo!" she said.

Thanking the luck that her roommate was elsewhere, Theo cleared the light and sprinted for the door. Asu need never know!

Theo's walk back was more of a trot, the small packet tucked securely into her day bag. The whole proceeding had taken but a moment: Theo entered and there was no line in front of her, the student on desk recognized her on sight, and the packet was produced with a simple "Sign here, Pilot" request.

Lieutenant Win Ton yo'Vala—she spotted it even before it was in her hands, and on signing, she almost fumbled her signature.

Silly Theo, she told herself, just a note, that's all! After all, he owes you a bit of mail...

The mailing labels had been printed and signed by Win Ton

beneath their protective tapes and there were four additional signatures: a Scout captain, a pilot first class, the student shuttle pilot, and the student on desk, who was a pilot.

She cradled the packet, which was slightly flexible and thicker than a mere sheet or two of paper, but had very little weight.

Not a bowli ball, she thought, but there was...something in the packet. Another pair of wings?

It took great control for her not to tear the thing open then and there, but she wanted privacy—suppose he'd sent her a flatpic of him at the beach or something?

Back in quarters, with the door closed and locked, Theo used her boot knife to open the packet, finding paper, folded in half, like a proper letter, and more paper, sealed around a solid lump. She thought for a moment before putting the lump back in the envelope and unfolding the letter.

The paper was so fine it was almost cloth. The fibers glowed with a creamy warmth, and it released a scent that was subtle and charming, with undertones not unlike *vya*, but not nearly so challenging to the comfortable nose. Just holding it was a sensuous experience.

Sweetest of Mysteries, the missive began, in Win Ton's angular Terran script.

Well you may wonder that I still recall your face and address after such a time. In the way of things I calculate that you've experienced perhaps eighty percent of your school life since you last were kind enough to touch my hand. Count me pleased beyond measure that your days, at least, have been spent among pilots and the striving for knowledge. Mine, I admit, have been full of the tasting of the three hundred teas most suited to polite society, and to the drinking of wine from a cellar whose best days were perhaps some time before the coalescence of the first black hole.

I discover, now that I am again free to access my mail drop, several letters of yours, long held for me; I thank you for writing of the commonplace as well as the adventures and wish there had been some way for me, with decorum and according to the Code, to have done the same for you. I can, with no great damage to the Code, choose now a random day from my recent past and let you imagine that most days were much like it, once in fact my

*most major duty was done, which alas required both more time
and effort than I would have expected.*

*In any case, we would share a lakefront vista from the deep-porch
opening onto the joint chambers; tapping a bell would summon
several teas and a grudging morning wine, and each day I might
request as much or as little of a breakfast as I wished. Alas, the
Scout in me made an unusual request or two over time, but my
hosts fed me all with aplomb, from full-dinner pasta to crackers
and fish paste, always with a complement of juices, marmalades,
jellies, and breads enough to have brought the whole of one of our
dinner tables on* Vashtara *to full-belly belching.*

This came at the page turn and Theo laughed, admitting to
herself that far too many of the cruise passengers they had traveled
with had indeed overfed. But here before her, she had the account
of his adventure, which was far less boring than he pretended.

*This delightful repast is to consume near the whole of the morn-
ing, though I was able to carve out for myself time for proper
exercise both morning and afternoon by assuming the practice of
surf-swimming, as my running was seen as a provocation to the
good nature of the small but always elegant community where
we resided. Only once did I make the mistake of returning from
my swim with a finned creature I thought suitable for dinner, for
the cook surely has a better eye than mine for what is finest in a
fresh fish.*

*The company most mornings included the two of us and a smat-
tering of available house kin; on a few memorable days we also
shared time with various medicos and consultants, but the less of
that, the better.*

*Of the afternoons, when not whiling away the time identifying
craft from their contrails and altitude, I sometimes read of the
popular literature so that of the evening I might discourse properly.
While the fact that I am a pilot weighed heavily in my choosing,
the larger clan wished to know next to nothing about what it is
that pilots do, and the fact that I am a Scout was shared most
quietly indeed.*

*Afternoons were often social affairs; here it was that the Lady
shone in her knowledge of teas, and I met the very heart of the
insipid community which I had already fled to become a pilot.*

*I warn you, Sweetness, the society of pilots is loud, boisterous,
bawdy, challenging, and dangerous. While the High Houses of Liad*

may be no less dangerous and challenging, they lack the social graces of loud, boisterous, and bawdy; most of them assume competencies never aspired to and lack an understanding of what the word "survive" means unless it involves a multi-year multi-clan Balance. While one should never underestimate a Liaden—or anyone!—the assumption that survival is implicit in position is surely difficult to maintain over time.

This on the page turn; she was momentarily distracted by some curious marginal marks; almost it seemed hand-talk brought down to paper, as if Win Ton had paused in his narrative to argue briefly with himself.

The evening discussions were mixed events. If I have not mentioned it before, I will now: we, the hopeful couple, were situated in a summer cottage large enough to house my clan entire, and perhaps yours, too, had you one. It shared a bay with a few similar houses, and a truly wondrous view of ocean. The lady's clan sent various of her kin to us from time to time, and from discussion not well hid from me I discovered the lady's need for a child was becoming urgent and the choice of myself, younger than she by a dozen Standards, was seen as means to incite success in one with little hope.

Thus some evenings were full of busy clan members, and others to clinical attempts to achieve mood, or will. Later, once intent, at least, was successful, the waiting was in many ways harder, for the lady had little need of my company other than in polite gatherings; I sometimes swam in the surf late as well as early, and there were times I would walk on the beach and think of mysteries such as yourself while naming stars, observing the weather and tides, and cataloging shells on the wave fringe.

In all of this, the lady was quiet, respectful, and not so much willing or even interestingly submissive, but ultimately level-headed. She was not one to play games of chance, she was not competent at games of physical skill, nor was she, aside from her tea, a lady of passions. Memory of her pales and fades far more rapidly than that of our times together, which I treasure.

I now turn to matters more of concern to we two as pilots. You have mentioned several pilots who have come to your attention and names are always good to share. I appreciate the depth of your reports and your wit as well. Having said that, I must come the Scout at this point about the pilot Brine Batzer.

As you have sat second for me and have dealt well with pilots I trust, I was compelled to research this Batzer. His license, which was current some few moments ago, is of first class, though the unfortunate treatment of ship and staff you detailed seems hardly that of such a pilot! Though there, it is said on Liad that many of us have mothers with their own kitchens, meaning that habits are both born and trained, so who knows where this man may have become who he is, eh? Obviously he was not trained at my school or yours!

Batzer very rarely comes to Liaden ports. Though scant, his record has not been good; it shows fines for minor cargo violations, fines for shipyard arguments, actions for refusal to pay standard fees, he has . . . Well, I make him sound the criminal in all of this, and you must not say to anyone that he is a criminal, for all of these infractions are at levels below that.

He is, in a way I do not understand, well placed on certain planets of Terran extraction: at least once he was "bailed out" of an issue by appealing to a traveling Terran official. One must assume him highborn or well placed for I see him listed as pilot of several ships, all of them as owner.

Having traversed history, and traded pilot lore, I speak now of my current estate.

My delm has again released me to the Scouts, as I am no longer of immediate use to the clan. You may imagine with what speed I presented myself to Headquarters and requested an assignment.

I was gifted with a garbage run, and sweet it was to be alone inside my own ship, concerned only with the simplicities of my assignment. More, having finished transporting a Torvin-class vessel to a Scout base from whence this is delivered into the hands of a pilot heading your way, I now assist in preparations for a working investigation. And such a one! I am made third in the command chain despite my admitted youth, this because the mission to hand is one I myself proposed!

But there, I go on about myself. It pleases me to hear of your continued success at school, of your third class rating provisional and your plans for the second, and your willingness to take on tutoring—

Tutoring!

Chaos!

Theo looked to the chrono. If she ran *now* she'd be on time for Claudy's refresher on the Star King. After the lecture she'd given the kid last time on precision and punctuality, she'd better *not* be late!

Locking the letter and envelope into her drawer safe, Theo fled for the airfield.

TWENTY-THREE

. . . .

Erkes Dormitory, Suite 302
Anlingdin Piloting Academy

THE LETTER WAS STILL PRECIOUS WHEN THEO CAME BACK TO IT, later that afternoon. Claudy's refresh was an ugly memory: you'd have suspected the kid had spent the semester flying kites instead of studying navigation. Rocky as she was, Claudy did pass, though Theo'd drawn black looks and a suppressed curse for requiring a mandatory review before semester end. Really, if the kid wanted to stay current, she shouldn't *play* it, she should *do* it!

And so Win Ton's letter—she started again with the first word, luxuriating again in the feel of the paper and the subtle, oh-so-subtle touch of scent. Theo was becoming fond of subtlety, having recently become aware of how fine a sense of timing and nuance Win Ton possessed, of how careful even his passionate words were. That his sense of smell, his understanding of color, and his advertent approach to the universe was superior to many who considered themselves pilots was without doubt.

That made her sigh, and miss Win Ton in a way she hadn't for a long time.

She came again to the point where she'd rushed off to deal with immediate concerns. Indeed, she felt some guilt, because she hadn't updated him entirely over these last semesters. Her third class was now firm and it would take time in grade, and a couple more trips as PIC for her to up the second class from trainee to provisional operator.

Theo had retrieved the sealed packet from the envelope, and tumbled it in her hand as she read. It was soothing in a curious way, almost like stroking a cat.

There were the other things she hadn't filled him in on, just as he'd not been particularly explicit about his duties as a husband— surely he would have been able to bring some joy to the pairing! Now she read on hoping for something more about his travels, his route, or when they...

Alas, I am not able to convince any of the mapping computers, nor my superiors, of any route wherein Anlingdin Academy is a way point for my journey to the assembly site. As your own location is still based on the needs of tuition, and as I am not at liberty to disclose my tour destinations, immediate, intermediate, or final, there seems little likelihood that we shall see each other in the near term, as dear as that thought has been to me since we last parted.

For a moment she felt like she'd hit free fall; but her stomach settled, and Theo sighed, closed her eyes briefly and opened them.

If you have not already opened the packet sealed with wax from my dinner candle, I pray that you will do so now. I consider it a great favor you do me, if you will.

Though only partway down the lovely page the letter continued on the next sheet, as Win Tin meant her not to read beyond until she had complied—or not.

With growing curiosity she put the letter aside, broke the waxed seam, and smoothed the paper away from an inner wrapping of metal foil, the whole coated thinly in wax that verged on the liquid.

It took a moment to find the seam. She peeled it back carefully, discovering within a coil—not a coil! A chain, like a necklace, chill against her fingers as she raised it. Pendant from the chain was a cerametal chunk that was not simply raw metal but formed and shaped with notches and ridges around a small central cylinder.

She let the foil drop and took the cylinder between her fingers, rolled it, felt the crisp edges of the metal. It felt good, like it should do something, rather than just be...interesting to look at. More, it felt *old*, much older than the chain. It wasn't pretty, exactly, but she liked it, if one could *like* a thing.

Still, thinking advertently, she held it in her hand rather than putting it on immediately, and returned to Win Ton's letter.

Theo, it would be both a favor and honor to me if you will hold this, and perhaps wear it and keep it with you. I discovered it during my brief garbage run, and it is to all appearances twin to one I wear about my own neck. Let us say that, as soon as I held it in my hand, I thought of you. Indeed, I can think of none other that I would see hold it. As the pair is to my knowledge unique, and found in an out-of-the-way place rarely visited by tourists or ordinary travelers, I hope it does not offend you to share such a thing with me.

We need not speak of these again until we are together, but I feel they are a bond we can share, one that has already helped me focus on the necessities of my immediate plans, and of my plans beyond. Call it celebration, plan, or sympathetic magic, I vow I will not be separated from mine and I hope you will keep yours by you at all times.

Though she wasn't talking, Theo *felt* speechless. Unique, and something Win Ton treasured, something very special.

She sighed and felt stupid as tears fell down her face, onto her hands, onto the necklace. Happy tears, yes, but it felt so good to be—cherished.

She brought the necklace close, peered at it, smiled, and had the silliest feeling that it returned her regard, or that Win Ton had infused it with his own.

Shaking her head to settle her hair as best as could be done, Theo spread the chain between her two hands and put it over her head. The cylinder fell comfortably between her breasts, not cold at all, or warm, but exactly the temperature of her own body. She regretted that Win Ton hadn't been there to help her put it on—but that thought should probably wait, at least until she had finished reading his letter.

Meanwhile, it is my hope and wish that you continue to stay in touch with me at this address; only understand that my mission may make it difficult for me to reply for dozens or perhaps hundreds of days at a time. That I cannot immediately answer, or perhaps even receive, your messages in timely fashion makes no difference to my regard for you, nor my desire to hear from you.

Clan, mission, and duty permitting, as well as your agreement, of course, I shall again someday be by your side for a quiet breakfast.

Yours in many ways,

Win Ton

*　　*　*

She thought of calling the hopeful proto-pilots with whom she'd recently shared bed-time—first thought of one, then the other.

Then, she thought of Win Ton, and shook her head. Her friends would only be an annoyance to her, in this state of mind. And, since they *were* friends, she didn't call.

Which didn't change the fact that her mind was unsettled, and her body too, as if she'd spent the morning ingesting caffeine and sugar treats. She wanted to move, to dance, to not be right here with the letter, which she'd unfolded and read yet again, and refolded, hands caressing the lines that Win Ton had inked.

Kara. Kara might provide some comfort, or at least a willing ear—and it was obvious that her deep sky navigation problem was not happening right now!

It was work of a moment to slip the letter back into the lock-drawer. She pulled the chain up until Win Ton's gift was spinning before her eyes. Frowning, she tried to see through the patina of age and mysterious origin to whatever it was that he thought was there, or meant to be there. She thought of writing back immediately—but what was the use in that? He was already on the way to his assembly point.

She stood, and danced a few steps, which didn't calm her, exactly.

Air, she thought. Air would be good; air and color and the sight of craft overhead.

She closed the quietly behind her.

As she walked Theo felt like her shoes picked up extra energy from the ground, and when she stood still it felt like her blood vessels and muscles were full of energy. The calming steps she danced became attack variations as soon as she moved, the quieting motions of pretest relaxation flowed into dance which flowed back into power moves, which flowed into kicks and stunts.

Finally she admitted defeat and walked fast, striding toward the Culture Club at a ground-eating pace, forcing the energy in her arms and legs into the pace of her march. She was going the long way, hoping to calm herself before she encountered anyone else.

She heard the sounds long before she saw it: the quick steps, the laughter and crowing, the grunts and curses, the silences of waiting. She rounded the shrubbery that defined the big side lawn, where a crowd surrounded the action.

Bowli ball! And by the tenor of things, a match well in progress. Or maybe a match well out of hand.

Kara was the first she saw; the only one of the standing players she knew by name. Sprawled around the grass were seven other DCCT members in various states of disarray ranging from bloody nose to ripped shirts to grass-and-mud-stained pants. One, Yberna, was curled on her side, like she might have taken a shot in the gut.

There were three standees in the playing zone; two of them, both guys she didn't know, were playing a back and forth together that meant they were teaming it against Kara, trying to make it as hard as possible for her to know when the ball was hers. Sweat streamed down her face, and if she saw Theo, she was too busy to show it.

Suddenly, the ball was in play, heading for Kara; too fast and too wobbly to deal with cleanly. It struck her high on the shoulders, knocking her off-center and rebounded straight above her. Theo yelled, Kara looked up and managed a one-handed slap that sent the ball back to the originial thrower with considerable energy. It wasn't elegant, but it was enough to "keep bowli," as Kara found center again, and the crowd cheered.

"Kara's still in!"

"Clean clothes," yelled the taller of the two guys, showing his teeth in what he might've thought was a grin. "Play if you dare!"

The ball was on the way before the tall player finished yelling, and Theo charged, recognizing at the last moment that the spin was not quite what she'd expected.

"Kara," she called, and saw the fleeting nod and hand flash as Theo fed the ball to her as lightly as she could, allowing her a moment's respite; Kara returned the favor soundlessly and this time Theo flung the ball to the short guy.

Even as it left her hand Theo felt the odd pull, as if the normal permutations of spin and power of a bowli ball were off somehow. Maybe the ball wasn't true; maybe...

That fast it was back, and thrown not to her, but *at* her. These guys were playing bloodball; no wonder the usually happy crew from the Club was scattered—

"Take him, Theo!" The crowd was surely partisan, the encouragement was Bova at full voice.

The ball danced; she grabbed it, felt the thing slip even after the catch; her toss was meant to go toward Kara but the ball was beyond, meaning it was up for grabs and the tall guy did just that, charging and faking toward Theo while slamming it at Kara.

"Grah!" was about what Kara managed, taking the ball with her left hand and barely getting it along toward Theo.

The spin went wonky, and the bowli ball shot off with an unexpected burst of energy. Which was just—wrong.

Theo lunged, snatched, and spun, meaning to return to Kara—but Kara was down, struggling to get her feet under her, to get back into play.

The ball in Theo's hands twisted and growled, like it was fighting her. She tried to gentle it, almost lost it, and danced in a quick circle, barely containing it inside her own motion, her mind suddenly considering board drills. In particular, the bad gravity board drill; the equation for near-limit Jumps—and suddenly she had it! It was like the ball had two drivers!

Her mind flung itself around the ball's absurd motion, as her body reacted, took the ball and spun it against the spin it demanded, nearly catching the tall guy in the head, his touch more a pass than a catch, so the short guy could take it, and Theo was charging for the point where the ball had to go, when—

"Full halt!"

Theo went down on one knee, obeying that order. She shook her hair out of her face, and looked up, not at the short guy, but at Pilot yos'Senchul—but no, it wasn't.

In one hand, the pilot held the bowli ball, hard and steady, though Theo knew it was kicking to get free. In the other hand, the pilot held a data transport bag.

Theo took a breath and climbed to her feet. It *was* yos'Senchul, but—two hands?

He shook the ball at the assembly. "No one leaves until I have some answers. First. This ball—it has an owner? Someone who should claim it?"

The question was penetrating and serious.

The tall guy cleared his throat. "That girl there, sir, she threw the toss and should get the return."

yos'Senchul looked to Theo, grim.

"Pilot Waitley, do you own this object?"

Theo shook her head.

"Sir, no. I just got in the game. It *is* my catch and toss, and I've got it figured now so—"

"Yes, Pilot, I could see that you have it figured." yos'Senchul turned, holding the ball out like a weapon.

"Pilot ven'Arith, does this bowli ball belong to you?"

Kara was on her feet, breathing hard, her face wet with sweat. She bowed, some special thing with hand motions, and knee tucks, performed without a stutter, though an instant before she'd been shaking.

"Master Pilot, it was brought to the game by someone else."

yos'Senchul turned to the tall guy.

"You, sir, who wished the ball returned to Pilot Waitley?"

He gulped. "I brought the ball, but I don't own it, I mean I got it from—"

"I see," yos'Senchul interrupted. He looked to the shorter player, who was staring at the ground. "And you?"

"I've had the ball awhile," the guy muttered. "I mean, you know, a guy needs an edge."

"Ah. Tell me, how long have you had a death wish?"

The short guy looked up, eyes wide. "Death wish, sir?"

"Surely, a death wish. It is one thing to play a clean, high stakes game among pilots; for surely pilots delight in such things. It is another thing to bring into play between uninformed pilots an amateurishly modified gladiator ball. I have saved your life, not because I am your friend, but because Pilot Waitley would have blamed herself for your suicide or that of your comrade."

The man went pale but said nothing.

"Did you not hear Pilot Waitley say she had figured the ball out? Look!"

yos'Senchul put the data case down against his knee, and pulled back his other sleeve, revealing a metal and ceramic arm adorned with a plethora of readouts.

"As I hold this ball, it contains enough stored energy to launch itself to the nearest town. Pilot Waitley says, and I trust her enough to have her pilot my own craft, that she has figured the ball out."

The instructor bowed toward Theo, gently.

"Tell us, Pilot: what do you see?"

Theo returned the bow.

"There's something extra in the ball, like a resonance. It takes the ordinary changes and, I sort of plotted it, I think. The more often the ball is thrown quickly, the more energy it takes from the spin and every so often the energy comes out in a throw. I can see the timing of that release."

"Enough. Close enough. And your strategy?"

He looked at her expectantly, and Theo raised both hands, weighing the phrasing.

"I was going to take the pass from the shorter player, dive, roll, and give the ball to the taller, chest high. He keeps his hands too far on the fringe, and he's not quick—"

Enough, yos'Senchul signed. He bowed again.

"Pilot, thank you. An able strategy, indeed, and more than sufficient to have told the tale."

Turning to the two men, now standing well isolated from the DCCT players, yos'Senchul waved them casually before him with the admonition, "Sirs, you may thank me for saving your lives, while we walk together to the Commander's office. A discussion of the source of the modification kit will not be out of order."

TWENTY-FOUR

· ·

Diverse Cultures Celebration Team
Anlingdin Piloting Academy

YBERNA WAS MORE THAN JUST TIRED, SHE WAS *ILL*. THEO DIDN'T think she'd ever seen anyone that exact shade of yellow, especially considering how pale the girl usually was, and the color didn't go well at all with scrapes and bruises. With yos'Senchul gone DCCT was acting like a team, indeed—someone had broken out extra oxygen and there were a couple first aid kits circulating among the combatants.

"I'll be fine," Yberna said, her hands trembling and her lips going blue, "I just need a little oxygen."

But oxygen didn't help, nor did the simple remedy of keeping calm that some were loudly advocating. Even before yos'Senchul and his wards were out of sight, Kara was on the comm with the infirmary, demanding an emergency pickup at DCCT.

"Yes, we have first aid providers," her voice rose, shutting down adjacent conversations, "but none of us has prenatal training and Yberna is pregnant."

The words struck Theo's ears like a sonic boom, and she wasn't the only one whose near-squeaked "pregnant?" broke the air. She managed not to ask "how" as a follow-up, but surely Yberna wouldn't have *planned* a pregnancy for this late in her school career!

"It isn't *silly* to rest, Yberna," Kara was saying, "and we're not going to carry you down the hill over our backs like a day pack!

177

Here, use this for a pillow, and try the relaxation exercises for concentration. They've got a crew out the door already."

"Thank you, Pilot Waitley, you have done well for your friend, and you, Kara ven'Arith, you have great empathy!"

Theo nodded to the crew chief's bow, pleased to see him, surprised to be recalled.

"Theo? Theo, please? Did you really know? Were you going to knock him down?"

Yberna was being tucked into the stretcher, monitors squinching closed on her wrists as she peered around the medical staff, trying to move against the pressure pads that held her still. The one who had bowed to them—Theo saw a name tag reading "Healer el'Kemin"—fluttered a vague hand-sign, perhaps meant to be *say please in truth*.

Theo nodded vigorously. "On the next throw, Yberna. He had it coming to him."

Yberna attempted a smile.

"Good! We can't let them win, you know!"

The stretcher was locked to the pallet attach points and the hoverlift smoothly rose.

The med tech—Healer el'Kemin—and one of the other staffers got up behind the driver; the other two ran outrigger and Yberna was away, weakly trying to wave. Healer el'Kemin, reached down to touch her head, likely adjusting a medication, because the girl went quiet, as if she'd suddenly fallen asleep. "Make way, clear, make way, clear!"

The sled was gone, moving briskly down the hill toward the dispensary.

Kara took a step after them. "I should—" she began, and was intercepted by Vin, wielding a med kit.

"Kara, hold still; you're bleeding."

DCCT's common room was alive with swirling conversations, the galaxy-portrait end walls giving back echoes and the knots of noise moving and coagulating. Theo'd never seen the group so animated. It was almost as if they'd won something, despite Yberna's difficulties.

Freck was almost bouncing.

"Did you *see* that? Theo was going to take them out big time. Think they can run up here from their silly club and take all of DCCT with one trick? I think this planet loyalty stuff is way overrated for pilots!"

Theo hadn't recognized them but enough of the crew had: two of the Young Pilots of Eylot, membership restricted to those born on Eylot of Terran descent.

The sudden holiday mood was helped by Bova and assorted helpers rushing around with sweet rolls, served with creamy topping and an accompanying hit of oxygen.

Theo took the roll, and spurned the oxy, frustrated that so many conversations were going on at once that she couldn't get more than the gist of things. She gathered that the Young Pilots had a complaint—DCCT got first shot at the break jobs at Hugglelans. That, they claimed, was a right of the planet-born.

Trying to follow the discussion got more frustrating as Bova played wrong-side advocate and took up the Young Pilots' argument, which felt a lot like a Simple sermon to Theo.

"I *should* have gone with her! I got in the game to let her drop out!"

Theo turned and touched her friend's shoulder.

"Two problems: no room for a copilot on the sled—and she was already asleep. You'd have slowed the ship."

Kara closed her eyes, and maybe she did a dance move in her head, because Theo saw some of the tension flow out of her. Eyes open, she moved her hands: *truth*.

"How did you figure out what was wrong with the ball? I saw—and felt!—that it was moving strangely, but I couldn't understand it. You just grabbed it and went, like you knew exactly what was going to happen!"

Theo shrugged.

"I didn't know, *exactly*; I was just reacting to what the ball was really doing, and not what it *should have* been doing. It's like dance competition stuff—at some point *something's* got to vary, so you have to be patient, and alert, and when the vary comes, deal with it. I *did* know that we were getting acceleration in there, and I'm afraid I was already running with a lot of energy when I came looking for you, so I was primed to run the numbers, and that's the course I saw. I didn't have time to calculate all of the variables, just that I could return it to him with spin and velocity he couldn't handle. Mostly I wanted to stop the game long enough to be sure you were just winded."

"*Just* winded? I wish I could say that. I was going to half measures, to just keep the ball in play. You were right on top of it compared to the rest of us."

Theo sighed, held out a hand. It was absolutely steady. Kara held out her hand, holding it still, and laughed as she rippled those fingers into some kind of nonsense rhyme about *pilot's choice copilot's bad dream.*

Kara lifted her hand toward her face, then made a fist and forced it down to her side.

"Guess they didn't give me a full numb on this thing. Is it awful?"

Theo leaned in closer, shook her head.

"Looks raw, but not drippy or anything. It ought to hurt, I'd say."

"Itches." She chewed her lip, then took a deep, deliberate breath, like she was putting something aside to worry about later.

"You said you were coming to see me?"

"I was," Theo admitted. "I had to get out of the dorm, and I wanted to . . . check custom. You're looking pretty shook, though. Maybe you should lie down."

"No," Kara said definitively. "I should *not* lie down. Come on, let's find someplace where we can hear each other speak."

The language room was vacant. They shut the door and sat on one of the tables, Theo cross-legged, and Kara swinging her feet, like she still had excess energy to burn.

Kara listened, her face far more serious than usual, quite in what Theo thought of now as *Liaden face*: bland and careful. It reminded her of Father's face when he was being particularly himself: almost a mask without a hint of what he was thinking. She'd always thought of it as something personal, belonging only to him; discovering that he shared it, not only with Kara, but with yos'Senchul, and apparently the whole race of Liadens had been . . . strange, at first. Also familiar, and obscurely comforting, was the slight tilt of Kara's head, indicating attention to Theo's concern.

Theo finished in a rush.

"But this gift—is it too much? What do I promise by accepting it?"

Kara moved her shoulders, her gaze focused maybe on her alternating boot tips, maybe on lessons so deep-learned it took effort to pull them out where they could be explained.

"The Code," she said slowly. "The Code lists many occasions upon which the giving of a gift is either appropriate or required. There is another list, matching gift to occasion, so that one neither presumes by too much generosity, nor insults by too little. The occasions: an evening visit, to seal a contract marriage, to end an affair of pleasure—there are, as I say, many such." She paused, and looked to Theo.

"Your Win Ton being a Scout, it is perhaps wrong of us to expect him to hold entirely by Code, especially in matters concerning one who is outside of Liaden custom. He would, being a Scout, wish to deal rightly with you according to your own custom. So I ask—is there a custom of Delgado that might make sense of this gift?"

Theo nodded. "A keepsake; sort of a reminder—like keeping pics of family and favored friends."

"So there is custom." Theo got the feeling that Kara was relieved, though her friend was still in Liaden face. "This letter—does it seem that he assumes *obligation* of you?"

Theo felt her ears heat.

"Obligation—no. He specifically said that it was my choice whether or not to wear the gift. He was also clear that he had an interest in us being together to . . . enjoy each other again—and I'm interested in that, too."

"Your courses align, then. I would say, in that case, that the gift is neither too much nor too little, but well given as a promise of desire and intent. But—" Kara stopped.

Theo considered her. "But?"

Kara sighed. "At the risk of telling you something you already know—remember that we—that Liadens—*belong to* our clans. This means that your Win Ton, Scout though he be, is bound by the order of his delm. Everything—promises, partnerships and plans—must be set aside, should the clan call one to duty. Remember that, about Liadens, Theo. It's just—it might help. Later."

"I—"

A quick rap on the door was immediately followed by the entrance of Pilot yos'Senchul, two-armed still, data carrier in hand.

He bowed to the pair of them, his free hand describing the Liaden bow-sign for *necessity*.

"Pilots, you will forgive the intrusion. Pilot Waitley, I assume you have not been to your room, and thus have not seen my request. I am in need of someone to pilot me to Codrescu, leaving yesterday, if not sooner. Your class schedule being clear for forty-three hours, I wonder if you might do the honors?"

TWENTY-FIVE

· ·

Codrescu Station
Eylot Nearspace

THEY GOT TO ORBIT IN A SPRIGHTLY FASHION, *CHERPA*'S SPOT ON a hotpad meaning Theo slotted the ship into a launch window quickly, even if that window wasn't optimum from a fuel viewpoint.

yos'Senchul gave her initial lift plan a vague glance, praising it as textbook perfect. Then he'd gone on:

"This is not an exercise for finding fuel efficient launches, Pilot. Consider your necessity as a PIC to be conserving time, rather than energy. Once lifted, please find us the fastest way to docking. Consider me your client and your payload for an express delivery."

Pilot Waitley had followed those instructions implicitly, allowing the routing to include what was, as she considered it, an expensive burn from what would have been a higher elliptical orbit to arrive at the proper orbit more quickly.

Cherpa's boards felt more familiar than the shuttle's had last time she'd flown it—all the sim time she'd put in recently meant she expected a ship scan to include more than nearby space; expected it to have warning for Jump, expected what was in front of her. What she hadn't *quite* expected was how much of her scan was blocked by Eylot's presence, nor the sudden change in comm traffic when their destination rose above the horizon.

Theo spent some small time studying the scans to see if she could figure which ships were actually going somewhere in system and which were transiting to Jump points. *Cherpa*'s navsystem was immensely helpful in this; she could, with the touch of a button, plot a dozen ships likely outbound and a few more than that likely inbound from Jump. As she watched the scan fill in, a ship seemed to fuzz into existence outside local space but—according to the scan grid—well inside regular Jump space. Experimentally she ran the scan back—yes. There was the place where the new ship wasn't—and, suddenly, without glare, flare, or warning, there it was.

"Second," she said to yos'Senchul, "is there a reason the ship that just showed up without Jump glare isn't tagged with a name or ID number?"

"Pilot, I will explore this. It does happen, from time to time, that what appears on screen is a 'ghost ship.'"

She glanced from her screen to him quizzically,

The instructor gave her a wry grin. "It is a bad name, I admit. I believe this term was coined by a Terran, many Standards ago."

He adjusted something on his board, frowned momentarily.

"The Liaden phrase is *ekly'teriva*, which would translate as *the ship unseen*, perhaps, or *shadow ship*. Still, there are times—the math is intricate well beyond simple piloting equations, as I understand it. Basically, there are conditions that may occur in Jump that can cast an image of a ship ahead or behind itself; though it is very rare."

Theo sighed, considering her threaded webwork, and wondering if that might enable her to conceivably get a handle on...

"Another, more likely, possibility is that there is a scan error, Pilot. A misplaced bit or byte in the computer memory, a flaw in the scan head, a tracking overlay retained. I have created an incident report and am scheduling the scanner for maintenance on our return."

Theo looked at the screen with the numerous objects and projected courses...

"That one has no course? The ghost ship?" Her hands said *explain explain*.

"As I say, scanner error, Pilot. The object in question seems to have the same proper motion *Cherpa* enjoys. For this to be true of a ship just out of Jump would be...extremely unlikely."

"Tag it," she said finally, "it annoys me."

"Local scan will not show it," yos'Senchul told her the obvious, politely.

"Good. Tag it *Shadow Ship*, then go to local scan."

"Pilot," the instructor acknowledged.

Eylot nearspace zoomed in, Codrescu grew larger, and the shadow ship dutifully dropped out of scan so she could concentrate on the mission to hand.

The place that was Codrescu wasn't pretty, and the approach wasn't neat and tidy, like bringing the shuttle into one of the three shuttle-only bays at the so-called "big orbit" a full planetary diameter higher.

While the basics of matching orbits were the same, the fact was that this was crowded space: ships and satellites, work crews, stockpiled supplies netted with warn-aways, and then more of the same, all of it in vague joint revolution around Eylot with the amalgamation that was Codrescu Station proper. Theo was glad of something concrete to do, and something to think about other than the security walk-around, the silly politics . . . and too, the pilot's card she'd have soon enough along with her degree, if the stupid planet didn't close the academy down first.

"Bringo wants to know who is that First Board on *Cherpa*?"

From the corner of her eye Theo saw finger flicks from yos'Senchul; glanced aside to see the confirming *not required, chatter* and tucked her *affirm, yes* into a reaching touch for the close-up of the red-and-blue-lighted swarm that was someone's unpressurized warehouse in orbit. That close-up brought with it fine detail of the thing's local motions: as long as Theo moved the ship along smartly there'd be no problem from that quarter. In a moment or two she'd killed off more of the overspeed and was on a slow drift toward a pattern of green and white lights, with flashing red at the corners. That would be *Cherpa*'s immediate goal.

It didn't matter that she hadn't answered Bringo; in a moment a cascade of replies came at mixed volumes:

"Says here T. Waitley, Provisional Two, out of Anlingdin . . ." That voice, strong, professional, and likely male, from somewhere close; and "Thet'd be a tray-nee fline a awful cutesey line inter Berty Saixteen . . ." which was a lot weaker signal and harder to decipher—both probable gender and probable meaning—and then a "Welcome to Eylot's back pocket, Pilot. If you've lost sumpon it's prolly here and if you hain't lost anythin you darndy well will."

Over it all, crisp, clear, and unconcerned, came Station Ops:

"*Cherpa*, your alignment is good and you've got the choice of manual or automatic clip-on. You're in Berth Sixteen space, we confirm. I suggest manual if you need points or automatic if you're getting hungry. Slot billing has started."

"Thank you on the confirm. I'm on manual in twenty-two ticks."

Cherpa was small and quick to answer the board, but Theo felt like the controls were a bit slow here in close orbit. The feeling grew as the clock ticked down and she made her approach to Berth Sixteen.

"No clip, Pilot," said her second; and she sighed. They'd jostled the bumpers ever so slightly and rather than trying to force things she backed away to try again.

"Thet-away, pert close, pert close," came the chatter and Theo wagged fingers in the direction of volume, heard yos'Senchul's "Yes, Pilot, confirm volume down," as she located her ship within the beacon field and, after a count to ten, tried again.

This time was worse rather than better, worse in that she could see even before the final moment of closing that the alignment was off, high.

"Does the station *bounce*?"

She looked directly at her second, whose hands were poised over, but not on, the board.

"Very good question," he said carefully. He scanned his instruments, observed her hands well away from the controls and sat back, flexing his new hand. The new hand was why she was Pilot In Command: yos'Senchul had been called to travel while the nerve meld was yet healing, and while his strength and base control were good, he lacked yet the hundred hours of adjustment and training that must be certified for flight.

"It seems to depend on the time of the day as well as location in orbit. Bounce, wiggle, vibrate, shake, shimmy, what you will call it, there is sometimes but not always motion on these loading arms. The locals attribute the problem to ghosts, to not having had enough to drink, or to the result of buying local goods for construction."

"Pharsts!" she muttered, then bit her lip, remembering company, then forgetting it again as she thought about the problem.

Finally, she sighed, motioned her copilot back to the board, promising *good insert next*. She stretched briefly, and looked back to her own board.

Theo brought the front screen into close-up mode and ratcheted the controls down to their finest levels, permitting the thrust gauge to fluster itself as she moved *Cherpa* very gently forward, eyes on her readouts.

Yes! There it was: sensors reacting to velocity—and *there*, the radar showing odd pauses as something, somewhere, flexed a minute amount ahead of them.

The ship's distance was perhaps a hand's breadth and closing, a finger width and closing...

Theo reached a hand out to the board and held it there as she watched tight-lipped. The vaguest tingle touched the tip of her finger and she gently tapped a single side jet.

Lights flashed and changed color. Local comm flickered to life, displaying offers for dockside air and power, and...

"We lock now," she announced triumphantly.

With that she palm-slapped the proper control, watching another set of lights, feeling the light *chunk* through the hand on the board.

"*Cherpa*, we have solid connects all around. Station billing has started. Welcome to Codrescu."

Low in the background someone was cackling, "Bringo, you gottsa pay attention. Owe my lungs a week's air you do! Right there in the records, Waitley, T. done her shuttles twicet and more, and aside that, she sat second on *Torvin* a couple orbits."

"You and your lists, like you the only one with a database! Anyhow, don't you owe me a week still, anyhow? I got that wrote down somewhere..."

Theo looked to yos'Senchul, who gave a wry grin.

"Everything that is not emergency is entertainment for a yard pilot, Pilot. Everything."

yos'Senchul was off to conclude his business, whatever it was. Theo sat with eyes half-closed, having counted hours and duties. She could add those to her skill count immediately, which made her very happy...and she thought back over the last few hours, getting them firm in her memory.

When yos'Senchul had offered her the chance to pilot for him, she'd assumed the Star King until he said Codrescu.

"Shall we meet at the field after you change," he'd asked, "and get your cards and—"

Theo shook her head, "I'm fine now, as long as we're not going to fancy dinner or something."

He laughed, "But you have with you—"

"Father didn't tell me a lot about piloting, but he did say that a pilot should always be able to lift immediately."

She patted the pockets of her vest and slacks, "My cards, up to date, here. I have a couple ration bars, I have the emergency transceiver under the lining of the vest, the nearspace chart in flimsy and the updated stick, with the comm freqs for the system, too, the..."

"Ah. Then your father was a courier pilot. It can be good to follow a clan's..."

She'd flushed.

"I don't know," she admitted.

yos'Senchul had hesitated, as if he'd felt her discomfort, and bowed, gently, maybe meaning to soothe her.

"As the pilot is well prepared, we shall leave on the instant. There will be some introduction to the craft, of course."

The introduction to the craft had been scary in its sketchiness once they got past the security check. They did a manual walk-around first, with yos'Senchul clearly taking it seriously, down to inspecting the still-connected power and comm loops as well as the tie-downs.

Once on board he was as thorough, directing her to follow his lead. Not only did he review the ship's own records and images, which Theo thought was careful enough, but he downloaded the field's view of the ship back to his last exit, certifying that he'd been the last person on board. In all of this he was as businesslike as always, yet less calming than Theo usually found him. He seemed infused with a strange energy, as if he'd been playing bowli ball.

But of the *Cherpa*, the basics: how to recognize engine failure and abort limits, clarity on the locations of emergency equipment, a reminder of which air controllers she'd need to speak to, then systems check to launch-readiness once, with her call in as Pilot-in-Command, and systems check and security scan again as they lifted.

Theo had been busy enough for the lift and the first overboost; it was not until they'd passed into the "wings don't work here" of the mesosphere that yos'Senchul relaxed. Theo was certain that she'd made him nervous, that she'd missed some important procedure, but when he spoke to her it was as if to a comrade.

"Pilot," he said, "it always cheers me to have more of the atmosphere below me than above; and cheers me more to orbit. I'm told I share this weakness with other pilots, but truth told, some pilots are not like you and I, but are always looking down instead of up or out."

Theo'd been looking down right then, needing to confirm leaving controlled airspace behind, but she'd happily flashed an *all agree all agree* at him. A few moments later the ship began its slow throttle down, to the comfortable moment when it stopped as orbit was attained.

"This is good," Theo said then. "So far this is my favorite spot in a flight. The spot where weightless is normal."

She checked the boards one more time, recalled herself, and announced, "For the log, we are orbited and crew movement is now unrestricted."

She'd thought that was when the "hard work" of the trip would be over until landing, but yos'Senchul's elegant bow—he stood to deliver it!—and careful demeanor immediately chipped away at that feeling.

"It struck me, Pilot, that perhaps I have overstepped somehow, and that perhaps I will again. Forgive me, if you will, if my mention of your father was off-*melant'i* on Delgado; I had forgotten that the line of trace there was through Mother lines and not through clan. Yet your father, who did not teach you of hand-talk, nor of Liaden, but did teach of tea and gave excellent advice, did he not speak to you of other Liaden things, or of the news of clan that surely..."

Theo shook her head, suddenly missing Father immensely.

"He's never mentioned his clan. He helped me with the math, and convinced Kamele that Anlingdin was likely safe enough. He told me to keep the bowli ball hidden from civilians, to carry what I really needed on me at all times, and to always know where the back door is."

There was a moment of silence and a slow movement of the new hand.

"I see. The advice is good advice, I assure you."

He sat again, suddenly flipping his new hand through a series of hand-signs as if testing it as he watched. *Caution Warning Alert Caution Warning Alert Caution Warning Alert Danger.*

"In which case, not attached to clan as an offspring of Liad, and having given over the lifeworks of your mothers, there is information you will find useful and necessary, and which I, as a member of the Pilots Guild should share with you."

He looked at her seriously.

"This 'safe enough' you mentioned...it is not what I would call Eylot at the moment, though all at Anlingdin are not actively hostile. The display this day, a display of contempt, to bring such a device directly to the DCCT...ah...an attempt to produce random disruption among those most comfortable with...looking up and out. Not a welcome event, however well disguised as a mere prank."

"They were trying to hurt Kara? Or after Yberna?"

The instructor raised his hands. "Without a proper Healer to interpret, who can say? I think there was no single target, Pilot, but the group: who can know when which pilot will take up a bowli ball, eh?"

Theo nodded, but her hands were talking, suddenly echoing *alert query, warning query, caution query, danger query.*

"Yes," he allowed. "All of that. I can say, Pilot, that Eylot is becoming..." He paused, finger-talk describing the motion *unstable*, "Let us say *disbalanced*. Not physically, you understand," having seen her rapid glance at the board, "but the politics. Those of the Clans do not expand as rapidly, or as radically, as do some of the elements which desire to celebrate other genes.

"There are small efforts under way to do things which have heretofore been unnecessary. In some areas citizens wish to declare certain languages superior, in others to enact laws regarding access to schooling. And, given the rule of voting here, there are areas where the majority of the residents who may vote are of Terran extraction, and they are being given more opportunity to take advantage."

He looked at her carefully.

"You will note that in the past there may have been efforts by certain members of let us say, 'the other camp' to arrange things for their own benefit. It is what groups do. But, the focus of late has been on commerce, and on controlling commerce. And to control commerce..."

"...you try to control pilots and ships," Theo finished the sentence, recalling the flaming debris of a small jet falling down a mountainside. "Will they stop—the guys with the bowli ball? I mean they're in such trouble!"

The instructor exhaled slowly.

"Yes, those two will likely stop. If the academy isn't able to remove them, surely their keepers will assure that they lie quiet, for a while. The major goal is to take control of pilots on planet, to require planetary registrations, to, in fact, require that all student slots at the academy go first to citizens of Eylot, and then to 'approved' groups."

Theo stared, considering Wilsmyth and his connections, and—

"This will take some time to happen, if it does happen. There will need to be votes, there will need to be legislation . . ." yos'Senchul paused as Theo took in the board for a moment. When she turned back, he signed, two-handed and elegant: *objects moving keep moving.*

"But it will happen, you're sure?" Theo leaned into the control chair, considering her own future.

"Soon. Soon enough that I have agreed to have the nerve implants made so that I will, if needed, be able to work as a yard pilot or such; since among the suggestions made is that Anlingdin should, of course, be staffed first with the best the planet itself can offer, and only then . . ."

Theo caught her breath.

"They'd rip the school apart!"

True course, he signed, attempting a simultaneous Terran shrug.

"The timetable is not perfect, and indeed, there are those who say the effort will fall short for years, and never succeed."

He was silent for a moment, and went on.

"I have told you before not to trust Liadens simply because they are Liadens. The same is true of those in DCCT, and those of Terra, and . . . in all cases, a pilot must—as your father suggested to you—have a contingency plan. I suggest, as an instructor who wishes to see an exceptional student prosper, and as a pilot who has an interest in knowing that there are worthy pilots in the skies, that you join the Pilots Guild. You have achieved third class, and there is a truth that time-as-member comes into play if time-in-grade is similar. Guild supports Guild, as best can."

The ship chirped, indicating the orbital approach was nearing.

"Pilot to pilot I say: have your contingency plan in place. Do not dawdle documenting any skill you may rightly claim."

Cherpa had really needed herding, then, and Theo had returned to the task at hand.

TWENTY-SIX

. . . .

Codrescu Station
Eylot Nearspace

THE SO-CALLED FRONT HALL OF CODRESCU CENTER WAS ABOUT THE size of the few back halls Theo'd seen on the *Vashtara* and the back halls were wonders to behold, with crew signs in Terran, Trade, Liaden, and at least one she was unsure of as well as handholds and rungs on all the walls. There was gravity, but it was very light and somewhat spotty, with some quirkiness, perhaps because the halls actually had humps and ridges as well as numerous access ports. In fact, as she thought about it, she realized that the hall, or the deck, or the whole of the establishment, was subject to exactly the kind of tiny twitches the docking ring exhibited.

What she'd not expected were the sounds. Codrescu was smaller than Delgado Station, and the ports she'd been in traveling on *Vashtara*, but the sounds were more frequent, and less differentiated. From class and from her travels she could tell the warning sounds of ship counts, and it sounded like there were three different counts within hearing, and then the *beep-beep-beep* of a door-lock warning echoed from somewhere and she passed several busy people with voices seemingly speaking numbers to thin air and getting replies from their shoulders.

She, at least, carried no live radio, and the background speaker news for ship folks that "*Thurstan*, green, thirty-seven, five green go. *Blueboy*, fifteen five five five, hold. *Drosselmare*, line seven forty-four, clear thirty-two, straight count," meant little to her other than connectors were connected, arrivals and departures were happening and would happen...but then this wasn't her community.

There were access ports on the walls, too, some raised, and airlocks in what seemed to be the oddest places. There were *lots* of doors, some numbered, some lettered, some anonymous, some color-coded, and even guards—live people—on duty outside some of them, which was surprising, on a space station, where people were surely expensive.

One bright blue door—no numbers, and the only one of that color she'd seen—had two guards flanking it, one with her hand on a holstered weapon. Of course, that was the door Theo needed to go through to pick up the Pilots Guild application in person.

yos'Senchul had been clear on this: she was to go herself, with all her ID, just to pick up the application.

"Given the mood on Eylot, applications are traveling by trusted hand and are kept in trusted hands, Pilot; you may carry with you my letter of reference, which is already on file, since I have this day proposed you for membership, also in person."

"Does this mean that untrustworthy people have been applying for Guild membership?"

He'd paused, looking down as if examining his new hand. She realized that he may well have *been* examining his hand—it *was* new, after all.

"It means, Pilot," he said slowly, "that the usual rules apply. We spoke of this earlier: don't trust anyone just because they appear to belong to a particular group. Have a contingency plan. Know as many back ways as you can to your ship and to another ship you can call on if there is need. Don't tell anyone about all of your weapons, nor all of your plans. I might go on at length, but they expect you at the Guild office shortly.

"You will want this token; have it in hand at the door, this glowing side up or forward." yos'Senchul pulled something from inside his jacket.

This "token" was a stubby rod with a handgrip, barely longer than her palm, looking for all the world like the top of a hand-stick for an aircraft; yos'Senchul tapped it several times on the instrument panel and handed it to her hilt first.

She took it, and weighed it, finding it heavier than she'd expected. She might be able to use it to clunk someone on the head with if she needed to—and wasn't that an antisocial thought! It immediately felt molded to her hand, with the supposed top glowing a dim green.

"Here's a map; as I say, they're expecting you, and the token."

He began to bow—stopping as Theo danced a kink out of her shoulder, and abruptly asked:

"How do I know the people there are who you say they are? Can I carry a key to the *Cherpa* with me? Will the *Cherpa* be here when I leave the office? Will they check me for weapons?"

He smiled, bowed fully this time, and held a key set out to her.

"Please, check that the hatch answers this key on the way out. I expect you will not be overlong, and as your copilot I will do everything in my power to have the *Cherpa* here and operable when you return. If it is not, I suggest that you yell for Bringo, who is boss of yard dogs this quarter moon. As to your other questions, the place I send you to is the most secure on Codrescu as far as I know. If they'll do a weapons check depends on how they view the threat level, both of yourself and of the universe."

The air pressure on Codrescu was space normal, which meant low but with a little more oxygen than she was used to on Eylot. The extra oxygen was a good thing, Theo thought, since her walk, even with the map, was more stressful than she had expected, especially when she'd turned the last corner and found the guards, one looking eager for an excuse to use her sparker.

Theo'd been using the token as if it *was* a piloting stick, holding it in front of her and *zoommming* down straights, banking into turns. She hadn't realized that the Guild office was *quite* so close to that last kink in the corridor.

The guard with the gun glanced at Theo's hands even before Theo could recover a properly serious aspect; and with that glance removed her hand from the weapon and nodded, perhaps toward the token, which now was clearly emitting a green glow.

"Pilot, first time in?"

"Yes, Pilot," Theo replied serenely as she glided to a stop in front of the door, "my first time to the Guild. I'm told I am expected; I'm Theo Waitley."

＊　　＊　　＊

The guy at the front desk, like the guards outside, was a pilot. She hadn't noticed him at first, since she was overwhelmed by the sheer and unexpected luxuriousness of the room. It wasn't a big room, but the walls were paneled in what appeared to be wild-grown wood, and part of the floor was covered with carpets that made her own fine rug at home look shabby. There was artwork on the wall—like the wood, things that looked like they were real—*intentional* art and not simply office art meant to soothe or set a mood.

One wall display might be showing text of the messages she'd been hearing by speaker, but this place was quiet, overgrown and—a nice change from the stark halls.

The part of the floor that wasn't carpeted was covered in green plants, some showing flowers, some not. The room was filled with scents she associated with being outside, and something smelled like grass or bushes she might find at Leafydale Place. A small, carefully encased rock-lined waterfall with a tiny open pool with its own arm-thick mini-tree occupied that end of the room, and oh! A norbear!

The norbear was sitting quietly on a mat of vegetation beside the pool, gently chewing a long green plant with a bulb at the end. She looked shyly up at Theo and made a sort of chuckling noise, her thick brown-and-orange fur almost matching the rocks of the waterfall.

"Hello," Theo told the norbear, and the guy at the desk said, "Hello, Pilot, how may we assist you?"

She laughed, hand-flashing *see you Pilot,* and then said, "Excuse me, I—oh there's someone else! But I'm Theo Waitley. Here to apply . . ."

Tucked behind the tree in a very hard-to-see nest was a nearly colorless norbear, with wizened visage and slitted sleepy eyes. The color of her eyebrows—there was a touch of rust there, and the skin of her face showed clearly through the facial fur, as if the creature was so old she was—like Veradantha!

The old one stretched, slowly and thoroughly, as if she needed to recall exactly how it was done. Theo heard a low sound, more of a rasp than a burble, and the old norbear stood. She was skinny almost to the point of emaciation. Theo saw that this was no "hothouse norbear" as Win Ton had called the silky creatures on *Vashtara,* but someone who was looking at her as much as she was looking at her.

"Hevelin!" said the pilot behind the counter. "Hardly anybody sees him in there, and he hardly ever says anything. The hungry one's Podesta, Hevelin's great-granddaughter." He grinned and gave Theo a nod. "Please, sit where you will, and be comfortable."

"Here?" she asked, impulsively pointing to the matted plant beside the burbling water.

He shrugged, finger-spoke *seat is seat,* then laughed.

"But first I need your token and your cards, if you're here to apply. In fact, we ought to have enough time to finish the application right now, if you like. Give me those, please, else if the old guy gets to talking to you, you may fall asleep waiting for his next sentence!"

Theo rapidly discovered that the "old guy" did have a lot to say, or maybe a lot of questions to ask. Unlike the *Vashtara* norbears, who were smaller and much less seemly, Hevelin was dignified in his movements, and grasped rather than grabbed as he adjusted himself on Theo's lap. The resonance in her head was calm and thoughtful, more like Father's cat, Mandrin, than young Coyster, and sincerely inquisitive, as if everything was not only interesting, but *meant something.*

Puzzlement reached her; and she found herself closely recalling the norbears she'd met and seen; especially Threesome, the white and spotted one from *Vashtara* who apparently never went alone to a visitor, but always shared. There was something more going on that she couldn't identify, as if she was seeing older, larger norbears than she'd seen before, like Hevelin was asking her for a catalog of friends they might both have met—except coming up disappointed that she'd never met anyone he'd known....

But there was another catalog going on; even as her records were going to and fro in electronic pathways and being compared and cross-indexed by the Guild, Hevelin was seeking other acquaintances. She thought of yos'Senchul lecturing her, and felt as if there were an assent, and of Kara, who was not known as a game player but appreciated, and Win Ton, quite warmly, who was not known but gave off echoes of joy and something else, and then, since she was thinking Liadens at him, she thought of Father, carrying his cane and—

The norbear grabbed her hand and held it, and when she looked into those eyes she saw not Father, but a man who might have been Father, as if seen in a haze. Father with no sign of greying, spirited black hair in a tail falling over one shoulder. Father with a glow around him, and another face—female—sharing his space, peering down with amused green eyes, and more faces in the background. There was question in that, and she agreed that yes, Father may have been that person, there, moving lightly as a young pilot. The woman—she wasn't sure, not knowing all of Father's friends, after all.

There was more then: lots more norbears, and something that might have been a cat as seen through norbear understanding. More human faces—none familiar to her, and the sense of eager inquisitiveness fading into a ripple of raspy burbles...

"Pilot Waitley?"

The desk-pilot had already called her a couple times, the first to ask for a date check, the next to verify next of kin, Terran-style, not Delgado-style, and then in the midst of her dreamy listening to the norbear, to ask if she had plans for dinner. She'd managed to wake up enough to decline that, pointing out that she was on assignment, and got a slow finger-flash of *work, work, work* and a *see you next trip* alongside of, "I know the best bars and restaurants on Codrescu, Pilot. Just ask for Arndy Slayn."

She hadn't promised, but she hadn't outright rejected him, either, remembering that it was good for pilots to know people.

"Pilot Waitley, I think we're set."

The desk-pilot motioned her to come forward.

"The token gave us the palm print and fingerprints and some backup on the other ID readings, and of course we have yos'Senchul's vouchers and letters along with several other letters of support that have drifted in over the last few months waiting your application. Since you brought the token direct, and Hevelin passes you, I can give you your base Guild card, assuming you'll okay your dues payments."

Dues payments meant signatures and more ID verification, and after she managed to free her lap from Hevelin she had to extricate herself from the sudden attention of Podesta, who wanted to cling to her leg as she looked over the forms and explanations and signed away three percent of her base pay for the rest of her life.

With the signature came a card; an imbedded chip identifying her as a Guild member in good standing, certifying her record to date, and a code that he assured her was to a mailbox here on station—one good as long as she was a member, and any Guild office could forward to it or retrieve from it—and a key that would let her check available berths in almost any port in the known universe. Just showing her card ought to get her into the Guild Hall proper, which on Codrescu was down the other arm, since the Guild had some bunkrooms and a rec space there. There was also a slip guaranteeing her bail if she—

Theo laughed. "Guaranteeing my bail? Am I dangerous?"

He smiled. "Compared to most dirt-siders, you're dangerous. All pilots are. Not only that, you'll be a target sometimes, because some places think prices are high because pilots make so much money."

He laughed—he had a good laugh, Theo thought. "I've been a Guild member for seven years and they've never had to throw my bail. But knowing they will, that's good. Knowing they'll garnish my wages and come after me if I *skip* bail, that helps me stay honest."

He gave her a grin and a nod.

"You're good to go! Good lift!"

"Safe landing!"

She bent to unwrap Podesta again, bowed solemnly to Hevelin, who sat in his nest, watching her alertly, waved once more to Arndy Slayn, and left, a Guild member in good standing.

Among the info she had collected with her card was a complete map of Codrescu, which was both bigger and more complex than she'd realized. Arndy Slayn had pointed out several places as having decent launch food—that meant they specialized in not serving stimulants and sedatives along with their meals—in case she wanted to take something back to her ship.

A quick study of the map showed her a more straightforward route back to Berth Sixteen, and soon she was walking past shops displaying prices almost as bad as they were on *Vashtara*, and a couple of noisy bars. A small shop had maize buttons on offer, and she *had* to grab a dozen of those. Nibbling, she walked on, passing another noisy place, this one featuring music and dancing and other frivolities.

Behind the racket was the constant station talk, now letting her know that "*Thurstan*, eight clear clear green, *Drosselmare* four, clear clear yellow..." and more stuff she didn't need to know.

Cherpa's berth was down this way, the map illustrating a series of T-intersections as well as the semicircular way she'd gone to the office. There were north-south T's and east-west T's, each T offering berths at the ends of the T-arm. *Cherpa* was on the second east-west.

She sealed the rest of the maize buttons into their bag and turned into the first T-section, walking more briskly now, but still feeling mellow, which was probably Hevelin's influence.

From behind came the clattering of several people in a hurry. Theo glanced over her shoulder, seeing two uniformed men carrying gear and food. A two-minute gong sounded, and underneath it all she heard one man scolding the other:

"No girls for a billion miles where we're going and you gotta freak off the only one that even looked at us. We gonna be... look!"

"*Drosselmare*, two, clear clear yellow. *Thurstan*, six, clear clear clear."

The maize buttons felt heavy in her hands, and her back itched. Theo began moving a little faster, but they were hurrying for a ship and she really ought to give them right of way...

"Gazo, you think? We're away in a minute!" The sound of their footsteps increased.

"Hey, lady, you, girl! You need a new ride? Best thing that ever happened to you, a ship of eight—we'll make you a queen, we will..."

Theo glanced behind.

They were only a few steps away now, running, but not as steady as they might be. The second warning tick went off up one of the T-arms. The guy who might've been Gazo said, "Now!" and dropped his gear.

Theo swung to the side, her back against the wall. "You have right of way," she said, tensing, hoping the camera—but the other guy had his jacket over the camera, and—

The guy who'd dropped his gear was on her, now, arms wide, like he was going to get her in a hug, and it was already too late—she threw the maize buttons into his face and twitched to one side.

"Beecha da plaza!" he yelled, grabbing for her again, but even here in the low grav she felt the move coming, saw his fist as if it was some poorly thrown bowli ball, grabbed and threw him against the wall, danced the second motion, spinning, got a foot up in time to catch his arm there and—

Crack!

Somewhere, a gong chimed, and someone was yelling, "Gazo, you're dead if you don't make the tick!"

Gazo wailed, and went running; there was a bosun at the end of the T, waving at them as the next tick went off and...

The second man had a gun. Theo swung, faster than she expected in the lighter gravity, and slammed it out of his hand. He shouted; Theo grabbed his shoulders and threw him with all her might down the T-arm; her momentum taking her to the weapon. Instinct honed by dozens of bowli ball games scooped the thing up, and—

"Ferkistsake, don't shoot! We're gone!"

And they *were* gone, their backs disappearing into a hastily sealed airlock, the warning gong signaling closed and locked. Vibration ran down the hall and an odd *clang* sounded as the ship let go grapples, and then more noise nearby...

There was a noise behind her. She spun—

Arndy Slayn held up one hand, the other holding the twin of yos'Senchul's data case. He grinned.

"You are dangerous," he said approvingly. "And you really needed a gun."

TWENTY-SEVEN

. . . .

Codrescu Station
Eylot Nearspace

"BRINE BATZER."

Theo's hands moved on their own *say again repeat*.

Arndy Slayn laughed.

"It is an Eylot-sounding name, isn't it? Brine Batzer; I can't say this behind the desk, but he's one of the most active of the cheap pod-breaking ship agents. It's a wonder that he'd move two whole pods at the same time, but I guess he got lucky. Anyway, that's who you'd have to start with if you wanted to pursue something against *Drosslemare* as a ship—well, look at that!"

Theo was not as buzzed up as she thought she'd be nor feeling any need to explain herself. The pilots were treating this as a serious but manageable event; so could she.

Since Slayn was witness, he sat at ease on a chair half camouflaged by the norbear's greenery, using a mobile set, while Guild Master Peltzer stood unmoving with hand on ear, listening to news from Codrescu's control rooms.

When he did move, his fingers ordered, *back here, both*, while out loud he said, "Mister Slayn, please be careful. Batzer and Peltzer, Flatzer, Mertzer are all well-known, even historic names on Eylot; please do not dismiss someone because of the name, no matter how local it may be!"

As he spoke he pushed against a section of wall, which slid open to reveal a short hall. There was a snort, and Theo felt a tug at her knee—not a muscle strain or knee injury, but Hevelin, politely tapping, and pressing with his gripping paw.

Peltzer laughed.

"Let him come along if you like; but not Podesta. The yoster still needs to learn manners!"

Theo carried Hevelin, who weighed less than the gun she'd taken from the guy in the corridor, down the short hall, following the Guild Master.

At the end of the hall was a workmanlike office with multiple screens and a three-dimensional projection showing what must be Codrescu nearspace—and the chronometer ticking away said it was in real time.

"Pilot Waitley, since one of your admirers is to hand, we'll add him to the discussion; he already requested attention and he's on his way. What wonder have you discovered, Mister Slayn?"

Slayn stood near a screen, shaking his head.

"Batzer's not listed as agent for *Drosslemare* any longer; looks the termination was effective immediately the last pod-connect was confirmed. Since the incident occurred after that confirmation..."

"Mister Slayn, I suggest you do a statistical analysis of the 'pod-breakers' and see if you don't find a connect/disconnect relationship on many of the ships they handle. Some of them do trade for the family ships, that's true—they don't count for this—but the real meteor-shreds are almost as leery of their agents as their agents are of them."

Theo found herself and Hevelin a seat with a view of the projection, curling into a repurposed lift chair. As soon as she sat, she regretted not being more advertent: Slayn had dragged the recovered bag in with him and sat on one of the broad-cushioned file sections that lined one wall.

Peltzer's perch was just that: a tall stool that looked like it was stolen from a port bar. He sat, turned about, quick eyes checking the real time, hand tapping at the spot on his shoulder that brought him, and him alone, information from somewhere.

"Do you have that analysis?" Peltzer's voice was dulcet, while his fingers said *soon soon quick soon.*

"You're right of course," Slayn admitted. "I hadn't thought it through. Almost all of these contracts are on-delivery or on-event automatics; the funds transfer as things occur and the relationships are short-terms. No one is responsible for a breath longer than they have to be!"

"Codrescu's Council won't move on this: they've seen the records and feel like there's just a matter of drunk-boat behavior. I think that since they pulled a gun it might be more than that, but since they didn't actually gain control of you or maintain control of their weapons, the port's willing, and even eager, to let slide."

Peltzer handed a printout to Theo, who looked it over, seeing large tracts of fine print and not much sense to it.

Theo's so-called admirer, Qaichi Bringo, had joined them and sat beside Slayn on the broad cushions, slowly inventorying the contents of the bag Gazo had dropped with a scan-camera; he looked up at Theo and waved, vaguely shaping what looked like *confused unconfirmable paths*, other hand still shuffling through the bag. He was a greying and tidy man in an old uniform; the sleeve cuffs and collar were shiny with wear and his serviceable shoes were marked with the indents of guide pedals used frequently.

He'd arrived without fanfare, nodded as much at Hevelin as at Theo, after giving her one hard stare, as if storing her in memory, and had gotten right to work. He talked without looking at her.

"Pilots working the close-in stuff, I like to know who they are, Waitley. You was new, and not Guild yet, so I needed to ask, not being rude. I'm Chief Tugwhomper, see—"

"Tugwhomper?"

He smiled. "Local usage, Pilot. I'm overseeing the yard on all but three shift; and since you drew the hardest attach slot we got right now, thought I ought to know how close to run and if I ought to notch up the safety alert. Din't, on account of you was running with a good second and aside that, the Out-Lady had your record and was giving a thumbs-up."

He sorted rapidly, mostly one-handed, the other hand always slightly away from his body like he was used to moving in g lower even than station normal.

"But how can they get away with this?" Theo waved the flimsy, scowling. "I mean, what happens if they try this somewhere else? Can't the Guild act?"

Bringo looked up, a ghost of a smile on his face as he finished a scan and threw something back into the bag. He got serious, his free hand scratching at the side of his ear where his shipcomm would usually perch.

"Because none of them are Pilots Guild members, and none citizens, and none have ever been here before, nor likely to show face again, that's how they can get away with it. Come in with a two-can transfer and they're out. Filed no plans beyond Eylot's Jump, and then they hardly followed line on that, like to make it hard to trace. The pilots are rated, but not Guild. The crew: low port or worse, I'd say."

His sorting hand found something else that made him smile as he sorted, and then he looked hard at Theo. "You really wanna cure 'em, you can: but you'll have to post bond on the cost of rousing a three-ship intercept, and then you'll need a lawyer willing to take your money for the rest of your natural life and then some. Given the situation, you'd end up dealing with Brine Batzer if you did that."

Peltzer harrumphed. "Pilot Waitley may be *required* to deal with Brine Batzer. Drunk-boat or not, there will be an incident report. Batzer was agent of record so the port will be sending him a— let's call it a *note*—on this incident. This isn't the first time one of his contracts has acted up, and Codrescu will have to tell him *Drosselmare* and all her crew are banned, just so he doesn't get to thinking they're a fine and upstanding group of laddies, hey ho. In the meantime, we'll add them to the not-approved cloud for the next infoshare."

Peltzer stopped, peered at the projection, muttered into his shoulder, nodded, and looked up. "Batzer's within his rights to follow up on the actions of his contracted ships until they leave Eylot space, if he gets a warning. He may do that. He may be too busy.

"So, Pilot, since I'm informed you have an assignment which requires your immediate return to Eylot, and since we're not one of us related to you, bound to you, under contract to you, or contracted by you, we three can act as witness, in that Codrescu has approved of your claim to salvage. In the event that something untoward or illegal is here, we will witness that it was salvage and turn it over to the appropriate authorities, if any such exist."

"Salvage?" Theo turned to Slayn, who was now sitting with a gun in his lap, looking like a child with a new toy.

"I told you," he said. "You're dangerous, but you ought to

have a gun, anyway. You get salvage rights on account of being the subject of unruly behavior that is otherwise unresolved." He tapped the gun. "This, for example, appears to be a perfectly serviceable handarm for close work. You'll want to have an armorer do a refurbish for you, as a matter of course. Mark that it's a little more than a dozen years old, the holster could use some work, and you'll want to check your charges before you depend on it."

He snapped it open, showing her that it was unloaded before flipping it toward her. Surprisingly, Hevelin's tiny paw was on it as fast as she snagged it; he looked it over, sniffed it, peered into her face, then comfortably shrugged back into her lap.

She held the gun, absently catching the charges Arndy tossed to her. It was compact, it was, and not cold at all.

Pilot Bringo spread the rest of the bag and contents before her on a side table.

"Not a pilot's kit, but that's the pity. Got some clothes, won't likely fit you good, but can wear well enough. The station's Ref-itya Shop can use them; that bag, too. Got a couple names on it. Somebody just starting ought to not drag other names along and confuse things. Deep space isn't where you want people guessing who you are."

She looked at the remaining items: small metal clips and a personal knife, airtight containers of—

"Is any of this worth anything, really?"

Slayn took over, pointing.

"This seems to be *vya*, a commercial container, unopened. Always a friend of a pilot, for use or trade, this is a modest amount in moderate grade—but still, like the gun, having it will be worth more than sending it to consignment. This," he said, solemnly, unrolling a fancy tooled-leather packet, "is a set of matched firegems."

The three older pilots burst into laughter as one; inside Theo's head, Hevelin's amusement echoed theirs.

"Firegems?"

Arndy manipulated the packet. Light exploded from the gems, like a rainbow running loose. The colors sparkled and—there were seven of them; they seemed not only matched, but identical.

"They're very pretty, but I don't wear jewelry!"

This inspired another round of mirth.

"Pilot, of all the jewels and geegaws in the universe, a pilot should never be seen wearing firegems!"

Arndy Slayn was not laughing as hard as he might, Theo saw; in fact, he was blushing.

"I should apologize, Pilot," he said with a nod. "We *all* forget. Firegems *are* pretty and even attractive, but you could probably buy a double handful of these for the price of the cheapest ale on the station."

He held one out to her and the light played about so much that Hevelin leaned to look at it, too.

"But why the pouch—how did you know before you opened them?"

"Lotta crew members carry these," Bringo broke in, "and some pilots, sorry to say. They're trade, or more like bait, good for back worlds where travelers are news. And so someone in trouble or looking for some, might open a pouch like this and offer a gem in return for favors, or explain that they were going to get rich, soon, and borrow money on the contents. These things, pouches and all, sometimes with certificates of authenticity too, you find them in the cheap shops some spacers visit."

With some effort Theo rolled and sealed the firegems away in their pouch. She was about to throw it into the bag when Peltzer said, "And like *vya*, maybe something that can be carried if you have room and are not sure of your destination. At times a pilot must act for the ship, after all."

Theo looked at Peltzer, heard Hevelin's deep thrum... and tossed it back in the bag.

"Knowing choice is a better choice," Bringo said, nodding toward her. "Some solutions are better to not have in hand."

Slayn reached behind the bag—

"And finally, there are a few odds and ends of coins, and this which I cannot identify. A mechanical thing, a—"

Theo caught the object, and it was as if she felt a buzz in her ear, and a sudden distraction of thought. It felt—*dirty*. Reflexively, she threw it back, and the nasty feeling was gone.

"Don't want it," she said succinctly, and reached for the signing tablet to witness she'd made her choices.

At that Hevelin chuffed for attention, and images of those people he'd shown her earlier—maybe Father and those others— rose before her. There were also brief flashes of the men she'd fought, and even of Brine Batzer, but they faded. Theo ruefully admitted he had a point: the uglies were gone. This pleased her as much as him.

Getting out of Codrescu was easier than getting in. For one thing the clipping out was just that: turn off the connections, release to the acknowledgment that *Cherpa*'s port fees were now finalized, and twitch the merest touch of gyro. The ship spun the hand's breadth required to show clear and responded to the puff of gases released by the closed connections to begin a slow backing away.

yos'Senchul, Theo thought, was brooding. He'd all but hit his head on the deck bowing to her on her return, congratulating her both on her acceptance as a Guild member and her handling of the "unfortunate incident," the while indicating that she should sign in as soon as possible to maximize her ship time.

Theo cycled the scanner to local, overemphasized a touch and ended up with general—

As before, the screen showed incoming as blue and outgoing as green, and another touch brought up orbital elements and projected destination or outbound Jumps—and there in red was the incident report tagged *Shadow Ship*.

"Still here," Theo remarked.

"Yes, Pilot, it is. While the range seems to have changed in the interim, we're still improbably showing identical proper motion. Noted, and logged."

Theo heard an undercurrent in his voice and asked, "You're worried about it?"

His hands waffled, signing *no-and-yes*, balanced.

"Before you graduate, Pilot, we will have the discussion about the other possibilities a shadow ship might represent. Perhaps an Yxtrang surveillance device, or a leftover from the great wars, or a cloak for a smuggler. All of these and more, including a ship crewed by ghosts, which has been a tale of pilots for centuries.

"But now, we return to things more solid than *ekly'teriva*, Pilot. We have no need to make the full orbit from here—call ahead and we shall land in time for breakfast. And you will have time to visit the armorer before your first class."

TWENTY-EIGHT

· ·

Armorer's Forge
Anlingdin Piloting Academy

HER ANTICIPATED TARGET MOVED, SHAKING THE DUMP LID, BUT staying out of sight. She wasn't going to trust a sound shot or try a ricochet; she needed a clear view, and time...

The dark one she'd thought she'd already taken care of moved, standing with a lurch, arm swinging toward her, wild shot singing somewhere else. Without compunction she took him down with a three-shot volley, twisting in time to get off a shot at the other one, aiming at the gun itself in desperation—

A flash of blue filled the alleyway; she jerked back, sighed—and stood down.

"Clear on the range," she said, carefully sliding the gun into the unfamiliar holster. "Clear on the range."

"Thank you, Pilot. Clear on the range." That voice spoke into her left ear.

She removed the light goggles, blinked into the room that was really there instead of the alley and warehouse that weren't. There was the sound of a door unsealing, and a light step.

Tiffy Hasan stood about where Theo's last shot must've missed her target.

The armorer offered her the tablet with her scores on-screen, but she still had sweat in her eyes and she was breathing kind of fast, so she paid it no attention. Her muscles didn't exactly hurt, but her left hand was cramped, and she was pleased to let the tablet rest on her forearm and steady it with the fingers of her right hand.

"Four on one," Hasan said, "and that with a grip you're not comfortable with. We'll fix that; take an impression and get you something custom. Not sure *how* custom—you seem to be able to shoot with either hand, which isn't a bad thing at all. 'Course you don't want to change hands in the middle of things unless you have to. That last shot was a wingdinger, by the way, and a little too tricky for real shooting, 'cept if you're really desperate. You was aiming at the gun, right?"

"It was all I could see, Tiffy. Keep the head down, keep ..."

"Yah, right. Did what you wanted; the comp counted it as a disable three since your shot would have gone through the hand and put something on the gun, too."

Theo realized she was still breathing hard, threw a hand-signed *excuse this* toward the woman, and danced about three breaths' worth of relaxation. Her shoulders and arms crackled with the first moves, but by the end of the sequence she was feeling a lot more sure of her footing.

"So, you don't think you want to be a gunfighter?"

Theo laughed. "Give me a ship to fly. I'll be happy if I never have to pull a gun again."

"Excellent. The ones that scare me are the ones who think doing a sim is enough like the real thing to go out looking for trouble."

"I'd go to merc school if I really wanted to be a fighter."

Tiffy grinned. "I been to merc school. Say no if you get the chance, that's what I say. But then, that's experience for you."

Before Theo could answer, the armorer held her hand out for the gun.

"So, while I was waiting for you to finish cleaning up Trantor's docks, I ran the report on your gun. What's good is that we don't have any links to it; no law enforcement or military looking for it. What's bad is the last owner of record died a dozen years ago. That don't really matter—this is a case of who has it now owns it now, and that's you. The thing is—you listen up, Theo Waitley!—is that this weapon is *not* going to make muster as a day-carry here on Eylot. Most places won't measure the difference, but here, this is a what they call a *service weapon*. See, it's derived from a LaDemeter mini, uses the same basic design, even if there's no doubt that Ianic built it. That design is why you got that shot off at the end of the sim. That design also makes it too much gun for carrying on walkabouts for fun. If you're on duty, going to duty, or coming from duty—on Eylot you can carry it. Else you gotta leave it at home. That's official, and you'll sign a paper saying that."

Tiffy sighed gently.

"Me, I'd carry it. Get yourself an on-call notation somewhere, and that ought to cover, 'cause that's a technical duty level. I hate to travel without something on me. You can't always depend on hitting someone upside the head with your hand." She nodded. "Tell you what, let's make that impression, now. If you trust to leave it, I'll have it ready for this evening."

As it turned out, between "after breakfast" and "this evening" encompassed a long day filled with petty annoyances. She had to get her class schedule filed for next year, and every required course looked to be arranged as inconveniently as possible for people who were actually trying to fill their credit-hours with real work. Both the kids she was tutoring were late for their sessions, and Kon could just as well have stayed in bed and slept it off, for all the headway he made on his board drills. In retrospect, she probably hadn't been as sharp as she should've been, either—the adrenaline taking its balance.

After her last class, she went past the armorer's, though by then she could barely keep her eyes open. Her gun with its new grip was ready. She tried it, and Tiffy pronounced her "good to go."

Back at the dorm, it was her turn to fix the midweek, in-dorm meal she shared with Asu, the last vestige of their first year together. She laid down, figuring to take a short nap, and woke up, refreshed, and behind time for starting the meal.

Annoyed, she rushed the batch of maize buttons, and almost burned them while she was getting the rest of the meal together. A taste test showed they were a touch on the dry side so she made up a nice moist icing, using the last of her prized beth-berry jam, at which point Asu swung in, only a little late, ate a third of the icing before it could get on the maize buttons, and rushed off to her personal comm unit, leaving behind a cryptic, "Theo, you've got to be seen in public to stop all these rumors!"

"Dinner's almost ready!" Theo called at the blank faux wood;

whatever Asu was saying, which went on for some time, was muffled beyond recognition. Maybe she was on voice comm.

Now on task, Theo set the table, brewed tea for herself and Asu's special blend of coffee for her.

Asu reappeared, dressed to go partying. Theo stepped between her and the maize buttons, coffee in hand.

"Sit. I serve. You talk about rumors. Clear?"

Asu took the proffered cup, sipped, and sat as Theo brought the meal to the table.

"You know there's been some disquiet among the local Terran population; they have some grievances that they feel aren't being addressed, and they're starting to take action. I tried to introduce you, remember, and bring you along to some of their events, so you could meet people and they could get used to you, see that you weren't a threat?"

Theo sipped. Since they'd moved out of Erkes, it was true that Asu was always trying to drag her off to parties where she promised Theo would meet "interesting people," but—

"You're always *too busy*. And now look! Things are going to happen—everybody says so. Even some of the instructors are dropping hints that the school's changing direction, soon—and your name keeps coming up when students talk. The local kids think I'm local since I'm not into DCCT. They want to know why I'm still rooming with you when I had a chance to change things when we moved out and got the double together."

"But," Theo began as her hands said *stay course, Pilot,* "there wasn't any reason to change, I mean..."

"See, even there! Theo, you want to go to hand-talk all the time. You double-talk, hands and words at the same time. You started off bad in math and now you're doing special labs and *teaching* special labs. You get extra flight time—look at yos'Senchul having you haul him up to the little port! So what happens is that with all the political things and the social stuff where you aren't hanging around with your class, but always bucking for more work and more time and..." Asu shook her hands—not finger-talk, but simple frustration.

"I don't think you're deliberately trying to upstage the locals, Theo. I think you're just plain *not paying attention to life and to society*. It shows up all the time. You miss parties because you have work to do. You don't socialize nearly as much as most of us. You miss DCCT stuff, too, I guess, because your Kara is half the time calling here to see if I can roust you from your studies."

Theo took a deep breath, and put her teacup on the table.

"Asu, I'm not here to party. I'm here to be a pilot. And the DCCT people, some of them come from ships, or they've lived their life in trade families. Look at *you*; you have a tradeship named after you!"

Asu sat back, blushing.

"I didn't know you knew."

Theo suppressed the hand gesture *read the ship lists* and said with exasperation, "Why wouldn't I know? I've been reading job postings the last two semesters, for practice. You're going to have a spot to go to when you get out. But my family doesn't have ten tradeships to rub together in one port, and I can't make a living scraping my way up the teaching wall. As a pilot, I am what I am. I can do the math or I can't. I can handle the docking or I can't. When I get out of here, I'm going to be the best pilot I can be!

"This other stuff, the rumors here—I'm only going to worry about them if they get in my way. I don't have the energy for this superiority game. If the locals want to be better than I am, or better than DCCT, then all they have to do is the work!"

Asu squinched her eyes together, hard. When she opened them they looked watery.

"Theo, I'm in a spot. I keep telling people you're really not a bad person. *I tell them that.* I tell them that you're just really busy. *I tell them that.* What am I going to tell them now—that all the rumors about my roomie being a spy and a provocateur are wrong? *I tried telling them that.*"

Asu thunked her cup down hard.

"And they say that nobody's as good as you are. That you have to have help—outworld help. They say that you're part of a Liaden plot to take over Eylot and take over the rights of the local Terrans. And that—is crack-brained, frankly. I mean, if you're too busy to go to a class tea, when would you find the time to be an agent provocateur?" Asu shook her head. "They don't know that, though. They don't know *you*, and that's what makes it easy to set you up as a target."

Theo stared. "Asu—"

"I think you need to talk to the health people about your stress levels. I really do. And if you won't, you'll be looking for a new roomie for next year, because I have to live here too, and I am not superior to everyone else, and I do not live only for space, and I won't be lumped in with somebody that everybody else thinks is a threat."

Theo pushed her empty cup away.

Theo let her hands say *always have a backup plan.* "I see," she said quietly. "Thank you. I'll put in for space at DCCT next year."

TWENTY-NINE

. . . .

Anlingdin Piloting Academy
Eylot

ASU WAS GONE.

Always have a backup plan.

Staring at the table, at the uneaten meal, Theo realized that she'd never really *had* a backup plan when it came to next session, or even to what she'd do over the break. She'd *one* plan: to graduate, and graduate as soon as she could, with the highest-graded license she could earn. She'd known that she would have a spot at Hugglelans, since she was already on their lists; she'd known she'd have Asu in the other bunk; she knew—well, but it turned out she didn't know.

Theo sat looking at the remains of the maize buttons, then rose and swept them and the rest into recycling and headed for her own room.

Plans. Choices. Somehow that reminded her of Father and the time he'd pointed out the folly of her trying to stay with him instead of moving to the Wall with Kamele.

"To what extent are you willing to fund this choice? How much sorrow are you willing to cause?"

And now, someone seemed to be asking the same kind of question again, but this time she was able to "fund" the choice.

Funding. When she was a kid she'd thought Father had simply meant how would she pay for her school supplies. But that wasn't all he meant, after all, and she knew that now. She had funded

217

her choice through hard work. She'd come here, she'd fought her way through math courses, through red tape and through her own misconceptions. She'd fought with some people and made friends with others. She had, she thought, some allies. People who wished her well, who would help her, and whom she would help, in turn.

She was prepared to live with her decision, and if Asu couldn't live with Theo, then Asu was making a decision. Her decision. Theo hadn't come to the academy to be Asu: she'd come to be Theo.

Father's way of making choices was very advertent; and now she had to be advertent, too. If she was making people here in the main quad uncomfortable because she was more pilot than student—that seemed to be Asu's complaint, that Theo was doing too much and not being social enough—then she'd move to someplace where pilot and self-directed was more common—she'd see if there was room at DCCT. Last year Kara had mentioned the possibility, but she'd stuck with Asu, since they had come to the academy at the same time and they had managed to reach a certain comfort level. And there, did Asu really understand how much Theo'd put up with along the way? Did she?

Choice. Pilot's choice even. *Stay your course*, her hands counseled. *Stay your course.*

She danced a few moves, thought about lace, thought about Asu and her always going on about her boyfriends and her constant questions about Theo's weekends and about Win Ton. Thinking about Win Ton, what message could she send to him about this? Was it even important? He had work, work that was important to him, and needn't be concerned with the ways of students...

She touched Win Ton's gift, as if she would ask its advice. It felt good in her hand, and she was soothed. No, she decided. Win Ton didn't—couldn't—share with her the daily burdens of ship life and crew mates. There was no reason to write to him of this.

Advertency suggested she finish at least some of the studying in queue. There'd be time, later, to work out the details of next year's life.

She checked her pockets, which she did once or twice a day. And now, there it was, a gun. And three knives—although one would about slice maize buttons—and several disinfectant tubes and a small lace project wrapped in fine cloth and keys, and her key with pilot times on it, and the backup key, certified this morning as she and yos'Senchul passed through Ops, so it was up-to-date, and the suddenly comforting slickness of the Guild card reminding her that someone nearby *did* understand what she was doing, even if it was a norbear with near transparent fur, and then, the comm was in her hand, with Kara's account at the top of the list. A wave, and the comm was on; a click and it was answered.

"Hello," came Kara's voice, sounding young and a little silly, "you've reached my private backup message router at the ven'Arith residence. Your message is bouncing around the planet while it tries to find me. Please be patient because I'm probably bouncing around the planet, too."

Backup message router at her house? She'd never gotten that message before. Theo smiled. Maybe Kara was too busy with someone to answer the comm and didn't want to make promises. Not everyone had to be *arguing* this evening, after all.

Theo could bring no urgency to the studying she'd been trying to do. The energy she'd built up after talking with Asu was still there, still needing an outlet, and unrolling the lace had done nothing for her. She kept seeing star patterns, which reminded her that she needed to get Anlingdin Academy behind her, which meant getting organized for next year, which meant having an idea of where she was going be sleeping, which meant studying and having a plan which meant calming herself so she could . . .

She shook herself, realizing that she knew this pattern. In his best Jen-Sar-the-Professor mode, Father had pronounced this kind of thinking *circular logic*. His prescription for disrupting such damaging circularity was play or exercise. Theo didn't feel much like playing right now, which was why she was out on the campus in the dark, walking, walking, walking.

The academy at night was nothing new to her; she liked to be out alone, and the paths were old friends. She was used to hearing sounds from the airfield, but tonight there wasn't much going on there. Sometimes she could hear things happening at the stadium, but there wasn't much down that way tonight, either. There were people out: groups, couples, in the usual pathways, some more willing than others to be seen.

She had done the first of her usual routes, avoiding DCCT at first and skirting the field: she'd seen yos'Senchul's craft, and the shuttle being readied, and the usual evening maintenance crews on the tarmac. There were a few more people near the field; and there, a ten- or twelve-passenger airjet flowed overhead, banking into the landing pattern ... out beyond her view momentarily and ... it was funny the way she could visualize what the pilot had to be doing, how she must be *here* looking to the west and the beacon, *here* checking for visual hazards on the runway, *here* dropping the gear ...

The breeze was stronger than she'd expected, or the pilot very casual by the way the ship crabbed in, but then, it was down and running to the end pads.

She didn't want company, wondered if there'd been some great sport victory for the school earlier in the day, because that was the usual cause for group celebrations, but there, she didn't pay a lot of attention to such social things.

"Aliens," someone on the path ahead of her was saying. "I mean, in a lot of ways they're more alien than Clutch turtles or norbears or anything nixty like that, because, I mean, because *they look like us*. Like—"

"Parasites. That's the word you want. Like energy thieves. They come in here and make it hard for us natives to get through school, they make the grading harder, they..."

Theo made a face. Must be some more of the new kids. The new kids always complained about how hard school was. She took a light left, veering onto one of the lesser paths, toward DCCT. She walked quietly now, listening, feeling like there was movement going on around her, and with the night so busy there might well be a chance couple or two leaning against trees or ...

More people, talking low, somewhere ahead of her on the path.

"We've got be sure we let them know that this isn't just us, though. We all heard the news clips, we saw the charts, and there's been things going on for a while—this isn't, you know, *personal*, but we've—"

"Don't worry about. It's on the school channels, it's on the local channels. So we know something will be announced for first shift..."

Channels. Announcement. Now what? She hadn't caught up with the regular news, and wondered if she'd missed something urgent. She continued slowly on the path, knowing there was a cul-de-sac a little ahead. There, she could see a group in the dimness, moving in a bunch onto the path she was following.

"Anyway, they sent us the chant, so we can start it off right. And once we do, we're supposed to make noise until they come out and see the signs. We're already calling all their comms and keeping them busy."

Theo felt her energy level rise, and she could see someone in the group ahead of her waving something experimentally. They were going somewhere to make trouble, and the only thing out this way was DCCT.

The thing that was being waved suddenly burst into the brilliant actinic flare of an emergency wand. Patently something only to be used in time of dire distress, it cast tremendous shadows and Theo squinted against it, trying to see DCCT's building as something other than a mysterious blob hidden by great trees.

"Not yet!" someone yelled, too late, as other flares took fire and illuminated words glowed in the air: *Natives First! Solve Now!*

There was a rush from behind her, and a curse and someone saying, "They started without us!" and some cheers, and a general buzz of excitement and energy filled the land, and more of the lights flared. Theo stepped toward the now-empty side path and then a face she almost recognized ran by, paused, and yelled, "Watch out, it's Waitley!"

The buzz turned toward her then: ten, maybe a dozen, and the accusatory, "*She's one of them!*"

Theo started moving, toward DCCT, the dance informing her steps and energy firming her plans.

Two burly students wearing air masks and strike fatigues blocked her path, yelling, "Outsider, outsider, outsider!"

She tried to to duck around them but the crowd behind was thick. The two burly guys lunged; she caught scent of *vya* as she dodged again. Then there were fists and feet and she responded as best she could.

"There were too many."

Theo was battered, bruised, and tired; she ached everywhere. Her eyes were closed and the touch of hands near her lashes made her eyelids flutter.

"Yes, there were," said a soft and familiar voice. "Far too many. In fact, they got in their own way. Thank you for not killing anyone."

"I was just out for a walk. I—"

"Yes, I know. I was medico for the interrogation. You were quite clear."

"I didn't really hurt anyone, then? I can't see how I could have..."

"You did. You hurt several people quite professionally. I salute you."

Theo closed her eyes, realized she'd actually had them open a moment, and recognized that she was talking to the med tech. Healer el'Kemin.

"This keeps happening," she said.

"Yes. It seems that it does."

She came back to that other point, the professional thing he'd mentioned.

"Hurt them bad?"

"You are among the most proficient undergraduates I have had the honor to meet here. Had they come at you in less than waves of six or eight I suspect you could have stood your ground. The security cams will tell part of the story, I'm sure. Certainly they will bear out the fact that you did not charge the crowd to start the riot."

"I can't tell. I'm not sure I remember entirely..."

"You will; if you are permitted to see me in the next seven days—and if you have comfort issues about sleeping, *do* you see me. For the moment the drugs they gave you for questioning have addled you a bit. Be still a moment. Do you feel this?"

"Questioning. Am I under arrest? Riot?"

"Please answer the question."

"Yes, I feel it. That's where my cut is. Or was. That's not cut, too?"

"It is not. I am calibrating your responses."

She tried to say *pffft* or something similar, but it came out more like a sigh.

"How are my responses, then? What about my riot? Am I under arrest, really?"

Somehow the idea of having her own riot, of being her own riot, was both energizing and ridiculous. She giggled. It must be the drugs....

"Pilot Waitley, you are under security guard for your own benefit. There was a riot. You were at the center of it. I don't doubt the scorecard will make the rounds; three broken arms, several broken noses, multiple concussions. And that is just among those who admit to being there."

"I'm going to be thrown out as a danger to the school!"

"Pilot, please."

She looked up, saw his face serious rather than bland and medical.

"The school, indeed the planet, will take the wrong lesson," he said softly. "Yes, I fear you have it."

She closed here eyes again, realized she was carrying threads of thought at different levels. "Why were they wearing *vya*? Will it take seven days for me to stop hurting?"

He laughed, which surprised her, and she opened her eyes.

"Permission, lady, to answer briefly."

She nodded.

"*Vya* is sometimes used medically, and sometimes as an over-stimulant to create concentration or passion. Those of the broken noses were drunk on *vya* and other such stimulants and were therefore both unconquerable and heedless of danger. As for the seven days, the coming changes have become clear to me and I am among the first to have issued my resignation letter to the academy."

THIRTY

· · · · · · · · · · · ·

Administrative Hearing Room One
Anlingdin Piloting Academy

"MY ID *IS* AUTHENTIC!"

Theo schooled herself to calmness, thinking the dance moves rather than dancing them, remembering that she didn't need to always be ready to fight, feeling the aches that meant she'd just *been* in a fight.

The Anlingdin student ID wasn't the problem; that checked out. That she'd need to show *any* ID to get into her own hearing, accompanied by a well-known staff member, was on the far side of enough, already. But the demand had clearly been for "All academic and professional ID, please," and that had surely meant her Guild card, which she'd trumped with the Hugglelans Rotating Staff ID card. That card, too, had been accepted at face value, but the Guild card was another matter.

The guard in the unfamiliar uniform scanned the unmarred ID again, shaking his head.

"It does *appear* authentic. But it wasn't issued *on* Eylot, by the registry office here. It didn't go to the planet registry for approval. This one was processed *elsewhere,* so it didn't have local approval, and it's so recent that—"

"For *approval*?" It had taken her a moment to catch that. Theo fought hard to keep her face and eyes turned away from Veradantha, still standing silent beside her. "*Local* approval? The Pilots Guild is galactic."

Theo saw the guard lose concentration as he looked elsewhere for guidance and finally found it in a man in a business suit who lounged nearby. He moved forward, speaking firmly, to Theo and Verandatha as much as the guard.

"Yes, that has been the process here; any pilot with credentials and training might go to the local Guild office and join. Of late, however, an additional step has been added for those not from Eylot—they must meet piloting standards, of course, but they also must first have a job offer or a job and to get that they must be—"

The guard pointed to Theo's left hand, where the card bearing the crest of Howsenda Hugglelans was clenched firmly against her Anlingdin Academy credentials.

"Guide, the pilot does carry other, appropriate, ID."

The man in the suit nodded.

"You were correct in scanning her credentials, and correct that they are somewhat—out of the ordinary—for a student here. We shall make a note of that. As we should not start proceedings without her, you will admit her." He glanced at Veradantha, not politely.

"You will not be needed, counselor. Please return to your area."

The hearing hadn't taken long. In fact, Theo wondered why it had been called a "hearing" at all, since nobody had listened to *her*.

She walked—no! She *strode*. An eager calm infused her, dance was her being. The world went on all around her, voices and sounds, and as in a half-watched but well-known play. The theme of this play was an old one: Theo Waitley, threat and menace.

This episode was perhaps better scripted than the play as seen in her early days, when it was her hapless clumsiness that was cited. Now it was her pure potency that mattered—Theo Waitley, trained in unarmed combat, Theo Waitley, with a history of at least four violent incidents since she'd arrived on campus...

Four? There was her riot, of course, and then the incident of the stolen flight hours. But...

Somehow, for the purposes of this exercise, her infamous sailplane flight was linked to the general unrest being brought under control throughout the continent by the new policy rectifying the disadvantage and self-disadvantage Eylot had been laboring under. Then there was the recent incident, also linked to general unrest, in which a senior faculty member had intervened.

And now, of course, it was well known that this person with a history of violence was carrying a gun. True, as a pilot she might be permitted a gun, and clearly, she'd had the gun with her during the riot. That she hadn't brought it out and wounded dozens was considered by the panel to be a matter of oversight.

Commander Ronagy had not been present at the hearing; nor had there been anyone Theo knew in the room. Evidence was read by the man in the suit—the Guide—and no discussion was allowed. She sat in her chair while the Guide spoke, telling the room that in times of unrest it was necessary and purposeful to regard the precincts of academia as central to the future of the planet, and in particular, the precincts of any place producing pilots, who are the core of commerce. Acknowledging the speeches by the Guiding Council as authorizing immediate action by Guides in place...

"This hearing is to announce and confirm the decision of the Guides of Purpose on the immediate suspension of academic privilege, residence, and attendance of Theo Waitley at Anlingdin Academy, on the grounds of a history of her continued association with violent activity. Given the state of unrest facing Eylot we must act to make and keep Anlingdin an orderly institution and cannot countenance the existence of an ongoing nexus of violence. This suspension is to remain in force until the student can demonstrate two years of clean, nonviolent civil behavior records, after which reinstatement to the start of the equivalent semester may be considered upon proper application through recognized channels, assuming the state of unrest and threat is resolved. Failure to leave the premises on time or in good order will be considered a violent breach of the peace."

After that, they'd read the incidents, explained that in uncertain times order was necessary, and...

Dance. Thoughts of bowli ball, and a vague understanding that she'd really be needing a place to sleep. Tonight. She wondered if there was some kind of a rebound from the interrogation drugs that made her feel like this.

She'd been distracted several times during the proceedings, wondering who the Guides would report this to. Certainly they should report it to Captain Cho, who had seen her enrolled—so she would need to be informed, and of course Win Ton, once she was settled, somewhere. She would have to tell Kamele—and that was something Theo wasn't looking forward to. Father had worked so hard to bring Kamele around and—Father. She couldn't start to imagine what Father would say.

But there, that was later. Father would be fine; Kamele would—she would make Kamele understand. Just like the times with her mentor and the silly problems on Delgado. She'd get through this.

She would.

For now, she walked, with a single goal: get out. There was a shuttle flight in an hour; the Guides having preempted the first two jitneys to show up after the hearing.

Before her, there were footsteps. A lot of footsteps, being not at all quiet, and now, voices.

"There she is!"

She turned, calmly, ready, feeling the weight in her pocket as well as the energy in her arms, anticipating that the first move would be—

"Kara!"

As calm as she'd been about facing potential hostiles, she was unnerved to find a half-dozen members of DCCT.

"You're all going to get in trouble!"

"We're all in trouble already," Kara said, grimly, "every one of us in DCCT. They've tagged us with *association with recent violent activity*, and with *association with a known nexus of violence*."

They were walking rapidly, away from the hearing room and in the direction of the space field and dorms.

"Nexus of—"

Theo's temper flared.

"Someone brings a riot to DCCT and it's your fault? And *I'm* the nexus? *I* am the nexus?"

She stopped suddenly, eyes closed, the pause so rapid that several of the DCCT members jostled her.

"What are you doing, Theo? Are you going to be able to walk or should we call a cab?"

Kara was right next to her, looking intensely into her face, eyes grim when Theo opened her own.

"I was remembering names, Kara. Faces and names. I swear I will not forget this!"

Kara bowed, very formally.

"Yes, we have the names as well. The whole thing was live on the admin channel, you know!"

"Double," Theo said. "Double! I have their faces. They think I'm going to want to come back to this—"

"That is much Balance, Theo. Do not take on—"

Overhead a rotary wing was sweeping by, search beam bright.

"There, they said they were going to start security sweeps on groups of three or more."

That was Bova, echoed a heartbeat later by Freck.

Theo spun—"I'll be able to do this, just go. Don't get into more trouble on my—"

Kara turned as well, hands moving purposefully: *Split return careful I cover and report.*

A flutter of assents, and the two of them strode on alone, the sound of the rotary thrumming in the distance. When they reached the path leading toward the field Theo veered in that direction, while Kara strode on toward the dorms until realizing with a start that Theo's path had diverged.

"Theo," she half whispered after catching up at a run, "where are you going?"

"I've got to be out of here, so the field . . ."

"But your things! In the dorm!" Kara's hands enumerated *shirts jackets bags jewelry letters.*

Theo stood quiet, considering, did a quick pat of her person, felt the wings on her collar, made sure the necklace was around her neck, checked on pockets, marked the gun's still unusual presence.

"I'm set. I have most of what I need on me."

Kara uncharacteristically stamped her foot.

"And you are going to give them your belongings!"

Theo swallowed against a sudden urge to tears, and shook her head.

"Hug me," she said, "and then go get the stuff. Keep it, dispose of it as you will, start a legal fund, anything!" Theo thought for a moment, recalling the signs Kara had made, *shirts jackets bags jewelry letters.*

Letters.

"Wait, there is something else! Letters, Kara—two letters from Win Ton yo'Vala. Send them to me care of the Pilots Guild at Codrescu. They'll hold them for me. Do that, and all will be well for me. The rest, do as you see fit!"

Kara froze a moment, and then bowed, very deeply and with flourishes.

"If you are certain, Theo Waitley, I will do this. I will be the instrument of your will."

Theo felt her smile fade, heard the sounds of the night include the shuttle's tow machine.

"Yes, Kara. I'm sure. I give you my key, and my word."

They hugged quickly, and Kara made her repeat the statement into her comm, so she had Theo's word, and tucked the key away. She hugged Theo again, then bowed one more time.

"Pilot, good lift!"

Theo nodded. "And to you," she said, "safe landing."

THIRD LEAP

THIRTY-ONE

....

*Hugglelans Planetary
Conglomeration of Portcalay
Eylot*

THEO SLEPT ON THE SHUTTLE, CONTENT FOR ONCE TO HAVE someone else do the piloting; waking groggily at touchdown. Eyes closed, she listened to the sounds of her fellow travelers—ten or twelve students including three part-timers she knew from the repair bays who had taken seats together at the front, willfully ignoring her, never once overtly looking at the single passenger in the last row in the rear. The ship also carried a double training crew of her classmates. Asu could be among them for all she knew, but Asu was not among those who inspected the interior of the craft before liftoff, nor was she among those departing the craft ahead of her on landing.

The angry energy that had seen her through her hearing and its immediate aftermath had deserted her entirely; and she considered simply going back to sleep. But no, that wouldn't do, would it? The shuttle would be returning to the academy and she was banned from the grounds. Eyes still closed, she fingered the chair's controls, sighing as it folded out of its recline.

C'mon, Theo, stand up. You've got work to do. Another sigh and she opened her eyes, saw the commanding shuttle pilot doing his end-of-flight stretch as he walked the ship.

"Time to move out, Pilot," he said mildly.

"Right." That sounded a little surly in her own ears, so she

233

added, "Thanks," as she levered out of the chair, and moved down the aisle.

At the door she paused and looked back at him, surprising a look of sympathy on his face.

"Good lift," she said then, feeling like she owed him something for his concern.

"Safe landing," he answered quietly, as she dropped to the tarmac, waking the protest of six dozen bruises.

It wasn't a long walk to the office, but she was limping when she reached the door. There was a light on, of course; Hugglelans never closed. She set her hand against the door and pushed.

Aito glanced up from the console. He didn't look surprised to see her, even though she wasn't scheduled. On the other hand, he didn't look particularly *pleased* to see her, and Theo paused with her hand out, holding the door open.

"Should I go?" she asked him. "I don't want trouble."

He blinked, his professional smile snapping into place.

"Of course you don't want trouble," he said smoothly, gesturing her to come 'round the counter to the second chair. "You want a cup of tea and something to eat—and possibly an analgesic. I'll have a tray brought down from the kitchen. In the meantime, come and sit down, and tell me everything."

Splendid! she heard Father exclaim inside her head. *You must tell me everything!* She felt tears and a laugh rise together, coalescing in a sound something like a sneeze.

Aito raised his eyebrows.

"I'm sorry," she gasped, shaking her head. "It's just—you sounded so much like my father!"

He actually looked horrified. "That won't do at all," he managed, reaching out to flick a toggle on his board. "Come and sit down, Theo, before you fall down."

She did as she was told, settling into the old wooden chair with its short left leg. Tonight, the rocking motion was soothing and commonplace, when it was usually annoying. So she rocked, gently, and listened to Aito while he ordered food, and then called the restaurant main board, and arranged to shunt his console's business there.

"Until I take it back," he said, sharply, apparently in answer to how long this inconvenience was to go on.

Her fingers were twitching. Carefully, she folded them together on her knee. Aito hardly ever used the sharp side of his tongue; he must, she thought, be tired tonight.

"You may file a complaint with Father tomorrow if you—" He paused, maybe for an interruption, then continued with a full load of irony. "Yes. I thank you for your condescension, Seventh Daughter."

He closed the connection with a sharp move, and leaned back in his chair. Sighing, he lifted his hands and ran his fingers through his oiled hair, which didn't do anything more than make it sleeker.

"So," he said, giving her a grin that was less professional and more Aito. "What happened?"

The tray from the kitchen arrived while she was telling him everything; he poured tea for them both and shoved the plate of handwiches toward her. She took one, hardly attending what she did, and continued to talk.

When she was done, the plate was empty, a second hot pot of tea had arrived from the kitchen, and she felt—if not as energized as she had been after the hearing, then at least awake, on-task, and . . . determined.

"So, I'd like to put in my app for full time here at the yard," she finished, leaning forward, her cup cradled in both hands. "And to ask if I can claim a bed in the dorm—or rent a wayroom; I've got some money—"

Aito raised his hand, cutting her off. "One course at a time, Pilot. First, now that you are unburdened and fed—tell me how you feel. Do you require a physician? Will you have some painkillers?"

Theo considered that. Her hurts were mostly bruises and scrapes; while they nagged at her, she didn't think painkillers—no, she decided abruptly, *definitely* not painkillers. She needed to be alert.

It was an odd thing to think, here at Hugglelans, where she was safe, but she didn't question the rightness of her decision.

She looked to Aito and shook her head. "I'm . . . mostly all right. Healer el'Kemin said if I experienced any real trouble in the next seven days, then I should see him. If they'd let me."

Aito's eyes sharpened. "Seven days seems a peculiar figure," he noted.

Theo laughed slightly. "I said the same thing. It turns out he's put in his resignation, and he had to give academy admin seven days' notice."

"Oh," Aito said softly, and then, more loudly, "*Oh*." He snapped forward, fingers flickering as he entered a call code into the board. "Your pardon, Theo," he murmured, picking up the receiver.

The comm buzzed twice, then clicked as the connection was accepted.

"Father?" his voice was brisk. "It's Aito. I apologize for the— Yes. Anlingdin Academy's Healer has tendered his resignation, it— Seven days. Yes, sir. I have Theo Waitley here in the office. She has been dismissed for— I expect they are, sir. I— Inciting a riot and being a nexus of violence. No, sir. She has had tea and food. She reports herself capable and refuses painkillers, though she would like a job and a place to sle— Certainly, not. It would be most inappropriate. Indeed, I will tell her you said so, sir. About the Healer? Shall I— Ah. Thank you, sir. Your voice, of course, carries the— Pardon? One moment, if you please, I will ask."

Aito cradled the receiver against his shoulder and looked over to Theo. "What plans has Kara ven'Arith? Does she follow you here?"

Theo shook her head. "I don't know. She—I gave her leave to gather up my things and to do with them as she sees fit. But, her family's local!"

"Yes," Aito said seriously. "Her family is indeed local." He lifted the receiver to his lips again.

"Theo does not know her friend's precise plans, which is doubtless wise. The ven'Arith has accepted the burden of Theo's will, in the matter of private possessions left behind...yes. Good night, Father."

He cradled the receiver and sat staring at it for a moment before he raised his eyes to Theo.

"My father thanks you for your service to Hugglelans, and for bringing the news directly. We had, of course, heard rumors and rumbles, but we had not suspected that the explosion would occur so soon."

"I don't think anybody did," Theo said. "Pilot yos'Senchul thought something was...imminent, but not immediate. That's—I think that's why he had me get my card at the station."

"Short Wing is longsighted," Aito said, and Theo shook her head.

"You're going to have to find another nickname," she said. "He has both arms now. The new one's mech. Top grade, too."

Aito stared. "You tell me that yos'Senchul has accepted the

prosthetic? That—" He glanced toward the console, hesitated, and murmured, probably to himself, "No, it will wait."

"About a full-time job," Theo said, after a long moment had passed and Aito hadn't said anything else.

He started, looked to her and straightened in his chair.

"Ah, yes, the job," he said, and it was his professional smile he showed her, which didn't make much sense, Theo thought, though her stomach thought otherwise.

"Unfortunately, we cannot hire you here at Hugglelans Eylot," Aito said, so smoothly that the sense of his words almost slid past her.

She gasped, now realizing how much she had depended on Hugglelans—how certain she'd been that she had a place here. But, of course, she thought, painfully, they didn't want trouble. They were local, too.

"However," Aito was continuing, "it may be possible that you will qualify for an apprenticeship position with Hugglelans Galactica."

Theo stared, feeling slow and slightly stupid. "Hugglelans Galactica?" she repeated.

"In fact," Aito said briskly. "Did you think that this yard and the Howsenda was all there was? We span worlds, Theo Waitley. And, spanning worlds, we therefore have need of pilots."

"I thought you were a—service for pilots," Theo said. "The yard, the restaurant, the repair bays..."

"All of which we would need to maintain for our own ships! Why not extend the service and earn a fee to offset the cost of doing business?"

He stood. "We'll talk more of this after you've rested. I'm going to put you in the ready room."

Feeling not much less confused, Theo rose and followed him down the short hall to the rear.

"What about the pilot on call?" she asked, as Aito opened the door onto a room just big enough to hold a cot.

"The pilot on call this evening prefers to sleep other than in the ready room. As he's never missed a call and his partner is understanding of these things, Father accepts the arrangement." He pointed to the right. "Sanitary facilities at the end of the hall. You'll sleep safe tonight, Theo," he said, turning to look earnestly into her eyes. "Father is grateful for your service. After you've waked and broken your fast, ask whoever is out front to call me."

"Why?" Theo asked.

Aito smiled. "So that I can get you started on that application for full-time work you wanted." He inclined his head—half bow and half nod.

"Good night, sleep well."

"Good night, Aito," she answered, and stood in the doorway until he reached the top of the short hall, and the door closed behind him.

Please insert Howsenda Hugglelans employee card in the red slot, the instructions ran across the screen in rapid yellow letters. Theo complied.

Please insert Guild or other professional identification in the blue slot.

She slid the Guild card into the blue slot, feeling a pang as the machine accepted it. *You'll get it back*, she told herself sternly. *They just need to download your data.*

Please wait, the screen instructed her, the letters flowing into the Howsenda Hugglelans logo. The logo expanded, twinkling, against a black background, morphing into a blanket of stars spreading prettily, if not very realistically, into infinity.

Theo closed her eyes and counted to twenty-four. When she opened them, the graphic had faded, replaced by dignified blue-limned letters.

Welcome, Theo Waitley, Pilot Second Class. Your Guild license is active and cross-matches with your Howsenda Hugglelans employee identification. Following is the general piloting application for Hugglelans Galactica. Data gathered by this application resides, encrypted, in the Howsenda Hugglelans corporate database. Job applicants have the right to refuse three offered jobs before they are removed from the active database. Ready to proceed? Yes/No.

Theo thumbed *Yes*.

The questions were interesting, not all of them having to do with piloting, but a good number asking about her hobbies, whether she liked to be in a crowd or by herself, if she had any pets, if she'd taken self-defense. The "yes" on that question opened up a cluster of sub-questions: When? Which type? Was she proficient? Had she taught?

After that, there were more general questions, then the application program wanted to know if there were any planets she preferred not to travel to, if she had any outstanding local "rule violations," if so, what and where.

Finally, the screen flickered and one last question rose to its surface:

Are you qualified to carry a weapon?

Theo punched "yes" a little harder than was strictly necessary, and waited for a series of questions about her gun, her training with it, and her years of ownership.

Instead, the application program thanked her for her input and promised that a representative of Hugglelans Galactica would be contacting her with a job offer very soon.

It was, in fact, three days before she was contacted by a representative of Hugglelans Galactica, and that by proxy, in the person of Aito himself, who shook her awake on her cot in the on-call room, where she'd spent her time sleeping and working nav problems with her needles.

"Theo! Your ship is here!"

"What!" She was awake all at once, on her feet and stamping into her boots, her hands flew down her body, touching pockets, doing inventory. She grabbed her sweater off the hook and hauled it on as she followed Aito up the hall.

"I thought I got three refusals!" she said, as they came into the office.

He gave her a peculiar look over his shoulder. "Do you want to leave this planet?" he asked.

"Yes," she admitted.

"Do you," he asked, slotting a data card, glancing at the readout and nodding, "want to work as a pilot?"

"Yes!"

"Do you want to put your friends in peril?"

"What? No!"

"Good. Then you'll take this—" He flipped the card to her; she snatched it out of the air and stood holding it, watching him.

"That's your accumulated pay for unused vacation time, shift bonuses, and an override for a wayroom and a meal at any Hugglelans facility."

"Vacation time!" she exclaimed. "Bonuses? What—"

"Father," Aito interrupted, "is grateful for your service. I believe he said so previously." He tossed her another card, which she caught like the first.

"I am also grateful," he said quietly. "Listen, now, Theo. *Cameron*'s on Number Two Hot, lifting in five minutes. The pilots are willing to have you sit jump seat 'til Malta, where you'll disembark and report to the yard office. They'll have your papers, updated ID, all of it. You'll be 'prenticing to Pilot Rig Tranza—one of Hugglelans' long-time employees. You'll learn a lot from him."

"But, wait!" Theo cried. "What kind of ship? What kind of space? What—"

The board rang, and a man's voice rang out cheerily. "Our packet ready there, boss? We're coming up on a mark."

"Heading out now!" Aito said. He jerked his head toward the door.

Theo took a breath, held back the words in favor of a nod and a flashed *good lift!* and ran for the hotpad.

THIRTY-TWO

. . . .

Number Twelve Leafydale Place
Greensward-by-Efraim
Delgado

IT HAD LONG BECOME THE CUSTOM TO SHARE IN THE NEWS FROM Theo when it arrived, and to make it as festive an occasion as possible. The joint revelation of their offspring's latest adventures being such a habit, not even this evening's committee meeting in support of Chair Ella ben Suzan's important work reconfirming the department's accreditation would do more than put it off, despite Jen Sar's protestation that a letter marked for Kamele Waitley should be enjoyed by Kamele Waitley as soon as possible.

Kamele's not unexpected insistence meant that Jen Sar worked late in the fall garden, regretting his favorite jacket's location in a spaceship storage locker where it protected him from no wind at all. After, he showered, prepared in advance what he could of a simple repast, and graded student papers, enjoying the company of several cats and the scan of near-orbit action in space until his still-keen ears discerned Kamele's steps on the walk.

She's very tired. Aelliana stirred, concern tinging her thought.

Indeed, he answered, *I'm glad she's home, and with something to be pleased about!*

Kamele's face lit when she saw Jen Sar, but the first thing she said was, "I'm sorry."

He raised quizzical eyebrows. "Sorry?"

She stowed several bags through the simple expedient of dropping

241

them in front of the chair Coyster occupied, and then accepted Jen Sar's hug with warmth.

"Sorry I had yet another meeting, sorry the meeting went long again, sorry Ella's been quite so much in the midst of this, sorry Theo's letter arrived after you were gone for the day."

He hugged her again, which she accepted, just as she accepted their slow spin which brought them to the counter where the glasses were set and the bottle properly breathing.

"Ella is lucky to have you," he murmured, "and so is the Wall. Next year should see honest education out of all of you, with only a double dose of meetings instead of triple. Soon, all will return to normal!"

Kamele laughed softly. "Yes, a double dose of meetings does sound wonderful. It is really hard to remember sometimes that these people are all on our side!"

Soon they touched glasses and sipped, with Jen Sar all admiration of Kamele's attention to the glass.

Good, Aelliana observed, *she'll sleep well tonight.*

Distraction being the plan, Jen Sar tipped his head in Kamele's direction.

"Shall you read to me now, or shall we wait until after salad?"

"Let's see first if it is something to read or something to watch! Oh, and remind me to send on that clip we have from Bek; I'm sure she'll enjoy it!"

Kamele returned to her bags to retrieve the letter, while Jen Sar watched her.

"Well," he commented, "she's long put soarplanes behind her, so I think we don't need to worry on that score." After a pause, he added, "And really, as pretty a couple as they may have made for her *gigneri*, I doubt we can expect them to be much of a pair now, with him flying off stages and being an important artist, while she's going to settle on being a mere space pilot."

Kamele looked up from her rummaging to wrinkle her nose at him, and he smiled.

They had, he admitted, made a pretty couple, and the *gigneri* pairing had confirmed both Theo's independence, and her willingness to fly off on her own in pursuit of her own choices.

The letter discovered, Kamele settled on to a stool to peel the plastiskin cover open.

Aelliana's eyesight was no better than his these days, but she dealt with far less distractions; she caught the return routing address as Kamele set the envelope aside.

I haven't thought about that place in years, copilot—Staederport!

"A letter only," Kamele said, squeezing carefully to be sure there were no flatpics or mediachips enclosed. "We can trade reading paragraphs!"

Not quite idly, Jen Sar insisted, "No, no, please go ahead as you will. I'll just see where the letter's been—"

He snagged the envelope, a frisson of concern raising the hair on the back of his neck.

The envelope was franked at the Guild Hall on Staederport, for *Pilot 2 Theo Waitley, c/o Hugglelans Galactica/Light Courier Primadonna.*

Do you suppose it is still the same storefront, Pilot?

"Dear Kamele," she began, the thin page rustling between her fingers. "I'm sorry to have to tell you that there has been a riot at school, and I've been declared—"

Aelliana had been a courier pilot, as well, and they both read the words and the visible codes with no problem, she computing ahead of him to inform—

Second seat on a working courier, with a box on Staederport! She's—

"...a nexus of violence!"

Jen Sar was already at Kamele's side, who sat, white-faced, letter crumpled in hand.

"By the mothers, they've destroyed her!"

"Surely not," he said, easing her hand open to rescue the precious paper.

He wasn't certain how long it took, or whether it was his gentle insistence or Aelliana's firmer explanations that finally brought the rage to anger, the anger to acceptance. The wine sat forgotten for a while, and when recalled, was aimed at relaxing a mother's unrequited fury.

"Kamele," Jen Sar said, finally, "I swear to you this is true. The barbarians have *not* won. Theo may lack her degree, but she holds what she wants. She has her wings."

THIRTY-THREE

. . . .

Primadonna
Alanzia Port

TRANZA WAS OFF ON ANOTHER BINGE, THEO REALIZED DARKLY; she'd be lucky if she saw more than a passing wave of the hand acknowledging her dinner arrangements or that he'd be prepared any time soon to "study on" her proposed course and timelines. This time, besides laying out the course and schedule, she'd already had to balance the official delivery loads in their outboard minipods and fine-tune the more sensitive high-value stuff in the pressure pallets. Was that enough? No, then came the rebalance because the local office was shipping "internal matter" set to arrive after they were moved to hotpad, which meant it would have to find space in the tiny passenger cabin.

The last time they'd had "cabin goods," as Tranza would have them, it had been a load of *fron*, a spice so rare and potent that an amount matching Theo's own mass was sufficient to sustain the Howsenda's needs—the final destination—for a period of years. Whatever it was, it was probably the one thing that had gotten her outdoors—

That was another thing. When the trip came across the board originally it was a straight orbital pick-up from the outermost of the four transfer stations. So, she'd calculated for that on the Jump, getting nothing but an "I can get by with this, I guess" from Tranza. Then, he'd told her to push Jump and she brought them through a day later, within hailing distance and all he had

245

to say while they normalized the orbit was, "Hey, if we can get down there's usually some good play"—and he'd gone off to make a crew-rest request.

Crew rest was a joke; that meant Tranza got to visit friends and influence people while she tended the ship. If she was lucky, he'd bring back a new language module, and they could practice against each other.

If she wasn't lucky, he'd haul in a new set of silhouette training vids, not that she couldn't already identify forty-seven major ship styles and thirty-six uniques, including the top ten trade ships. Diamon Lines *Chanticleer City*? No problem. Korval's *Dutiful Passage*? She knew it from six directions, even though she'd never really seen *it*, either. Scout ships? She had them down by the dozen. Fah! That's what came of telling Tranza she'd caught a ghost ship in the screens when he was off-board and asleep. He wasn't going to let up until they found it all legal and ID'd in a sanctioned pack, since he'd taken polite leave to doubt the lacework sketch she'd provided.

Well, at least she hadn't had any repeat sightings in—well, in a good long while.

Once they'd dropped off their initial minipods they got that rest order, so on short notice she'd managed to cut to an inner orbit, and from there to the ground, with Theo getting a grand total of a walk to the local crew store and cafeteria and a visit to the pet library where she got to talk to a norbear for a few minutes between crowds of littlies on a field trip. That'd made her wonder why she'd never seen a norbear on Delgado but it was probably rules made up by the Safties.

The other good thing was that, after she visited the norbear, she'd gotten to see the birds, flying free, something that made her startlingly happy. Birds were oddities on Delgado, and the ones on Eylot were all tiny and stupid, but here on...wherever they were—Alanzia it must be. Here on Alanzia birds were protected as treasures, with even ship landings following paths strictly set to avoid nesting areas. Many of them had amazing wingspans and soaring habits that made them look like undergrown sailwings. Only good hearing had prevented her from being run down on the pathways, since she so often just stopped to take in the sight.

And then it was back to the ship, and now she could name Alanzia as planet number twenty-two that she'd set foot on, and likely number fourteen that she'd sat board for liftoff. Somewhere in her personal log she had a complete list of the ports, orbiting or not, and her time at the board and all that—but mostly she was keeping busy.

As for Tranza's binge, who could tell what it would be this time around? No doubt, it was something he'd picked up on Alanzia. He'd rushed back with several packages, asking after messages and delays, offering up advice to pull trip info on half a dozen potentials assuming a run to Volmer, of all places.

No, maybe she *could* guess. Her first trip out he'd mentioned music archives on half a dozen planets, Alanzia among them, since he'd just bought a run of a hundred different songs without instruments. He'd spent the first twelve-day with her breaking into what *he* assumed was singing at the oddest moments, and then he'd shown up for dinner with a tablet drum and some chimes so they could play music together, in between bouts of her learning, of course.

And that's the way it had been, him insisting that a pilot who wasn't learning was wasting what the universe was about, and periodically going off on tears of this or that amusement or pastime, in between bouts of sim flying, math games, and the like. He'd insisted that she keep up the ship-spotting regimen, saying that sometimes you needed to know without waiting for a computer to tell you, exactly what ship it was you'd got on the screen, or in your cross hairs. Some trips he'd spend all his time behind her shoulders, watching every move, and others he turned off the outer world and binged on drawing, or playing the flute. He'd tried to emulate her needle-play, but as good as he was at it, he didn't find it engaging. In fact they didn't agree on much in the way of music or art or theater or restful pastimes.

"Oh no," he told her the one time she dragged out a bowli ball, "not even a little bit, not on board *Primadonna*. We get to some place with room, I might play, but you come with a reputation, so maybe not. That goes away and I don't see it."

If Tranza was anything, it was protective of his ship.

"This vessel was first put in service the very day I got my jacket," he'd told her before she sat second board for the first time, "and I intend to see it in service the day I die. The company put me in here fifteen years ago and I won't have anyone at the controls who hasn't got a sense of proportion, control, and respect!"

The conversation had gotten a little odd after that, with him going on about her coming highly recommended, and asking why it was that they'd delivered her mid-session if she'd been at the academy.

"I'm suspended," she'd told him bleakly, knowing that someone should have given him a clue that she wasn't a top-scholar type of pilot, "and the folks at Hugglelans helped me get off-planet before I got in more trouble."

"Suspended? What did you do? Cheat on exams or—"

"Pilot, didn't anyone tell you? They say I started a riot!"

He'd sat back then, looking extremely solemn, and half-nodded.

"Started a riot. At Anlingdin Academy, was it?"

She'd flashed a hand-sign, *confirm*.

"Right. Well, here's the deal, Pilot Theo. You riot on your time, not on mine. If we're in port and you're a hellcat or a head-banging drunk, that's your problem until you get arrested and kept, or until you can't find the ship and be ready to fly it when the ship needs you. Portside I give you a comm, and you always have one ear for the ship: there's no such thing as unlimited liberty unless you're between runs, you got it? You and a choir can have plans for a Hundred Hours but if I call and say *Primadonna* needs you, you'll leave 'em all aching if that's where they are, because the ship's the thing. Right."

He tended to nod when he said *right*, and he looked at her, as if "right" was a command or a given and not a question.

With trepidation, knowing she was already too far away from everywhere and everybody she knew to say no, she'd agreed with a solemn nod and, "Right!"

Then he turned, pointed to the second seat, and said, "Sit. Get the seat adjusted. While you do that, I'll tell you about *my* first riot. I never did riot at school though, so you got me beat to start."

True to form, Tranza was humming as the ship moved to the pad, humming, breaking into bits of syncopated bops and boops, and doing something he rarely did, which was—dusting the bridge. He did like the ship to be clean, but now, in the reverie no doubt inspired by whatever music file he'd programmed into his ear buds he was actively dusting and shining things. He liked to be busy, but this—maybe he'd returned with something stronger than just music.

The trip info request that most got her interest was the run, here to Volmer to Clarion to Delgado to Vratha, though there was another one, starting from Volmer to Granby to Hellsport to Eylot that also caught her attention. She'd been kept away from Eylot these last two years and really didn't care to change that if she could avoid it. Kara's last bit of news from there indicated she'd gotten her second class rating and a temp job at Codrescu working as troubleshooter in the nearspace yard had been good, but seeing the new "block of 'crete" security building where DCCT had been was not in her plans.

The timeline was pretty short here, so as soon as she felt the ship halt, Theo flung herself into the seat, mindful of Tranza's earlier, "just sit First, I'll be busy during lift..." as he'd peered into a bag full of music chips.

She began before Tower did: It was time to get out of here as far as she was concerned.

"Theo Waitley, first seat *Primadonna*, acknowledging all connections lit, all connections good, all signal strength nominal, all ranging information green, sync green, we're on a rolling billable hold waiting a delivery."

Tranza was really going at the cleaning bit now, even wiping down the brightwork beneath the third and fourth seats in the back of the cabin, swiping down the seat tops—

"Heard here, Pilot Waitley is the contact, *Primadonna* is go except for paper hold billed by the second to Hugglelans Galactica. Your lift is approved to a 99-minute initial for the next two tenths... after that I'm afraid you'll be looking at an admin wait...."

The viewscreeens showed the port from five angles, and the close ramp was still docked to—

There!

Someone was hurrying, a pilot by the motion, wearing a hat and a backpack and pulling a small bright red-and-blue striped bag behind, the green jacket looking like a Hugglelans crew coat from any of two dozen worlds. The overemphasized hand-signal from the figure was clear enough, and the port call came through—

"Internal delivery from Hugglelans on the way, is this your package?"

Tranza was suddenly behind her shoulders, nodding, muttering,

"Striped bag it is, that'd be good; clear access, tell them clear access and ask for a three-hundred count and lift if it's available."

"Clear access," Theo repeated to Tower. "I'm opening for package, please give us a three-hundred count if you've got one."

Elsewhere in the screens there was motion as a ship lifted, and then the view of another landing, and the reply:

"You've got a three-twenty-five count on my mark. Three-twenty-five coming up—"

"Three-twenty-five, yes," Theo repeated, and she saw Tranza touch the stud to open the lower door, counting in her head that he ought to be *down* there if they were going to clear in time for the delivery person to get clear.

"Mark in five, please give full check, *Primadonna*."

The mark came in the middle of the check, actually, and she could hear Tranza's voice boom, "Damned striped bag still traveling, is it?"

The count went on, Theo now immersed in pointing the ship to a slot in a crowded sky, to a slot in a crowded orbit, to a run to a slightly less crowded Jump-safe zone.

The noises below subsided, Tranza yelled, "Commit."

One hundred and ten.

"We have commit," Theo said.

"Repeat, Pilot."

"We have commit."

There was sound in the cabin, the noise of feet, of a rolling bag, and Theo said "Tranza, strap in, Pilot."

There followed an unexpected melodious laugh, and another, and Theo's eyes left the board long enough to take in the sight of a woman with long fine black hair throwing her hat to the third seat, tying her bags there and flinging herself to the fourth, and Tranza, aglow, dropping into second seat.

"Ninety-two."

The woman leaned in Theo's direction, "Pilot, thank you for waiting. I am, in case you have not been informed, Master Pilot Mayko Ikari, Second Son of House Hugglelans."

Ground demanded attention then, and so did the ship as she did a fine rebalance for the new mass, and she glared at Tranza, to the amusement of their passenger.

"He's like this all the time, isn't he?" said Mayko Ikari from behind her. "But it will be fine, for I have discovered a master trove of music, and he will be singing in strange tongues for the next year, too busy to notice that you are rightly peeved!"

Theo formed a quick hand-sign of *welcome*, and another, aimed toward Tranza that translated roughly into *goat-furred ground-hugge*r.

"Glad to meet you, Second Son. I am acquainted with Aito, and—"

"Yes, I know, and that's why I hope to rescue you from Tranza's care. But we can speak later, Pilot. I'd not want to distract your liftoff."

The autocount went on, and Tranza's voice, low, asked—

"What do you have? Dances? Choir? Quartets or trios? I could use some—"

"Belt please, Tranza!" Theo demanded as his seat light was still orange.

The master pilot giggled, Tranza snapped his webbing, and *Primadonna* lifted.

THIRTY-FOUR

· ·

Primadonna
Out from Alanzia

"'PILOT,' PLEASE, PILOT, OR EVEN 'MAYKO,' IF YOU MAY BE THEO."

The master pilot sat second board while Tranza was off coaxing what he called a "quick picnic" from the small galley. The sounds—especially Tranza's complaints of the limitations of *Primadonna*'s oven and breadmaker—made it sound like he expected a dozen guests arriving to stay for a week of major merrymaking.

Theo, in the midst of calculating the newest suggestion from the woman because of what Theo considered avoidable congestion in the primary orbit, fluttered a *good plan* and then wrinkled her nose.

"I can't see why those ships are all over the place…" The chatter from those ships was live on all the hailing bands and seemed not to make much sense; lots of ships announcing they had pods and partial pods free, offering to broker, offering to subcontract, and Alanzia control all but throwing up their hands at making the flow of noise and ships work, other than multiple requests to tone down shields and please be sure weapons were offline.

"Many ships are arriving here, which is why we depart posthaste," Mayko said. "We will be much better positioned than they!"

"Positioned where?" Theo wondered aloud, "Is this the point you were suggesting?" she added, shuttling some figures over to the second screen. "I mean, if we need to be out soonest we can just request a release and cut away from the ecliptic; we can avoid the incoming rush and the ship's got the power to make that Jump as soon as we're out of range of anyone else." She sent a second set of figures: "Like this. It's expensive in power, but if time is of the essence..."

"Very good idea, Theo; that would work, too, and—well, what we would like is to be in someplace where we can get an advantage on the upwelling of new routes. You're the pilot, after all, so we should be clear what our goals are."

"New routes?"

"Yes, I suppose you are some behind on the news. What we have here are politics going on...extensively. The Yxtrang, some time ago they were beaten back from Lytaxin; it was a sudden attack and they were surprised by forces on-world. A mercenary unit was there, and of course Lytaxin is an ally of Korval. It was ill-advised of the Yxtrang, surely, to take on such. *Dutiful Passage* herself was called from shipping duty to become a battleship, and this...unbalanced other routes and schedules. Korval has recalled many ships from their usual routes. No one is quite sure where this is going, but everyone wishes to realize what profit they may!"

"Hah," Theo said softly, almost turning it into a sigh. "So the allies on Lytaxin took their problem to the Delm of Korval!"

"Well, yes," the pilot admitted after a pause, "or to the First Speaker; I gather there is much confusion in the ether about the situation with Delm Korval, but allies are allies, after all. Surely if Korval is arming ships and Liad is in turmoil because of it, there is money to be made in shipping!"

Armed ships were something they'd avoided talking about at the academy, and though she'd twice effectively fired the short range beams *Primadonna* carried, the pair of victims had been unsuspecting space junk in an asteroid belt, the better to demonstrate *Primadonna*'s meteor shields as well as its weapons.

Very early in her introduction to the ship Tranza had been really clear that *Primadonna* was built for agility and speed. "Run, right? *Run* is the advice I mostly have for you if you get in a spot where people are shooting at you in space. And if someone's running shields, there's no harm in having what shields you have on as well. See here, though, *Primadonna*'s not a warhorse, and we're not training for combat. We're just checking out the equipment, so you're up on it. No good reason to go shooting asteroids, too; some of them are pocked with gas and dust and can whump up a hell of a geyser on you if you aren't lucky. Best bet is to leave the weapons switches set to *off/off/disarmed* unless things are dicey."

Tranza ducked his head into view from the galley, waving what might have been a ball of dough.

"If pilots on the board would be so kind, I'd like to have an idea of likely meal schedules this shift. We have a lot to catch up on and I'd like the cooking to be done on time."

Tranza's schedule matched Theo's perfectly; they put the ship on auto, with a master pilot, a first class pilot, and a second class pilot all within quick reach of the boards and nothing but a half-shift's worth of just under one g acceleration on the agenda. The ship was full of the smell of bread, and the picnic was introduced with, "Right, we have two breads and dessert, and since we're just away from the gardens of Alanzia, we're full of fresh salad! I have to say this is a lot better lunch than I got my last shift with Mayko."

His hands were busy with hand-talk between handing over the vittles; Theo picked up something about *silly packing errors* and *always check invoice against items.*

Mayko laughed, which she did a lot, though she put her hand in front of her face when she did as if she was hiding.

"Rig put up with a lot with me, you know," she said, waving the roll he'd handed her at Theo as if it were evidence. "He had my training, as he has had yours, and toward the end I was doing all of the ship's ordering. I'm afraid I let my experience at the Howsenda overtake my mind and I ordered by number, from memory...we ended up with a five-day of young children's meals for the end of the run."

"Strained fruits and strained imitation meats with imitation sauce and imitation..."

She laughed again.

"No, Rig, say true. They were Howsenda meals, so they were all real. And for what they were, they were good."

"Right. They were real good and strained. And not much of them, either."

They bantered their way through two courses, with a remove of coffee for Rig and the master pilot, and tea for Theo. During the meal, Theo several times rose to manually check the instruments and did the same before dessert. It was with dessert that Mayko went from sudden passenger to official business, a flash of hand-talk becoming *mission information follows.*

"First, yes, first comes the Hugglelans business. I have brought with me, Theo, a lot of information that will be going out to all working pilots on routes. You will both get complete copies, of course, and I will expect you to know the information since your life may depend on it. In addition, route managers and lead pilots get an overview I expect you both to read, and I will of course expect both of you to be fully up-to-date on these by the time our trip is over.

"The short form is that there are, as I mentioned, major opportunities for shippers at the moment, and for pilots. We at Hugglelans are at a point that we hope to add an extra full-scale planetary base or two within the next decade, and certainly to add capacity and personnel to match. The alteration on the Liaden side of things makes this an excellent time for us to push forward. I have brought updated contracts for you, assuming you wish to continue employment with Hugglelans under these new circumstances, which we will have confirmed by the end of the trip. Rest assured that we value your service and wish you to be a part of the expansion program."

"New contract, huh? You got yourself a Liaden writing those things now?"

Mayko scolded Rig with severe fingers: *serious talk no joke read close consider.*

Nodding to Theo and then to Tranza, she said, "I think you'll both enjoy the new compensation package we are offering pilots with in-house experience, which of course you'll both qualify for. We do also expect to be hiring from outside, naturally.

"As to the rest of the business, Second Class Pilot Theo Waitley, in my capacity as a master pilot, I am here on the very ship where I earned my own first class card to test you for first class. I have flown several of your trips from log records..."

Theo felt a strange feeling in her stomach, like she'd just found a gravity vary while walking a gangway. First class! She glanced over to Tranza, who was looking elsewhere, and then grinned.

"In my contract, see," he said. "I assumed you'd earned a first class a few trips ago, but it pays to have someone fresh take a look, to be sure. You've seen my basic evals, Theo."

Well, and she had. Adequate and alert ship handling planetary. Adequate and alert ship handling docking. Adequate and alert ship maintenance procedures. Adequate...

"Adequate. That's what you said on the last three reports I saw. Adequate! Nothing about me being ready for..."

True course, he signed. "Right. Right. And if you looked you may have noticed 'conservative piloting for a pilot at this stage of career and training.' You weren't pushing so I wasn't going to push you."

"I thought that meant I needed work."

Her voice was low, and she felt the dance start to move, which brought Tranza immediately to attention.

"No, the alert part, and the conservative part, they're both good. The last three trips have you on command more than me and the trips would have been fine without me at all. Haven't you noticed how often you've signed for us?"

She nodded vigorously.

"I did. I thought that just meant I was doing my job."

A wave of hands from Mayko *communicate communicate good,* and she continued as she finished her coffee.

"So, time has not been adequate even if your piloting may be; these circumstances have kept the whole of my staff very busy. Theo, understand my time on this trip will be spent observing you more than testing; the real test for you has been putting up with the lessons and the cooking of Rig Tranza. And understand that 'adequate' from Rig is a rare and considered thing when it comes to young pilots. Didn't he work you scrubbing the deck and counting spares?"

Theo laughed despite herself. "And double-checking the food lockers for both catalog number and actual count."

"See, always check invoice against items! We share a lesson."

Mayko's hands moved to say *finish this session* and she leaned forward.

"So, the rest of this run is yours. Rig will have a holiday of sorts—he has new music, and he has been some time without vacation or proper leave. I am available to sit second at any moment, and at any moment I may ask for analysis of decision points. Calculations, your choice of beverage—anything. Do you understand?"

Something tickled the back of her mind. She nodded so gravely that it was almost a bow.

"Yes," she said, "I understand. The usual rules apply."

THIRTY-FIVE

. . . .

Primadonna
In Transit

THEO'S HANDS WERE DAMP WITH SWEAT AND HER MAIN COMPUTER was at least four screens deep on each of nine viewtops. She knew where things were but her astrogation instructor would have disowned her. Tranza was sitting back with his music, smiling.

She looked again at the screens, saw the solution, and began archiving like mad.

Let him laugh, Theo thought, he's got *his* jacket.

They'd got to Jump distance with no problems, a comfortable meal in their stomachs and her pair of companions only breaking into song three times in response to conversational cues Theo hadn't known were cues at all.

The thing was that after dinner, Theo began a mild stretching routine, letting it ratchet up to a little more of a workout so that she'd be done before they needed to get to actual work, like to a spot where Theo ought to soon be setting up for a Jump run or determining *Primadonna*'s long term orbit.

In the midst of that exercise, Mayko handed over the ship's run. Well, not exactly. What she did was hand over a list of places she needed to be within a more-or-less set time frame, with a bonus load of interdependent priorities, and a request that sooner would be better in all cases. All of the prefiled destinations were included, and a couple more.

"Pilot Theo, these are the needs of the company," Mayko had

said innocuously. "As the board is yours, this is clearly a pilot's choice situation. I think it best that we be outsystem in the next quarter shift."

Which would not have been Theo's usual choice with such a multiplicity of routes available, but if the ship was hers for the duration of the run—well, that clarified things immensely. Part of this was to push her, she knew. Part was real need. Mayko had said that Hugglelans needed to move in a hurry, while trade was still confused.

But there, the information was already gathered, the decision point just lacked confirmation.

"Mix and match?" she asked. "All of the destinations in the same run, priority fast and efficient?"

"Indeed, that would be best," Mayko allowed.

Theo nodded, raised her voice.

"First Board declares Jump check. Tranza, please secure the galley and confirm tie-downs, locks, goods and staterooms. The count to start our runout is two hundred, starting in seven."

"Right," he said and moved.

Next to her Mayko raised an eyebrow, began to speak, was overridden by Theo.

"Second, your main screen should match mine. Confirm Volmer coordinates, confirm ship safety, confirm scans."

Theo glanced toward the seat Tranza left empty in his rush; then toward Mayko, hands deftly touching the manual confirms on the automatics, readouts being echoed.

"Our route?" Mayko inquired, laughing as Tranza burst into song while he made some final seal in the galley, and dashed onto the flight deck.

"Volmer," Theo stated succinctly. "The coordinates are in, the ship is rigged, and there's eight flight plans ready to go once we get there. Volmer's closest in transit time, Volmer's in the priority loop, and Volmer it is."

Mayko opened her mouth again, but was cut off by Tranza's, "Confirming secure, Pilot Theo."

"Confirmed."

"But the route?" Mayko insisted.

Theo sighed.

"Unless this is a touch-and-go when we get to Volmer, we'd best calculate fresh when we have fresh news. I'll set two probables into the go-stack in case we need to move in a hurry, but we're set. We have a count of one hundred; I'll start the Jump on count."

"But my plans?"

"Your plans are to get there as quick as you can. We'll do that. Can't make the second Jump first though. Confirmation please, Second."

Tranza began to whistle a tune, and Mayko, studying the second board, joined in.

"Confirmed, Pilot Theo."

At this rate, they'd be out of the system in a tenth shift instead of a quarter, Theo thought, and that would do.

Theo lounged in the galley, eyes closed. On bridge, Tranza sat in the vacated First Chair, while Mayko retained Second.

"Pilot," came Mayko's call from the flight deck, "have you signed the contract yet? It would be good to—"

"I haven't," Theo admitted, "opened the file yet. Contracts are much harder for me than doing Jump equations in my head. I'll get six hours real downtime—at least—when we reach Volmer and look it over then."

"Pilot, when we reach Volmer we may want that done already in order to confirm—"

Somebody was pushing, Theo thought, around a spike of irritation. Did Mayko think she was going to *lose* the contract, or something?

"Sorry, Second," she said, "I'm on break unless there's a ship problem." She paused, counted to twelve, and asked, "Is there a ship problem?"

There was muttering in the background, Theo thought, and then realized it was Tranza singing one of his silly song snippets, something about "the ship *Jonny B.*"

"Rig, you're not helping!"

Theo waited a beat, then repeated her question.

"Is there a ship problem, flight deck?"

Again she could hear Tranza, this time singing something that sounded like "We had enough cooks for an army, and only one can of..."

"No, Pilot," came the reluctant reply, "there is not a ship problem."

"Right, Theo," Tranza confirmed. "None."

✴   ✴   ✴

"*Primadonna*, we've got all green for you, welcome. Please inspect your tie-down and sign for it at the gate; we're showing this a field stop charged to Hugglelans Galactica. You've got a cart on the way and a hot pad available for a turnaround tomorrow at this time."

"Thanks for the welcome—and for the cart."

"Cart comes gratis. Can we get our updates here on channels seven and nine?"

Theo keyed in the channels and the updates went through, showing Pilot in Command as Theo Waitley and dual seconds of Rig Tranza, Captain, and Master Pilot Mayko Ikari.

"Hey there, *Primadonna*," came another voice, this one full of energy. "We're holding high priority mail we can squirt through as soon as we get the certificates to talk to each other. One's a problem 'cause it's a special, may take a little time for that to finish up."

Problem mail?

Theo shrugged; she wasn't in a particular hurry to look at chained landing gear.

The trip to Volmer had gone without a ship problem, though Mayko managed to dredge up a fire alarm, two false positives on engine issues, a technical question on ship's financials, assorted runs of "what would you do if" and a really silly multilanguage drinking song that Tranza wouldn't stop humming once Mayko sang the first three verses.

Other than that—

The incoming screen lit, showing the Pilots Guild emblem.

"We have a private and confidential file for Pilot Theo Waitley, transcription through Pilots Guild encryption format. You'll need your card and certificate for this, and receive in person in the comm office."

"Theo," Mayko was saying, "we need to talk about the contract..."

"Right, you do," said Tranza, then saw the symbol on the screen. "I'll do tie-down, Theo" he said, suddenly all business. "Go!"

She went.

Finding the comm office was easy once she parked the cart and entered the Guild port area; what was hard was keeping herself calm as the rest of the process unfolded. A pinbeam message? For *her*? She'd never sent a pinbeam in her life and couldn't think of anyone she knew who'd send one, *especially* to her. Could something have happened to Father or to Kamele? Had Captain Cho and the Scouts decided to bill her for her failed education?

The Guild staffer checked her card, checked her against her card, checked her against the ship schedule, checked—she didn't know what they checked.

"RSVP," said the clerk neutrally. "That's free, well—prepaid. There's a return receipt that'll go as soon as you open it. You can take it in booth four; please record because we erase as it streams. You can send your reply any time within seventy-two Terran hours of receipt."

In the booth she inserted her card one more time, tagged her key to the connecting port, saw a series of letters go by and a warning that reading the following message without authorization was a breach of pilot ethics and...

Sweet Mystery, began the text, *you are an amazement beyond measure. Kara ven'Arith supplies me with the start of my search and a history worthy of a dancer such as yourself. I commend you. The Pilots Guild supplies me with the filed plans of the good ship* Primadonna, *and thus you are found.*

She took a breath, finally realizing she'd been holding it. Win Ton. Win Ton! Oh, what could be—

It is of utmost importance, my favorite dancer, that we meet together in person in the shortest possible time. I am prepared to meet you at any location you name, at Volmer if you like, to rendezvous on planet or station, to provide tickets for transportation from your current location to mine. Only tell me as soon as you may, I humbly beg of you, that you have received this message in good order and that you intend to be in touch with me in person, who gave you your first bowli ball. As friend and as pilot I swear that this is a necessary interruption of your life, and one that will not be forgotten.

There were so many hooks here, so many memories for someone she'd only spent a few days with, and a night.

I am and remain your friend and servant,
Win Ton yo'Vala

There followed a series of addresses she might reply to, starting with the autoreply and progressing four deep into what looked like port drop boxes in places he might expect to get to, including Solcintra, Liad.

She reread the message, from her own key, once it disappeared from the screen, and recalled that she still had copies of every message he'd ever sent.

She sighed, stood, stared at the empty screen. Maybe she could arrange to meet him at their next port, or something. She should answer him, quickly. Soon.

Yes, she should.

She danced a step to unkink her shoulder, and thoughtfully returned to *Primadonna*.

She felt that her arrival on-board had interrupted something. Tranza and Mayko lounged in the galley, hands moving energetically. She was good, but these two threw hand-signs fast as Jump, partial thoughts flying and being cut off by others, shared experience telling in the jabs and spikes of the motions, in the words left out.

Prominent in the first sighting had been *Theo* and also *pilot today now*; but as soon as she was evident Tranza folded his hands and lapsed into a sweetly sung song of conquest and pillage.

Mayko glared at him, and nodded to her.

"The pilot returns to us, sooner rather than later, which is always good in a pilot on port. As you are present, we shall move on to topics left off in midflight."

Theo nodded, pleased that Mayko hadn't asked about her message, and grabbed one of the trayful of landing-pastries on the table.

"We were discussing, right," Tranza broke in, "we were discussing the flight. A fine flight."

Mayko sniffed. She stood, smooth and graceful, deliberately turning away from Tranza, and giving Theo an easy nod.

"As Rig says, we were discussing the flight. It appears that Aito was correct, and despite your run-ins with academic authority in the past, you are exactly the kind of pilot that Hugglelans—especially Hugglelans Galactica—wishes to employ. I would like to insure that we are of a mind on this, and so I ask if you might, now that we are at Volmer, open your contract and sign it."

Win Ton. Somehow Theo kept seeing Win Ton's name on the screen and recalled his name as written on the card she'd gotten on *Vashtara*.

"I haven't read it yet," she said. "If I might have a few moments to look it over?"

Mayko smiled prettily. "It's our standard. We can sign it right now, then move on to—"

"No. Right? *No.*"

Tranza stood, making himself the third point in the triangle of pilots.

"I beg your pardon," began Mayko.

"Beg Theo's, right? You're doing it again. Trying to make the second Jump before the first."

Mayko straightened, mouth firming.

"All we need to do is settle the issue of a contract," she said, with what Theo thought was strained patience. "Once that is taken care of, we can..."

"*Wait*, right? Just wait."

Tranza broke from the triangle and dashed to his quarters. He slapped the door open, exclaiming, "Right, just wait!"

Mayko appeared as startled as Theo felt, especially when he backed out of the room a moment later, his pilot's jacket in his hand, gripped at the collar like he had an invisible pilot hard around the throat.

He shook the jacket at his boss, a hand flourish saying *now now now first.*

"This is what we're discussing first, Mayko. Her jacket."

Theo cast glances between the two.

"Rig, that's your jacket," Mayko said finally, with a sigh.

Tranza stared at her for a moment, began to sign, realized he needed two hands for what he wanted to say, and handed the jacket to Theo in a rush.

"Hold this," he said, and his hands flew into a rage of strenuous argument, reminding Theo forcefully of Captain Cho's assertion that hand-talk was good for many things, even philosophy.

Tranza's jacket, beat-up as it was, felt remarkably good in her hands, and heavier than she'd expected—but then he was a much larger person than she was.

The hand-signs were even faster than they had been when she walked in, and now punctuated in a way only hand-talk allowed. *Sneak. Steal. Hide. Wrong. My ship. My students. Know better.*

Tranza turned to Theo as if she had no inkling of what he'd just said.

"While you were away, me and Mayko were discussing that in fact without additional review, right, with no more testing needed, right, that you have been seen by this master pilot here, this Mayko Ikari, *who I taught*, to fly at first class level, which fact I have seen with my own eyes lo these months, right?"

It came to her that Tranza was *angry*. Theo raised her hands, fingers wide, and nodded, not sure what to say.

"I have my contracts to think of, Rig," Mayko said sternly.

"You want Hugglelans to have all the best pilots tied to you since Korval's got trouble. Business is business. Right. I see that. But you're a Master. You got duty on both screens. And you can't keep information away from her!"

He raised his hands toward the ship's ceiling, fluttered *this thought is mine* and started speaking, low and earnest.

"I have a contract, Mayko, and mine don't need to be signed. If you want Theo Waitley to sign a first class contract, give her what she's earned. A jacket. The raise. The respect."

Mayko sighed, loudly.

"Rig, we're renegotiating all the contracts. Galactic needs—"

"Will you," he interrupted, forcefully. "Will you tell Theo Waitley she's made first class and earned a jacket? Will you tell her that, *Master Ikari*?"

"When she signs the contract she'll be able to requisition a jacket, just like any first class..."

Tranza went suddenly and completely quiet. Theo looked at him worriedly. He stood entirely still for two long heartbeats, then extended his hand. She realized with a start that he was asking for the jacket, and handed it over. He stretched it in front of himself, shook it, opened it, did a dance move—

And hung the jacket around Theo's shoulders, firmly, like it was a cape. The inside was cool, the jacket long on her.

"The jacket fits, Pilot. Welcome."

He squeezed her shoulder and stepped back, hands enjoining her to *wear healthy long proud.*

Mayko's fingers were against her lips, a look of what might be horror on her face.

"Rig, you can't just give your jacket away!"

He turned on her with startling swiftness.

"I precertified your jacket, Mayko, and you still wear it. A pilot can give his jacket to a pilot. Theo's a pilot. She's got a jacket."

"Tranza, calm please," Theo said, genuinely alarmed. "I can't—"

"*Yours*," he interrupted. "I swear and witness it. And Mayko should know better than to pull this stuff!"

"But your jacket!" Mayko insisted.

"I'll requisition one, right?" He gave her a flat stare. "Just like any first class pilot. Right."

Mayko stilled her hands in mid-sign, mouth tight.

Theo cleared her throat. "I can't keep it, Tranza."

He laughed, suddenly empty of tension.

"You, Pilot, better call me Rig."

"But I don't have a card!"

There was silence.

Rig turned to Mayko, fingers terse.

Card.

Mayko put hand to forehead, then reached into her side pouch and extracted something.

"Pilot," she said, extending it, "may this bring you joy."

This was a pilot's license, handed to her own hand. Endorsed all the way around, and registered already according to the seal. *Theo Waitley, Pilot First Class.*

The words got kind of watery, and Theo blinked, looking aside.

Nothing to cry about, she told herself.

"Right," said Rig Tranza. "I owe us all a drink. We can read contracts later."

THIRTY-SIX

. . . .

Primadonna
Volmer

THEY'D HAD THEIR DRINKS—ONE GLASS OF WINE FOR EACH OF them, rather than the kynak Rig suggested—and then Theo called it a shift. She'd been long-shifting the whole trip and between the piloting, the argument surrounding the receipt of her first class ticket, and Win Ton's letter she was exhausted.

Retiring, she realized that on so-called solid ground the ship vibrated in ways it didn't in space, or docked to a station. While station docking often included swings and sways and even bounces, which the planet did not, the noises and vibrations emanating from the connect points as temperatures strove to balance in space were familiar.

On-planet noise snuck in from everywhere. The landing gear transmitted vibrations, the atmosphere vibrated against the ship's skin in the form of breeze and wind, and sounds traveled along and through the hull to fool the ear and excite sensors. Gauges flickered as air pressure changed; the ship's cooling from reentry generated creaks; on larger ships it was known to cause groans and crackles.

Theo's eyes were closed, which meant the sounds were all the more compelling. She wrinkled her nose against the distraction, and brought the question around to first things first, which ought to be sleep. She'd pointed out that regs were clear: she ought to be taking rest now, no matter what planetary time it was, and no matter Mayko's urgencies.

If she couldn't sleep, and Theo'd about given up on that, thinking of first things first meant rereading Win Ton's message with a little less surprise and a little more advertency. What might require a face-to-face meeting? An apology? If so for what? A proposal? Again, for what? Lust?

It was hard to believe that an accomplished pilot would be so bereft of company as to pine for her above all others.

So, she opened her eyes and sat up on the bunk. She yanked the reader onto her lap, and slapped the datakey home.

It is of utmost importance, my favorite dancer, that we meet together in person in the shortest possible time. I am prepared to meet you at any location you name, at Volmer if you like . . .

Theo blinked against the words and the desire. What better way to celebrate achieving her jacket than to see Win Ton? Win Ton had known her for a pilot before anyone else, perhaps, if she overlooked Father, who must also have known. Win Ton had recognized many things in her.

Her next breath was deep then, as she let the reader rest on the mattress. She closed her eyes, mentally stepping into a relaxation exercise as she sat with bare toes on an unstill floor, leaving the reader on so that she might look again at the mysteries it proposed.

She stood, eyes closed, the backs of her legs anchoring her to the ship and its minute vibrations while the darkness and the exercise fended off the need for immediate action. Her thoughts swept on despite the relaxation, bouncing between wariness and a growing awareness of her accomplishments.

Her time on Melchiza had first pointed up the necessity that had kept her not quite in tune with her compatriots and age-mates ever since: to be most responsible to the most number of people she had first to accept herself as potent and then to manage and expand that potency.

There'd been no good way to express that to Asu, nor to the team builders with their faith in doing well enough to get by in a group.

She considered Father, with his cars, his flowers, his garden—his work. As calm and reserved as he seemed, there was no sense that his first order of business was to please some ordinary standard. That must have been what brought him to Kamele, who also strove beyond the ordinary, finding time to sing in the choir while managing a child, and her career and an odd-world *onagrata*.

Dancer, Win Ton named her. *Pilot*.

She was both of those things. Also, she was Win Ton's friend, though she'd fallen out of the habit of writing to him. Right after she'd been expelled, she'd been too busy. And then—she'd been too busy. She might assume the same of him, who hadn't written again, after the letter bestowing the gift that she still wore 'round her neck.

Do you feel a connection to him? she asked herself, and answered: Yes. Yes, I do.

She opened her eyes.

It is of utmost importance, my favorite dancer, that we meet together . . .

It was true that she didn't know what he wanted from her. It was equally true that she would never know, unless she answered him. If he only wished to return a forgotten hair clip, like a proper *onagrata* out of a silly girl-book, so be it. If there was something more—there was an urgency, to both the letter, and its delivery. Pinbeams were expensive. Expense, in Theo's mind, suggested trouble.

She would answer him; a friend in trouble had that right. But she would answer him when she was rested, and clear in her mind.

That decided, she sighed, and stood in the darkness. Carefully, she did a small dance before stretching on the bed again, letting the words fade, dancing relaxation in her mind until she slept in truth.

"Rig," she said experimentally. "I—need to—"

He turned away from a screen full of legal-looking language, startled, already moving to balance and center and—

"Theo," he laughed, "what have you done now? I can't believe you could sneak up on me on *Primadonna!*"

She smiled, realized that she had been moving quietly, not wanting to rouse Mayko if she could help it.

"I'm awake and need to go back to the comm office before shift. But we didn't really settle what shifts we'd run today—"

"By all rights, you ought to be off-shift for a ten-day, I'd say. You haven't had a real break since we started flying together."

She smiled, raising her hands.

"Haven't got that far ahead," she admitted. "I need to go down

to the comm office and..." She hesitated, and he signed a quick
your call, your flight.

"Personal is personal. Get your comm work done, take a walk,
and we'll see about shifts after that. Mayko's already out so this
shift is mine, and it's about time I run one, huh?" He pointed
toward the lock, eloquent hands saying *go, go*—and, abruptly—*wait.*

He touched his forehead, the gesture meaning *my empty head,*
or sometimes, *I forgot.*

"If you need a comm room—let me call ahead to tell them
you're coming, tell them to reserve one for you, right? And I'll
call you a cart since Mayko's already got ours out on the port
somewhere."

Theo nodded. "Thank you, I should have thought..."

"No. You've been running first board, so this is my job, right?"

She hand-flashed *work work work* at him but he was already
singing as she moved—and he stopped suddenly, pointing back
toward her berth.

"Pilot, your jacket. You earned it. You're on port. Wear it!"

Theo opened her mouth to rebut and found his hands were
already replying with:

Order from shift captain!

She mocked a bow then, and went back to get her jacket.

The distance to the comm office was no shorter, but in the way
that even minor familiarity with a place will change perception, it
felt closer to the *Primadonna* this time. True, the cart attendant,
a young girl who drove a lot like Father, took her directly to the
Pilots Guild gate, and this time when Theo entered with card in
hand she was waved by as if they all knew who she was.

"Captain Tranza was to make..."

The clerk looked up from a desk full of screens.

"Yes, Pilot Waitley. With all the confusion going on I'm afraid
there'll be a wait; if you like, you can catch up on the news at
the café and we'll send someone, or listen for your call."

There was a lot of activity, and the tiny café was full of screens
and talk. There was a flutter of hands and nods when she entered,
and quick glances from those hoping to see a familiar face. In
fact, Theo did recognize several of the gathered pilots as having
been on route or in a bar or on port here at the same time in

the last year. If anybody thought her jacket too big, none said, and none challenged her when she grabbed a table with a multiscreen already scrolling streams.

Korval attacks Liad one stream was marked, and another screamed out *Scouts Repulse Armed Invasion at Nev'lorn*. The large *JONBA AGENCY First Class Pilots Wanted NOW Top Money Top Guarantee* ad bounced at the top of one screen while from the bottom a pulsing blue announced *Mercenaries. We Make Worlds Safe. Join Us. Your Bonus is Waiting.*

At the table to her right, a large woman was talking a little too loud, as if her coffee was boosted.

"Tell you true, I have this from clean source. Aelliana Caylon is back. They say she came busting in from Galaxy Nowhere with guns blazing and blew apart battleships with her little courier ship. These are great times we live in, friend, great times!"

One of her table mates was chuckling: "So when do we expect Bopper to show up, or the Second Terran Fleet?"

Theo touched the order board for the morning tea special, and leaned back. She could have read all this on *Primadonna* if she'd have known the comms were backed up.

"Punch up the register, sandfoot," the woman at the right-side table told her mate. "No? Then I will. I met the Caylon once myself, I did, her and her other. *Ride the Luck*. She was a pickup pilot, you know—just like us. Never missed a delivery, too!"

"She's been dead a long time, Casey. No matter how pretty she was, she's dead."

That voice was sad, and Theo glanced over to the table, where the louder woman—in Jump leather—was crowing, and the sad person craning her neck to see—

"Hah! Lookithere. *Ride the Luck*, Solcintra, Liad, Aelliana Caylon Pilot and Captain, Dock Sixteen-A Binjali Repair, Solcintra. Not Accepting.

"Tell me you see it! Right there in the register. Register don't carry ghosts, Tervot. And just like a Liaden to keep a working ship working, ain't it? Here, let's look for the big one! See it, see it? *Dutiful Passage*, Solcintra, Liad, Priscilla Mendoza Pilot and Captain, Orbit Seventeen Liad, Not Accepting."

There was a stunned silence, spreading over several adjacent tables.

"Mendoza's captain?" someone asked, somberly. "Where's Shan?"

"That's right," the loud woman said, not so loud, now. "yos'Galan was master—for how many years? Damn! They had all that fighting. You don't think—?"

There was a rustle two tables away and a plump man lurched to his feet. "I gotta get me a message out..."

"Queue's long on that," the sad-voiced person said, but the guy was already gone. She pulled the screen to her and threw in her own request. "Now look, Vitale, here's the news archive for when the Caylon got killed—"

The third occupant of the table laughed. "Won't take true for an answer," he said, as the conversations around started to pick up again.

The large woman shook her head.

"Hey, that's Korval-kin you're talking about. Korval is the most Liaden you can get, and if the registry says Aelliana Caylon's parked her ship at Binjali's, well I believe it, cause that's where she always flew from. You know better'n to trust news archives, Tervot!"

Theo sighed. Maybe she should go back to *Primadonna*, if the comm lines were *that* long. Or she could ask Tranza to authorize use of ship's comm; she trusted him not to snoop in her private messages.

Unfortunately, she didn't precisely trust Mayko to do the same.

Thinking of Mayko brought to mind that list of destinations, Delgado among them. Maybe she could get some crew rest herself—visit Father and Kamele. Coyster—Coyster was an elder cat now, looking like dignity itself in the last pics from—

"Vitale, shut your face!" came a vehement whisper from the table on her right.

She looked up in time to see the large woman blush, then push purposefully to her feet.

She nodded to Theo, hands asking *permission to approach.*

Theo granted it, warily sitting a little straighter though without resorting to dance.

The woman stepped closer, and attempted a bow.

"I'd like to let you know, Pilot, I wasn't talking personal. I'm just so glad to see the Caylon back that—well, I betcha most Liadens are glad that she's back, isn't that so? And if they managed to keep her hid so she *could* come back, why that's fine. I wasn't trying to, you know, impugn your *melant'i* or—"

Hold course hold course Theo signed, aware that everyone at the woman's table was watching with trepidation.

"I'm not a Liaden, Pilot. Please relax. I'm fine."

"Pilot, your tea, and handwich." The advertised items landed on the table before Theo, and the waiter was gone that quickly. The big woman nodded, glancing particularly at the tea.

"Yah, First, I see," she said, almost whispering. "Lots of folks are traveling quiet. Look, I'm Casey Vitale. Fly with Chenowith and Gladder. Right now I've got *Aldershot* on a coldpad until they get me new orders."

She handed over a card, and bowed again. "At your service. I get a little het up sometimes when I'm grounded, and right now, what with all the sudden traffic through here, I'm waiting for a beam."

Theo inclined her head, which was the proper answer to the bow—and exactly what a Liaden would have done. She sighed, reached into her pocket and returned the favor.

"Theo Waitley," she said.

Her card simply said: Primadonna, *Theo Waitley, Hugglelans Galactica*.

Casey Vitale grinned. "Hey, that's a good outfit. Good outfit. I—"

"Scouts!" came the call from somewhere near the door. "Crew of 'em! Weapons on display!"

That was enough to startle Theo, who looked away from Casey Vitale, trying to imagine a crew of Scouts so bold as to...

There *was* a crew of them, uniformed, and weapons in plain sight on their belts, a taller one in front pointing toward the single free table in the back corner, one with a view of the exit.

Hands fluttered all around, and nods, and murmurs as the café patrons took in the sight, and the silent march of the Scouts, as one wearing a half-plex goggle over his eyes and upper face made a large, shapeless motion with his hand. His wrists were encumbered with wraparound healing bracelets or supports, and his face mottled with fresh-grown skin still not toned. His signal, sloppy as it had been, halted the rest in mid-march.

The goggled one said something deep and quiet in Liaden, and threaded carefully through the close-set tables. Her attention on the approaching Scout, Theo felt, rather than saw, Casey Vitale step back to her own table.

He paused at her table, removed the goggle and bowed, deep

and wondrously slow, almost, Theo thought, as if it pained him to move.

"Pilot Waitley," he said in a hoarse, strained voice. He bowed again, not as deep, and corrected himself: "First Class Jump Pilot Waitley. Sweet Mystery. Words fail."

His eyes were brown, and strained, with wrinkles that stopped abruptly at the new skin; his upper lip had strange color where it, too, had been resurfaced. She searched his face and found him, behind the strain, and the patchwork.

Rising, she resisted the urge to throw herself on him, to touch him.

"Win Ton! Win Ton, what has happened?"

His grin was fleeting, and his voice even more of a croak.

"What has not happened?" he replied, and for that instant, he was Win Ton as she had first met him. Then he bowed, for yet a third time.

"Theo, I overstepped."

He glanced down at his wrists, and added, seriously. "I took damage. May I sit?"

Without waiting for permission—in fact, as if he *must* sit—he nearly fell into the chair beside her. She sank into her own chair, and put her hand over his, where it lay on the table.

He leaned toward her conspiratorially, his voice weaker even than his grin.

"We need to talk, pilot and friend. We need to talk."

THIRTY-SEVEN

. . . .

Conrad Café
Pilots Guild Hall
Volmer

"PRIMADONNA ISN'T EXACTLY NEUTRAL TERRITORY," WIN TON allowed. "Nor would our Scout rooms be, I gather," he said cautiously, glancing down-room to the table his companions had commandeered. "Certainly it is too public, here."

There was a dance or a game going on, beneath his words. Theo sensed it without understanding the rules. She agreed, though, that if she was going to be with him for the first time in, well, years, she'd rather it be somewhere other than a crowded café.

"Are we in competition?" she asked blandly, taking her hand off of his.

Win Ton, this apparition of a Win Ton, sighed lightly, eye wrinkles tightening as he leaned toward her, speaking as low as might be heard in the cramped room.

"We are not in competition." His shoulders moved in what might be a shrug as he weighed his words with care. "We are, however, working on multiple balances and necessities, which might put us at odds, and so should not be dealt with in a place as distracting as this one, nor in a place—"

"*First*, you said you wanted some place quieter."

He didn't argue, his left hand making an exaggerated and unformed attempt at *acknowledged*.

"We can use a comm booth then, or a conference room." The thought that had been niggling at her back brain surfaced and spoke itself: "What are you *doing* here, anyway?"

"Speaking with one of my favorite people."

Theo frowned.

"This is complex." He pursed his lips. "I am willing to have you choose a location, Theo, but really, no more, here, if I may be so bold. I'll order another tray of tea and—"

Theo motioned, not at Win Ton but at the waiter.

"Guild conference room? Is one available?"

The waiter looked at Win Ton, in uniform, and at the other Scouts, again at Theo in her leather, and hitched his neck in an odd motion, using his head to point.

"Upper left quad of the display. Looks like there's two available— the blue lights. One's clear until next shift, the other's got...a while, that's the numbers on the right column. Other four are solid. Show your card at the desk."

"So, yes, it is complex. I am at fault in some things, for which I will plead necessity and also admit that I have overstepped, and offer to hear your balance on the issues as time permits."

They were seated, just the two of them, across the table of the conference room. There'd been an awkward moment when the door closed, leaving the Scouts with their weapons and aware-ness behind, and Theo'd wanted to fling herself into his arms, a moment made more awkward by his apparent realization and careful half turn offering her the choice of seats, and the fact that she carried the tray with the tea and snacks.

"I, who, why..." she began, and sputtered out; the look of intense concentration on Win Ton's patched face silencing her.

"I honor you, Theo Waitley, I honor you immensely. You quite properly have many questions, and I will attempt to answer them as quickly as I may, in as clear a fashion as I may. I request your patience. Please believe me in all ways eager to explain a situation that is as complex as it is nearly inexplicable."

Theo danced in her mind, calling on the routine she called *inner calm*. She hadn't realized before how many cues about Win Ton she took from his hands and shoulders. Now, with his hands—not fully operational...

There on the chair, she centered herself, and looked to his face, with patience.

"Would you like some tea?" she asked.

He inclined his head. "I would very much like some tea. Thank you."

She poured for both of them, and sat back, cup held in one hand.

"I'm ready when you are," she said.

He smiled weakly, though to Theo's eye, with honest intent, and sipped his tea, some of the tension easing out of his shoulders.

"The easiest questions may be your most recent. The Scouts I travel with are, as a unit, security and support. One is a med tech, each is a specialist. Consider them for argument sake, if you will permit yourself a moment of absurdity, my bodyguards."

Theo thought about that; sighed and acknowledged, *accept*.

"Excellent. I am here, we are here, because it was likely that in fact *you* would be here or within hailing distance, and because the task I am set to by the Scouts has a thread which runs through Volmer. As a haven for Juntavas in the past it has been a place where Scouts and the even less reputable might from time to time have discourse on many subjects.

"So, that is the immediate why of here and who."

He paused, and surprised her by reaching inside the collar of his shirt and pulling out a necklace matching her own. Made clumsy by the wrist shields, he pulled the chain over his head and placed it on the table between them, one finger on the pendant cylinder. He looked into her eyes.

"This, my friend, and the one you wear, are the start of all of it, as well as I can manage the story. I will tell it to you, requesting you share the information only on a true need-to-know basis."

She nodded, but he was already moving on, seeming to look at her and through her at the same time.

"In my travels immediately after my contract wedding, I was started as a courier to deliver a ship, before my long-term assignment was to begin. I had cause to visit a—let me call it a site—requiring periodic maintenance of various reporting equipment. This site is one where, in the distant past, various objects and devices of doubtful source and design were sequestered from polite commerce, and in that distant past the planetary site was manned. My duties were simple: to be assured that the airlocks still functioned, that the holds still held, and that the sovereignty of our organization over it was not in doubt. This particular assignment was one of what they call the 'garbage runs' that Scouts must make from time to time, personal observations being important, and besides, Scouts need to be kept busy and in training, even between long-term assignments."

Theo tried to concentrate on Win Ton's words and not on his face. There was something there she wasn't used to seeing in him, a reserve beyond simple attention to his own story, or a distraction.

Impulsively she asked, "Are you in pain?"

Win Ton bowed slightly to her.

"Another question we shall arrive at in good time. Suffice it to say that at the moment I feel no pain. And that so, we continue."

Theo felt the hair on the back of her neck tingle and involuntarily looked behind her, perhaps to the very spot Win Ton looked, for again he was not looking directly at her. If there was anything there, it was invisible to her eyes, and she returned her attention to his face.

"While I arrived at the happy news that most of the items on my checklist and inventory were in fine order, I discovered much to my surprise that there was, among the expected items, one that was listed on no manifest. It being anomalous, I explored.

"I am not quite the aficionado of ancient technology that Captain sig'Radia is, but what I found in plain sight appeared to be an antique ship."

He smiled, as if there was an amusing secret to be revealed.

"When I say antique I mean one in which the mount points for add-ons are all of what we now think of as 'legacy' and inadequate; but still the lines were attractive and it sat close enough to the rest of the assemblage that I considered its location not an accident. There were no signs of egress or return, and conditions were such that when I approached, I left footprints in the surface dust."

He smiled again. "Indeed, I was pleased to leave footprints, to and fro. In any case, in size my mystery was no battleship or trade monster, let us say just large enough to carry *Torvin* in the main hold."

The mention of *Torvin* made her smile, and gave her useful scale. Not a tiny ship, just sitting—

"No pad, no guidance markers, no—?"

He waved his hands lightly. "No, no...not a place outwardly inviting landing, I think. Certainly there are no current incoming guidance or landing markers which might be regarded as invitation...

"Standard hailing having failed, despite the signs of the ship being on low power, and finding no signs of human life on the various scans available to me, I approached, with imaging on. And arriving at an available airlock, I pressed cycle, fully expecting the works to fail."

He glanced toward the ceiling, then gave her a strained grin.

"My expectations were dashed. The ship opened to me. As it did I could feel systems working within, and thus welcomed, I toured it.

"The crew quarters were fit for six or eight, with a separate family suite. In addition, there was a small passenger section which might hold perhaps six more. There was one large hold, as I said, and several smaller. There was a medical tech room with a quite amazing array of equipment—and I was dutifully amazed by it. The bridge itself was for the most part dark when I entered, and more crowded than we are used to, but lights came up and I...overstepped."

Theo raised an eyebrow. "You sat at the captain's console, and the defenses nearly killed you?"

He blew air through his lips lightly, a long sigh.

"No," he said slowly. "No. Your story would be happier than mine, I fear. True, I did sit, and I *thought* I sat in the captain's chair, at the front, with the copilot's seat to the left and a worktable with odds and ends upon it between. As I settled, the screens before me lit.

"Antique Terran ships have not, until now, been my specialty, Theo. I saw the letter approximating B on screen and discovered that I taken the copilot's place, as Terrans and Liadens oft mirror-image things. The screen politely requested that the copilot insert a command key. On the table between there were two chains with keys, each in their own depressions, and several cups in cup tunnels, and I grabbed up the key closest to me, which was the one I could reach, and I held it in my hands for some moments, considering that I should not, perhaps—and then considering that I must, after all, make a report and a fuller report would be better than none.

"So, grasping the key, I inserted it, firmly, and turned it to the right."

He paused to attend to his tea, raising the cup in two hands and sipping uncertainly.

Theo sighed. "It did occur to you that this wasn't smart, but you did it anyway."

He lowered his cup to the tabletop and looked into her eyes. "I cannot help myself, Theo. The curiosity overrules sense, which is ridiculous."

She nodded. "Then what?"

"Then, the ship asked for my palm on an outlined reader surface. I did as it asked, and felt several tingles of low-dose static, and then the screen turned several colors under my palm. I was even sampled for blood, I believe, as I got nicked! A light went on, and a nice musical note sounded.

"I raised my hand and the ship truly woke. The screen displayed a new message: '*Bechimo* welcomes our copilot. Registry in progress.' Then, it proceeded to detail to me the state of the vessel, which considered itself fully fueled and at one hundred and thirty-seven percent of rated power. It showed condition of airlocks, of scan cameras and radar and vision checks, rated the meteor shields and defense screens, and proceeded to offer six different weapons systems.

"At that point, I thought it best to call in the experts. The tech which the Scouts had stored at this site was all Old Tech, and I had no reason to consider this ship anything but more of the same, despite it telling me that it was willing to fly; despite that it was suggesting courses, despite that it was updating star charts and energy field information to match current observations.

"Cautious too late, I turned the interlock, and turned the key to off."

He demonstrated at the nonexistent console in front of him.

"The ship noted this, and requested that I remove my key."

He waved his hand at the screen that was not there.

"This, I did." He shook his head, slowly.

"*Registry complete*, is what it told me, Theo, *registry complete*."

She shrugged. The ship would have had to acknowledge, after all . . .

"Ah, but you see, the ship continued with its work. Star chart systems continued to function. Air gauges proved the ship habitable. Defense systems were now *on*."

That was wrong. Theo opened her mouth to say so, then simply shook her head.

"Yes," he said wearily, "overstepped, and an idiot besides. And now, rather than having only my single ship to worry about I had two live ships on the surface, and one of them I knew nothing about. Surely the systems were close enough that I might fly *Bechimo*, if I dared, but what then of the remainder of my assignment?

"Thus I hit on the plan of removing the keys, both copilot and captain, locking the ship behind me, and continuing my rounds."

Theo touched the chain around her neck.

"*This?* You sent me a ship's key to an antique ship sitting on a planet in the middle of nowhere? Why?"

He lifted his hands limply.

"Because I had realized—not my error; that came later—say that I realized I had awoken something best left drowsing and sought to be certain that no one else found it aware. However it was, I took possession of those keys, the B key and the A key, and I sent in my reports, with images, as I continued my run, expecting at every turn to be asked to bring the keys in, or to take them to someone, or to leave them somewhere.

"No one got back to me, and I was near the end of my interim mission, arriving on what would be a long mission. So I sent you the captain's key, knowing you would keep it safe. And I kept my own key, knowing that I would keep it safe."

Theo stared at him, hard.

"This is true? All of it?" Her hand-signs alternated between *full power* and *one hundred percent*.

"One hundred percent," he said, and again lifted his cup in two hands.

"So that's the problem?" she asked. "That you acted hastily? That no one cared about your work?"

"Eventually someone at Scout Headquarters *did* read the report," he said, looking at her over the rim of his cup. "It had been misfiled... perhaps even purposefully hidden—altered. I refiled the complete report, at the direction of Headquarters."

He drank the last of the tea, sloppily, and lowered the cup to the table.

"Theo, there are people after what I carry—what *we* carry. They want the keys to that ship."

Theo took a very deep breath.

"If it belongs to them, then we should—"

Win Ton raised his voice, or tried to: "It does *not* belong to them."
He paused, his eyes downcast, then looked into her face.

"There are rogues, rogues working from Liad, and even from
within the Scouts. They want that ship because it is a hybrid of
Old Tech and more current technology, and because that ship
has already cost them dozens of agents. Dozens."

"I don't understand this, Win Ton. You've lost me here."

He sighed, looking exhausted and frail behind his scars.

"Yes, because I have not told it all. Your pardon, Pilot." He
took a moment to recruit himself, again daring to look into her
face. "To continue, Headquarters is very concerned about that
ship. *Bechimo* was built at a period when the Terran trading
families were trying to reassert their trade routes; it used Old
tech, stolen, perhaps dangerous tech. The ship owners and the
ship builders hid it because they were under pressure and then
they were . . . suppressed."

"Suppressed?" She shuddered, remembering some of the histories
she'd read at the academy.

"The regional Terran trade cartels had them hounded, drove
some into bankruptcy, them and their families, some perhaps
were forcefully removed and blackmailed.

"This was several centuries ago, you see, and the *Bechimo* was
never flown beyond proof flights; never in actual service. According to the stories, the crew meant for *Bechimo* was raided and
arrested, and a lien put on the ship. Whereupon, the ship disappeared. Rumor said it could fly rings around other tradeships
of like capacity. It was all that was better—and more dangerous
because its builders dared to use some of the Old Tech that went
into the original Terran fleets, that destroyed each other in the
big war, and things even older and more dangerous.

"My research says that *Bechimo* has an onboard AI. More likely,
it *is* an AI. *Bechimo* the ship—it can fly itself."

"Well, there are ships now that—"

"No. Well, yes. I can program a ship to take me somewhere,
and if I fall over dead with poison it will still get there, in some
case even over multiple Jumps. Lacking a pilot, *Bechimo* will itself
decide where to go, and what to do when it arrives. With owners
dead, perhaps it owns itself!"

"What was it doing at the Scout site?" Theo asked. "Looking for a party?"

He smiled, palely.

"Very close to that, I think. I gather that what it was doing there was that an agent from the Department—one of the rogues—had been last on the garbage run before me—several Standards before me, in fact. Given leave to look about, that agent investigated the cache of old equipment. They were testing and trying things, copying things, copying records. Inadvertently or not, they had activated the call signal, and did not know that it had finally been answered. I was first on the scene, after it had waited . . . and it imprinted on me."

Theo thought back to school, wagged her body from side to side in the chair and said, "Quack, quack, quack, gooselets on parade?"

Win Ton gave a bow so light it was barely a nod.

"Indeed. But then the rogues saw the report, hid it, shared the information among themselves, and went back for the ship."

"Which didn't acknowledge them?" Theo said helpfully.

"In a manner of speaking."

Win Ton paused, poured himself more tea from the pot, appearing somewhat steadier.

"*Bechimo* did not allow them aboard. When they attempted to force entry, it resisted, inflicting minor injuries as a warning. When they tried something more forceful, it wiped out the boarding party."

Theo blinked.

"Had you programmed the defenses?"

"Until now, recall, I have not had the study of antique Terran ships close to my heart."

"But how do you know this, about the landing party?"

"The survivors decided that what had worked once, would do so again. They came looking for me, Theo—and they found me."

Theo looked to the hall in horror. Win Ton raised his hands and signed heavily—*not those*, wincing as he did.

"I escaped, but they know that there were two keys. They believe that the second is still with the ship." He paused. "I believe I convinced them of that."

She sipped her tea, which was cold; sipped again and put the empty cup on the table.

"Thank you," she said, because she felt she had to acknowledge his last statement. She took a breath. "How do you have *your* key with you, if you were captured?"

He sighed. "It is Old Tech, and it is imprinted on me. It returned itself to me as it was able." He used his chin to point at it, there on the table between them. "There, take it up."

She picked it up, feeling a sense of relaxation, of welcome—and something more. Her key warmed agreeably between her breasts, and she heard a buzz, as if the captain's key was . . . acknowledging the copilot's.

"I feel it," she murmured, hardly aware that she spoke aloud.

"No difficulty?" Win Ton asked. "No headache?"

She shook her head, and put his key back on the table, not really wanting to. Her fingers moved gently—*all fine better good.*

He sighed, quite loudly. "May I hold yours?"

Reluctantly she drew the necklace, and handed to him.

He held it in his fist a moment, then returned it across his open palm, face gone Liaden bland.

"What's wrong?" she asked, holding the chain in her hand.

"Yes, Pilot, that is the question. The answer is like the birds you mentioned, Theo, the gooselets. That key, it has imprinted on you. I did not think—but there, that is given, is it not?" He moved his head, maybe he meant to shake it. "You not only hold the captain's key, Theo, but the key has also been imprinted. *Bechimo* accepts you as her captain."

THIRTY-EIGHT

. . . .

Conference Room Able
Pilots Guildhall
Volmer

"THEO?"

The chain was bright, the odd-shaped pendant familiar and comforting. In fact, so comforting that she was inclined to accept Win Ton's tale of Old Tech imprinting; the key almost *radiated* comfort...which was enough to set her teeth on edge when she thought about it. Theo glanced between her chain and his, seeing not much visible to set them apart. What would happen, she wondered, if they switched keys or got them mixed up by accident?

Win Ton's voice was more insistent this time, a little stronger. That was better—he almost sounded like his old self for a moment.

"Theo?"

She looked up into his face across the scarred table, feeling the smile trying to twitch at the corners of her mouth despite the annoyance that informed her shoulders.

"What am I supposed to do, Win Ton? You're not looking up to sitting a board and I—I don't know where this ship *is*, I haven't the first clue where to find it. You knew where it was, and now you don't; now you know who the pilot is but not where she can board it! What a pair of First and Second we'd make for *Bechimo*, eh? A pilot who wouldn't recognize her ship and a Second—well, if *I'm* the captain, what am I supposed to do with you?"

"Theo, I am a Scout. A Scout on duty..."

"How can you be on duty, Win Ton? Look at you!"

That hit him like a blow; if he'd been feeling stronger she was afraid she'd taken it all back from him with an ill-timed word.

He bowed one of his consequential bows, and spoke with eyes down, voice low.

"Pilot, I doubt anyone is more aware than I of my state."

"Then surely you know you need more than a pilot for a missing ship!"

"Theo, I am here to meet with a . . ." He hesitated, the pause stretching; and Theo couldn't tell if it was his vocabulary or his attention that was failing him. He raised his hands, fingers stuttering through something she couldn't catch. He drew a hard breath and lowered his hands, pressing palms flat.

"My team is here to meet with a person of special knowledge, one of those fringe type who exist, but who are rarely mentioned in reports or acknowledged in public. This one fell heir to a title belonging to one who aided in the building of *Bechimo*. An owner—this we think not. Yet there are features on the *Bechimo* . . . that this one has particular knowledge of. Features which speak to my thriving again, Theo. Which speak to my survival."

Dread flooded her and she dared to lean toward him, reaching toward his hands pressed against the table.

"Survival?"

"My captors insisted on my assistance, Theo. They assumed they could compel it quickly enough that I would be in their thrall when they recovered the ship."

"I don't understand, Win Ton."

He nodded a firm Terran *yes*. "No, you do not. May I have some tea, please? It is well chosen."

"Thank you."

She poured again for them both, hands flippantly presenting *continue at will* as soon as they had each sipped from their fresh cup.

Win Ton allowed his mouth to curl into the veriest ghost of a smile.

"This is not easy for any of us. The crew that travels with me does so to keep me alive insofar as they may, because of the problems I have caused, and the solution only I may effect. If I die, well then, *Bechimo* would be free in the galaxy with no guidance at all from a Scout, and with the danger that it may take some other group of people—these not attempting a forced entry—into dislike and eliminate them. Only my key, and yours, stand between this ghost ship becoming released to do whatever bidding it gives to itself."

"My key—" she began.

He shook his head. "Your key—is not widely known. It is in fact, underreported."

"I still am missing pieces of this...why can you not be cured? Why am I so bound up in this?"

"The *melant'i* of the situation is complex. We have sat at the same board, and because of my overstep, we sit at a new and strange board in absentia. Worse, and more complex, is the mix of the Old Tech in this, which inspires Headquarters to lend energy to a scheme depending on the trustworthiness of scoundrels and the very technology the Scouts wish to dispense with entirely."

The tea *was* having a bracing effect; his voice was clearer now.

"After my report reached a dishonest agent within Headquarters and was noted, waves happened. While the actual administrator was attempting to route me to a safe place to be questioned, this group, this Department, captured me and inflicted torture in the hope that I could, and would, give them *Bechimo*. They used Old Technology and new in service of their goal, but I was truly ignorant. Alas, the Old Tech they wished to embrace did as Old Tech so often does; it moved to its own whim, or to a design so grand it is beyond us all.

"In the course of this...questioning, I was injected, on purpose, with a slow-growing set of nanobugs. They—the rogues—had a controller, and could make me sicker, and better, or so they thought, and they used them to change functions, and even to hide and replace certain DNA, they claimed."

Theo kept her tone even, and only succeeded in making herself tenser as she heard her own words. "They were wrong? If you're sick to being in danger of your life..."

"The Old Tech, Theo, it—interacts with other devices of its kind, and not always at direction. The key—our keys—they are aware of our presence, or even our distance; in some fashion I do not understand. They interact with each other and they draw on the power and ability of other Old Tech. How else would the key forcibly taken from me keep returning to my cell? And when it returned the final time, why, the hand of the man who sought to reclaim it was burned as if he grabbed a live torch, while the necklace was cool and comforting to me."

"Is the key keeping you alive?"

"I do not know that. Neither do the techs, nor the Scouts who specialize in the study of Old Tech. But the ship on which I was captive—it orbited a world that held Old Tech in abundance, and my keepers told me they would unleash these devices they had collected to destroy Liad. They promised—as if it were a *chernubia!*—to allow me to *help*. All I need do was give them *Bechimo* and my future would be returned to me.

"They would fix me, cure me, make me whole. And that ship that these rogues held me upon, it suffered when I suffered; the Old Tech systems were changed while I was there. It would whisper to me, in Terran sometimes, or else dementia from the nanobugs did, but it mentioned names and repeated words."

"Words?"

"'There are secrets in all families,' it said to me, and whenever it did, there was a change. The first time it told me was when the food robot brought me dinner with my key buried in the food. The next time was just before the air-leak alarms went off. I am not certain of the next time—but they left that planet when a ship without call signs kept appearing at the limits of scans, appearing and then moving elsewhere. I suspect it was *Bechimo*. But I was kept well away from any comm devices or viewers.

"We grounded at Caratunk, for emergency repairs. The ship let me out, Theo, the ship and the food robot conspired and let me out."

He paused there, watching her. Not trusting her voice, Theo let her fingers reply: *continue information I copy.*

She could see his eyes follow her hands, but it was as if he needed to *translate* what she said, instead of just absorbing it, and when he looked into her face before going on she knew that it was so.

His words came, slowly.

"I ran, as well as I could. The observatory staff hid me and eventually Scouts came, and they failed to believe my story. They thought me an agent or an enemy, and then they took me for debriefing to Nev'lorn, the reserve headquarters, under guard. The agents of the Department came there, and my key whispered to me, and we had fighting..."

"Then *Ride the Luck* arrived, and turned the battle," Theo suggested, remembering Casey Vitale's excitement.

Win Ton sighed.

"Perhaps it did; for my part, I was involved in the fighting on station. I robbed the dead of their weapons. There were injured and wounded all around. I defended a hallway leading to the administrators who were holding me as prisoner, because the attackers were this same Department that had tortured me.

"Of course, the important news to the universe was that the Caylon's ship broke the back of the enemy, and that there is a missing yos'Phelium returned to Korval." There was real annoyance in his voice; he gave a half laugh, and a shrug.

"Far more important to me was the understanding that the catastrophic healing units were first for the casualties of the battle. Understand, Theo, that meant for the people they knew might benefit. But these things I've been infected with—the ordinary units, even the catastrophe units, they are not adequate."

"The healing units don't work?" Theo barely heard her own whisper.

"They stall matters for a while, it seems. Every time a fresh series begins, there's something new, as if the bugs learn the unit's cure, and so have restructured themselves. The techs therefore have held me free of autodocs and the like, afraid the bugs might learn all that the unit might do."

"And this place—Volmer. There's someone here with a cure?"

Win Ton sighed. "Not, I think, a cure. A lead, a chance. Headquarters cannot afford to have me take up healing space that is needed for others, and they do not want the Department to control *Bechimo*. They want *no one* to control *Bechimo*. And thus they mean to find it, and kill it—which they consider me too ill or too stupid to have deduced. So we come here; which intercepted your course—a bonus for me."

Theo touched her necklace, the familiar weight of it calming, soothing—active.

"Do they expect me to hand this over to them, then?"

Win Ton looked startled.

"Who? The crew with me? As I said, it is...not well known that there is a second key. Those who travel with me are doing a favor for a comrade who may not have much time left, by allowing me to meet with you for whatever we might bring to such a meeting. Call it a casting of Balances, and celebration of my life."

Theo reached for his hand then, barely covering his right hand with the strange scarring. His skin felt cool to her, even cold.

"And you, do you expect this to be our last meeting?"

That sounded hollow to her, but she didn't want to say...

"Do I expect to die? Yes—we all do, and pilots often earlier than others, it seems. I am not...advocating my death now, and I have an account I would prefer to Balance."

"Then this meeting delays you? You must get to your contact, Win Ton, because I'm not advocating your death, either. I'd rather settle accounts, if we have them, in proper time, than rattle off some unthoughtful words just to..." She stopped.

"Just to settle a dying man's mind?" Oddly, he smiled. "Sweet Mystery, yes, this heartens me. We will come into Balance, I have no doubt. And I cannot meet with this person, until they announce their presence to us—my crew is waiting for news now."

Barely were these words spoken when a knock came at the door, and a respectful two heartbeats after, one of the Scouts stepped in, with a Guild staffer.

Theo thought they'd overstayed their time, and rose to leave.

"Forgive us, Pilots. There is a message, the Guild holds a message, for Pilot Waitley."

The staffer showed the memory pad he held, and spoke with animation.

"Pilot, I can't believe this—someone has sent you a message marked urgent, but it's not pinbeamed and it isn't properly addressed! It goes by relay to the whole route of your ship, I gather. But you are here, I knew, and rather than send it on to the ship, or wait until I saw you again, I thought to gain what speed I could by bringing it now, here."

He handed the pad to Theo.

"Wipe and return before you leave, or if you must, take it and we'll deduct it from your credits."

Theo received the pad, staring at it like she'd never seen one before. A route-following message for her? But—if it was so important it couldn't be sent to her mail drop, why *not* a pinbeam?

The Scout and the staffer left. Win Ton was making a painful motion with his hand, and this time she could read the signs: *privacy query.*

She shook her head, tucked the pad against her side so she could sign—*a moment only*—and touched hand to key plate.

URGENT for Pilot THEO WAITLEY Hugglelans Lines from KAMELE WAITLEY.

She sat, heavily, waiting for the rest of the message to resolve. From across the table, she heard heavy breathing.

The message was short and wrenching, with the unsaid as unsettling as the said.

Daughter Theo, I am sending this to Hugglelans and to your Guild, and apologize if multiple messages reach you, or if the cost seems exorbitant. I act as your mother in this, and not as an accountant.

Jen Sar has disappeared in midsemester, without notice to me or to the Administration, on his off day before mid-tests. The only clue I can gather is of a small and dilapidated spaceship long unflown, departing Delgado the same day, from an airfield within easy drive, flown by one of his description. His car, keys on seat, fishing gear in place, sat in an assigned spot there. The spaceship, so station informs me, is not in Delgado space.

Within a day of his departure, I discovered that the house on Leafydale Place, all possessions, and especially the cats, are gifts to me. I continue the tea run, with fading hopes. I felt that you must be told, and can only hope your connections with your father are not as fully disrupted as my own.

Kamele

Theo banged the pad on the table as if the message might be shaken into something other, and then grabbed it up again and reread it, the sense of it the same, the whole of it senseless. Father wouldn't just *leave*!

"Theo?"

Win Ton was standing quite near; she'd been so concentrated on Kamele's letter that she hadn't heard him move. He was doing his best not to look at the memo screen, so much so that she struggled against a laugh and lost to a resulting snarfing giggle.

"Theo, is there...a problem?"

He stood with a steadying hand on table, and she managed to strangle the giggle into words.

"Win Ton, my father's gone."

His mottled face showed a change from intent interest to

blandness back to some emotion she couldn't name, as if his ill-
ness betrayed his training.

Hand still braced against the table, he bowed a special bow,
indicating respect for the elders, and said something in Liaden
which she understood part of, and something else in Liaden,
which got by her ear entirely. Within a heartbeat, he bowed again,
murmuring in Terran, what must have been the translation: "May
you have all joy in the memory of your loved one."

"No," she burst out. "He's not dead! He's *gone*. Missing! Run
away from his classes in a beat-up spaceship and—*his classes!*"

Win Ton went through another set of changes, relief perhaps
coming into his shoulders, while his eyebrows drew painfully
together.

"And has he never before—"

"No, not ever not ever!"

Theo realized that she'd banged the memo pad onto the table
again.

"Sorry," she said, very low, and then took it to Liaden, with
proper gravity, "Forgive me if I offend in this moment of uncer-
tainty."

"No offense," he murmured, inclining his head.

Theo closed her eyes momentarily. *Inner calm*, she told herself,
deliberately relaxing tight muscles. She opened her eyes. Win Ton
was still standing, braced against the table, his arm trembling
with strain.

"Please," she said, alarmed, "sit. This—this is not your problem.
I'm not sure it's my problem, except—"

Win Ton stood away from the table carefully, a soothing hand
barely touching hers before he moved back to his chair.

"Your father, this is the Jen Sar Kiladi you spoke of?"

Theo nodded, staring again at the screen and Kamele's last,
accusatory sentence. *I felt that you must be told, and can only
hope your connections with your father are not as fully disrupted
as my own.*

"Kamele thinks I must have known," she said. "He had a *spaceship* on world, and he never mentioned it."

Win Ton's hands now soothed her from a distance, his fingers
moved, maybe trying to form words. After a moment, he folded
them together on the table.

She looked down at the pad again, trying to think clearly.

What *could* she do, after all? Go to Delgado and stare at a car full of fishing poles? Witness an empty spot in a ship park she'd never known of?

"I repeat, Sweet Mystery." The irony in his hoarse voice penetrated and brought her eyes to Win Ton's face.

"By all understanding your father is Liaden, whether he properly wears a clan name out of history, or not. It is obvious that his clan has called him home. The delm has the right to demand, and the clan member has the duty to return."

"No," she said. "He wouldn't—"

She stopped, hearing Kara's voice, speaking very seriously, warning her—warning her about Liadens.

Everything—promises, partnerships and plans—must be set aside, should the clan call one to duty. Remember that, about Liadens, Theo. It's just—it might help. Later.

She closed her eyes, trying to accommodate a universe in which *Father* could be commanded—compelled. Father had always been a force unto himself—like a law of nature, Kamele used to say.

"Theo?"

Her hand moved of itself, fingers forming *pause*.

Contract, she thought. Win Ton. Father. *Bechimo*. Four problems, pulling in different directions, and no clear solution to any of them. She needed—

She needed time. Focus.

Theo rose, memo pad in hand, sparing Win Ton a nod that was far more curt than she intended.

"And by this you mean?" he asked with some perspicacity.

She took a breath.

"I mean that I need time to think. I'm missing a father. There's a ghost ship looking for me. I have a friend who is dying. I have a contract to read and a future to decide. Right?"

She stared at the cuff of Rig's jacket—*her* jacket—and looked back at him.

He rose, shaky, but determined.

"Be as well as you can, my friend," she said, softly. "We *will* sit board together again. I *want* that. If there's anything I can do to make that happen, be sure I'll do it."

He bowed then, perhaps with a bit of energy.

"You have my direction, Theo. I will contact you as soon as I may, if you cannot contact me."

Theo sighed, and gave him the pilot's salute she'd learned on Melchiza.

"I'm due back on *Primadonna*," she said. Chaos! Tranza would think she'd been taken by slavers!

"If you do not return or reply, Sweet Mystery, what shall I assume? That you have decided that my plight is beyond your care?"

She took the question, looked at it advertently, felt the terrors around the edge of it. Carefully, she extended her hand, and took his cold, weak one. He did not withdraw.

"Win Ton. Pilot yo'Vala. Friend. I will reply as soon as I may. If I do not reply it is because the solution is one beyond me, and I've gone—gone for help. Is that acceptable?"

His eyes widened very briefly, and he bowed a stately bow on unsteady legs.

"Pilot's choice, Theo. As I sit your second, it must be acceptable."

THIRTY-NINE

. . . .

Primadonna
Volmer

"RIGHT."

Rig stood with arms crossing his chest, noting the board feed Theo was taking from Volmer's orbiting station. She could see him reflected in the screens—a not-unusual thing for her this past year.

"It makes sense to see what they're looking for there, but, Theo, the real action's right there in the bar, right? They got the same feed you got from station and they got bidders and askers looking for work right now. The usual applies, of course—makes sense to get a checkup on the ship if you can, and know the crew if there is one—but here you can find something you can check before lunch and sign before dinner if you need to, and you don't have to pay a fare or pull a favor to get there, and you're not paying for your own air while you wait. Right. Station-waiting can be a big drain on the accounts!"

That made good pilot sense, even if her mood now was to get off-planet as soon as she could. With no need to go to Delgado, no real need to be *anywhere* except at the board of a ship...and coming up with a plan to find her father, of course. And figure out a way to help Win Ton, and *Bechimo*, if it existed, and for which, she had realized on her ride back to *Primadonna*, she only had the word of a very ill and perhaps unstable man.

"Guild member to Guild member, Rig, am I reading this right?" She flicked to the screen displaying the new Hugglelans contract.

"Right. See, historically, the whole trip run gets credited to whoever runs the board, with time as PIC. This contract, I think they want to make it so they can keep running to places like Eylot and Tourmalin and—well, these places that want to look at the ship's log for the last ten years and see if you've ever been anywhere they don't like. So see, they'd not mention that you was even on board here at Volmer if they wanted you to be PIC when we got to, say, Tourmalin, who don't hold with trading someplace where the Juntavas is quite so thick on the ground. Thing is, by this contract they could hide that, and once you hide that on the ship records, then it gets pretty easy to hide or steal flight time from pilots, or release it only under seal to the Guild and such."

"That's what I thought I was seeing, like here—" Theo pulled a second screen live, several sections highlighted in the ugliest pink she could find. "Which, it looks to me, means they could cut my pay if I'm aboard a ship going to Eylot, by cutting me out of the in-and-out loop there so Eylot Admin wouldn't see my name and number; they wouldn't need to give me full time-in-grade points and—"

Rig tapped his ear, which meant his volume must be wrong or—no, the sound of footsteps in the corridor reached her.

"Pilot Tranza, I believe you are duty pilot, are you not? Would you care to share with me the status of the ship? This chitchat—"

"Pilot Mayko," he replied without turning, "a Guild member has asked my advice on a matter of current interest to both of us, and one which affects this ship intimately. As you are returned I assume that our immediate mission here is done and we can begin implementing the routes and procedures outlined for this vessel by Pilot Waitley. Shift sequence alone requires the PIC—that's me—to be aware of staffing availability."

"Pilot," Mayko began, and now Theo could see her approaching reflection, "you seem to be counseling a crew member to seek work elsewhere. That could be—"

"Oh hush, right, Mayko?"

Rig turned to her smoothly, arms still crossed over his chest as he leaned in her direction. Mayko took a half step back, and he leaned even more in her direction.

"The contract she's working under gives Theo a trip to the nearest employment center following the end of her employment. That means *Primadonna* is liable right now, if Theo Waitley wishes, to take her to orbit. If she finds something here, well then, she can walk out under her own power and precious Hugglelans Galactica don't have to feed her for the next day. But this is still the contract offer period, *boss*, and you offered her a contract. She's got the right to consider, to get advice, to look for competing offers. Right. Let her look. She'll likely find there's nothing out there near as cushy as a job hooked up to the Howsenda...and then your problem is finding her a ship!"

He turned his back on Mayko.

"Now, Pilot," he said to Theo, "if you want an actual legal analysis of that contract you could always take it to the Guild office proper and pay that fee—"

Mayko gasped. "You wouldn't!" she said. "You singsong—"

Rig's face broke up into a laugh.

"You never were all that good in cussing battle with me, Mayko. Let's fix us something to eat and let the girl take her jacket to the bar. The ship can fly as soon as we get topped off foodwise, elsewise, since you asked."

Mayko looked around him, to wave a come-on motion to Theo.

"Pilot, if you hurry you can probably catch the cart before it goes back...the girl was checking on the steering when I left."

The "girl" was of indeterminate age, as far as Theo could tell, but certainly older than her, and she had one of the front panels on the cart open and an instrument Theo didn't recognize in her hand while she swept the interior with a scan wand. The breeze made the driver's extra-dark hair swirl so she had to shake her head to see around it, and if the earrings she wore were real she'd need a guard for them on a couple ports Theo knew.

The driver reached into the panel and Theo grimaced, wondering how many more things could go off in the wrong direction—she'd nearly forgotten to bring her crew kit, and then...

"Bad jets?" she asked. "Down for repairs? Are you the driver?"

The breeze, or concentration and the normal noise of a port in action, must have swallowed the words since the driver didn't react, and Theo repeated herself.

The woman, for now Theo was sure she was older than any mere girl, swept around elegantly as if surprised to discover anyone near. Wand held before her, still watching the instrument, she had a gentle smile on her face.

Theo relaxed. The woman was showing no signs of concern and her calm made Theo feel better.

"Yes, Pilot. I can drive you. Indeed not on the repairs; the sensor was getting an anomalous reading, but with so many extra ships on port these days, and so many security scans, unexpected readings will occur. Please, strap in and I will seal this instantly. You may call me Dulsey."

Theo sat in the passenger seat, strapped in, and watched the special elegance of this person who...was a pilot, and a dancer. Why then was she driving pilots about the port? She answered her own question—after all did not Aito wait tables at the Howsenda? Clearly though, this was no mere dayworker.

"May I drive you to the hiring hall, Pilot?"

Theo looked into the woman's face, but she was intent on starting, making sure the driving line was clear.

"Do I look like I'm leaving home?"

The driver glanced at her, still with that smile on her face.

"The hiring hall is a very popular destination, Pilot, especially today, and your shipmate came from there most recently, as I may be permitted to recall."

Mayko had been to the hiring hall? Of course, one way or another, Theo's spot on *Primadonna* would need filling.

"I understand there are several—but, yes, take me to a hiring hall."

The driver moved a hand used to work over the controls and the cart shot forward. Clearly the steering had no troubles, and after several sharp turns and dashes around other carts Theo began to assume that it was the brakes that needed looking into.

A few moments into the trip, after a sudden winding turn into a ramp new to her, Theo asked, "What hall are we going to? I thought they were mostly—"

The inner workings of the port came into view and flashed by: cables and pipes, ramps and people, warning signs and strange markings meant only for those who worked there.

"Ah, Pilot, since you come from the ship of the Hugglelans I thought it perhaps not best to travel to the hall where they hire now. Instead, I know a private party interested in hiring a pilot of special caliber such as yourself."

Theo held on as the cart lost altitude, taking a turn into a tunnel off of the ramp, tires' noise rising as the speed increased yet again. "Is this private party known onworld, and at the Guild hall? May I get a name?"

"Surely known on-world, Pilot. Why just a few hours ago, I drove there some Scouts."

Before the last word was fully annunciated, Theo gently moved her hand toward her pocket, saying, "I'm not sure that I'm interested in visiting this place, having recently taken leave of a Scout. Please take me elsewhere."

"Alas, Pilot Waitley, I believe you are committed now," said Dulsey, as the cart came to a squealing halt beneath the open bay door of a ship type Theo, despite her intensive study of silhouettes, couldn't identify.

"We have already copies of your records, and it behooves you to at least listen to our offer, which I assure you is far more interesting than the ordinary low-grade smuggler's contract offered in the halls here."

The driver used calming motions in Terran, then in Liaden, and then in Trade.

"You will not need your weapon here, Theo Waitley, only your wits. Uncle is waiting and there is much to be done."

Theo felt a thrumming, and wondered briefly if it was her own heartbeat. But no. It was the key around her neck, singing low. She danced a move to calm herself, knowing that she did not face thieves or ordinary brigands, for such would hardly bother to learn her name, nor would they likely speak of the Scouts.

Well. She still had her comm for *Primadonna*, and the ship's key. It was unlikely Rig Tranza would abandon her, though she wasn't so sure about Mayko.

Theo nodded to Dulsey who waited with patience as well as an impatient person might.

"I will listen to bona fide offers, Dulsey. If I have none, you will take me back to my ship."

Dulsey inclined her head.

"As you say, Pilot; it will be as you say."

Amazed, Theo stared around at what looked a museum more than a ship. There were carpets, deep rugs, and furs on the deck; there were ornate pieces of sculptural art, and there was wood.

Wood! Desks made of wood and chairs made of wood and inlaid deck portions of wood. There were hangings on the walls and soft music in the air. The air carried with it the scent of the growing things which were evident in such profusion. These weren't mundane plants grown for morale and oxygen, these were bushes and extravagances as well as pots of simpler things like Father might grow at home at Leafydale Place. She almost expected to find a norbear in the forest by the time she'd turned around once.

"Uncle will arrive shortly, Theo Waitley. Please, if you like, it is the custom of many to go barefoot here, for the ship is comfortable. Make yourself at ease in our atrium."

Dulsey was gone, she herself barefoot, her shoes left on a mat by the door. Theo had heard of such customs on worlds, and on old-style family ships from the years of the Terran loop traders. She, however, might want to leave fast, and having to put on her shoes would surely slow her down.

There must be cameras and sensors here, she realized, there must be ways to keep the curious from feeling the surfaces of the art.

Alone in this atrium, Theo kept her shoes on, despite temptation. Still she wandered among the nooks and crannies that made the careful planning of a great cruise ship look like amateur design. There were myriads of things to look at, and none of them by accident, she was sure.

From her left, a sound, and a man with carefully trimmed hair and a sketch of a beard stood at the mouth of the corridor Dulsey had disappeared into. Like Dulsey, he was neither old nor young, and he was dressed simply, not in imitation of a Guild driver, but in something that looked like it might be dance class clothes. He had deliberately made the sound that alerted her, for he walked, silent and barefoot, over the rugs and furs. A pilot, yes, but not a strong pilot; a dancer, perhaps, but not strong at that either, she gauged. Dulsey had perhaps walked and moved better, yet here was someone before whom Mayko might shrink.

Theo turned carefully to face this person. He smiled and gave a half bow that was neither Liaden nor yet simply Terran.

"I see your relatives in you, Theo Waitley," he said, his bare toenails showing glossy, as if they were waxed. "Your face is more comely than most of them, but you carry yourself every bit as dangerous, which is fine news indeed. I am Uncle, and I am very pleased to meet you."

FORTY

· · · · · · · · · · ·

Volmer
Underport

THEO'S HANDS WANTED TO TO ASK HOW UNCLE MIGHT KNOW HER family, but she held them firmly around the excellent cup of tea Dulsey had brought, sipping with appreciation while Uncle sat across from her, comfortable amusement on his face.

Beside her was a key and the contract he'd offered her; she'd not looked at either yet.

"Really, it was more than chance that brought you to this interview, and so we were prepared to make an offer for your services long before you were committed to making a change. The truth is that we've been on the lookout for you, or someone very much like you, for some time. We knew that Hugglelans was moving a pilot up—I can't tell you how, sorry—and we knew that there was a good chance Mayko Ikari would make that move here."

Theo sat forward, used a gesture of inquiry she'd learned from yos'Senchul to lead into her next question.

"There are a lot of pilots, and even a lot of Jump pilots—why would you be so sure that I'd be along? Aren't there more usual ways of finding pilots then hoping one walks off a ship looking for work?"

He laughed, very gently, and gave her another of his half bows, seated though he was.

Theo offered a nod to the half bow, polite interest to the smile, and permitted him the moment to continue.

"The first thing is that we've been wanting for some time to have a ship moved as quietly as possible, which means we needed someone to fly solo, and many pilots will not fly solo. We needed someone who might have special need or tendency of their own to privacy, for while our organization is not unknown, it is one that we try to keep as low profile as possible. We need, if you will forgive me, someone who is competent—even dangerous. Of those pilots coming to Volmer for Hugglelans, the profile fit—you."

Trim as it was, Uncle fiddled with his dark hair, as if he missed something he was used to at his ear or on his head, perhaps a turban, or an earring. He held a cup of tea served from the same pot in his other hand, moving it in careful emphasis as he went on.

"Understand, I find *advertising* such a plebeian approach to the problem that I never seriously considered it, and while I find sorting the dregs of on-file job hunters interesting for the information it brings me, information by itself is so much fog in the viewport. But here, now, I have been accumulating news, which is information in action, and I have been long in the habit of making things happen rather than waiting for them to occur. And so, records in hand, so to speak, I did even more research spurred on by event. You are a very good match for this job."

Theo sighed to herself; fascinated by the Uncle and his approach to hiring, concerned about what he seemed to know about *her*.

"I think no one considers my mother *dangerous*, Uncle, nor my grandmother, nor ever did! My family is very well documented, and very respectable—my mother and her mother and her mother before her are all scholars! Cite and location, date and degree, it's all there and all public, after all. No pilots among them, no tendency toward violence..."

It was his turn to lean forward, using his cup to point to her before he spoke.

"Ah, I forget, you were very much raised as a child of Delgado, as ill as it suited you. Of your maternal side I know only that it was sufficient to the task of birthing you. But no, I look to the paternal side here, Pilot."

The slight to her mother was almost lost in the twist of pain associated with Father.

"Jen Sar Kiladi," she said coolly, "is also a scholar, Uncle, and a retired pilot." She took a careful breath. "Do you know my father?"

"*Know* your father? No, not your father, if you mean to ask if we have met in person. However, your gene lines are hardly so short that your sire marks the length of the shadow, and I have met others in the line . . . some years before you were born, I daresay. As is illustrated by your own performance, the line is one prone to survival. Guild records indicate you carry at least one weapon you took barehanded from the care of a previous owner."

Theo started to speak, held it back—at least he hadn't mentioned her riot!

"But you see, your records are just updated, and trustworthy Jump pilots being at a premium, there are ways to achieve as much assurance ahead of time as possible. As an employer willing to trust into your care a vessel of both monetary and sentimental value, I feel that such records ought to be available. It helped, of course, that the Scouts were willing to assist."

"Scouts? What Scouts?"

Uncle smiled, precisely as if he saw through her, but was willing to give her points for trying to play the game.

"Your Win Ton, for one. He sleeps just beyond your view at the end of the hall, guarded by the chief of his medical team."

Theo's glance was unsubtle.

"I'd not be so cruel as to say so, and not prove it, Pilot Waitley." He motioned, giving her permission to investigate, just as Dulsey appeared at the end of the way.

Theo nodded to Uncle, rose not as steadily as she might like, saw Dulsey's face go bland as they passed each other in the lushly carpeted hall.

Around that corner the hall turned utilitarian, with beige walls and floor; bulkheads and pressure doors obvious. Sitting neatly cross-legged athwart the first double-wide door Theo came to was the same Scout who'd disturbed her and Win Ton with the news of a message.

The Scout rose languidly and bowed in recognition to Theo.

"Pilot, I see you. Alas, Scout yo'Vala is not receiving visitors."

Dulsey spoke from behind Theo's shoulder.

"The Uncle decides, Scout. You may permit entry."

Theo glanced aside. In fact both Dulsey and Uncle were behind her, bare feet on the plain decking, the Uncle gesturing a clipped *open*.

*   *   *

Theo read rapidly, finding the usages no stranger than contracts she'd read in class, and certainly better paid than Hugglelans' newest offer. The confidentiality agreement carried with it an extra payment, but—

"And so," Uncle went on, "we both have more information than we did before. The Scouts have entrusted me with some news, of course, but they cannot hide from me, as much as they might wish to do so, the identity of the pilot to whom your Win Ton has given the second key—actually, the first key—because the keys speak to this ship, which was built at the same yard as *Bechimo*."

Theo glanced up, seeing no joy of surprise in the man's face, but rather serious intent.

"They speak?" Win Ton had said that, hadn't he? That his key had talked to and manipulated the Old Tech devices on his prison ship?

"Yes. I understand, from the man himself, that he entrusted you with one of the phrases, and I find it compelling."

His hands motioned a *repeat please.*

There was no reason she knew of not to. Theo shrugged. "'There are secrets in all families.'"

"Wonderful. A phrase so old it is new again. So, we soon come to the truths we share and the truths you need to know. First though, is the contract reasonable?"

"A cantra for going to Liad?"

"Liad is a war zone, Pilot. I cannot say it will be without risk." He sipped his tea.

"The rest meets with your approval? In short: I provide a ship, a destination for the ship, and a list of items or documents to be delivered or picked up. At each port you will have a public pickup or delivery; which permits you to claim time, ports, from the Guild; as well as a reason to be in system. From time to time I may provide a 'wait for' order as items must reach your location, at times I may issue a 'skip run' and you will then not follow the previous route but move beyond, or rendezvous as is pertinent. You provide piloting, care of my ship, and act as delivery or receiving agent. You will be issued three pinbeam codes for use as required in emergencies or other exigencies, which you will use with care."

"What will I be carrying, Uncle?"

He smiled, and raised his hand like a lecturer looking for attention from a class.

"To the best of your knowledge you will be carrying rare books, special or unique reference items, and the occasional replacement part. Some of these are antiques, some are reproductions, some are both. You will not be carrying drugs, jewels, or other material generally considered illicit."

"This is good pay."

"A good pilot is worth good pay."

"What about Win Ton?"

He raised both hands as if weighing an invisible cat.

"Yes, you see, these things are all run together. Win Ton has saved the Scouts, and myself, some difficulty by acting with haste. His actions have brought to him the problems he discussed with you—but see, I tell you that he is not giving away confidences, but rather was subject to an interview after he was given a drug to relax him into the device in which he now sleeps. It is not a mere med unit like the best ships and hospitals have, it is a med unit of the type the Scouts have long abjured and fought against, in that it uses forbidden, even secret, technology."

He paused, seeing her concentrate, spun the *comment query* off of his fingers in that clipped accent of his.

"How can you forbid technology?" Theo asked. "How can you keep it secret? If someone can make something, so can someone else, eventually."

Uncle nodded slightly.

"That would be my understanding, as well, Theo Waitley. The med unit operating on your Win Ton is something more than a standard autodoc unit in that, if required, it can replace tissue to the point of...let us say near to the point of creating a clone. Our med unit onboard, as it stands, is Win Ton's best chance to survive the next two Standards or so."

Theo eyes widen, hope quickening. "It will cure him?"

"It will *not* cure him!"

At this Uncle rose, and began to pace, hands making rhythmic motions as if he posted to a keyboard, or struck a small drum set.

"If I had been permitted to work with and collect this technology several hundred years ago when I wished to, we might again be at that point. But I was not and in any case—at hand what we have is a machine which is far more powerful than the Scout catastrophe units; if you have a brain to hand, almost any other injury you might name can be healed over time; if you have time, even aging can be reduced considerably. But to do that, we need a very complete sample, a very secure sample."

He paced, and Theo's hands won the race with her mouth, *confirm data several hundred years* outpacing her spoken, "Sample?"

He paused, and smiled slowly.

"In fact, a secure sample: what we have now of your Win Ton is contaminated; his blood and his cells carry within them the very things of which we need to cure him. The Win Ton you saw in the viewport of the machine, that Win Ton, the biologic system, has been altered to hide what is new among what is old, to make all of him somewhat other than the Win Ton you knew previously."

Theo shuddered, wondering, saw *data confirmed* go past as she considered—

"Clones, people clones, aren't legal, are they?"

He waved his hand with no meaning other than frustration, walking a few steps away and back as he thought.

"Fashion," he said finally. "It is a matter of fashion to make these rules. Cloning has been legal, it has been illegal. Good people have died a final death because they might not be cloned, my relatives among them—and for that matter, yours. Progress has been held back until the point that these Liaden fools Win Ton has been tangled with can threaten everything out of ignorance!"

"The Scouts?"

He sat suddenly, anger leached into an earnest and almost beseeching tone.

"The dissidents, the Department of the Interior. The fools who have collected good and bad Old Tech without discrimination and use it without understanding. The Scouts, the old Scouts, made it easy for them by putting these devices in *safe places* where they thought no one would find them, not knowing that technology cannot be suppressed over time. Banned, perhaps, outlawed certainly, but that's a passing thing waiting for the right person or group to write new rules.

"What may cure your Win Ton is what the Scouts are afraid of. *Bechimo* has a med unit that far surpasses even the unit on this ship, upon which both Dulsey and I depend. More! *Bechimo* certified Win Ton yo'Vala as copilot. It holds a sample—a secure sample—enough to rebuild him completely, properly, and without contamination."

Theo took a breath.

"You believe in this *Bechimo* then? It isn't just a coping—an artifact of his wanting to survive?"

Uncle leaned forward, his old-young face earnest.

"Please, listen and hear, Theo Waitley. The keys, both of them together, are Old Technology, *good* technology, and they speak to some of the devices in this ship which are also Old Technology. *Bechimo* is the next step; it was a hybrid built of the Old Tech that was fading of age and very advanced current tech of its time. And that is its danger to the Scouts, and to these dissidents, that what we built really was, and is, better than what they have and treasure."

Uncle's hands tussled with words or ideas she couldn't read.

"*We?*" she ventured, at last.

He sighed, gently.

"Call it *we*, if you like, Pilot. I believe in the *Bechimo* because I stood on her deck as she was being finished, so I know she exists. We can discuss the philosophy of these things called *existence* and *self* over a drink sometime, or a pot of tea, if you like. In the meantime, there is an issue of time, on several accounts.

"Win Ton yo'Vala's prognosis if I turn him back to the Scouts is not good: perhaps two hundred or three hundred Standard days, maybe four hundred if they are content to allow him to stay in the machine until he dies, useless and helpless, inside a cocoon. My machine—well, the machine calculates that at the current rate Win Ton will have a series of dozens of good days, and then of tens, and then of fours or threes, all interspersed with more and longer time within the med unit. With good food, diet, exercise, care, he may well have a thousand days or more of interrupted, painful survival.

"If we can get him to *Bechimo*, the ship should be able to restore him. It may well improve him. Then he may have centuries, as you should."

Theo bit her lip.

"Win Ton said *Bechimo* was looking for me."

"Yes, that's true. And with both of you together here it may well find you—and quickly! Which we can by no means allow!"

"Whyever not? If Win Ton needs the ship, then let it come here. I'll open it, we'll get him into this super-rated autodoc, and—"

"Think, Pilot. What happens here or anywhere public when a self-controlled ship comes to port demanding a space, or just taking a space? If someone warns it away, and it assumes you, or Win Ton, is in danger, it may attack—surely if someone tries to board it without your permission, it will repel boarders again!" He tapped the table for emphasis. "If you do not know this, know it now. *Bechimo* is self-aware. It is also ignorant, having been reft of an association which would have taught manners and something of human interaction."

"Win Ton said it was an AI," she admitted, and sighed. Uncle was right. Better to let the ship find her in . . . less crowded conditions.

"How will I know it?" she asked. "*Bechimo.*"

"We can provide a matching program," Uncle said, and reached further, to tap the contract at her elbow.

"What I want you to do, Theo Waitley, is to accept my contract. There is a ship in orbit, an old ship but serviceable and proud. The port records are open to you ahead of time and you may check it thoroughly. It is built on an old Terran commissioner's ship plan, and is mostly standard, aside it has had several power upgrades. Accept the contract, and go. *Bechimo* will find you, I make no doubt. Be canny and choose your time and location. Once you have it in hand, then the choice of what you will do is, as every choice a pilot makes, your own."

He paused, regarded his hand a moment, then looked at Theo with no sign of anything but seriousness.

"In the meantime, it is best, I believe, for all of us, that you accept my contract."

Theo looked down at the contract, the phrase *Solcintra, Liad* coming into sharp focus. Clan Korval was based in Solcintra, Liad, as she knew from the news reports. Delm Korval—who was delm to pilotkind, wasn't that what Kara had said? Her father, Win Ton—pilots both. Would it be possible—?

And what could it hurt, she thought suddenly, to ask? Neither Father's disappearance nor Win Ton's circumstance was something that Sam Tim could solve on his own!

"I'll do it," she said.

Uncle inclined his head, and offered her a pen.

"Your signature, please." He produced a pouch from somewhere, and dumped its contents on the table before her: five cantra pieces, a ship's key, and what looked like a clay game piece.

"The ship I wish you to pilot is *Arin's Toss*, Pilot. Dulsey, please bring a screen, so that the pilot may review the records."

Theo looked at the small fortune sitting beside her, idly reaching out and touching the mint-fresh coins with the stern face on it, and then the key . . . and then the clay piece, which felt oddly fuzzy for something so hard, which felt comforting, the way the key round her neck had felt when she'd looked at Win Ton, who would be her copilot if he could . . .

Now that she had decided, now that all of her problems seemed to be pointing in the same direction, she wanted to lift, to fly, to be *doing something*.

She stood.

"Just a moment, Pilot; Dulsey will be here—"

"That's fine," she interrupted. "If the ship will fly, I'll fly it."

She picked up the game piece, and flipped it. It snugged into her hand like a norbear.

"The usual rules apply," she said. "Let's go."

SALTATION

FORTY-ONE

· · · · · · · · · · · · · · · · · ·

Arin's Toss
Volmer

THE BOOK OF SHIPS WORKNET DESCRIPTION OF ARIN'S TOSS, OUT
of Bluestone, Waymart, called it

> *an excellent example of the early trade-merge ship, with the*
> *courier-weight vessel built on Terran proportions, denominated*
> *and calibrated with Terran mensuration, and reminiscent of*
> *the family-vessel forbears it descended from. The ship has*
> *been surveyed as recently as Standard Year 1389, when its*
> *single classic Class Three mount point was replaced with a*
> *more modern Class Two mount during refitting that included*
> *installation of a dual core drive to replace what was claimed*
> *to be an original Terran Sentry-Overbrook.*

Reading about it, though, was nothing like being there. Theo
had in hand already the hard-copy printout and three reader
versions of the ship's details, down to replacement part numbers,
lists of shops that had worked on it in the last century, and the
promised pinbeam info as well.

They'd toured the ship first, inspecting it externally on the way
in as Dulsey piloted the minishuttle belonging to Crystal Energy
Consultants.

For the initial runthrough, Theo sat second seat, Dulsey demon-
strating the few nonstandard board-set items the antique retained

with the ship quiet. Some of the surfaces were polished metal, some were clearly refits, but the entirety made the ships she trained on at the academy look old and grubby, and *Primadonna* just a little... dowdy.

Theo frowned, the memory of her last visit to *Primadonna* was still uncomfortable. Rig had taken her comm, her key and her news of a ship with a wide grin, and the advice to "fly her like she's part of you, Pilot Theo, because that's what she'll be, so soon it'll make your head spin!"

Mayko...had not been pleased. She demanded to know who had hired her, and how she felt, after Hugglelans had taken her aboard and trained her, to be signing with another company. Until Rig told her to put it in a can, that was, and Theo was left to pack in peace.

Arin's Toss, though— They did a full run to Jump sequence with the board on neutral and Theo sitting second; then brought it down to quiet again. Theo took over, reset the board to zero and did the entire sequence again, adjusting toggle strengths and seating and light angles and straps to things that would be comfortable to her.

The intro time flew by; and on the morrow Theo would—
GAWGAWGAW.

Theo snatched for the comm—but it wasn't lit! She looked to Dulsey, who pointed.

Right, she thought. Pinbeam.

"Test message?"

Dulsey's hands were eloquent: *Live message get.*

Theo signed *accept* and pressed the read now button, glad to see open text in Terran.

++Request/require immediate shipment pallet fifteen++new local conditions++arrive shields up++doubled terms arrive on-before Day 201 Standard 1393++haste++purple44+arrival Day 203 Standard 1393/later unacceptable++listening++

Theo glanced to the other pilot, surprised to see reaction on that normally serene face. Dulsey brought the second board live just in time to catch an incoming comm call which she flashed to the open speaker. Uncle's voice was clear.

"Hello, *Arin's Toss*. We'll have to rendezvous for a transfer; are systems good there?"

Dulsey looked to Theo, answered, "We have done first sequencing and introduction. There should be a dozen more hours or longer—"

"You can do the math; we are attempting a very finite deadline on a unique item."

"Waitley, can you get the *Toss* to—that would be Solcintra, Liad, planetside port by darkest night, day two-oh-one, if we can get *Toss* loaded?"

For a moment Theo flashed on stuffing the Slipper on the plateau; her hands running the board for fine coordinates.

"There's some leeway," Uncle continued. "Darkest quarter of the morning before dawn is client preference."

"Yes," Theo said, absolutely certain. "Yes, if the ship's up to spec and we can load within the next two orbits, I can make delivery. If there's food on board. But it'll have to be five Jumps."

There was a pause and Uncle's voice came through with a hint of something besides calm control.

"I'm bribing the Tower now and will lift soonest. Get clear of the station and intercept. Dulsey, you'll play tug."

"Waitley, I don't think there's any coffee on board. You'll have to do with whatever tea is in the stasis tins."

Theo looked to Dulsey. Shrugged. Replied:

"I'll manage."

In the middle of the third Jump—the longest one—Theo broke open the second stasis tin, not because she was out of tea in the first tin, but because she'd never had Supa Oong Dark before and had been told it was the best tea in the universe...from someone who'd lived on the planet where it was grown.

She could use something right now, all things considered, because she'd fudged her figures slightly and the recalculations were showing that she'd need a really good run-in from Jump if she was to make the schedule. That the *Toss* was equal to it, she had no doubt, having already developed a deep respect for the abilities and heart of her vessel. That the *pilot* was equal—

"Well," she said, "you'll just have to be."

She laughed, and wondered if this was why Tranza had taken up singing: to avoid talking to himself.

Theory is that any single Jump is physiologically neutral. Practice said that a single Jump was physiologically neutral. Timing was everything, after all, and there needed, for some reason, to be some time between the end of one Jump and the start of the next else . . . else the body was not entirely recovered from the experience. Time being measured in heartbeats or orbits or—

Third Jump ended, and *Arin's Toss* was real again, really here, really able to be seen. Theo checked the prefed coordinates, the destination coordinates, caught the gross arrival coords, compared them, corrected them, checked herself twice, had the *Toss* check itself. Satisfied, she pressed the go-button, throwing her ship into the fourth Jump—and reached for some tea.

Jump glare faded and she'd recalled the rules: she arrived with shields up and all channels open, and with the understanding that purple44 specified a night landing and she checked local time, throwing herself into the First Seat with a will and watching the time count down toward dawn someplace she'd never been.

Coming in at close to two gravity acceleration was tiring, but not as bad as missing the deadline.

There were things to see though, and she took feeds from the planet, mighty Liad itself.

Of ships, there were many she'd never seen before: mining ships, and Clutch asteroids and Juntavas ships openly advertising their affiliation. There were Scout ships and there the silhouette, so long studied: *Dutiful Passage*!

Other than having no second, the landing sequence was routine; she made contact with planetary control, agreed to drop shields within the planetary defense net, caught her time signals, dropped the ship down, down through nightside to a well-lit landing zone, only to be directed to the darkest corner of the port.

She didn't witness the pallet transfer except by camera: there a remote vehicle of some kind, there a lift working, there the transfer and acknowledgement.

The feeds were on the while, and when she was done, *Arin's Toss* was quiet. Tea would be good. Breakfast . . . she'd lost track, inside the Jumps, of meals, but she wasn't hungry, really—or tired. She did make tea, and tapped up the news feed for the headlines.

Korval Mystery Move on Tap was the first. *Delm Korval Talks to Pilots and Clan, Ignores the World*, another. *Liad Abandoned*, claimed a third.

She tapped that one, scanning the story rapidly.

It turned out that the headline was a little misleading—a lot misleading. Clan Korval had been given a deadline to leave Liad with all its possessions. It seemed that agents of the clan had blown a hole in Solcintra City, which the ruling body—the Council of Clans—had taken badly. Theo could see their point. She paused the scroll.

She'd heard stories about the Tree-and-Dragon, which was how spacers had referred to Clan Korval. They were... unpredictable, and, while admired, it was generally agreed that the best course included a wide margin given to Korval. She'd never heard that they were... antisocial. But—a hole in the planet? She started the scroll going again.

At the hearing, Delm Korval hadn't bothered to deny or explain the action of the clan, with the result that the Council had acted as they had, to protect the homeworld, and Korval was to leave Liad no later than—

Theo leaned forward and slapped up the local date and time.

Tomorrow.

Her stomach clenched.

"Now, Theo," she said, drinking what was left of her tea. "Or never."

She stood, hesitated, thought of Win Ton, asleep inside the med unit that was only keeping him, barely, alive.

She thought of Kamele, she thought of Father, and she thought of a ship, self-aware and unsocialized, that was out there, somewhere, looking for *her*.

"Korval is ships," she said.

She went to the galley and made herself another cup of tea. Then, with dawn giving way to day, Theo Waitley called a taxi.

FORTY-TWO

. . . .

Day 201
Standard Year 1393
Solcintra
Liad

THERE WAS A GUARD ON THE FRONT DOOR OF THE HOUSE—JELAZA Kazone was its name, according to the taxi driver—a plump man with a greying ginger mustache and speculative taffy-colored eyes. He wore a Jump pilot's jacket nearly as battered as her own, and a pellet gun openly on his belt.

"And you are?" he asked in plain Terran, sounding only curious.

"Theo Waitley," she answered.

He tipped his head. "Are you, indeed? And your purpose here, Theo Waitley?"

"I need to see the Delm of Korval," she said.

"As does half the planet. Alas, Korval is just a trifle busy at the moment—moving house, you know. You *have* seen the news feeds?"

"I have," she admitted. "That's why I'm here, now."

The guard considered her seriously. "Is it? What an *interesting* sense of timing. Have you ID, Theo Waitley?"

One eye on the gun, which stayed peaceably in its holster, Theo put her hand inside her jacket and pulled out her license. She handed it to the guard, not without a pang.

He scanned it, then looked back to her. "The license is newer than the jacket."

"That's because Rig Tranza gave me the jacket off his back when I got the license." Theo was beginning to feel irritable. Also, her knees were starting to shake. Maybe she should have had a meal, after all.

The guard nodded and flipped the card back to her. She snatched it out the air and slipped it back into its pocket.

"Armed, Theo Waitley?"

She looked at him. "Of course."

He laughed, which increased her irritation, then bowed, abruptly formal.

"What matter do you bring before Korval, Pilot?"

She was beginning to suspect that the guard was amusing himself at her expense. "Are you Korval?" she asked.

"Gods forfend!"

"My business," Theo said, trying to sound patient and probably, she thought, not doing that good a job of it, "is with Delm Korval."

It was like she'd passed a test, or maybe he figured he'd gotten all the fun out of her he could. Whichever, he turned his head and called over his shoulder.

"Jarn!"

The door at his back came open and another pilot stepped out, leathers gleaming, gun holstered and very apparent.

"Master Clonak?"

He moved a pudgy hand, directing Jarn's attention to Theo, like she was an interesting kind of flower. "Please take Pilot Waitley to the inner garden and point her on her way."

The garden reminded her of home, with the flowers let to go almost wild, and the bushes trimmed only enough to keep branches out of the faces of the unwary. Jarn's instructions had been to "keep to the path," which sounded simple enough. The challenge was finding the path among the overgrowth of vegetation.

She figured that there were cameras on her, and watchful eyes nearby. Not that she intended any harm to Delm Korval, but it was comforting to think that somebody would come find her, if she got lost.

By the second turn, she realized that she was on course for the tree that was improbably growing out of the center of the house.

It had seemed as big as one of Codrescu's arms when she'd seen it from the taxi. Looking up now into a sky lacy with branch and leaf, she thought it might be bigger.

Theo swayed a little when she brought her sights down closer to her level, and closed her eyes until she felt steadier.

The path turned again, tighter and again, drawing her in closer to the center every time. She took a deep breath, trying to clear a head suddenly a bit too heavy, and reviewed her points, carefully worked out during the long Jumps. It stood to reason that Delm Korval was busy; she had to be concise. State her case and stop, that was it.

She heard voices now, or, rather, *a* voice, so deep that it shook the flowers at the edge of the path.

"Ephemeral and multistranded, it wends through time, space, and song," the voice boomed, "altering the very fabric of the universe. As I see, each day brings a new thread."

Abruptly, the path ended, but that was fine. Right before her was the tree, and—it must be a Clutch turtle! She'd never seen one—well, hardly anyone had. Her eyes on this wonder, Theo stumbled on a surface root, recovered—and almost stumbled again.

Almost invisible beside the Clutch turtle, two people stood hand in hand. They turned, as if they'd heard her stumble, pilot smooth and perfectly in time.

More guards, Theo thought. She continued, carefully, across the root-rumpled lawn. When she judged she was at the proper distance, for people who wanted to talk to Liadens who were neither kin nor comrades, she bowed, as from junior to senior.

Straightening, she found the phrase in Liaden, which she'd've given to the guard at the gate, if he hadn't thrown her by speaking Terran.

"It is necessary that I speak to the Delm of Korval, on business of the clan."

The woman—red hair, grey eyes, and just visibly pregnant—nodded, did a double-take, and looked up to the man.

"*Another* one?"

Theo tensed.

"Shall you like odds?" he asked, his voice soft. He gave Theo a nod, like they were pilots chance-met on port.

"You are addressing the Delm of Korval," he said in unaccented Terran. "May we know your name?"

Here we go again.

"Theo Waitley," she said, groping after the concise statement she'd put together and memorized.

It was gone—and the guy was looking at her, face oddly familiar, and green eyes serious.

"I'm here because my father's missing," she blurted. "And he told me—he always told me—to go to the Delm of Korval, if ever there was really bad trouble."

She paused, running one hand distractedly through her hair.

Finish what you started, she told herself. *Then go on to the rest.*

"My father's name is Jen Sar Kiladi," she told the pair of them—were they *both* the Delm of Korval? Or had she muddled that, too? "He teaches—"

"He teaches cultural genetics," the man interrupted gently, and Theo felt a twist of hope. Father was known here!

"Right," she said. "I mean, you might not think it was a big problem, if your father wasn't where you left him—" What was she *saying*?

"No, acquit me," the man said. "I would think it a very large problem, indeed."

Was he laughing at her? "He's never done anything like this before—just up and left, in the midle of the term and—"

She stopped, took a breath and forced herself to say calmly, "I got trouble, and since I can't find him..."

The man was looking beyond her, and the woman, too—was there a guard behind her? Had she lost it all, Win Ton and *Bechimo*, with any chance of finding Father?

"Theo," the man said, in his soft voice. "Look behind you."

Stupid! she told herself, and did as he ordered.

A man was walking over the uneven grass; she didn't need the jacket to see that he was a pilot. Dark hair going grey, angular, interesting face—

"Father!"

She leapt, slamming him into a full body hug, feeling the tears, and the joy, and—

"Father, where the *hell* have you been?"

Strong arms were around her, then she felt him tousle her hair, like she was a kid, and set her back from him.

"I've been busy, child," he said. He paused, and shook his head, a half smile on his lips.

"I can't tell you how glad I am to see you, Theo. And sorry, as well."

"Sorry!" She stared at him, suddenly afraid, recalling bar stories told of Liaden Balances and lives called forfeit over matters of trade...

Father touched her cheek.

"Gently," he murmured. "Sorry because you would not be here if there wasn't really bad trouble."

She nodded. "It's kind of complicated," she began...